Robert Derry is in his fifties and is a Human Res Somerset, England. He was educated at Lancaster London, where he worked in the City of London, t. - The Waterman - published by Austin Macauley Publishers Ltd. in 2021. He is an avid supporter of Aston Villa Football Club, who hail from his hometown of Birmingham, England and of the NFL, following the Green Bay Packers, from a distance. He is married to Tina with two grown-up children and two troublesome cats.

Robert Derry

The Burning

Every house has a Heart

Copyright © Robert Derry (2023)

The right of Robert Derry to be identified as author of this work has been asserted by the author in accordance with section 77 and 78 of the Copyright, Designs and Patents Act 1988.

All rights reserved. No part of this publication may be reproduced, stored in a retrieval system, or transmitted in any form or by any means, electronic, mechanical, photocopying, recording, or otherwise, without the prior permission of the author.

Any person who commits any unauthorised act in relation to this publication may be liable to criminal prosecution and civil claims for damages.

The Burning is a work of fiction. Any names or characters, businesses or places, events, or incidents, are fictitious. Any resemblance to actual persons, living or dead, or actual events is purely coincidental.

FOR MY DAD, MICHAEL JOHN DERRY, 1941-2023

AN UNEDUCATED MAN WHO TAUGHT ME EVERYTHING I EVER NEEDED TO KNOW.

Monday 23rd March 2020

FIRST DAY OF UK LOCKDOWN - DAY 1

188 deaths reported in the UK – the total number of deaths due to COVID19 now stands at 930 with 11,138 people testing positive for the disease.

PROLOGUE

"An Acte against Conjuration, Witchcrafte and dealing with evill and wicked Spirits."

"That if any person or persons, after the said Feast of St. Michael the Archangell next coming, shall use, practise, or exercise any invocation or conjuration of any evil and wicked spirit: or shall consult, covenant with, entertaine, imploy, feed, or reward any evil and wicked spirit, to or for any intent or purpose; or take up any dead man, woman, or child, out of his, her, or their grave, or any other place where the dead body resteth; or the skin, bone, or any other part of any dead person, to be imployed, or used in any manner of Witchcraft, Sorcery, Charme, or Inchantment, or shall use, practise, or exercise, any Witchcraft, Inchantment, Charme or Sorcery, whereby any person shall be Killed, Destroyed, Wasted, Consumed, Pined, or Lamed, in His or Her body, or any part therof; that then every such Offender, or Offenders, their Ayders, Abettors, and Counsellors, being of the said offences duly and lawfully Convicted and Attainted, shall suffer paines of death as a Felon or Felons, and shall lose the priviledge and benefit of Clergy and Sanctuary."

Passed by James I and his Parliament in the session that began on March 19, 1603, and ended July 7, 1604

CHAPTER 1

"We need to go."

Anthony had been mulling things over as the nationwide crisis became ever more serious and now that the Prime Minister had declared a full lockdown, he was certain that it was their only option.

"We have to get out of London, before things get out of control," he whispered so that only his wife could hear him, but she was much less certain.

"What about the kids? Won't we get in trouble if they're not around when the schools reopen?"

"They're not going to reopen for weeks." said Anthony, convinced that they were in it for the long haul. "It could be months before things get back to normal, now let's get out of here before the motorway gets busy."

"Do you think it will?" his wife asked fearfully. "Boris just said that we should all stay at home. Don't you think that the police will stop anyone that's trying to make a run for it?"

"Not if we're quick.," Anthony snapped back. Only his mother called him Anthony these days, even though his business cards, his passport and his birth certificate all begged to differ. He was Tony to his friends, to his wife, and sometimes even to his kids, though he preferred it when they called him Dad.

"Come on kids." he shouted up the stairs, deciding in a split second that he would make the decision for all of them. His command was met with the usual silence. "Get your things, we're going to the cottage!"

That one word did the trick, and they came bounding down the stairs like excited puppies, battling for supremacy at the top as they fought for territorial advantage, until the younger one conceded ground and they each tumbled like an avalanche into the hall.

"Can I take my Switch, please?" begged Arthur, thrilled by the prospect of an unexpected visit to their holiday let where he knew he'd be left to his own devices for hours on end. He always was, so why would this time be any different?

"I'm taking mine." said his older sister triumphantly, waving the small rectangular gadget in the air like a trophy. She had long since learned that asking for permission was only ever likely to end in disappointment.

"I don't care what you take, so long as you're ready to go in five minutes," yelled their father, at which they started to run, "and so long as it doesn't take up too much room in the car."

Tony was already stockpiling his own essentials on the coffee table, striking each item from his mental checklist as he retrieved it from the far corners of the house. It wasn't long before the table was piled high with gadgets and equipment, various chargers for a whole plethora of mobile technology that were now considered essential travel items for the twenty first century family.

His wife was upstairs frantically throwing together a ramshackle collection of her own. Clothes for the four of them, a task that only her daughter seemed to be taking any interest in and one in which her husband rarely engaged. Their annual holiday in the sun would always see him forget something important, for which she would then get the blame. One year it was his swim-shorts, on another his contact lenses, and in one unforgettable catastrophe in the Algarve, not a single pair of underpants had made the flight leaving him to 'go commando' for the whole two weeks after he decided that the locally available style was not to his liking.

"Do you want your hoodies?" Charlie hollered down the stairs, incensed at the realisation that she was on packing duty for four and still horrified at the prospect of an unplanned getaway.

"Just the red one," hollered an oblivious Tony from the kitchen. He was hastily assembling a few culinary essentials, including his cherished coffee maker, which he could not do without, even for a day. "Oh, and my green one."

Fifteen minutes of chaos ensued, until the family were finally encamped at the foot of their stairs, like students about to embark on a field trip, fully prepared for a spring break and ready for anything that the British weather could throw at them. Walking boots, raincoats, hats, and gloves lay heaped on top of a multi-coloured array of rucksacks, that Tony would somehow have to find room for in the back of the family car.

"What about Bruce, we have to take Bruce." It was Lottie and she was almost distraught at the prospect that – in this the most unusual of vacations - they might be about to leave the family dog behind.

"Of course, we're taking Bruce," her father assured her, wondering to himself quite how he was going to fit a family of four and a large and hairy dog in amongst enough luggage to fill a small passenger plane. "We wouldn't leave him behind now would we. C'mon fella, let's go."

Their long-haired German Shepherd had been beside himself for the last hour, sensing that something was about to go down and increasingly distraught at the thought that he might not be part of it, but now he was at the door, his tail spinning at the prospect. He was a fine animal, fiercely loyal of his pack, especially the two children, who together represented the only humans that were ever permitted to get too close, especially to his ears, which were a no-go zone for almost anyone else.

"Right." said Tony, his grey hairline tinged with perspiration, "Kids, don't start if you've forgotten something, we won't be coming back. Have you picked up your phones and your chargers?"

They each nodded rather theatrically.

"Check." shouted Arthur in time-honoured fashion. "Bruce said 'check' too dad."

"Well done, Arthur." chimed Tony reminding him that at least one essential item had been overlooked and he returned from the kitchen seconds later with the dog's lead raised high in the air, dangling like a noose. "Almost forgot it." he announced, as the dog sprung up at him, his wet nose buffeting the leash until his master commanded him to stop.

Charlie looked frazzled. She hated doing anything on the spur of the moment, but this was taking it to the extreme. "I'm bound to have forgotten something." she wailed, brushing away an unkempt length of recently highlighted hair from her forehead. "Oh shit, my hairdryer, the one in the cottage is crap, I can't manage without one for three months." and she fled the scene, in search of the more expensive alternative.

"Three months." Lottie screamed in horror, her bright blue eyes wide and worried. "We're going for three months?"

"Yes." said Arthur punching the air in delight.

"We have no idea how long we'll be," admitted their father, "but the man on the news said that it could be up to twelve weeks, yes." He tried to hide his own concern at the very idea of three months without income, but although his son was oblivious to it, his daughter had seen the same worry lines on his face before, and it was catching.

"What am I going to do down there for three whole months."

"We'll be fine," said Tony, doing his best to brush his own fears aside as he called upstairs to hurry his wife along, knowing full well that she would have become distracted. She returned a few moments later with yet another carrier bag, crammed full of additional items that were now cosied up to the hair dryer like a generous donation to a jumble sale.

"Are we ready?" she asked, sensing a change in the mood in the few minutes that she'd been away.

Tony didn't give anyone the chance to object. "As ready as we'll ever be."

CHAPTER 2

The roads were eerily quiet, and they reached the M3 in record speed, passing two other cars that had been stopped by the police at the side of the road. Heated exchanges were taking place between the boys-in-blue and those unfortunate members of the general public whose civil liberties were being brought into question for the first time in a generation or two.

Tony was just grateful that it wasn't them.

"Do you think we'll get turned around?" asked Charlie, shooting a concerned look at her husband who was seated in his customary position at the wheel of their expensive family saloon.

"There's a chance," he conceded. "Maybe we should get off the motorway, head down the back roads? Less conspicuous."

"I think so," his wife agreed. The kids weren't consulted. Neither of them was in any position to offer an opinion anyway as they were already engrossed in their own personal choice of movies, their headphones blocking out all unwelcome noise from the surrounding world.

Entertained. Oblivious. Vulnerable.

For them the journey would go by in the blink of an eye, as both would soon be soothed to sleep nestled against the warm leather, but for their parents, every mile would feel like a marathon. They felt like fugitives in their own land, and it was a new feeling for them both, one that they didn't much like.

"Sat Nav." Tony said clearly. "New Route. Cottage. Avoid Motorways." The navigation system immediately heeded his command, taking no more than twenty seconds to replot their route, before replying in a friendly but familiar voice.

"Route set. One hundred and twenty-seven miles. Two hours and fifteen minutes. Traffic is light. Leave motorway at next junction."

They followed the electronic instructions to the letter, exiting the motorway at speed and tracing a spider's web of A-roads and back streets, that would eventually lead them all the way to their second home, deep in the English countryside.

They didn't encounter a single additional traffic officer enroute, and even the secondary roads were much quieter than normal, the local populous following the government's bidding like the good citizens that they were, as freedom gave way to fear. The British people had all been urged to do it for their elderly parents or for their vulnerable friends, and the vast majority had complied, though some - like the Mountford's and certain government ministers – had been quick to make an exception in their own case.

"Once we're there we'll hole up and follow the guidelines," said Tony, excusing his actions in a rare moment of self-doubt.

"But won't the locals object?" argued his wife, already getting nervous at the reception that might be waiting for them in the picturesque village where comers-in were still seldom made welcome. It had been described as a 'chocolate box' cottage, the kind that the big manufacturers in Birmingham and the West of England used to put on the front of their biscuit tins in the days when metal containers for such things were in fashion. It was still possible to find examples from the forties or fifties, but most are now to be found squirrelled away in sheds, attics, or garages, crammed full of nails, screws or wall plugs, or have long since been melted down for scrap.

"Well, we're hardly going to see too many of them, are we?" quipped Tony. "They will all be holed up as well, so we may as well be down there as in London," but his wife of fifteen years standing wasn't convinced.

"We've broken the law." she said nervously, but her husband was having none of it and he laughed out loud at the very suggestion.

"Of course, we haven't." he said, "not everyone has got a second home. Those that have will be doing the same, you'll see. What's the point of having a bolthole if you can't use it when you need to bolt for the first time ever and anyway, we might as well; we've had to cancel all our bookings for the foreseeable future, and I can finish up a few jobs about the place whilst I'm down there. It makes perfect sense, doesn't it?" They could kill two birds with one stone, whatever the hell that meant.

Charlie didn't answer, but instead peered out of the window into the darkness as they sped down yet another empty country lane, and even though the car's navigation system indicated that they were headed in a south westerly direction, she failed to take any comfort from it. For the first time in her life, she felt genuinely scared, and it wasn't a feeling that she liked.

They had bought the cottage before the kids were born, snapping up a derelict shell of a house for a song, and then spending a vast sum in bringing it up to standard. In fact, once it had been fitted out with what were then the latest mod-cons it was way above the usual standard for holiday homes in the area. Tony had spent a large portion of his redundancy money on it, a healthy payoff from an investment bank whose fortunes had sunk in the wake of the dot-com crisis and rather than waste it on expensive holidays, they had decided to take advantage of the short-lived slump in property prices to snap themselves up a bargain.

To begin with, it hadn't looked like much, but it had benefited from that all-important quality that all sharp investors looked for; it had an abundance of land. Room to grow. A couple of extensions were quickly added to create the cross-shaped footprint around the ancient L-shaped building, its rotting roof was replaced, and its thatched splendour restored. The new look was not lost on their immediate neighbours, who could see the benefits that the substantial upgrade would have on their village, though few cared to comment, and most had continued to give them the cold-shoulder for another ten years or more. Only now were relations starting to thaw.

Its kitchen had been transformed from a dishevelled collection of mismatched units into a plush modern room, the adjacent extension adding the luxury of space to a once cramped corner. Even the stairs had been ripped out and replaced, and not a moment too soon; several treads were so badly worn that a few more footfalls would have resulted in a broken leg or worse. In their place, a chrome and glass balustrade now nestled up against the angle of lounge and snug, a fashionable wrought iron handrail guarding the side to guide the weary up to bed.

Three sizeable bedrooms on the first floor, and an optional space downstairs had put the let into the realms of the 'large family holiday' class, its six-to-eight berth category offering a far more lucrative return than would have been possible without the extra floor space and although only two were original, the new ones had been fitted out with similar Victorian-style fireplaces to give the impression that all was of its time.

Tony had been very hands-on with the renovation at first, his six-foot frame and rugby-player physique well-suited to physical work and as a younger man, he had been more than willing to get his hands dirty. Though he'd had to employ some specialist craftsmen to achieve the required finish, he had refused to pay out hand-over-fist for labour and so, along with some willing friends-of-the-family – who were paid mainly in cider and fried breakfasts on many a long weekend in the west country – they had made short work of stripping the ancient structure back into an empty shell.

Devoid of all life, as if nothing living had ever dwelled there.

It had certainly been a labour-of-love and though they ended up being overspent by quite some margin, going into debt to the tune of a few hundred thousand on an unwanted second mortgage, Tony had known from the start that they were onto a winner. In the height of summer, he'd always suspected that a rental with a newly installed outdoor pool and hot tub, would easily command a whopping four thousand pounds per week, especially when shared between two families who were more than happy to avoid the cost and hassle of flights abroad to stay in the lap of luxury, within half an hour's drive of some of the best beaches in England.

And so, it had proved.

In subsequent years, in the height of the season a week had rarely passed when the house had lain empty and many families would soon be snapping it up a year or two in advance, returning year after year to relax in its solitude and to bathe in its sumptuous elegance. The mortgage had long since been paid off with the proceeds and although the taxman took his share of their profits in January and July, much to Tony's disdain, it had proved to be every bit the wise investment that he had always known it would be.

Though the cottage was not everybody's cup of tea, and there were some unwitting guests who had made their feelings known by jotting down their *'experiences'* in the visitors' book, the owners had always been quite open with everyone that called to make an enquiry, before relieving them of a hefty down payment on a reservation. Money that was now having to be refunded in the tens of thousands thanks to the pandemic.

"Now we like to be very transparent about everything," was always Tony's opening line whenever he picked up the phone to field a call, or when responding by email. "We do have a resident ghost, though people do say that it's a friendly one."

Reactions varied. Some people were intrigued by it, asking all sorts of questions, whilst others were immediately put off. The majority didn't seem to mind at all though, in fact, some had left disappointed when the apparition failed to put in an appearance and after a while - once it became clear that there would be no adverse impact on their bookings - Tony and Charlie had even included it in their adverts. After all, old houses needed a ghost or two, real or imagined; it added to the character of the place and to the excitement of the holiday for many of their satisfied customers.

> *Idyllic country cottage, ideal for large families or two families sharing. Perfectly situated, close to the town centre and several pubs and restaurants, and within a few miles of one of the best beaches in England. Four well-sized bedrooms comfortably sleep six to eight adults, with a sofa-bed available in the lounge for additional space if required. All the mod-cons including cable TV, swimming pool, hot-tub and pool table provide the entertainment when you're not on the beach or enjoying a refreshing pint of cider or tasty lunch at the nearby Kings Head Tavern. Oh, and one relatively well-behaved ghost'.*

"Are you sure that won't put people off?" Charlie had asked, the first time that Tony had insisted on including it, but he had a ready-made answer to convince her otherwise.

"I think we have to be transparent about it." said Tony, as he repeated his well-worn 'dad joke' for the umpteenth time.

"What if they leave early because of it and ask for their money back?" was Charlie's only real objection at the time, but her objection had fallen on deaf ears.

"And what if they leave early because of it and we haven't told them about it?"

His argument had won the day, but whenever they returned to the cottage, she always made a point of reviewing the comments that had been left by their guests in the visitors' book, just in case. It was always good to find out what people thought of the house and of the area and most entries were polite and complementary; some were even grateful. Surprisingly few ever mentioned the ghost, and those that did, were often simply voicing their disappointment at the lack of any sightings.

"No ghost. ☹." The most frequent entry, with some accusing their hosts of making the whole thing up, just to improve their booking history.

Every now and again though, someone would leave an account that was always eerily like the previous happenings, the details contained in other annals that were kept back in London, as the latest guests made their mark for posterity.

"Cold spot in the kitchen, was sure someone was behind me whenever I made dinner, didn't like it, won't be coming back," was one version, and many variations on that theme had been reported over the years.

"Bedsheets pulled off, front bedroom – slept on the sofa-bed for the rest of the holiday," was another oft-reported incident. *"Lights always on when we came down in the morning – know that we turned them off before we went to bed"* was also a common claim. *"Snug door opened on its own, there was no wind outside, closed it when I went to get a beer, open again when I got back. Gave me the shivers."*

All regular occurrences in the house that they simply christened, *The Cottage*.

20

CHAPTER 3

When the Mountford family finally reached their second home it was very late, and the winding lane was its usual spooky self. The lane was always lined with hidden potholes that jerked the kids from their slumber, whilst unkempt trees leaned in from either side to tap and tickle the paintwork as they went by. As they drew up outside, they each hoisted a child out into the night air and edged towards the light of the standard lamp, that had been left on in the snug for their arrival by their devoted housekeeper, Mrs Illsley.

It was only just spring, and there was a coldness about the March night that had them shivering on the doorstep as Tony strained for his keys. They were all more anxious than usual to get inside, as if there were something out there in the dark, lurking just out of sight and as the front door fell inwards, the dog stormed across the threshold, like an infantry captain in a World War One battle. He surveyed the house, darting into the corners to complete his sniff-check before settling uneasily in his customary place by the fire.

The log-burner was still glowing in a furious shade of red, though it was no longer blazing, and Tony wasted no time in adding a couple more logs from the stand beside the fireplace. Thanks to Mrs Illsley, the snug was living up to its name and after emptying the car of its contents and dumping them onto every unsuspecting surface where they would stay until the morning, the kids made themselves at home without delay, as their parents completed a quick tour of the house to ensure that everything was all as they had last left it.

Most of their guests could always be relied upon to leave the house exactly as they'd found it, and after the close attentions of their housekeeper, it would always be looking like a show-home again within a few hours of every departure, ready for the next arrivals. Occasionally there were breakages though, and whilst most people were honest enough to own up to such things, some weren't and so a quick survey was usually enough to identify any missing objects or out-of-place items. They had decided early on to leave the house well-furnished and comfortable, the walls adorned with their own family pictures and the furniture to the same standard as if it were their own regular abode.

"No flat packs here." Tony had insisted from the start and so there was not a stick of furniture in the place that could be traced back to any such supplier, Scandinavian or otherwise. Whenever they were out-and-about on their travels around the country, or across Europe on weekend breaks, they often came across paintings that took their fancy or ornaments which they agreed would contribute to the olde-worlde feel of The Cottage. It was rare that they did not agree when it came to furnishings having realised early on in their relationship that their tastes were very similar and so, whilst there had been many moments of tension between them over the years, it was never about how best to dress their homes.

They never hesitated when it came to spending, and so the shelves and fireplaces were packed full of curiosities, items that would look out-of-place in their London terrace, but which fitted right in here, amongst the landscapes, ceramics, and other arts-and-crafts of their future retirement pad.

In many ways, it was a perfect cottage, the sort that visitors to England always swoon over. It would not have looked out of place in the Cotswolds, or in the Lake District, up high on the North York Moors or hidden away down the rugged lanes of a Cornish village. It was a typical English cottage, stone-built and solid, its thick walls offering effective insulation against the coldest of storm surge winds and a cool escape in the heat of the summer.

"It was just right." An oft repeated observation in the visitors' book, but perfect, it was not.

"Who wants tea?" shouted Charlie as she made her way into the kitchen, delighted to see that despite the sudden shortages of everyday essentials in the shops, Mrs Illsley had stocked them up with enough provisions to last them for the first week at least. "And we've got CHOCOLATE hobnobs."

"Me, me, me." It was the children and at the very mention of their favourite biscuits, they were both off the sofa in a jiffy, the distractions of the wi-fi instantly forgotten. "Can I have a hot chocolate instead?" asked Arthur, pushing his luck, but his mother was feeling relieved to have arrived safely and so was more than happy to indulge him with his favourite drink.

They had stopped at a local service station on the way down and had filled up on burgers and fries in one of the few rest-stops that were still open. It was the unhealthiest of options, but if there was ever an excuse for fast-food this was it, and a quick fix of caffeine and instant calories had been just what the doctor had ordered. A 'necessary evil' was how her husband had described it and it had felt surprisingly apt in the moment.

"Put the news on love." Charlie instructed, "let's see if there have been any developments."

He did, and there weren't. Just more scaremongering on the back of some dreadful news from mainland Europe, where the deathrate in Italy and Spain was seemingly spiralling out of control and panic was beginning to set in.

"Turn it off." she said just a minute or two later. She had seen and heard enough.

"I thought you wanted to know what was going on?" gulped her husband, midway through a long swig of his cooling tea and although he tried hard to take it all in the spirit in which it was intended, he could not resist a small side swipe. He was tired and it showed. "Make your bloody mind up. It's all bad news. Now that we're here let's just try to forget it all for a while, eh?"

It seemed like a good suggestion; now that they were safely tucked away in their country retreat, the world could get on perfectly well without them. It was their usual habit and though there were three TVs of various standards placed strategically about the house, they were rarely used, other than for gaming which was their son's favourite pastime. An old Game-Cube and a Wii meant that they were spoilt for choice and although the games were now long since out-of-date, they still provided the kids and their house guests with hours of fun, whenever they were pressed into service, especially on rainy days for which the English counties are famous.

Before long, the kids were reluctantly tucked up in bed, but as their noisy remonstrations began to fade, neither adult believed that either one would stay awake for long. They hadn't slept that much on the journey down and so both were left yawning, reading themselves to sleep, but still finding the energy to protest that they 'weren't a bit tired' as each bedroom door was pulled slowly and silently into its fake 'period-style' frame.

"I'm having a whisky," declared Tony, already half-way to the kitchen where a few bottles of single malt were locked away for moments such as this.

"It'll have to be neat." his wife answered, her voice muted through restored layers of wooden lath, horsehair and lime plaster that still cloaked much of the wooden skeleton of the Grade II listed house. "There are no ice cubes, the big fridge hasn't been switched on."

"Bummer." The 'big fridge' was always left on. It was one of those double fronted American jobbies, complete with an inbuilt ice dispenser, but it had been laying empty for a week or more after their last booking was forced to cancel due to the pandemic, and so Mrs Illsley would no doubt have taken the opportunity to disinfect it and had almost certainly left it turned off to save on the electric bill. She was prudent like that. "Do you want one?"

"Go on then, I'll be down in a bit, I'm just going to jump in the shower."

He poured himself a large one, at least a treble or maybe even a quadruple by Pub standards, but it was his first in a while and he told himself that he needed it. It had been a fraught day, and though he may have been successful in giving the impression to his wife and children that he wasn't worried about the crisis and its potential ruinous impact on their business, nothing could have been further from the truth.

He was quaking in his boots.

Events management was his 'bag', and thanks to the worst health scare since the Spanish Flu, there were now no events planned for the foreseeable future. For how long, nobody seemed to know, and though he was clinging to the possibility that the outbreak was going to be short-lived, all the indications were to the contrary.

They were in this for the long haul and the "new normal," whatever that was, could mean the end of his long and prosperous 'bull run'. All bookings for the house had now been cancelled for the next three months, meaning no second revenue to make up for the loss of the first, but their expenses were not going to disappear. There was the mortgage to pay on their London house, the rental on the lock-up where he kept all his gear for the extravagant outdoor events for which his firm was famous, their multiple insurances, school-fees, council tax on both properties, as well as utility bills for both properties. The list was endless. He was starting to panic.

He took a large swig from the cut-glass tumbler and swilled it around his mouth, enjoying its bittersweet tang, before swallowing hard to let his throat share in the sensation.

Charlie returned from the upstairs bathroom, a beige towel wrapped around her head and sporting a fluffy pink dressing gown with matching slippers. "Water was cold." she complained, "started off hot, but then went lukewarm and then it was freezing. I've put the immersion heater back on again."

"The log burner is blazing now," said Tony hardly listening, lost in thought, and consumed with worry. "That'll get the back burner going, it'll be back to normal by morning. No one has complained about the heating for years, have they? Not since Bill fixed it. I'm sure it's fine."

They settled down on the comfy sofa in the snug, a most apt name for the cosy room at the front of the house, which had once been the family parlour in Victorian times. There was only room for a two-seater sofa and a single armchair, which crowded in on the double-fronted log-burner that was set back into the base of the chimney to illuminate the inner frame of a large imitation Adams-style fireplace. The fire cast its shadows about the darkened room, its mesmerising flames licking at the plain painted walls and providing a cosy ambiance that they had never grown tired of.

The lane was always unnaturally quiet, even in the pre-COVID world, and an absence of streetlights or the occasional sweep of nearby headlights from the main road, meant that the fire was the only source of light. Tony had turned the standard lamp off for maximum effect minutes before, and the two of them were soon entangled, her feet on his lap and his curled up beneath her thighs.

The orange glow illuminated the faintest red tinge on their Alsatian's back, the rest of him almost invisible in the dark, as the dog soaked up the heat and began to snore, his legs galloping off after every imaginary rabbit and his lips quivering at the very thought of catching one.

For a moment, they just sat there, enjoying the near complete silence, the chatter from upstairs long since subsided. Charlie had picked up a book from the shelf in the hall, one that she hadn't seen before and which she presumed had been left behind by one of the families. It wasn't unusual for visitors to leave their holiday reads behind or to swap them for others that had been similarly deposited. In fact, it was something that they had openly encouraged, a note on the wall inviting their paying guests to do exactly that; it ensured that there was always a fresh supply of reading material for those that came back year after year and there was often something unusual to be found, lurking amongst the well-thumbed paperbacks.

Tony sat brooding over a final mouthful of whisky. He was staring into the middle distance, playing things over in his mind, his fingers tapping on the side of the glass. From the hallway, he could hear the faintest heartbeat of their grandfather clock, a French-style reproduction that they had rescued from a second-hand shop many years before, its lengthy pendulum swinging back and forth as its wrought-iron hands marked time across its finely decorated face. They'd had to saw a few inches off its base to make it fit in this the oldest part of the house, its ornately carved frame too tall to slide comfortably beneath the low ceiling, which remained bowed despite the best efforts of their builder to bring it to heel.

"You know what I don't get?" blurted Tony, the silence finally becoming too heavy.

"What honey?"

"Why didn't they lock us down sooner? The Chinese were building hospitals in November for goodness sake. It's not like we didn't get advance warning. Why did it take dozens of deaths on our own doorstep to force them into action?"

His wife shook her head, sharing his bewilderment at the government's apparent inertia. "Who knows," she answered sleepily, "maybe they just didn't think it was going to get this bad? It's a new disease they say, so it's easy to be wise after the fact."

"I suppose," mumbled Tony, downing the last of his drink. He looked over at his wife, instantly aroused by a familiar glimpse of breast peeping from beneath the nape of her dressing gown.

"Oh hello." said Charlie playfully, glancing down at her husband's straining shorts, her eyes wide and welcoming. "Looks like somebody wants to come out to play."

It was all the invitation he needed, and he moved in like a horny teenager, pressing his lips against hers and forcing his hand beneath her towelling gown to squeeze her ample breast. It was an urgent embrace, a deep and needy engagement. His tongue did battle with hers, as he switched positions and forced her down onto the short sofa, her feet dangling over the end as her covering fell apart to reveal her nakedness. Immediately he went down on her, burying his face into the space between her legs, tasting her as his nose nuzzled into her wispy brown bush of pubic hair.

Charlie moaned louder than she had intended within earshot of the kids, and her body tensed as she pulled him up by the shoulders and yanked down his shorts to release him, and in a second, he was inside her, his hips thrusting in time with hers.

"Fuck me." she sighed, an almost inaudible plea as she nibbled on his ear and squeezed his firm torso tightly to her. "Fuck me." she said more loudly, more urgently. "Do it."

He didn't hesitate to do as he was told, ramming himself higher and higher inside her and grinding his hips against hers, then holding back to keep himself from ejaculating too soon. "You dirty bitch." he whispered, knowing how much she loved to be scolded at the height of their passions. "You little tart. Are you enjoying this you slut?" Such "quickies" – that is, sex when she least expected it - were always her favourite and he wasn't about to disappoint.

She was almost lost in the moment, and her voice had risen a couple of decibels when she next cried out. "Yes." she screamed."

He lifted her waist up from the sofa, his ample penis still inside her and slapped her hard two or three times across her upturned backside. His right hand kneaded at her buttocks, his fingers tracing the line between them as his left grasped her waist, to pull her into him. He kissed and caressed her neck and shoulder, his hands busy about her body, just as another closed around her neck and began to burn against her bare skin.

As she screamed, the dog barked and he came, a powerful burst of semen that had him groaning in uncontrollable pleasure, and which drowned out the terror that his wife was now feeling at the alien touch of a third hand.

The close-fitting clutch of fingers around her throat.

She pulled herself up on the sofa and he fell away in surprise. She always liked him to stay inside her for as long as possible afterwards, but not this time. This time he was dumped unceremoniously to the floor, her legs kicking out at him like a swimmer who is frantically treading water in panic, as the sight of land recedes beyond the horizon. Bruce was barking frantically, leaping up onto the sofa and over the back, snarling and barking at nothing, his teeth bared and his hackles high.

"What." was the only word that Tony could find to say in the moment. "What's wrong?" he said recovering some of his composure, as he reached for the light on the lampstand beside them. "Shit. What's that on your neck?" In the now illuminated room the clear imprint of four red lines stood out beneath her jawline; the unmistakeable shadow of a human hand.

His wife was sobbing now, unable to get her words out, but even through her tears he could sense her fear and it was obvious to him that he was not the source of her terror.

Bruce had stopped barking now, but he was still patrolling, circling the room on high alert, his eyes blazing in the firelight. Finally, as Tony's calming voice began to take effect, his hand stroking his wife's hair and his lips planting gentle kisses upon her forehead, she recovered enough to speak, but what she had to say would not be to his liking.

"There was someone else here." she spurted, as the dog nuzzled at her hand, and she pulled him closer. "I felt a hand, around my neck, and it was cold, as cold as ice."

Tuesday 24th to Thursday 26th March 2020

DAY 2 TO DAY 4 OF UK LOCKDOWN

370 deaths reported in the UK – the total number of deaths due to COVID19 now stands at 1,836 with 18,096 people testing positive for the disease.

CHAPTER 4

The next few days were sunny with just a light easterly wind, and each one passed without further incident at The Cottage, but the moment in the snug was not easily forgotten, at least not for the humans. Although the episode had left them all feeling unnerved and uneasy in their own home-away-from-home, Bruce had shown no ill-effects; he had been his usual inquisitive self, unperturbed by any of the new sights, smells, or sounds.

Yet as the wave of anxiety swept across the country, it had already begun to rattle the windows of their pragmatic down-to-earth existence and so that friendly spirit, which they had often laughed about with friends, no longer seemed so benign. As a result, Tony and Charlie were both 'on edge' in the days that followed and though the root cause of their unease seemed to ebb and flow, shifting from an uncertain future to their unnamed house guest, and back again, it did so without warning.

They had never indulged in any form of supernatural shenanigans, despite the prompting of some of their more adventurous friends to bring in a medium or to have a séance. They had preferred instead to let things lie in the belief that their invisible visitor would not bother them if they didn't bother it. In the past, they had always been convinced that the presence was simply standing guard over them and their property, keeping a permanent vigil, rather than posing any kind of threat to them or to their friends and family. It was a conclusion that no longer passed muster, but they chose to cling onto it, in the hope that as the physical evidence faded, so the lingering memory would go the same way. The handprint had all but gone by morning and so, outright denial seemed the best remedy.

The very next morning, Tony asked his wife if she wanted to go home, but she was made of stronger stuff. It was their house, their investment, and their life, and she was not about to let one unfathomable experience put a dampener on twenty years of grit and graft. She was what his mother would have called a 'brick' – his rock, with an unshakable and unflappable personality, and it had come as no surprise to Tony that his wife would not be scared off after one inexplicable occurrence, however freaky it had been. Not for the first time in their marriage, he was astounded by her resolve and by her determination to focus on the long-term gain, whatever the short-term pain.

In the intervening days he had set up his office in the conservatory, a brand-new addition for the new season, that sat astride the kitchen, and which provided the most comfortable of environments in which to work. The wi-fi was strongest at the rear of the house and so it was a prime spot to connect to the firm's server and to communicate with the remaining skeleton crew of staff, the handful of workers that had not been immediately furloughed following the outbreak. Sadly, he feared, that they would soon share the same fate as their former colleagues.

"Morning Mike.," he hailed through the Zoom connection, a company that was set fair to do very well out of the pandemic and one that Tony had already included in his share portfolio. Along with some of the other technology giants of the world, he was certain that in a world where remote working was about to become the norm, those firms that were supplying the services that underpinned the latest in a long line of technological revolutions were going to be very well-positioned to reap the rewards.

"Hey Tony, how's it going?" came the cheery response, his co-worker looking like he had only just got out of bed, judging by his unshaven face and steaming cup of coffee.

"Late night?" Tony asked, ignoring his colleague's question.

"Couldn't sleep," the bearded man admitted, "too much on my mind – this thing has got me really worried. What about you, how are you feeling about it all now?"

"Same," said Tony. "We are just going to have to sit it out. I've had an official email to say that we should not be expecting the situation to change any time soon. We can assume that all indoor events will be off for the long-term and in the short-to-medium term, most large outdoor events will also be banned."

"Shit." said Mike solemnly. "That's it then, isn't it? We've got to put everything on hold."

"I think so," said Tony sadly. "I wanted to let you know face-to-face, so to speak, that I'm going to have to put everyone on enforced absence for now. At least you'll get eighty percent for a while, until this thing blows over."

"What about you and Charlie?"

"We're directors.," said Tony. "We get nothing. Don't they say that a good captain always goes down with the ship?"

"Shit." said Mike again, in what was clearly becoming his choice of word for the morning. "I'm sorry mate. Let's hope they find a cure or a vaccine or something, sooner rather than later."

"We can but hope," smiled Tony, but the smile did not sit well on his face.

"Listen, I've got to call a few more people to give them the bad news, so I have to drop off, but let's stay in touch. Find yourself a hobby, you've always said you wanted to take up gardening, so now's your chance."

"Cheers mate." said Mike, "I will, and good luck."

The rest of the calls took up most of the morning and by the time he'd finished informing the remainder of his team that they were now on enforced leave he was left emotionally drained. Some had taken it better than others, but all had expressed their concern for him and for Charlie, one or two even asking after the kids and how they were bearing up. He had always been proud to say that theirs was a 'family business', one in which every member of the team was treated as if they were part of one extended family, and he found himself hoping that he'd still be able to say the same, once this unforeseen nightmare was at an end.

His back ached royally as he stood up from three hours on an uncomfortable chair, that was better suited to a dinner party than office work, and he extended his shoulders and arched his back to relieve the muscle tension that had taken hold, flexing his fingers into a cat's cradle to complete the stretch. He could hear the kids arguing upstairs, a common enough occurrence at the best of times, but after a few days cooped up in unfamiliar surroundings and without their vast array of toys from home, it was unlikely to be the last time. He feared that boredom was already setting in.

He heard Charlie's shrill voice echo through the house as her limit was finally reached. He smiled to himself as he heard Lottie storm down the stairs to hurl herself in front of the TV, snapping up the remote control in mid-strop, and he guessed correctly that they had each been banished in opposite directions. It wasn't long before his wife trailed downstairs in the wake of their eldest child, with a look on her face that said she was at the end of her tether.

"Those bloody kids of yours." she yelled, picking up the kettle and filling it from the sharply contoured tap above the butler sink, where her husband stood ready for an onslaught that never came. Whenever the two of them argued as children do, they were always his and never hers, and today was to be no exception. "I tell you; the world of high finance is a walk-in-the-park compared to a day with those two when they're in this mood." That said, her own mood remained remarkably chipper despite the upheaval and with her recent fright seemingly consigned to history, she made them both a brew, reaching out for the biscuit tin that was no longer where she had left it.

Neither of them was prepared for what the day had in store for them.

"Let's sit out back," gestured Tony, making a move to unlock the double doors to the rear of the house, where an ornate two-seater table sat invitingly in front of the revitalised yard. "I'll have a coffee please, but hold the sugar, I've got to cut down or I'll be the size of a house after two months of this." Bruce followed him out, heading straight into the bushes to do his business, before completing two circuits of the table and easing himself to the ground with an audible groan.

The garden had been last to feel the full weight of the overhaul, but it was now much better and the quadrangle in which they were soon seated like bookends had been refashioned into a neat and attractive pot-garden. The only thing that remained were some of the flagstones beneath their feet, though they were not in their original position, having once made up the base for the kitchen. Set at intervals between these large sandstone slabs, a series of more modern, but irregular stones were laid down in coloured patterns, giving the whole thing a rather haphazard look, which somehow worked. Pots of various sizes were scattered around and about, all in need of some attention now that spring was here, but the unseasonable sunshine was already coaxing several plants from their winter rest, which always added a touch of glam to the garden.

"At least we can spend some time getting all this in order," said Charlie, glancing around at the criss-crossed lines of trellis that acted as a scenic backdrop to the low brick lined borders of their flowerbeds. "Shame the garden centres are all closed, we could do with some potting compost, though I expect we have plenty in the composters."

Tony was just turning to look in the general direction of the rundown greenhouse, a maintenance job that was high on his hit list, when a shrill scream rang out from inside the house and for a split second, they didn't recognise it for what it was.

Bruce was off to the races in an instant, dashing indoors ahead of them, his ears pricked up and barking wildly. It was the unmistakeable cry of a child and both parents were on their feet and running at pace behind the dog, long before the shriek began to fade, to be replaced by a rapid patter of footsteps that grew louder as they drew near.

They clattered into each other's arms at the base of the stairs, just where the extended kitchen met with the old part of the house, and for nigh-on a minute it proved quite impossible to decipher the cause of her distress. Lottie was in floods of tears and there was no doubting that whatever it was, it wasn't simply another case of sibling rivalry.

"It moved." she sobbed, her chest heaving with the effort of it, her hands clutching Bruce's fur for comfort. "On its own."

"What did?" asked her father, concerned, and confused at the same time.

"What moved darling?" It was her mother this time, sunk down on her knees, her twelve-year-old daughter in her arms as if she was a toddler once more, with all sense of bravado gone and wanting nothing more than to be safe and secure in the face of danger.

"The book, on the table," she spluttered, "it opened all by itself and then it snapped shut again. And then it fell off the table and onto the floor. I didn't touch it honest; it just fell all by itself." They must have looked like they didn't believe a word, because a moment later and Lottie lost control of her emotions again, but this time it was in frustration, prompting Tony to head into the snug to investigate for himself.

"It's okay honey," said her mother, soothing her hair as she used to when she was a little girl. "We believe you - we do. Dad's just going to look. Where is your brother, was he there too?"

Lottie shook her head and with a pointed finger indicated that her arch enemy was still upstairs, no doubt with his gaming earphones surgically attached to his head and missing every minute of the drama that was unfolding in the room below.

"It was this one, was it?" asked Tony, returning less than a minute later with a hard-backed copy of a Dickens classic in his hands. She nodded in confirmation, and he leafed through its pages, as if checking for strings or batteries or something, but there was nothing there to see; it was just a plain and dusty old book, illustrated throughout with cartoons of Nicholas Nickleby and his many adventures.

"That's odd." he said, turning to his wife for corroboration. "Does this feel cold to you?"

"Freezing." said Charlie, taking the book into her hands with a shiver and turning it over to inspect its faded red spine. The dust cover had been misplaced long before and all that was left was the hardback itself, the many layers of yellowing pages caught in between like layers of dried lasagne. "Where was it?"

"In front of the fireplace," he said, pointing at the floor, "just there, squared up perfectly like it had been placed there."

"Dad."

This time it was their son, hailing them cheerily from the top of the stairwell, a rectangular box clutched in his outstretched hands. "What's this?"

"I dunno Skip." said Tony, trying his best not to spook his boy into the bargain. One freaked out child was enough to be going on with, but the boy didn't look scared, he looked excited, and Tony hoped that it would prove interesting enough to capture his sister's attention too. "Bring it down, let's take a look at it."

The boy came down the stairs at breakneck speed, leaping from the third rung from the bottom and onto the carpet beneath.

"SLOWLY." his mother shrieked, fearful of a more earthly trauma but far too late to have any hope of changing the outcome. Arthur came up smiling, as he handed the board game to his dad for closer scrutiny. He hadn't even been able to read the name on the front, as if the game was written in some foreign language or something, but if the scary man in the pale blue hood on the cover was anything to go by, it looked fab.

"Where did you get this Skip?" asked Tony trying to retain a modicum of outward indifference as he looked across at the boy's mother, an expression of surprise and no little worry etched into his expression. His son's nickname was short for 'Skipper', a pet name that only Tony used and which he had adopted instinctively, almost from the day he'd come home from the maternity hospital.

"It was in the toy box under all of the other stuff," said Arthur quite honestly. "Can you show me it Dad, can you, please?"

"No Skip." said Tony, fashioning a look on his face that was stern enough to scold, but not enough to scare his young son. "This sort of thing isn't for children, it's a grown-up game."

"What is it dad?" Lottie could sense her father's anxiety and given her only too recent experience, she was keener than ever to know more about it, especially if it was going upset the 'boy-wonder'.

"It's not a toy." said Tony, more sharply than he had intended. "I can't believe it was up there. We need to find out which of our *guests* brought this here Charlie. I don't care who they are, they're not welcome here again. They're barred."

CHAPTER 5

"It's a Ouija Board," explained Tony later that night, once the kids had been settled into bed. They'd gone up rather earlier than usual, citing the excuse that tomorrow they would be venturing out for the first time since the start of lockdown, but in reality, their parents just needed some grown-up time.

The box looked intriguing, consisting of a dark grey backdrop with large red letters spelling out the word OUIJA, overprinted onto a silhouetted figure in black, his right hand raised aloft in greeting, or in warning. The manufacturer was proudly proclaimed beneath – a familiar name that he'd seen many times before over the years, though he couldn't quite place it, certain that he had never seen this particular product before in his life. It was further described as a 'psychic odyssey' or 'visionary board set' and as he turned it over in his hands, pausing to read what would now be called its USP – or unique selling points – a coldness came over him as he recalled something that he had seen about them years before.

"These things were marketed on an unsuspecting public in the sixties," said Tony, as he remembered a documentary that he'd seen on one of the dedicated history channels. "They were banned shortly afterwards after hundreds of complaints were received from worried parents."

"Complaints about what?" asked his wife, assuming that there were small parts or sharp edges to it, on which children had choked or cut themselves.

"Weird shit." It wasn't much of an explanation, but it seemed to do the trick as his wife was stunned into silence. "This one looks like an original American version," he said as he slipped the limited contents from the box; a heart-shaped piece of plastic with a hole in its centre and a beige coloured board, on which an array of letters, numbers and words were laid out in an orderly fashion. He peered closely at the elongated grey planchette and read the inscription aloud to his wife.

"OUIJA. TRADEMARK REG. US. PATENT OFFICE. WILLIAM FULD, whoever that was; MESSAGE INDICATOR; MADE IN USA."

The planchette itself had a large circular hole – or window as the description on the box described it - towards its narrowest end, about the size of an old half-crown, its underside supported on three free-moving ball-bearings, which allowed it to glide in any direction at will, supposedly at the direction of the spirit world.

"What does 'Ouija' mean?" Charlie asked bemused.

"In simple terms, it means 'Yes-Yes, would you believe.

It wasn't difficult. It was simply a combination of the French and German words for 'yes' and together, they hinted at the board's primary purpose, which was to ask questions and to receive answers.

Answers from the realm of spirits.

Answers from beyond the grave.

Tony flipped the box over, where a limited set of instructions could be seen, though there was no hint therein of the more macabre purpose with which such things are often associated. In the absence of any form of warning, Tony could see just how the unwary might have been led into a world that they were quite unprepared for. The two of them continued to read it quietly to themselves, speaking aloud occasional words and phrases that caught their attention as the marketing blurb piqued their interest.

"The OUIJA witching board provides endless hours of entertainment for you and your friends and family. It brings the two people closer together in a sense of mystery that is unrivalled by any other game."

"Can you believe this?" said Tony, incredulously. "Amusement and recreation; what were these people on?"

"I don't understand," said Charlie, still perplexed by the whole thing. "Are you really saying that they marketed this as a 'toy' for children?"

"Fun for the whole family, apparently," said Tony sarcastically. "Well, I think we've seen the results of some of that fun, haven't we?"

"What do you mean?" said Charlie, still unsure if she really wanted to put two and two together to make four.

"Isn't it obvious?" asked her husband, doing what he could to bring her up to speed without scaring her out of her wits. "Someone, one of our previous paying guests no doubt, has brought this into our house and tried it out, and has got far more than they bargained for, leaving us to sort out the mess."

"What, do you mean that they've conjured something up?" asked Charlie, unsure if it was a question that she really wanted answered, but it was too late to back out now. It was said. "Something that's still here?"

"It's got to be possible, right?" whispered Tony, conscious that one or both children might still be listening. They had learned from bitter experience that sound carried in this house, as if it were somehow transported along the lengths of the wooden beams, like muted conversations on a telegraph line. "If they read about our resident ghost and thought it might be fun to try to speak with it, to ask it questions and to get some answers," he continued in the same subdued tones. "'Did you die in this house'; 'how old were you when you died'; 'what year did you live here'; that sort of thing."

"There are some directions, what do they say?" Charlie had no intention of following any instructions, however simple they might seem to be and had no interest whatsoever in the *'hours of fun, anticipation and stimulation'* that were on offer to anyone who dared to engage with it. But she remained curious and hoped that, in her case, such curiosity would not prove fatal.

"Put the board between two people who are sat facing each other across the table," her husband announced, reading the list aloud.

"I'd rather not." said Charlie, in a forlorn attempt to lighten the mood as her husband continued to read from the fifty-year-old box that had somehow found its way into their house.

> *'Put the OUIJA message indicator at the centre of board, with fingers lightly placed upon it, so that it can move without obstruction in all directions. Then start your questioning and within a few moments the planchette will begin to vibrate, at first slowly, then moving faster, spelling out, through a series of letters, a message from another realm'.*

"This is all very damn peculiar if you ask me," said Charlie, "It's got to be a hoax, hasn't it? You don't really believe that these things work, do you?"

Tony shot her a pensive look, indicating that he was clearly more open minded than she was when it came to supernatural matters. "There are more things in heaven and earth." he said, cutting short a famous quote from the Bard himself, as he reached out to fuss the dog, who was suddenly more agitated and was busily pacing the room, stopping to sniff for a moment in every corner before moving onto the next.

"But it's just a cheap piece of wood and plastic.," scoffed Charlie. "Isn't it?"

"And the handprint on your neck was just in your head, was it?" he teased, knowing that he might live to regret the jibe, but his sudden spate of bravado didn't stop there. "Did you imagine it? And the incident with the book – our level-headed daughter dreamt that one up by herself, did she?"

"I don't bloody well know Tone, sod off." It was a rubbish answer, but it was all she had and so, somewhat reluctantly, she gave him the green light to continue. "What else does the little box of tricks have to tell us then, seeing as you're such a know-it-all on the subject all of a sudden? Does it tell us how to rid our house of whatever has been invited in?"

"Well, unfortunately, no. It doesn't make any such claims to anything that we might call 'paranormal'," admitted Tony, a little surprised. "It seems to be suggesting that it's somehow linking the minds of the two people involved. There's no mention of ghosts or spirits anywhere on the box. It's only hinted at, but they might argue that it's more about telepathy than anything else."

He continued to read from the official directions provided.

'2nd – be sure to avoid confusion by keeping your questions simple – do not speak over one another.

3rd – take the game as seriously as you can – avoid asking silly questions, concentrate and avoid any distractions.

4th – we cannot guarantee a response each time you use it but persevere and you will see results that will surprise and amaze.

5th – don't be surprised if secrets are revealed from your most innermost consciousness and of those around you.

6th – keep the board free from dust and moisture, so as to maintain an ideal surface for the planchette. Clean it with a soft dry cloth before storing away in a dry enclosed space'.

"Shall we give it a go then?" said Charlie with some trepidation, but even though she wasn't expecting him to say yes, she was taken aback by the force of her husband's refusal.

"No, we bloody well won't." It wasn't an answer to be argued with, in fact, it was clear to both of them that it wasn't even up for discussion. "This is going on top of the wardrobe where the kids can't find it and that's where it's staying. We are going to find out which idiot brought it here and then, they can either take it back or it's going in the bin."

"Okay, I only asked." said Charlie, who had not seen her husband snap like that in years. "I just thought we could see for ourselves what all the fuss was about. Maybe there's a 'Strip-Ouija' version we could try out?"

They both laughed at that, a timely and welcome break in the tension that had been building between them ever since the kids had gone to bed, and Tony quickly apologised for his outburst.

"Well, that's definitely not a 'game for all the family'," he replied, squeezing his wife's hand and smirking like a schoolboy as he allowed his mind to wander off. Of course, she wasn't being serious in the slightest, but that didn't stop him from wrestling with the conundrum of how the rules to such a game might work just in case she ever was.

In fact, nothing could have been further from her mind, but in the end, none of it mattered, because Bruce was stood stock still at the bottom of the stairs, his head raised and his hackles up, as a deep guttural growl put a timely pin into Tony's rising passion.

"Dad." It was their son, calling for attention from the top of the stairs, his long-suffering comfort blanket scrunched up in his hand. It was a mood killing moment for everyone.

"What's up Skip?" his dad called to him, expecting to be summoned with a glass of water or for a late-night story. But what their eight-year-old had to say would chill them to their bones.

"Daddy, there's a man in my room."

CHAPTER 6

If there had been something there, it was there no more and although their son was insistent that he had not dreamt it, an over-active imagination seemed to be the only logical explanation for the apparent late-night visitation. Although it had been his dad that he had called to his side, Arthur only had eyes for his mum. After he'd calmed down enough for her to coax him back into bed, she attended lovingly to his every need, tucking him up tightly beneath the duvet and showering him in kisses to banish any lingering memories that might otherwise have led to nightmares.

As Charlie fussed over his small form, his dad scoured the room, looking for anything that was out of place, even checking that the windows were securely fastened and that the small wardrobe wasn't acting as a refuge for anything other than a pile of clothes and a few assorted boxes of miniature cars and action-hero figurines. Within minutes, Arthur was well on the way back to the land-of-nod, and as they backed quietly from the room, they left the night-light on and the door slightly ajar. The boy shifted onto his side as they exited, pulling his blankie up under his chin, the silky label caught between his thumb and forefinger as he had done ever since he was a babe-in-arms.

In the distance they could hear the faint metallic clatter of the local villagers, as they beat out their appreciation for the NHS in what had become a weekly tradition across the cities of Europe. Even so, they spoke in whispered tones, just in case either disturbance had roused their eldest child from sleep, not wanting to have to explain another noise on top of her own trauma.

As they talked, Charlie made herself a cup of tea, whilst Tony drained the last of the whisky into his tumbler and followed her trail back into the lounge where his agitated wife was wearing a desperate look all of her own.

"Is this how we left it?" she asked, her eyes fixed on the Ouija board that was still laid out on the small glass topped coffee table, the planchette placed carefully in the top left quadrant. "It seems to have answered us."

Its circular window had stalled above the word 'Yes', but Tony could not remember asking it a question and he looked at his wife, hoping that her short-term memory would prove to be better than his.

"You said, 'do you really think he might have seen a ghost?'" she reminded him, "just then in the kitchen. You didn't say it loud enough for anyone to hear, but maybe it doesn't need things to be said within earshot – I'm sure that we didn't leave the board set up like this, the planchette wasn't even out, was it?"

"I don't remember," her husband confessed. "We left in such a rush; I could have knocked it or pushed the table as I went by. It could be a coincidence. Let's not spook ourselves any more with this thing." and at that he picked up the board with its self-styled 'mysterious message indicator', and dropped them unceremoniously into the box, sealing the top with the pristinely preserved cardboard catch. For good measure he retrieved a roll of Sellotape from the bureau drawer and bound it like a heretic to a stake, using up the whole roll in a frenzied attempt to seal the box shut for eternity.

"So, what do we do now?" Mrs Mountford asked, at a loss to know where they should go from here. "I don't want to worry the kids with this, let's try to keep it to ourselves as much as possible. If they don't mention anything, we shouldn't remind either of them of it. Or of what they think they've seen."

Tony nodded in agreement, but he'd been plotting, and he was now ready to share his fledgling plans. "Have you been through the latest visitor book entries yet? For the ones who've stayed here since we were last down?"

49

"No, not yet," she answered, immediately catching his drift. "How many bookings have we had since October half term? Ten, twelve maybe?"

"Yes, I think so. Last time we were here, there was nothing untoward was there? No signs of any goings-on. Nothing that could be remotely described as 'supernatural'?" He was certain that there had been nothing at all that had unnerved him during their last, or on any recent visits for that matter, though he could recall a few incidents during the renovation work a decade and a half earlier.

"No," agreed Charlie, "and the kids have always loved the place, they've never been scared to come. They always jump at the chance."

"Though Lottie did used to have an imaginary friend, didn't she?," recalled Tony quizzically, rubbing his stubble for effect.

"Yes, she did, but she also played with her up in London," said Charlie, "I can't believe that ghosts can hitch a lift up-and-down the motorway, can they?"

"I wouldn't have thought so." Tony mused, suddenly recalling the girl's name. "It was Tabitha, wasn't it? I remember now because the only other Tabitha that I've ever heard of was in that American comedy series from the 1960's, the one that they made into a film recently."

"Bewitched." answered Charlie, biting her lip in an unsuccessful attempt at self-censorship. "Great – so now you're bringing a witch into the conversation, maybe you can think of a few ghoulish demons as well to stop me from sleeping tonight. Any werewolves? What about vampires?"

"Don't let's get side-tracked," he laughed, kissing his wife on the forehead before continuing to lay out his master plan. "Tomorrow, not tonight I don't want any more drama today, let's go through the entries and see if anyone has reported anything these last few months. Maybe someone might even have owned up to bringing that sodding board into the house, which will save us a lot of time and effort. Whatever, we can then contact all of them – we have their email addresses, don't we?" His wife nodded and so he continued. "Let's email the lot of them and ask them outright – did they bring it here; did they use it here or did they see it here? That will help us to narrow down the search to a point in time, so if the culprit doesn't own up by themselves, we might be able to tell from their responses the first time that anyone clapped eyes on it. And then, bingo."

"Very true," Charlie said, feeling a little better now that they had agreed on a sensible way forward. It was at least worth a try. "Maybe we can ask them if they noticed anything different about their stay this time, if they have been here before that is. Get them to help with the detective work. We don't want to put them off staying again though, so we'll need to be careful with our choice of words."

"I'll work on it first thing," said Tony, knowing full well that his wife and son would not stir until at least nine o'clock, giving him a couple of hours at least to focus on getting it right, especially as Lottie would be parked in front of the TV and unlikely to stray from there until lunchtime at the earliest. It wasn't much of a plan, but at least it was something.

Soon afterwards the house was once more in darkness, the electric lights turned off for the night and the dying embers of a once roaring fire ebbing into potash. There was still enough of a glow to lick at the edges of all but the most distant furniture, and so familiar to the early hours that Bruce remained undisturbed. He was laid flat out in front of the fireplace, his fur coat keeping him warm despite the fading heat and his ears flat, a faintly contented snore keeping time with the clock's steady heartbeat.

Every now and again his ears would be alerted by movement from above or below, a contracting timber, or the tired spring of a mattress as a sleeping occupant fought hard to stay on the other side of consciousness, but each stirring was recognised for what it was without rousing him from rest. The faithful dog slept on into the small hours, his steadfast form rising and falling like a set of bellows as his dreamt of familiar smells and the soft touch of his mother's nose on his.

It was the scratching that egged him from his slumber, the faintest clawing of nails on glass that seemed to seep up from beneath his makeshift bed, and although his eyes scanned the room and his nose twitched in vain to sniff out the cause, his senses drew a blank. Once or twice, he lifted his head and looked about him, but satisfied that there was nothing out of the ordinary that would endanger him or his sleeping charges, he ignored the continuing sound and with an indignant snort, he settled down until the dawn.

Even then, as the faintest light began to crawl inwards to the spot where he lay and the cautious call of birds broke through the silence, it didn't encroach on his rest. It only made him think of what lay outside, an intrusion of wet grass and the fragrant rush of other springtime scents as he barged between them. His tail wagged out an involuntary beat as these succulent images crowded in on him, but still he didn't budge an inch, though he thought that he could hear human noises from below that whispered and wept up at him through the folds of time.

He had heard them before of course, and so, he was used to their pleading tones. He no longer paid them much attention, though the hearing always left him with an uneasy feeling, as if he'd let them down somehow in his canine duty to protect and serve, but it was just another noise of the night that would soon disappear with the darkness and be forgotten.

F̲r̲i̲d̲a̲y̲ ̲2̲7̲t̲h̲ ̲M̲a̲r̲c̲h̲ ̲2̲0̲2̲0̲ ̲D̲A̲Y̲ ̲5̲ ̲–̲ ̲U̲K̲ ̲L̲O̲C̲K̲D̲O̲W̲N̲

416 deaths reported in the UK – the total number of deaths due to COVID19 now stands at 2,252 with 20,768 people testing positive for the disease.

CHAPTER 7

Both parents passed a peaceful and uninterrupted night in the comfort of their king-sized bed. They would never have fitted it into the old bedroom at the cottage, but with the addition of the front extension, it took centre stage and provided just a short hop to Mrs Mountford's flamboyant balcony of which Juliet Capulet would have been proud.

Tony rose early, as was his habit, and after releasing the dog for his morning constitutional, he had spent the first hour lost in thought. Seated in the spacious conservatory, he had enjoyed the early sunshine in contemplative mood, but work worries continued to lay siege to his mind, to batter any sense of satisfaction he might be feeling into submission. By the time he heard the first movement from upstairs, he'd already seen off more than half of the fresh filter coffee that had been percolating since first light, as he laid a mental bet on which member of his family would be the first to join him.

He loved their cottage, despite the recent goings-on, and he remained determined not to let anything spoil that fact. He had long since come to believe that these four walls would be the place where he and Charlie would eventually see out their days, however long into the future that might turn out to be. For a moment or two, he allowed himself to wonder how many years he had left, a morose moment that he would later put down to the pandemic and the realisation that the rising death rate was not simply a grim statistic for the elderly and infirm. The number of deaths observed amongst otherwise fit and healthy people was also stacking up and it wasn't a headline that he had expected to be reading on the digital edition of his favourite newspaper that morning.

The cottage had become a much anticipated bi-annual retreat for him and his family and every year they had been able to add to its charms, to make it increasingly 'of them'. In some ways he hated having to rent it out at all, but he was now on first name terms with many of their regulars, so much so that some of them had become friends. They had even enjoyed a couple of new year's eves and one momentous Christmas here, when Charlie had announced – much to his surprise – that she was expecting a 'mini me'.

The reference had stuck, so much so that when they had discovered they were expecting a girl, it had seemed only right to name her after her mother, though she had been a Lottie from the very start. Charlotte had seemed to be way too formal a name for a little girl, let alone a baby, and so almost overnight it had been Charlie and Lottie. His wife's pregnancy had been relatively uneventful and though childbirth would prove to be a very stressful experience, for both of them, Lottie had been a delight from day one, sleeping through the night at just two weeks old and taking to the bottle ahead of time to give her weary mother a much-needed break.

As he reflected on those early years, he remembered, quite out of nowhere, that the only times that Lottie had ever been any trouble at night was when they had come to stay at the cottage. At home she would go down at night as good as gold, but down at their bolthole, she would often be restless and tearful, sometimes waking in the night and once she could walk, she had wandered into their room and into their bed on a regular basis. There was never any explanation required and they had just hoped she would grow out of it, and she had; in fact, he could not recall the last time she had been of any bother at all on their spring or autumn breaks.

They rarely came down in high season, the rental incomes were way too high to ever consider losing out on that lucrative trade, and so they would always pencil themselves in for a week in February or March and again in October, to coincide with the half-term holidays. It was always perfect timing, allowing him to ready the property for the summer surge or to batten down the hatches for the winter trade, which tended to be restricted to Christmas and new year's eve.

This week's weather had been widely predicted to get unseasonably hot and he made a mental note to get the swimming pool ready for the kids that afternoon, so that they could do what-kids-do-best for the rest of the week and get from under Charlie's feet. He suspected that he would need to change the filter after draining and disinfecting it, but it was usually a two-to-three-hour job and so he was determined to get to it right after breakfast, before the mercury topped out.

For a minute his thoughts returned to the creepy Ouija board that he had left on top of the wardrobe in their bedroom, out of the reach of inquisitive hands. It wasn't even visible at his head height, the pelmet of the old-fashioned cupboard rising a good inch above the top and so even a teenager standing on a stool would not have been able to see it. He'd never liked to hear about people dabbling with that sort of thing, and although he wasn't a religious or superstitious type, he had heard enough stories and watched enough TV shows to knows that the occult was not something to mess with. He didn't know if he believed in ghosts as such, but he believed in something, another dimension that lay beyond the current understanding of human beings. Whatever, the game – if that's what it was - was now stored firmly out of harm's way and there it would stay until someone came along to claim it back, and if they didn't, he would take it to the tip or to the end of the garden where it would end its days as kindling.

It was now 8:45 and he had an email to write.

He poured himself another mug of steaming black coffee, straight from the hot plate, and after sweetening it and adding a dash of milk, it still looked strong enough to stand a spoon in, as his mother used to say. He flipped open his laptop and logged in at the prompt, opening his email and clicking on the compose-message option. He began to type.

Dear Guests

I hope you enjoyed your recent stay at The Cottage.

Sorry to contact you at this difficult time, but an item has been discovered in the children's toy box, which we feel is a little out of place. Whilst we don't mind receiving a few contributions, and many of you have been kind enough to leave toys and books over the years, when it comes to this kind of thing, I have to draw the line. Rather than describe it, I have inserted a picture as I'm sure that if you take a look, you'll know what it is and if you don't know what it is, then I suggest you delete this email and forget I mentioned it.

If you do recognise it and want to have it returned, then please let me know and I will send it to you at the next opportunity – once the post offices re-open – don't worry about the P&P, I just want it out of the house. If I don't hear back by the time we leave the property in a few weeks' time, then I will take the opportunity to destroy it, lest it falls into unsuspecting hands.

Just one final thing – if any of you have 'played' with it during your stay here, even if you were not responsible for it being here, please could you give me a call. The numbers on which I can be reached are mentioned below.

We hope to be able to welcome you back to The Cottage soon.

Kind Regards and stay safe,

Mr Anthony Mountford.

Anthony sounded much more official than Tony, as on this occasion he wanted the full weight of formality to back up his rather stern circular.

He bcc'd all their known guests and addressed it to his wife's email address instead, not wanting to reveal the addresses of all their guests to the world. For a minute he thought about waiting for his wife to surface, to get her to give it the once over before sending it on its way, but in a sudden rush of self-assurance, he acted on impulse and pressed the send button to let the message do its worst.

"It's a bit brusque, isn't it?" his wife complained as she read it over at breakfast an hour or so later. "Someone might take offence at that. It's only one of them that's left it here, by the tone of this, it seems like we are taking a swipe at all of them. Tony, why didn't you let me look at it first?"

"It's fine," said her husband defensively, "I've already had two replies look and neither of them seem at all upset by it. In fact, they seem quite intrigued to me."

She read the two responses in turn, and both were pleasant enough, wishing them well in the current climate and sending them their very best for the months ahead. Neither of them could offer any explanation for the board's presence in the house and had not even noticed it during their stay, never mind had it out for a séance.

"Well, it's done now," she said, "I suppose it's okay, at least whoever is responsible might now have a guilty conscience about it and will hopefully own up to having left it behind. You never know, maybe they'll even come and fetch it."

"I doubt it" said her husband, "not in lockdown they won't, haven't you been reading any of the news. Traffic is down to ten percent of where it was before, and the police *are* stopping people and turning them around on the motorways. If they haven't got a good reason to be travelling, they're sending them home again."

"Yes, so I hear," said Charlie, "I've been reading about it on Facebook. We were so lucky we didn't get stopped, we'd have been going stir crazy at home, at least here we've got the garden and the pool, if it's ever warm enough to use." At the very mention of the words, the kids came screaming and yelling into the kitchen in fits of joy at the prospect, proving to their parents that their children's hearing was in full working order.

"When can we go in Daddy?" screamed Lottie, almost in his ear.

"When will it be ready?" said Arthur, his excitement almost causing him to burst in anticipation. "Did you pack my swimming trunks mum?" and as she nodded, he punched the air and ran back to his room to change.

"Not for another hour or two at least." his dad shouted after him. "I've got to change the filters and unblock the drain, and it'll need a while to warm up. It's not going to be that warm today."

The boy was back inside a minute, but his shorts were on back-to-front, and he was still in his socks. He was at least wearing his goggles though, which was something. At the sight, his parents fell about in fits of laughter, and even his sister couldn't help but join in, snapping a picture of him with her phone to post on Instagram later. With a few essential digital adjustments, for her own amusement, of course.

Like most children when it comes to water, they couldn't contain themselves for a full two hours and so, an hour and a half later the first sounds of splashing could be heard from the back of the house. The shocked screams of two delighted children followed on quickly behind, as the still cold water took their breath away and Charlie went out to check on them, just to make sure that they were set up safely for as long as they could manage.

"That should keep them happy for a while at least," said Charlie, when she got back, turning her attention to the washing up with a hefty sigh. "What are you going to do with the rest of the day? Other than fielding complaints from angry former guests."

Tony ignored the well-timed dig, choosing instead to take the moral high ground. "I'm going to get started on some of the maintenance jobs, I think. The gutters need clearing, they haven't been done since the start of the winter, so they're bound to be full of leaves again, and then I'll get started in the garden. We could do with a nice big bonfire at the end of the week, so I can burn that bloody board game, if no one has come back to claim it."

Right on cue, his laptop pinged, but it wasn't the only sound. Another chimed out at the very same moment that put him in mind of a tinkling of glasses coming together at midnight in a toast to the new year. It was just the faintest echo, and it went almost unnoticed, as Tony chose instead to focus his full attention on the incoming message, but over the coming days he would hear the other sound again, until he would eventually take heed, though by then, it would be too late to matter.

Charlie on the other hand remained oblivious to both.

She was up to her elbows in washing up, a chore that she hated with a vengeance and so had allowed her thoughts to stray once more to her own career and the life that she had left behind.

She didn't doubt that raising a family was indeed a noble pursuit, as her mother had reminded her on so many occasions, there were still times like this when she begged to differ. Instead, she wished that she was back in the City of

London, racing from meeting to meeting across the Square Mile, hailing down taxicabs, and chasing up leads, her head spinning with the rush of adrenalin that accompanied every deal done.

Having children was meant to have been a career break for her, but the break had turned out to be permanent, as the fine art of juggling home life and work life proved too much for everyone. She missed her independence; she missed the buzz of the office; she even missed the commute, and whilst she enjoyed her husband's company most of the time, there were times, especially of late, when she had come to realise that she preferred her own.

In that moment weeks without end loomed large, and the thought of being cooped up day after day with him and two stroppy kids, suddenly started to fill her with a sense of foreboding that far outweighed anything that even a haunted house could throw at her.

CHAPTER 8

"So, you're telling me that you hadn't seen it before that moment?" pressed Tony, his mobile phone at his ear. "It wasn't in the toy box under the bay window as far as you know?"

"I can't say for sure Tone," muttered the flustered caller. "I can't say that I'd looked or anything, but we'd been there a week and until then, nobody had mentioned it. When we got back from the pub, they'd set it up in the lounge and they were all scaring themselves stupid with it. It was all light-hearted stuff though, nothing heavy. *'Is there anybody there?'* and all that, you know how it goes."

"And was there?"

"Was there what?"

"Was there anybody there Phil, did they get a response?"

"Well, the wotsit, thing, was moving about," said Phil, "if that's what you mean?"

"The planchette?"

"Yes, that's the thing. The planchette. It kept going up to the 'yes' and 'no' answers whenever they asked it something and we all thought it was a bit of a laugh really," he explained, but somehow it didn't seem all that funny anymore. "Lucy was blaming Emily and Emily was blaming Gaynor, all saying that it was the other one that was moving it about. We didn't really know what to think, we'd had a few, if you know what I mean, and that local brew is so strong as you know, I just sat down in the comfy chair, and I was off."

"Asleep you mean" asked Tony.

"Yes, didn't wake up until three in the morning," he laughed. "They'd all trooped off to bed a few hours beforehand. I remember having to pick up the board and the, the thing, off the floor. Not sure what it was doing down there, they denied it the next day, said they'd left it on the table, but it wasn't on the table, it was on the floor. I set it right and went to bed, slept like a log. I love the bed in that house."

"And that was the only time? The only time it got played with whilst you were there?"

"Well, no, not quite," Phil admitted with growing embarrassment. "Me and Joanie had a go at it too, one night when the kids had gone to bed. Thought we'd have a laugh with it, give ourselves the willies before we went to bed. After all, you've always said, you'd got a ghost and so we thought we'd see if we could, you know, make contact with it."

"Go on," said Tony, annoyed at the turn of events and the fact that one of his oldest and closest friends were amongst the guilty.

"I nearly shit myself."

It was a horrible thought, but having reeled him in, he wasn't about to let him off the hook so easily. "What happened?" asked Tony, "and don't spare me any of the details. I want to know exactly what happened, every little detail, however small or insignificant."

"Sure mate, I'll do my best. Well, at first, nothing happened." It was an inauspicious start, but it wasn't going to stay that way. "We did it exactly as the instructions said, we sat down in front of the fire. It had turned a bit cold as it happens and so we chucked another log on and had it balanced between us on our laps like, so a gust of wind would have blown it over. We sat facing each other on the kitchen chairs which we'd moved into the lounge and had our knees touching so that there was no gap, and the board was perched on top. We had our fingers lightly touching the plastic thing and we started asking it some questions – I don't remember exactly what we asked at first, but nothing happened anyway, so I don't suppose that matters much."

"Go on," said Tony, anticipating that a turn in events was due any moment.

"Well, it all kicked off when Joanie asked a question."

"What did she ask it?"

"She said, something like, 'did you die in this house?'" he recalled, his throat dry and his voice rattling on a sharp intake of breath. "It went mental, I mean really crazy. First it moved up to the 'yes' answer, and then it darted back and forth into each corner and back to the middle again. I looked at Joanie, because I thought that she was pushing it, but by the look on her face I knew that she wasn't, and I knew for certain that I wasn't. It was really freaky."

"And then what happened?" asked Tony, desperate for the answers that he knew were coming. The silence prompted him to repeat himself for a second time. "What happened Phil?"

"I asked for its name. I can't remember exactly how I put it, but I said something like 'can you spell out your name'. I may have even said 'please', I was so terrified I didn't want to upset it any more than we already had."

"Tell me," said Tony, his heart in his mouth, breathing heavily in expectation.

"It spelled something out, but we could make any sense of it, at first" Phil admitted, not enjoying the retelling one little bit. "First it went to the letter 'H', very clearly, stopped right over it. Then to the 'C' – we thought then that it must be wrong, as there are no words that start 'HC' but we thought that maybe it was spelling out its initials, but then came the letter 'T', followed quickly afterwards by an 'I' and then after a second or two, the 'W'."

"That doesn't make any sense," said Tony, his annoyance bubbling over.

"Not unless you read it backwards it doesn't." his friend informed him, "and Joanie had been writing down the letters with her free hand. It was Joanie who twigged it and just as she started to speak, the freakiest thing ever happened and after that we didn't touch it again."

Tony had just deciphered the word, but he was still processing the implications of it and so stayed quiet, which Phil took as his invitation to complete the retelling.

"The board flew off our knees, as if someone had just grabbed it and thrown it against the far wall." he whimpered, the terror of the memory still fresh in his mind. "It clattered onto the carpet and that's where it stayed until morning, because neither of us could pluck up the courage to touch it again. We just ran up the stairs like frightened kids and jumped into bed. Joanie was almost in tears. I wasn't much better. We didn't sleep well and kept imagining that we could hear movement coming from the snug beneath, I don't know if we did or not, you know how it is with old houses, they're always creaking and settling in the night. Something to do with the moisture in the air and the changing temperature I think."

"Witch." said Tony, still pondering the word and its implications. "Are you sure that's what it spelled out in reverse? Are you sure you didn't get the letters mixed up and it wasn't just some random muddle?"

"I'm sure," said Phil, still a little flustered. "You can ask Joanie, though she refuses point blank to speak about it now, even to me."

"So why didn't you tell me about it straight away? Why didn't you let me know?"

There was a momentary pause as Phil thought about his answer. "I guess I was too embarrassed to say. I'm sorry mate, I just thought that no one would believe me and as you'd never mentioned any weird goings on in the house, other than the resident 'happy ghost' that you include in the blurb, I didn't want to disturb you with it. After all, what could you have done about it? Joanie wrote a cryptic message in the visitors' book, and we packed away the board and stuffed it at the bottom of the toy box, hoping that would put anyone else off using it. We thought about writing a warning on a piece of paper and leaving it inside, but we decided against it, as we didn't want to spook anyone unnecessarily. Or to encourage them to go thrill seeking themselves. You know how people are."

"Yeh, I know," said Tony, with as much sarcasm as he could muster.

A few more forced pleasantries passed between them, but the rest of the conversation didn't last long. Tony had what he needed, and he was left fuming at his friend for leaving him in the dark about it for so long. His anger wouldn't last, but for now he wanted him to feel the full force of his fury and planned on leaving him to stew for a few weeks at least before burying the hatchet.

"Bloody idiot." he said to his wife as he recounted the tale a little later in the day. He had considered not telling her any of it, but he figured that doing so would make him no better than Phil and Joanie for choosing to keep it to themselves and so he had spilled the beans, leaving nothing out and adding no embellishments of his own. After all, none were needed. It was scary enough.

"What are we dealing with here Tony?" his wife asked him straight, scared out of her wits. "I really don't like the sound of this. Is it dangerous? Should we be taking the kids home?"

"I don't know," said her husband, equally uncertain as to the right course of action. He could see that it wasn't the answer that she wanted, but he was right out of solutions. "Trouble is, we can't go anywhere, can we? Lockdown is being rigorously enforced they said on the news this morning. We could get half-way home and they could just send us back again?" He was feeling trapped, and he didn't like it.

"Or would they send us home?" wondered Charlie aloud. "Could we say that we were already down here when the situation began, and we are only now making our way back?"

"Haven't got a clue." Tony shrugged, "but running away doesn't solve the problem, does it? We can't leave things like this. Once things get back to normal in the world outside, people will start coming here again for a relaxing break. What are we supposed to tell them? That our friendly ghost has 'gone rogue'? We need to find out which idiot brought that bloody thing here as I'm sure that whoever it was, they kicked this whole thing off. They wouldn't have brought it and not used it. They must have brought it and used it here for the first time and when they did, it opened this whole can of worms."

It was then that they heard it clearly for the first time and the sound sent a shiver through their bones. At first, it reminded Charlie of the sound of wind chimes moving gently in the breeze, or a crate of beer bottles being hauled up the cellar steps at the nearby pub to slate the thirst of the waiting locals.

"What the hell was that?" asked Tony, leaping to his feet as the dog started to bark once more.

"Oh my God." said Charlie, knowing full well what she had heard but not wanting to admit it, even to herself. "It came from the snug. From the inglenooks in the fireplace."

Immediately, Tony knew that she was right.

CHAPTER 9

Tony wasn't hungry. He was playing with his food, pushing the constituents of his dinner around on his plate, taking only the occasional morsel with an unenthusiastic prod of his fork. Food for thought.

The kids had enjoyed their day in the pool and were now suitably tired, each already in their pyjamas and looking forward to a promised Disney movie, whilst their distracted parents were hoping for an early and peaceful night. The two of them looked done-in, and so did their parents, exhausted by the day's recreations and revelations respectively.

During the year of renovation, they had found what they later learned were 'witches bottles' all over the house, hidden within the lath and plaster walls and beneath the flagstone floors. They had accidentally smashed the first one they'd unearthed, but from then on had been more careful and eleven more had come out whole. As each one saw the light of day again for the first time in hundreds of years, they could tell that they were old, the thick green glass a dead giveaway for their ancient tenure. It was their builder who had identified them, having come across them several times before when doing refurbs of old properties in the local area and he was in no doubt as to their purpose or antiquity.

"They were placed there to ward off evil spirits." he informed them with a straight face that showed no hint of humour. "They're kind of good luck charms really, but they shouldn't be removed from the house. If I were you, I'd bury them again behind the new plasterboard but if you want to keep them on show, then that's fine too, just don't open them."

"Why ever not?" asked Tony, his pragmatism coming to the fore once more. "What's inside them then?"

"I always assumed that it was just water," Bill said, admitting that he didn't know for sure, "but also pressed flowers, herbs and occasionally human hair or fingernails." He saw the look on his client's face and realised that more was needed by way of explanation and so he did his best to enlighten them. "The locals say that it was the hair and fingernails, or other bodily bits and pieces, of the witch purified with flowers from her grave, sometimes shards of wood from the scaffolds on which she was hung, and a concoction of herbs, which together would ensure that the witch, or wizard, stayed put. In the ground."

Tony had told him straight that he didn't believe in such mumbo jumbo, but the bottles were a rare find and a great talking point for the many dinner parties that they planned to hold in The Cottage over years to come, and so he'd agreed that they deserved to be out in the open where everyone could see them. Six bottles would have pride of place on one side of the stone fireplace, set back in an inglenook where they would remain out of reach of small hands and five on the other side. Each one uniquely different, even in their density, and so each caught the light in a different way as the evening sun shone through the house casting rainbows onto the bowed ceiling and out into the room whenever the sun pierced them at just the right angle.

But until recently, they had never been moved. Until this week they had never made a sound. Until now they had remained as they had been left, like a troop of sentries standing guard on either side of an entrance to some fortification or to a castle's keep.

"Did you take a look at the visitors' book?" Tony asked his wife, as he pushed the memory to the back of his mind where it would incubate for a while longer.

71

"Not yet no, just a minute." She made a quick return trip to the telephone stand in the hall, where the most recent books were stored, a framed handwritten note encouraging their guests to complete it on departure. She sat down and began to leaf through the pages, finally opening it on the blank page where the most recent write-up had been entered. "Now let's see, when did the Hills stay here, it was November wasn't it?"

"Something like that," said Tony, unsure of the exact date.

"Yes, here it is," said Charlie triumphantly. "It's been written by Joanie, not surprisingly." It was always the women who filled in the book, either the mother or the eldest daughter, sometimes the grandmother. It was rarely the men, who never seemed to have the time or the interest to be bothered with such niceties.

> *'November 16th, 2019; 'The Hill Family', 'Great stay as always, even the weather wasn't too bad for once, can recommend the local pub for its draught beers and cider and scrumptious pub grub. The 'friendly' ghost put in an appearance this time, though it didn't seem very friendly'.*

"Well, that's not going to help with business, is it?" bemoaned Tony, wondering to himself how easy it would be to strike it from the record. "That doesn't leave all that many people before them, does it? I mean since the last time that we were here?"

"Just two I think." reasoned Charlie, "but neither of them has bothered to fill it in by the looks of it." She scanned through the rest of the entries for the subsequent months, looking for anything that seemed out of the ordinary. Only a handful caught her eye, and each was a little disturbing, strongly suggesting that they had no plans for a repeat visit in the future.

'January 4th, 2020; 'The Jackson Five'; London; an eventful week, New Year was a blast in the village pub – disturbances at night spooked us all a bit though. An uncomfortable time in an otherwise very comfortable setting.'

'January 25th, 2020; The Smith Family; Hampshire; not so sure that your ghost is all that 'friendly' after all. Please don't put us on your mailing list. Lovely house, lovely welcome, not so lovely atmosphere.'

'February 22nd, 2020; The McMillans; Bristol; we were a bit spooked after we read this book, but we had a lovely week. Not the best weather but great spot for walking and for the beach. We'll be back. Light downstairs kept coming on at night – is it on a timer or something?'

'March 14th, 2020; Mr & Mrs Wilson; London; we quite fancied the idea of staying in a haunted house, but we think we'll give it a miss next time. Left early, didn't get too much sleep after the 3rd night. Didn't see anything, but nasty feeling about the place, especially in the snug. Lovely welcome though and thanks to the housekeeper (can't remember her name) for all her efforts, did her best to sort everything out for us.'

"This isn't good Tony," was all that Charlie could think of to say as she finished the readings.

"And not a clue as to how all this got stirred up either." Tony sat down in a huff, deflated at the thought of another business that might be about to take a nosedive into bankruptcy, pandemic, or no. "Have you spoken yet with Mrs Illsley, maybe she can shed some light on things. After all, she has more to do with the guests than we do."

"Only on the phone when we arrived," said Charlie, trying to recall if their long-standing housekeeper had mentioned anything at all that could be considered as 'unusual' during their brief conversation. "She seemed fine, as far as I can remember, she said that she could arrange for deliveries, if we needed anything."

"That was all?"

"Yes," said Charlie, her brains fully racked. "That was all."

"Well let's see if we can get hold of her today," said Tony, "see how she responds to some direct questioning."

"Sounds like an interrogation Tony.," snapped Charlie. "You need to calm it down a bit, this isn't her fault. We can't afford to lose our housekeeper on top of everything else and what if she hasn't been made aware, we don't want to scare her off too. You know what villages are like, once a rumour like this gets started it'll spread like wildfire and before we know it, the local papers will be knocking on our door."

"Didn't someone once say that 'all publicity is good publicity'?"

"Well, if they did, whoever it was, he was a bloody idiot." It was Charlie's turn to get irate. This was their investment. Their nest egg. And she wasn't about to let a few ghostly goings-on get in the way of their retirement fund.

"I never said it was a man who said it, did I?"

"Bound to have been," quipped Charlie. "A woman would never say anything so blatantly stupid as that."

Mrs Illsley wasn't all too keen on any face-to-face interaction, reminding them both that she was well into her sixties and so was keen to heed the official government advice to maintain a safe social distance until further notice. "Yes, the last few people have seemed a little bit odd my dear, I have to say," she informed them, when asked if she had noticed any changes about the place since their last visit. "One family in particular, if I can just recall their names.

Stayed late last year, but I can't remember the month. Nice couple, from up north somewhere, two teenage boys, but they left in a bit of a hurry and so I didn't get a chance to check in with them before they went. I suspect it was November – yes that's right."

"The family from Biggleswade." said Charlie, remembering the name of their home village, before being able to bring them to mind. "The Waltons, was it?"

"Not Walton, Watson," her husband corrected her from nearby, doing his best to listen in to the conversation. "They booked last minute, if I remember, we'd had a cancellation and we'd advertised on one of those cut-price holiday websites – they got quite a discount."

Mrs Illsley could remember no more, and though Charlie was sure she was holding something back, something that might have helped them to figure things out, she decided against pressing her any further. Instead, she thanked her for her time and wished her well, reiterating that if there was anything they could do for her, she only had to ask.

"So, I'd say that they're our prime suspects," said Tony, convinced that the Watsons were at the root of their current malaise. "If you can dig out a phone number for them, I'll give them a call now, I've had enough of beating around the bush."

Charlie stomped off into the kitchen, a little tired of being ordered about like an under-valued secretary, and after going online to retrieve the details of their paying guests from their company database, she scribbled down the Watson's landline number and handed it over to her husband. "This is not all my fault you know." she fumed, as she slapped the scrap of paper against his chest like a proclamation to a church door. "It's not going to help you getting all stroppy with me about it, it's not my fault that some moron has been using our house as a set for a paranormal panto."

"I know, I'm sorry." he said, backing down as his temper subsided. "I just want to get things back to normal. I love this house. I'm not having some jerk messing with our plans, that's all. Let me make this call and then I'll make us a drink. I don't know about you, but I'm gagging."

He dialled the number from his cell phone and the call-tone started, the same monotonous double ring that he'd heard a thousand times before. Just as he was expecting it to switch to voicemail and as he began to mentally prepare for what he was about to say, a solemn female voice spoke up on the other end of the line, and for a minute it knocked him right off his stride.

"Oh, hello," he muttered awkwardly. "I, is Mr or Mrs Watson there please?"

There was a silence on the other end, followed by what sounded like a heaving sob, the faintest catch in the throat of someone who had also been caught off guard and wasn't sure how to respond. In the end, he received a blunt answer, and it made his blood run cold.

"I'm sorry," said the anonymous female, choking back the tears. "They're both dead."

Tony Mountford felt his legs give way beneath him, and he sat down on the arm of the chair before they could. In the end, he didn't have to worry about how he was going to ask the obvious question as she proved more than willing to impart the whole story. It wasn't the first time she'd been forced to do so, and it wouldn't be the last.

"They died a few months back, before Christmas. In a car accident on the motorway. They were coming back from holidays with their two sons. It was a head on collision. There were no survivors."

"I'm so sorry," he stammered, the standard response that all strangers give when faced with such dreadful news, whether he meant it or not, it was the only decent thing to say in the circumstances. Charlie was looking at him in disbelief, knowing that something awful had happened and judging by the way that the colour had drained from her husband's face, she could see that he was having some trouble believing it too.

"I'm sorry for your loss. Are you a relative or friend of theirs?"

He knew that he was now over-stepping the mark and he should have simply ended his enquiries there and then, but he couldn't help himself. He had a feeling that she knew more, and he was determined to glean as much information from her as he could, before putting down the phone. He instinctively knew that it might be his best and only chance.

"I'm Will's sister – Mr Watson's that is – I'm just looking after his affairs for a while, sorting out the sale of the house and suchlike." It was obvious that she wanted to end the conversation there, but she was being polite, for now, and so she asked if there was anything else that she could help them with.

Tony's response was crass, unnecessary, and totally selfish, as his wife would soon be telling him. "Do you know if they, the family that is, ever owned a Ouija board?"

"A what? No, sorry." Her patience had been balanced on a knife edge as it was, and as the meaning behind the caller's words sank in, what little poise she had possessed was finally broken, leaving her on the edge of tears. "Look, unless it's something urgent, I've got things to do." She didn't bother to say goodbye, and so that would have to be the end of the matter whether he liked it or not. A curt 'good day' followed.

"Dead?" asked his disbelieving wife, as her husband began to nod. "What, all of them?" He continued nodding. In fact, he carried on nodding, for far longer than he should have, completely lost in his own thoughts.

"Dad." It was their daughter, and she was clearly upset. "Daddy."

"What's up Pumpkin?" he called trying to sound as unfazed as possible, as the sound of her voice cut through his melancholic mood.

"I don't like it." she said, handing him her phone, her lip trembling and her eyes welling with tears. She ran into her mother's arms as Tony looked down in growing disbelief at the photograph that stared right back at him, almost daring him to deny what he was seeing with his own eyes.

It was the picture that she had taken of her brother the day before. He was standing in the kitchen, his goggles strapped over his eyes, bare-chested with his azure blue spiderman shorts on back-to-front and his socks at half-mast. And behind him, against the far wall not far from the grandfather clock that stood on the opposite side of the room, a dark mass had formed.

Not quite a figure, but enough of one to conjure up an abstract outline. A vertical oil slick or ink blot. It had the faintest outline of arms held tightly within its form, a bulbous head that lolled to the side like an alien in that seventies movie and a thick, impenetrable blackness. It looked a little like smoke, but it was more solid, though without any real substance to it, and yet it retained an illusion of movement that put him in mind of a fine oil painting by Turner.

Whatever it was, it was like nothing that he had ever seen before. It was not of this world.

CHAPTER 10

"Right, that's it." Tony fumed his fists clenched like clams. His wife had only just managed to placate their daughter with a hot chocolate and a reassuring cuddle, so she was in no position to argue with whatever decision her husband had made. "You're going back. Lockdown or no lockdown, this is getting too weird for my liking. You and the kids are not staying another minute. There's something badly wrong around here."

"And what about you?" said Charlie, beginning to realise that he wasn't planning on joining them. "Aren't you coming with us?"

"No. I'm staying put. I'm getting to the bottom of this." he insisted, in words that made him sound far braver than he really felt. "I'm not letting that, that thing ruin us. I'm going to stay here, I'm going to do some research on this house and this land, and I'm going to get to grips with this whole sorry mess."

"How are you going to do that?" asked Charlie, "all the local libraries and museums are shut aren't they?"

"Isn't that what the internet is for?"

"Yes, but can't you do that from London. Why do you need to be down here, on your own? I don't like it Tony, I'm not going to leave you here to face this on your own."

"I'm not on my own," he said calling Bruce over, much to the dog's delight as his master knelt to fuss his neck and ears. "I've got old Bruce here haven't I – you don't think I'd be staying here without him, do you? I'm not stupid." She hurled herself at him then, as reality began to bite, giving him the hardest hug that she'd ever mustered in the hope that it might yet bring him to his senses. She wasn't all that sure that she could even face their London home alone at night, but she knew where she'd rather be, and that if it came down to a straight choice, there was only ever going to be one winner.

"Thanks love," he said, "but if I did go now, then I don't think that I'd ever pluck up the courage to come back. We've been happy here for years haven't we, it's our bolthole, it's our retirement home; and up until now we've been happy with our friendly ghost. Something has changed, and if it changed once, then it can be changed back. I've just got to work out what 'it' is and how to put it right."

"Okay," said Charlie, knowing that once he'd set his mind on something, he was never one for turning. "Well, what can I do then, when I'm back at home? There must be something that I can do to help. After all, two heads are better than one, aren't they?"

"I'll give it some thought. We can talk tonight or in the morning. But I want you gone with the kids and home before dark."

She feigned to protest once more, but he was having none of it and secretly she was glad. "No Charlotte." She knew that using her formal name was a sure-fire sign that he was in no mood to argue. "No, you need to get packed now, get the kids in the car and head home. If the police stop you, just say what we said, I'm sure that'll be fine."

"Should I go on the A roads again?"

"No, go on the motorway, it's quicker." said Tony. "It'll be empty, and I don't want you out there in the dark, don't ask me why. I just want you home for teatime. I'll call the neighbours, maybe they'll be okay to come round, they're not the nervous types."

At that Charlie gave in and went upstairs to pack, instructing both kids to do the same but omitting to tell them that their father wasn't going with them. Consequently, as they gathered their things and began to repack the car, the pent-up tears began as soon as Lottie twigged that her Daddy was going to be left to face their demons alone. She was old enough to realise that something wasn't right, and she wasn't about to be fobbed off with a hot drink and a few of her favourite biscuits.

"I'll be along in a couple of days Pumpkin," he assured her, not at all sure that he would be. "I've got a few things to do first. I won't be on my own, I've got Bruce and don't forget, I've got Mrs Illsley."

"Dad." Lottie said summoning up her sternest look. "Mrs Illsley is an old lady and she's not even living here. She lives up the lane."

"Exactly, so I can always pop up to see her, if I need to, can't I?" he said forcing a smile. "She's not far away, is she?"

Just as he said it the rattling started again, only this time it sounded like it was coming from inside the walls. No one moved a muscle, and even Bruce pricked up his ears, listening intently, but the subsequent silence stirred them into life and before long, three quarters of the human side of the family were once again ready for the road.

"Right, have you got everything?" asked Tony, kissing his wife on the cheek and each of his children on the tops of their heads, as they clambered into the back of their family car.

"I think so." Charlie answered. "Kids, have you got all your things? Have you got your Switches? Your phones? Your chargers? Arthur, have you got your blankie?" They all nodded or waved them in the air to show that they were all accounted for. "Are you sure you won't come with us?" she pleaded, in one last effort to change his mind, but she knew it was futile to even try. He was staying put.

"No," he said stoically. "I'm going to fix this. One way or another. Just a few days, that's all I need, and then I'll be home - I can get a lift to the train station. There's a direct line to London. The trains are still running, I've checked. I'll be back before you know it."

His wife had started to cry now, but she pulled herself together for the sake of the children if nothing else, snapped on her seat belt and got ready to leave. The car hummed into life and with one last despondent look at her husband, she pushed the gearstick into first, and set out on what would prove to be a long and uneventful journey back to London.

"Right, you fucker." Tony shouted as he re-entered the house, his dog once more on point. He was suddenly flushed with a real sense of bravado, determined not to be scared out of his own second home by some troublesome ghost. "No one messes with my family and lives to tell the tale."

As the words left his lips, he sensed the stupidity in them.

Whatever was messing with his family, was long since dead.

CHAPTER 11

That night, he made a plan.

He always liked to have a plan. It wasn't the best laid plan he'd ever put together, but it was something, and having scribbled down the outline of a mind map, containing everything that he knew, or thought he knew, about the house and the haunting, he set about prioritising his to-do list.

He was anxious to know that his family had arrived home safely though, and so for the next couple of hours he couldn't settle to the task at hand. He was on edge throughout, regularly checking the traffic news in case of accidents or hold ups on their route and was more than relieved when the sound of an incoming text message broke the self-enforced silence.

> *[HOME. ROADS ARE QUIET. KIDS SLEPT ALL THE WAY BACK. LOCAL PIZZA IS DELIVERING AGAIN SO ORDERING ONE IN. SORRY YOU'RE NOT HERE XXX]*

He texted back that he was fine and that he was glad they were home and that she should call both sets of grandparents just to put their minds at ease, knowing full well that they'd be worried. His ears would soon be burning as his mother-in-law gave her unsolicited views on his decision to stay behind and for once, he found that he could see things from her perspective. What *had* he been thinking? He promised that he would call before he went to bed and she wished him a restful evening, as she always did whenever they were apart, but the sentiment now carried with it a more sinister overtone.

Now it seemed to harbour an ominous warning and a real risk that it may turn out to be anything but restful.

He numbered his priorities one to ten, figuring that any more than that would prove too much and would be closer to a shopping list than a running order for a research project. Outside of the top three, he wasn't sure if the ones at the top were more important than those further down the list or not, but it gave him something to shoot for and that would do for starters. He even scheduled in some times and days when he wanted to be done with each item, just to help to keep him on track over the coming week.

1. *Ouija – what's is all about? #1 need to get to the bottom of this... What are the do's and don'ts – there must be some rules.*
2. *Who the hell was William Fuld? Might not be relevant but it shouldn't take long to find out online.*
3. *Who has lived in this House before? #2 one for Charlie – she can do this on the genealogy site that she uses. I think?*
4. *What's this House been used for in the past? I remember Mrs Illsley saying once that it used to be a meeting house or something.*
5. *Mrs Illsley knows more than she's letting on. #3 find out more, use your charms.*
6. *See if there are any details about the Watson's accident online – there must be some news on a fatal accident that killed 4 people.*
7. *Is it worth looking further back in the visitors books? Maybe there's a pattern? Something about the time of year? #4 Charlie can do this too – she has all the oldest registers at home.*
8. *Talk to Bill – he helped with all the renovations years ago. What does he remember? Didn't he used to refuse to work in the cottage alone.? #5*
9. *What did it mean when it said 'hctiw' – did it really mean 'Witch'? If so, were there ever any local witch trials around here? Long shot. Internet?*
10. *... Bound to think of something else later.*

'All good lists had ten points' Tony told himself as he scribbled down his thoughts in a notebook. He would have been better served to do it online, just so he could more easily share it with his wife, but old habits die hard. Instead, he took the nearly blank exercise book from the top shelf and tore out the used pages, lobbing the screwed-up ball of paper into the log basket before jotting down his thoughts on each point.

He didn't get far before he was interrupted by a noise that seemed to be coming from upstairs. He ignored it, refusing to be drawn, sensing somehow that it was toying with him, trying to entice him away from his self-appointed mission. But it put him off his game sufficiently to require a change of air, telling himself that Bruce was long overdue a walk. A long walk. At the very mention of the word, the dog began turning in circles and as Tony fastened the lead, he started to berate himself for his own bravado. He was no longer feeling quite so bold, and he resolved not to let the dog leave his side for the remainder of his stay. In that moment, he decided that on his return he would move the dog's bed from its customary place in front of the log-burner, to a new more strategic location at the top of the stairs, where he could block the path of any intruder, living or dead.

He wasn't sure if a brutish looking dog would prove to be much of a deterrent should this haunting turn nasty, but as Scooby Doo was still going strong after fifty years of ghost hunting, he figured that his own canine sidekick was well cast for the role. After all, one was a spook-shy Great Dane, whereas his was a military grade pedigree paw patrol.

"C'mon Bruce." he called, as the crack of a smile began to break across his face for the first time in a few days as he recalled the untold hours spent watching those cartoons with his kids. "Let's hit the road." He grabbed a scraggy looking tennis ball as they made their way out of the back door, turning the key to set the deadlock behind them, as they ventured out into the cooling afternoon air.

The temperature had thankfully dropped a few degrees to something more seasonal, much to the dog's relief. He was no longer panting for air, his long tongue lolling now only in excitement and not in a silent plea for water, though he still took every opportunity to lap at the stream as they criss-crossed its path through the meadow towards the village. In the end they walked for miles, enjoying the freedom of the abandoned lanes as the force of the breeze, which ruffled Bruce's fur, reminded Tony of just how much he himself needed a trim – but the barber shops were all closed. He hurled the bright yellow ball into the distance at every opportunity and the dog never failed to chase it down, racing after it and flicking it up again, catching it skilfully in mid-air, before returning it in a long curving arc to his master's feet.

Their permitted 'daily exercise' gave him time to think and to plan, mentally reviewing his hastily assembled options in the hope that he would soon be able to connect all the dots. He made a snap decision there and then to call Bill, despite an intermittent signal and the interference of the wind, which he knew might cut them off at any time. Suddenly, he needed to hear another human voice to chase away the memory of one misspelt word that he was finding hard to forget. The house may have been out of sight, but it was certainly not out of mind, as he found himself casting his mind back to the early days of its renovation. He knew that there must be more to it; things that he had forgotten to remember or had simply chosen to forget. He looked towards the steeply angled cliffs in the gloomy mid-distance, where layer-upon-layer of sedimentary rock concealed the outlines of long dead dinosaurs; monsters from the past, whose bones had been pressed into dust to leave only a stubborn imprint as evidence of a once glorious past.

"Tony." hailed Bill as he picked up the call and immediately recognised his old friend's voice. One of the rare clients that had been promoted to *friend* over the years. "How are you doing, it's been years. How's Charlotte, how are the kids?"

He was the only one who called his wife that. There was no explanation for it, only that he had once known a Charlie, a famous sportsman and serial playboy who had retired to his village and whose antics would forever be synonymous with the name in his mind at least.

"Yes, they're all fine," Tony lied, sparing his long-time friend the traumatic details for now. "We have a new member of the family too – I'm just out walking him actually, his name his Bruce, so if you hear him barking, you know who it is though after you hear what I've got to say, you might think it's me that's barking; mad that is."

"Oh, that sounds interesting," said Bill, his stubborn Yorkshire accent still prominent in his voice despite decades spent down south. "You wouldn't be out of place; the whole world has gone mad. This virus thing has got folk in a right tizz."

"You remember the cottage, don't you?" said Tony, refusing the temptation to dive into a tiring discussion about the causes and effects of COVID19. That could wait for another time.

"Of course, how could I forget."

"Well, that's what I was hoping for," said Tony, getting straight to the point. "I'm down here at the moment actually."

"Oh right," said Bill, "down with the family, until it all blows over?"

"Well, I was, but they've hot footed it back to London, so it's just me and Bruce now." He paused to consider what he was about to say next, but he knew that it was time to throw caution to the wind. In for a penny in for a pound, he thought to himself. "And the resident ghost."

"Oh that." said Bill with a shiver. "Now that's something that I do remember. That place always gave me goose bumps. You're not wanting more work doing, are you? If so, sorry, I'm up to my neck right now, and I'm not sure I'd want to set foot in that place again, and not on my own. Not for all the tea in China."

"And that's where it's always been a bit strange," laughed Tony nervously, "it's never been like that for us. We love the place, always have, and rarely did we ever get any complaints from our guests either. Though lately, well lately things have changed a bit."

"How do you mean?"

"Well, it doesn't seem like such a 'friendly' ghost anymore," said Tony, a trace of tension in his voice. "And we have seen things, we never used to see things. No one did. We only ever heard things or had things moved about."

"Well, I bloody well did." said Bill, determined not to have his experiences overlooked. "I saw something twice, I told you about it, remember?"

"To be honest Bill," said Tony a little guiltily. "I don't. I know you didn't like being there on your own and I remember you telling a few tales over a beer, but I can't remember any of the details. You know me, here and now and all that. Sorry mate, I wish I'd listened more now."

"That's okay, no apology needed, most people think I'm crackers anyway, so whenever I dine out on this one, they all look at me like I'm a few bricks short of a bungalow."

"Do you mind telling me again?" asked Tony, "and if the phone cuts out I'll call you back. As I say, I'm outside and it's blowing up a bit of a storm."

"Sure, well I tell you what," said Bill. "I've just got a bit of an errand to run before the rain starts. How are you fixed in about an hour, or so? I should be back by then; I've just got to pop to the chemist to get a prescription and that could take a while what with all this social distancing. You can call me on the landline, and we can take our time over a cup of tea. What do they call it these days? A virtual cuppa?"

Tony smiled to himself and agreed to his old friend's suggestion, ending the call there and turning for home in the same instant. He called Bruce to heel, and his faithful friend was soon speeding towards him, kicking up tufts of grass like a greyhound in hot pursuit of a cut-out rabbit.

The circular route led them back over rutted fields, through hardy clumps of grass and deep bunkers that were the remains of old surface mining activities from the middle-ages, but which now resembled the aftermath of a World War One battlefield, minus the tanks and the barbed wire.

Bruce continued to dodge between the mounds, momentarily disappearing and then popping up again, turning his shaggy head back into the wind to check that his master was still hot on his tail. A couple of times, he stopped dead in his tracks, as if he was checking out the scene behind him, but it wasn't Tony that he was regarding with his dark brown eyes. His stare was fixed beyond his human companion, far into the distance, so much so that Tony did an about turn more than once, just in case the dog had seen something that he hadn't.

They were alone, he was sure of it, but the dog's persistence had set him on edge, and he quickened his pace, his calf muscles straining like old leather as the heavy terrain began to take its toll.

As they made their way into the town from the opposite end, he was surprised to find the streets so deserted, but as most of the shops were boarded shut, he reasoned that most people had little reason to venture out that day, even if they were allowed to. The lack of any kind of meaningful tourist trade would hit the town hard in the coming weeks, and he found himself feeling increasingly fearful that some of his favourite coffee shops and restaurants might not survive.

As Bruce sat to allow his lead to be secured, Tony flipped his own hood over his head to ward off the first signs of rain that had been forecast to become torrential by the end of the evening, with high winds and heavy downpours predicted to bring flash floods and high tides to the southwestern counties.

"Better get a move on Brucie-boy." Tony bellowed, as the wind began to drive the rising drizzle directly into their faces. It wasn't yet a gale, but it was heading that way and Tony had no intention of getting caught out in it any longer that he had to. "C'mon, let's get back." he said, knowing full well that the dog did not have a clue what he was saying, but he said it all the same. It made him feel better even if the dog was none the wiser for the one-way conversation.

Tony made an unplanned stop for bread and milk at the local Cooperative, socially distancing himself as he joined the queue and leaving Bruce to sit it out in the wet, his lead tied up in a makeshift knot around the bike stand. It was good to see that the British love for queuing had again found a purpose for the first time since the long-gone days of rationing, and Tony passed the time making small talk with some of the locals, who somehow seemed far friendlier than they had ever been in the past.

Something about the 'Dunkirk spirit', he reasoned to himself, as he gathered up his small basket of shopping, some chewy treats for Bruce and a large bar of chocolate for himself. Or maybe there was just something now that they all had in common. A common enemy always did have a habit of uniting people, even if it was of the viral variety.

As they approached the house, he found himself regarding it in a new light. It was as if he was about to be sentenced after being found guilty of a crime that he had not committed, and as he inched along the unmade road, closer to its picture-postcard front elevation his sense of trepidation reached a new pitch. The stone-fronted extension with its elegant bay window stood proud, perfectly complemented by two matching dormer windows that protruded through the reed-covered roof, around which a skilled thatcher had painstakingly carved a series of beautifully bevelled returns. Even the downpipes were ornate, reclaimed Victorian remnants from other more opulent buildings that now adorned his humble abode, adding perfectly to the sense of place, as if they had always been there. As if they belonged there and, in that moment, they were doing a splendid job, routing the increasingly heavy rainfall from the tightly packed reeds, along the guttering and down into the secure soak-away that had been strategically positioned far from the building's ancient foundations.

Damp had been a big problem in the beginning and he and Bill had hired a JCB with which to dig a deep and lengthy pit, into which a plethora of building refuse had been dumped to act as an effective sump for the water. The spare soil had been used to landscape the surrounding grounds, creating the raised beds in the footprint of old foundations and the rocky backdrop from which an abundance of small trees and shrubs had now outgrown their carefully planned out setting.

A tug on the lead reminded him that the dog did not have the luxury of a water-proof mackintosh, and as Tony delved into its pocket to pull out the door keys, he was suddenly overcome with an overpowering sense that he was being watched. It was not the first time, and as he glanced up again at the window casements, he was reminded of how both he and Bill had often complained of such a feeling throughout the renovations.

"Do you remember," recalled Bill a few moments later, once Tony was back indoors, with a newly laid fire roaring and a steaming dog jostling for position in front of its warming glow. "There was always an uncomfortable feeling in the very heart of the house, in front of the fireplace, in the snug?"

"Yes," said Tony, reaching for his tea and setting himself down in the armchair beside the very same fire. "Though I have to say that until just now I hadn't thought of it for years. I've honestly not felt it in all the years we've been coming here, and I'm certain that it became less and less noticeable as we got closer to completion."

"For you maybe." said Bill, "but you were never much of a believer. I was still getting the chills right up until the end. There were times when you were back in London and I was there on my own, finishing up the carpentry or painting, when I could have sworn that there was someone standing right behind me."

"And was there?"

"No," Bill admitted. "Never. I'd turn around in the same instant and there'd be nothing. Nothing at all. Except that's not entirely true you know?"

"Go on," Tony prompted, more invitingly than he felt.

93

"There was often a smell of rotting, something.," Bill recalled. "A pungent smell of decomposing vegetation, like you sometimes get in the fridge when the salad has gone over its date."

"I can't say that I've ever," Tony started to say, before stopping mid-sentence as he recalled his wife's horrid experience from a few days before.

"What?"

"I was going to say that I'd never experienced it myself," said Tony a little sheepishly, "but that wouldn't exactly be true anymore either. Charlie said she could smell something 'nasty', the other day after her experience on the sofa." He opted not to elaborate, and though Bill asked about it straight away, Tony didn't want to embarrass him with the details, choosing instead to focus again on Bill's own experiences.

"Most of the time, it was just more of the same," said Bill, thinking back to a time in his life when he was a much fitter man. "Most days, I suppose, there'd be one thing or another. A feeling of being watched. A sense that I wasn't alone. Sometimes a strange noise upstairs when I was downstairs or from downstairs when I was upstairs. I never bothered to look after a while, I always told myself that it was just the wind, and I'd often put the radio on full blast to drown out anything else. Sometimes the radio would get switched off, I remember that, usually it was just the on/off switch, but sometimes the switch on the wall had been tripped – that would always freak me out. Happened a few times that."

"Did you ever see anything though?" asked Tony, his voice cracking as he spoke the words. "You hinted earlier that you had, seen something?"

At first Bill didn't answer, as if he didn't want to think about it again or didn't want to bring it up for fear of unsettling his friend who after all, had to turn off the lights in the cottage that night.

"Twice." said Bill somewhat ominously. "First time, I was coming down the stairs and I swear I saw something standing by the wall, where you have the clock now, I think. It was one of those, corner-of-the-eye things. I'd had a peaceful day and I was thinking about clocking off and looking forward to a beer or two on the way home. I think I was looking down and I caught sight of movement, I glanced up and saw an outline or shape."

"What kind of shape?"

"That's the weird thing, it didn't really have a clear form," gulped Bill. "Like its shape wasn't fixed, you know how they say that your mind tries to classify things that you see based on what it expects to see? Well, because I think that I expected to see a figure, I think of it like that, but in fact, I think it was just a thick black nothing. Impenetrable. Not one of these transparent ghostlike mists that people talk about, this was thick, black and, well, solid."

"I think our Lottie saw something very similar the other day," admitted Tony. "In fact, she caught it on camera. I'll send you over a snap of it, she did that Bluetooth thing on her phone with it, so I've now got it on mine."

"I'm not all that sure that I want it." said Bill, without a trace of humour in his voice. "Really, please don't, it sounds like the same thing and so let's leave it at that. You can show it me when we see each other next, whenever that might be." He sounded really shaken up, as if just thinking about the place had brought back some memories that had lain undisturbed for years, along with the rubble of a once decrepit house.

"And the next time?"

"The next time, well, the next time was as clear as day and I have absolutely no doubt what I saw and I never want to see it again," Bill whimpered without drawing breath. "And if you have a picture of that, then I don't want to see it, ever."

"Okay Bill," said Tony, trying to offer a calming word. "I won't. I don't, but if I ever do, I won't."

"I was working in the bathroom, putting the finishing touches to the plumbing," he recalled. "I was laid under the sink, tightening up the u-bend, which if you remember was an awkward cuss, I hadn't got a spanner the right size to give me the purchase that I needed, and it was proving to be a proverbial pain in the arse. Well as I turned my head to reach for my tool bag, there it was, large as life."

"It?" questioned Tony. "I thought you said it was a woman?"

"I don't know what it was," said Bill with a nervous laugh. "Whatever it was, or wasn't, I wouldn't like to say, but it was looking straight at me and as I tried to get to my feet, I banged my head on the underside of the basin and saw stars. Creepy thing is that I was sure I heard a sound as I did so, and it wasn't dissimilar to a laugh, but it was a nasty laugh, like a cackle. Dry, grating, callous. Like it was laughing at my misfortune."

"Shit." said Tony, "you've not told me that before."

"No, I know," said Bill a little ashamed that he had kept it to himself all these years. "I didn't want to scare you. You'd poured so much money into that place and you had a family on the way, I didn't want to put the dampeners on things."

"Fair enough mate." said Tony, not in the mood for a blame game. "I appreciate that you didn't want to burden me with it. But now it's started to affect my family, I must try to get to the bottom of it all, somehow. How would you describe this thing?"

Bill hesitated for a moment, gathering his thoughts, planning on choosing his words very carefully. After a while he spoke up, and the description had Tony glancing about the room, starting at every unsettling creak from within the walls of the oak framed house.

"It wasn't like before," he remembered. "It wasn't an outline, or a blackened blob. It was a clear image, faint in the torso and arms, though she was wearing an old-fashioned dress, like the kind that they had in the Puritan days, you know black with white trimmings. But her face, I'll never forget her face. It wasn't faded or transparent or anything, it was fully solid and though it wasn't ugly or scary, her eyes were looking straight at me, wide and bulging in her head, and her thin and ashen lips were just slightly turned up at the ends as if they'd been told to smile but weren't sure that they wanted to."

"Oh crap." said Tony, "That's horrible."

"Do you remember the old woman in the Hansel and Gretel fairy story? That's what it put me in mind of and do you know what?"

"What?" said Tony.

"I couldn't help but think, that she wanted to eat me."

"That's ridiculous." snapped Tony, more unnerved by it than he wanted to admit. "What in hell's name made you think that?"

"She seemed so thin," said Bill sadly. "Like she was starving, maybe through some famine or other, or maybe she had been denied food or water for a while, but she looked desperately thin and terribly sad. Terribly, terribly sad."

CHAPTER 12

"Oh, that's just your imagination running wild," argued Tony, wishing that Bill had not been quite so open after all. "It made you think of the fairy tale, like you said, and so you associated what you'd seen there with what happens in the story. You don't need to be a psychologist to work that one out."

"Well maybe you're right," said Bill, sensing that he had overstepped the mark, and recognising the need to backtrack. "Yeh, you're probably right, but it scared the living daylights out of me I can tell you."

"I bet it did.," said Tony. "So, what happened next?"

"I got the hell out of there. When my head had stopped spinning, I was left with a nasty bump, but I hauled myself to my feet and scarpered."

"And she had just vanished?"

"Yep," said Bill, "completely. As if she'd not been there at all. I grabbed the keys, locked up, jumped in the car, and left it in the pub carpark for the night. Started on the double brandies and didn't look back after that. The wife had to fetch me back, I was smashed before dinner."

"I bet that raised a few eyebrows."

"It did," the old landlord asked me if I was okay as soon as I arrived. "'You look like you've seen a ghost.' he said, "I didn't have the gumption to tell him that I had; knew that I'd be the laughingstock of the village if I did. So, I just sat in the corner until my hands had stopped shaking, eventually ordered myself sausage and mash for my tea and they called Rosemary to pick me up at closing time."

"Did you ever tell anyone about it?"

"Eventually," said Bill. "I told Rosemary the next day, the rest of them I think I told one Halloween, when we were all sharing scary stories after hours a few years later."

"And did they laugh at you?"

"Funnily enough, no they didn't." said Bill, "in fact, a few of the older villagers weren't surprised to hear it. Said that the place had been known to be haunted for years."

"Really?" said Tony, annoyed that the current owners had seemingly been the last to know the finer details. "So why didn't they tell us about it, I drink in there most nights when we're down here?"

"Most of the old timers are all dead now." explained Bill. "The new missus wouldn't know much about it, and I can't think of any of the regulars who would remember it as it was. Don't forget you've been the owner for more than fifteen years now."

"Anything else?" shrugged Tony, smarting at the fact that he was still seen as a comer-in by the locals after a decade and a half of generous investment in the local economy.

"Nope," said Bill with a sigh that sounded a lot like relief. "Went back the next day to finish off and to pick up my tools. That's when I told you that I wouldn't work there on my own ever again, remember?"

"Yes," said Tony, "that I do remember."

"I was almost finished anyway, and if I remember it well, it was all done-and-dusted a month or so later, bar for the usual snagging."

"And we started renting it out not long afterwards," said Tony, "and up until very recently I can't say that we've had too many scares to speak of. A few things moved about, items going missing and then reappearing in odd places, that sort of thing, but we always told ourselves it was the kids. We knew it wasn't, deep down we always knew, but it was much easier to think that it was them. Never paid it much mind, I have to say."

"So, what's changed?"

"That's what I'm trying to figure out," explained Tony, "but I must admit, I'm drawing a bit of a blank. There's no doubt in my mind, that something's been put out of kilter here, and once this pandemic thing is out of the way, there's no way we can continue to rent it out with the 'friendly ghost' tagline. I'll be had under the trades descriptions act. It's like the mood has changed, the equilibrium of the place has shifted and not in a good way, but I don't know how to get it back to how it was. It's like a ship that's run aground."

"Well, if there's anything that me and Rosemary can do, you know, to help out," said Bill nervously, regretting the offer as it left his lips. "So long as you're not expecting me to do any lone vigils or anything."

"No," laughed Tony despite himself. "I think you've done your last lone vigil in our house. But thanks, I may take you up on your kind offer once this lockdown business is done with. Maybe we could meet up with the dogs once we're allowed to meet outside again, it would be good to see you, if nothing else."

They exchanged pleasantries for a few more minutes, but the conversation was exhausted, and Tony was starting to feel much the same way. Drained would have been a better way to describe how he felt, his nerves frazzled, and his confidence shot. He no longer knew which he was more worried about – his financial wellbeing or his emotional stability, and a constant sense of fear had begun to weigh him down. The fear that his events management business would be bankrupt by the end of 2020 simply refused to be ignored, but the fear that there was something not of this world watching his every move and listening to his every word now seemed a far more terrifying prospect than financial ruin.

He felt trapped. Ensnared. Cornered. His primal instincts to fight or flee had been awoken, but he could do neither. There was nowhere to run to, the world outside was in turmoil and there was no way out of it. He couldn't fight, his enemies were invisible; a virus that was lurking in every public place and some demonic presence, ghoul or witch, whose presence was hiding within the restored stonework of his own private nirvana.

He forced himself to eat, fixing up a basic meal of baked beans on toast and served Bruce with his usual diet of dried biscuits, which he wolfed down in seconds as if he had not eaten for a week or more. The dog was a huge comfort; a four-legged early warning system for supernatural goings-on and a must-have accessory for all owners of old houses, haunted or not.

Night was drawing in and the log-burner was already ablaze, much to Bruce's delight as he spread himself out before it like a sacrificial offering to the god of fire. By contrast Tony was far less settled, seated in front of his laptop in the conservatory with his to-do list in front of him, perched like a reporter at a long-awaited press conference that is just minutes away.

Tony found himself thinking back to his earlier conversation as he waited for his wife to call. It seemed a strange thing to say, that the apparition that Bill had seen looked like she had been 'denied food and water'. Such a turn of phrase had all the hallmarks of a torture chamber, the kind of thing that prisoners-of-war had had to endure when they were under interrogation. "We have ways of making you talk." he said aloud in a mock German accent, whilst looking at Bruce who just stared back at him and wagged his tail.

Then, tired of waiting, he clicked on a younger image of his wife, one taken several years before on a sun-baked holiday to Rhodes, her hair a few shades lighter and her skin a few shades darker and waited for a more up to date visage to materialise before his eyes.

"Hey." she smiled, "how are you doing?"

"I'm okay," he sighed, suddenly realising just how lonely he was really feeling. "Missing you and the kids if I'm honest," he said returning a forced smile of his own.

"We're all missing you too," said Charlie, "loads more than you think. The kids keep asking when you're coming back, and they're really missing Bruce. How is he?"

"Oh, he's fine," reported Tony, "he's crashed out by the fire. I took him on a long walk earlier, I think it's tired him out. I also talked to Bill." He filled his wife in on their conversation, leaving nothing out, and she nodded in all the right places, admitting afterwards that she'd heard much of it before from Rosemary who had been a little less circumspect with the tales. In fact, it seemed that Bill's wife had hammed them up a bit, so much so, that for Charlie at least, they were less unnerving in the retelling. A moth was beating its floury wings against the broad expanse of the conservatory glass, in a suicidal irregular clatter, seemingly begging for permission to come into the light. "So why didn't you tell me if you'd heard all about it from Rosemary?"

"I think I did," said Charlie, "but you just dismissed it as idle gossip, and anyway, you know how she exaggerates everything, I probably didn't think it was worth the effort. What's that noise?" asked Charlie fearfully, even though the sound was on her husband's side of their technological divide.

"Just a moth." said Tony, unperturbed by the insistent flurry of floury wings. "Or probably a whole squadron of them judging by the noise they're making." He wasn't a fan, but his wife was positively terrified of their unpredictable flightpaths, and he had lost count of the number of times that he'd had to capture them in his hands from a bathroom or bedroom as they beat themselves into a powdery frenzy in his grasp. "At least they're outside."

Charlie gave an involuntary shudder as she began to recount the events of her day, one that had revolved almost entirely around the kids. "I did get time to do a bit of research though," she admitted after a while, "though I'm not sure if it helps much. I looked up the name of that William Fuld fella; it seems that he patented the Ouija board in the US back in the day. Created quite a few different versions of it, marketing it as a parlour game, before it was picked up by a big games company in the early years of the twentieth century. It seems like he made a lot of money out of it, though he came to a particularly nasty end."

"What happened to him?"

"It seems that he died in a fall, from the roof of his factory" explained Charlie. "You can read all about it on the internet. There's a website with his name and biography."

"Nothing untoward in it?" asked Tony, expecting there to be some mystery connected to the name.

"Not that I could find, it all seemed fairly mundane, just a tragic accident that's all. Just one of those things. I'd say that one's a dead end." He didn't laugh at her half-hearted joke, but then again, she hadn't expected him to. "What about you, did you find anything out?"

"Other than what Bill had to say, I heard back from a couple more guests but no luck, they both say that they didn't see the board and they didn't use it." explained Tony, his email account otherwise empty now that all business-related enquiries had dried up. "I did find a rather upsetting account of the accident though; it was quite easy to find as it happens. Just searched for the date in question and 'fatal motorway accident' and it came straight up. There was a photo of the burned-out car – it had rolled over and smashed into the central reservation, where it burst into flames. There was no way out."

"Any idea what caused it?" sighed Charlie, crossing herself as she spoke.

"Driver error," said Tony. "There was no one else on the road, it was deserted they say. It seems it was very late. They must have decided to drive back overnight to avoid the traffic and so they'd surmised that the father had fallen asleep at the wheel."

"But they don't know for sure?"

"Well, no, how could they?" said Tony, a little less interested than his wife appeared to be in pursuing it any further, though she was about to become a lot more engaged. "There was one witness who had something very strange to say though. A passing driver on the opposite carriageway reporting seeing the interior of the car in flames, as it sped along in the outside lane."

"What do you mean?" she said after a second's hesitation to allow the image time to blister up before her eyes.

"Well, he said that he thought he had seen the driver, on fire."

"What?" snapped Charlie, "that's impossible isn't it? How could that happen? He must have been mistaken. It was late. It was dark. That can't be true, can it?"

Tony let the question hang between them for a minute, but if truth be told, he no longer wanted to think about it, so he shrugged his shoulders and tried to think of something else, something that would help turn their conversation onto a less disturbing tack. A solitary fly divebombed him like some kamikaze pilot from another age, repeatedly returning despite Tony's failed attempts to swat it in mid-air. It was a big bluebottle, seemingly angry that it had emerged out of season, its instincts in turmoil after the unseasonably warm March, which had fooled it into life too soon.

"I looked back through the old visitors' books," explained his wife, as he waved his hands frantically around his head like some sectioned lunatic.

"Anything of interest?" he asked, though his attention was firmly elsewhere, as the unsuspecting fly met a particularly quick demise beneath his outstretched palm. "Die you bastard." he muttered under his breath, wiping the aftermath of bloody mucus and broken wings onto his jeans.

"Not really," said Charlie, ignoring the fatal disturbance at the other end. "More of the same. A few comments from people who said that they'd seen or heard something strange, and some wishing that they had, the fools. To be honest, mostly they are just happy reports of relaxing holidays and promises to come back again in the future."

"Which only goes to show that something has changed," said Tony wearily, becoming fed up with trailing out the same old line. As he pondered his next move, he noticed a change in his wife's expression, an intense look that said that she'd seen something as she leant in towards her screen and opened her

106

mouth to speak. Instinctively, he turned around to look behind him but there was nothing there, nothing that was visible anyway. "What?" he said, becoming more alert to the unseen threat, as his wife raised her finger to point and stammered her response.

"What's that?" Her eyes had widened and even over the ether he could see that she was no longer looking at him, but beyond him. Over his shoulders and into the depths of the room.

He turned again to scan to deepest reaches of the open stairwell and the compact room beyond, the flickering flames of the fire dancing around the walls like some atmospheric film noir. "I don't see anything Charlie, what are you seeing?" he turned around to meet her eyes once more and was shocked by what he saw. Just a few feet behind his wife, on her side of the technological expanse that divided them, a darkness was rising from the corner of the room. He watched speechless as it grew up out of the floor, formless and thick, devouring everything in its path.

"Charlie." he screamed, "behind you." She turned to display her carefully tied bunch of expensively highlighted hair, a silky silhouette against a spreading black satin backdrop.

"What, there's nothing there." she said turning back to face him, her eyes reacting in terror before she could form the words of warning that she so desperately wanted to say. "Please Tony." she sobbed, "behind you."

"Charlie." he screeched, watching as the blackness in the room behind his wife closed in around her. "Get out of there."

As she turned around once more to face the invisible threat that had now almost swallowed her whole, he switched his attention to his own image captured in a minimised miniature in the corner of the screen, a head and shoulders view that was also now completely enveloped in darkness. As he turned once more to stare perplexed at the orange glow from the fireplace that caught the edges of stairwell and sofa like the sun behind rainclouds, an awful sense of helplessness bore down on him, just as an almighty bang brought their creepy conference call to an abrupt and unexpected end.

The electricity had been cut off.

CHAPTER 13

Bruce was barking now, stirred from sleep by the snap of the trip switch under the stairs. Tony leapt to his feet and bolted towards the sound, unsure whether he was more fearful for his own safety or for that of his wife and children. Later he would be certain that his primal instinct to protect and serve his family was at the forefront of his mind as he felt his way through the moody darkness, thankful at least for the life-giving light from the fireplace.

He pulled open the double-fronted cupboard doors, an artfully decorative feature that an inspired Bill had crafted to cover the electricity board at its point of entry into the cottage. The trip switch was indeed in the off position, and Tony wasted no time in springing it back into action. A ping from his laptop told him that normal service had been resumed, and the kitchen LEDs were also back on, as he dashed back to the place where he had left his phone, determined to speak to Charlie as fast as the best of his technology would allow.

He hit the speed dial button #1 on his mobile phone, and his heart skipped a beat as he was met with the automated message telling him that her phone was switched off. "Shit." He tried again, hoping against hope that she would soon realise her mistake and would at that very moment be scrambling around in her handbag to retrieve the handset.

"Shit, shit, shit." he yelled, "Charlie come on, switch your frigging phone on." He found himself wishing that they hadn't had the land line disconnected only months before, believing that in the age of Wi-Fi, the wired world of telecommunications had had its day. He turned his hopes back to the laptop as the operating system whirred into life, bringing up the home screen and automatically launching the communications centre. "C'mon, come on." he flapped, the pre-set routines not functioning fast enough for his liking, as he double-clicked on the icon that offered him a tantalising glimpse of his younger wife's smiling face. He was to be disappointed.

'Internet is not connected' flashed up before his eyes, a message that seemed intended only to frustrate him, though he knew that the network always took a few minutes to reset itself after a crash as it ran through its pre-programmed validations.

It was then that his own phone trilled out his wife's assigned ringtone and in pure relief he reached frantically across the table to grab the handset.

"Charlie." he shouted, "are you okay."

He'd heard the chuckle before, a low mean cackle that froze the blood in his veins.

"Yes. Thank God. Are you okay? What happened?" It was Charlie. It was his wife. The sniggering had been smothered by her familiar voice in an instant if it had even been there at all.

"The electric tripped." he explained in a garbled rush.

"Mine too."

"That's impossible."

"I know."

They were both silent for a moment after that, lost in thought, both contemplating the apparent impossibility of such a coincidence. As realisation dawned, they were both gripped by a shared panic, that whatever was haunting them was not in any way restricted by the earthly limitations of time and space.

"Tony.," whimpered Charlie, hesitating to give the thought life. "Has it followed us home?"

"Well, if it has," her husband answered, refusing to accept the possibility, "then it's somehow managed to be in two places at once. What you were seeing coming for me, I could see coming for you."

"What did you see?" she asked, knowing that it was a question that she really did not want him to answer. She already knew the answer. She had seen it with her own eyes.

"A darkness," he said in grim remembrance. "A thick, blackness, but I could see a shape of some kind in its centre, like there was something inside it. Getting closer and closer until it filled the screen behind you. It was like, like an approaching storm."

"Don't." she cried out, not wanting it to be true but knowing all the same that it was. "That's exactly what I saw, behind you. It started out like a black patch in the corner of the room, but it seemed to break out of there, and expand like a raging ball of dark water, but there was something there. An outline of a shape, that seemed to turn and run, from a standing start, until it was looming over you, behind you, spreading itself like a black mass."

"But now, it's all fine again." said Tony, in an attempt at reassurance that would do little to help either of them sleep that night. "Even Bruce has settled back down by the fire. I heard him bark when the lights went off, but I don't think he was roused before then, not before the bang. Did you hear a bang too? Or was it just at this end?"

"I don't know, I don't think so," said Charlie, trying to remember for certain the events of just a few minutes before. "The screen just went blank, and the lights went out, that's all I can remember. I didn't hear anything, I'm pretty sure I didn't anyway."

"Are the kids okay?"

"Yes, they're both fast asleep," said his wife. "I went straight up there after I flicked the trip switch back on, thank God you thought to leave the torch on the side. I'd have been petrified if I'd had to find my way in the dark. Even more petrified, I mean."

"This is crazy." said Tony.

"I know. What are we going to do Tony? I'm scared."

"Do you want me to come home?" asked Tony in desperation.

"How can you? It's essential travel only, even on the trains." It was hopeless, but Charlie found that she was still more fearful for her husband's safety than she was for her own. "Are there any hotels open? They must have vacancies if they are?"

"I'm pretty sure they've all been forced to close," he said, "and even if they're not, we don't have the spare cash right now to waste on a hotel room. Not when we've got two homes to keep. No, I've just got to sit this one out. We've got to get to the bottom of what's going on here, I keep saying it I know, but I mean it. I am not going to be chased out of my own home by some spook."

"So, what can I do?" pleaded Charlie, still desperate to help. "There must be something that I can do from here, on the internet maybe?"

"There is," said Tony. "You can access all the census records online, right? Going back to 1841. See if you can trace back the owners of this house, every ten years from the latest available one, which I'm pretty sure is 1911, unless the 1921 release is out yet?"

"It might be, I'll check," said Charlie, anything in the last one hundred years is still subject to censorship so the 1921 one will be the last if it's out, though the 1939 register will also tell us who was living here at the start of the second world war too."

"And we might be able to get some information from the voting registrations as well, won't we?" asked Tony, remembering the work that his wife had put into uncovering her family tree a few years before. "They're available for the pre-war years I think, and there are some trade directories and suchlike that cover the fifties and sixties."

"That's right," she replied. "Every ten years or so we should be able to get something that will take us back to the mid nineteenth century at least. I don't know what it will tell us, other than names and occupations and we'll probably find that most of them were Agricultural Labourers, but it's got to be worth a go."

"While you're doing that, I'm going to bleed Mrs Illsley dry." said Tony, a little too melodramatically for his wife's liking.

"I hope you don't."

"You know what I mean," he smirked. "She must know more than she's letting on, she's lived around here for years and her family before her, I think. I'll call her tomorrow and see if she'd be willing to join me on a walk with Bruce. Out in the open air, she can't object to that surely?"

"She might," his wife said, doubting that the old lady would agree to it, but trying her very best to stay positive. "It's got to be worth a try, but just do one thing for me Tony, please. Be careful."

"I will," he promised. He'd try, at least.

For a second or two, Tony simply sat and stared into the depths of the room, as a deep sense of sadness wrapped itself around him like a shroud. He had never been one for wallowing, but in that moment, he could think of nothing else that he'd rather do, as his sense of isolation deepened. He sat like that for a while, marooned in his thoughts, until he began to realise that he hadn't eaten in hours and that most basic of instincts forced him onto his feet and into the kitchen in search of sustenance.

He was running low on essentials and with just a few slices of bread, the last scrapings of butter and a solitary tin of beans, he fixed himself up a plate of his go-to comfort food for the second time that day. A piping hot cup of tea followed and with the aid of a Union Jack tray, he proceeded to the snug where he would at least be able to enjoy it by a smouldering fire, his trusty companion at his feet.

As he made short work of the toasted treat, he turned his attention to the list that he had placed on the tray, half hidden beneath his meagre feast and as he pulled it fully into view, his last forkful dropped onto the tray with a dull plop.

The final item had been completed and where the words once read '*bound to think of something later*', the whole line had been scribbled out in a frenzy of charcoal black lines that had been applied so vigorously that the paper beneath had torn through. But that was not the worst of it; it was not what had caused his fingers to loosen their grip around the touch-cold cutlery as it closed in on his gaping mouth. It was what had replaced it.

There in capital letters and bold black ink, alongside the now extinguished sentence, his own words had been inscribed in someone else's hand, as if that someone had been taking notes. An ephemeral secretary, sent from who-knows-where to minute his actions and his words, for the record; for a testimony; for eternity.

"DIE YOU BASTARD."

Saturday 28th March 2020

DAY 6 OF UK LOCKDOWN

449 deaths reported in the UK – the total number of deaths due to COVID19 now stands at 2,701 with 23,147 people testing positive for the disease.

CHAPTER 14

The night inched by at a snail's pace, but the inclement weather wasn't the sole reason behind his insomnia.

He'd heard their grandfather clock strike every hour and though he knew that he must have slumbered in between, it wasn't until the dawn chorus came that Tony finally drifted off. He'd managed to convince himself that he must have written the words down after all, as he'd had the list and pen at the ready at the start of the call with his wife and so it wasn't impossible that the words had been written and spoken in the same moment, but deep down he knew that it was unlikely. He had swatted the fly with his right hand; he had wiped the same hand on his right leg; after all, he was right-handed, and he was not ambidextrous. He couldn't have written it as he said it, not with his left hand, but maybe he'd written it down afterwards. Maybe.

Even with an infamous breed of guard dog on duty at the bedroom's threshold, he did not rest easy and was startled by every creak and knock for which old houses are renowned. The respite from the rain had been short lived, and as the wind howled in accompaniment through the twisted eaves that underpinned the thatched roof, he had lain awake and fearful in the hollow darkness as the rain beat like a drum against the window.

For his part Bruce lay undisturbed. Only once did he start to stir, his pointed ears pricked and a low growl emanating from his throat that didn't quite materialise into full-on barking. Instead, after a minute or two, he had settled back down, and was soon back in the land of nod, as evidenced by his loud canine snoring and occasional scampering, his paws scuffing along the carpet in pursuit of nocturnal rabbits. Or something less fluffy.

Consequently, it was far beyond Tony's usual time, when he was finally roused by the wet nose of his canine companion, urging his master to get up and attend to his needs. It was a rude awakening, hauling him up from the depths of an unsettling dream, the details of which were completely forgotten by the time he reached the back door where he allowed Bruce outside to do his business. On the dog's return a full bowl of dried biscuits was waiting for him, but the sense of unease lingered long after his second cup of coffee had topped off a meagre breakfast of toast and jam.

A gap in the cloud cover welcomed in the sun as it streamed through the conservatory windows and a week of unseasonably warm weather was once again on the cards, urging Tony to turn his attention back to the task at hand. He had sat for a while, watching the morning news with an increasing sense of panic as it became clear that the pandemic remained in full swing with no end in sight. The populations of Spain and Italy continued to suffer under an unrelenting tide of infections and the now infamous 'R-rate' for the UK showed no signs of falling below its high watermark. As a result, there was no imminent end to lockdown in sight and so, with fears for his livelihood resurgent and his prospects for the rest of the year hanging by a thread, Tony hit the off button and lobbed the remote control onto the sofa in disgust.

On a brief call after breakfast, his wife had done her best to help him to look on the bright side, and as Tony did not want to bring her down too, he chose not to share the curious case of item #10 on his list. But after trying to cheer him up with news that petrol prices were at an all-time low and that the station closest to home was 'practically giving it away', even the prospect of cheap heating oil for the cottage failed to shine a silver lining on their predicament. He was in no mood to make small talk, and before his irritation could turn to anger, she elected not to poke the bear any further and so left him to his own devices for the day.

Tony on the other hand wasn't yet done, and he remained determined to find out more from their long-term housekeeper. And so, despite his worsening mood and his wife's words of warning, he wasted no time in following up his first call of the day with another.

"Mrs Illsley," he said as an older female voice cut short the ring tone after just two bursts of an old fashioned bakelite trill. "It's Tony Mountford here, how are you keeping?"

"As well as can be expected," she said sharply, in a tone that could have cut glass. "Charlotte didn't hang about for long I see, is everything ship-shape over there or is there something the matter?" Mrs Illsley rarely missed a thing and even now that opportunities for active surveillance were severely curtailed, she had still somehow managed to notice that all was not as it should be. "You'll be wanting to know if I've noticed anything amiss, I don't doubt?"

It was uncanny how she always seemed to be a step ahead of them, even in the current climate that must have had a limiting effect on the abundant fruit that always grew so well on the local grapevine. Tony hadn't been too sure how he was going to get the conversation started, but he needn't have worried - she had saved him the trouble.

"Well, after a fashion, yes I would," he conceded. "You see, until recently we'd never had any reason to be concerned about any ghostly goings-on here and as you know, we have never tried to hide it from our guests. Some have even made bookings because of it, but lately, things have taken a turn, and I'd like to get things back to the way they were, if I'm being honest with you."

For a moment there was just an empty silence, broken only by the intermittent sound of raised voices in the background, which Tony put down to a daytime TV show or radio broadcast. Mrs Illsley had always been a big fan of the radio plays on the wireless, as she still called it, but it proved a timely reminder and Tony made a mental note to see what he could find online that might help to take his mind off things too.

"I can't say that I've noticed anything," said the housekeeper. "But the Watsons did leave in quite a hurry as I recall. There was even unfinished dinner left on the table and leftovers on the stove, and the beds were all unstripped and unmade. They left a few books behind as well and I took some items of clothing to the charity shop that they'd forgotten, including a nice pair of trainers, that were left in full view in the middle of the lounge. As I say, it looked to me like they'd left in a hurry. I talked to your wife about it, and suggested that she withhold their deposit, but I don't know if she did or not?"

"I don't think so," said Tony, knowing full well that they had never even discussed it, "she never mentioned it anyway, but I'll check when I speak to her." Most likely Charlie had thought that it was just the same old Mrs Illsley, fussing over nothing and talking up her part and so, not wanting to sour the relationship with their paying guests, had opted to let sleeping dogs lie.

"No, I didn't think so." she sighed, a judgmental edge to her voice. "Well, if you had, maybe you'd have found out what had happened to them."

Tony ignored the thinly veiled rebuke, instead choosing to push home his advantage now that he'd finally got her talking. "Mrs Illsley, I remember you telling me that this place was once a meeting house, or something, can you tell me anything about that?"

"Not a meeting house." she snapped, frustrated that he hadn't been interested enough to listen attentively. "It was a courthouse. The local Justices of the Peace used to sit in sessions there to issue fines and suchlike for petty offences and disputes. Not in your house though, there was a far grander house that used to stand on the same plot."

"Wow, that's very interesting, I never knew that." said Tony, not meaning to sound condescending. "Do you know what sort of cases they would have looked at? I'm assuming that it wouldn't have been for serious things like murder, would it?"

"I doubt it very much," she answered, sensing that he was getting ahead of himself. "I don't know for sure, but there's a local historian in the village who has done quite a bit of research for the local historical society. He's even done some talks on it in the past at the local village hall, but not for a while now. He's getting a bit unsteady on his feet these days, so he finds it hard to get about, but he might be willing to tell you what he knows."

"Do you think he'd be willing to meet me?"

"No, I doubt it very much," said Mrs Illsley. "He's been quite poorly over the last few years so I'm sure he'll be shielding, but I will give him a call and ask him to call you, if he's up to it. I'm sure he won't mind though; he likes nothing better than to tell people what he knows about our village and given that he'll be bored silly at the moment, being locked indoors, it might be a nice thing for him too."

"That's fantastic," said a genuinely pleased Tony, as he trapped another lone fly with an upturned glass, prompting him to try his luck with one more direct question. "Mrs Illsley, have there ever been any recorded cases of witchcraft in this village? You know, the sort of things that they used to burn people at the stake for in the olden days."

For a moment or two, she went quiet again, though he could still hear her breathing, in spite of the radio play that had reached a dramatic point where the sound-effects team were in full swing.

"No," she said finally, though she didn't sound certain, dragging the word out for far longer than was necessary. "I can't recall there ever being anything like that. Though I can say that the duck pond next to the pub is reputed to have once been used to test suspected witches and the village stocks that are still there, were also used to punish anyone who stepped out of line." Tony had seen the stocks many times before, even having had his photo taken next to them. They had snapped one or two of the kids there too, squealing in delight with their heads poking through the holes that were once meant for punishment.

"By the 'test', do you mean where the suspected witch was dunked?"

"Yes, that's it and if she drowned, well she was innocent and if she didn't, then she was guilty," but it would prove to be a short-lived recital of village folklore. "Now if you don't mind Tony, I need to be getting on, I've got cakes to bake. I'll ask Mr. Humphreys to give you a call, but I can't say when he'll get around to it, you'll just have to be patient I'm afraid. He's exactly the kind of person who wouldn't survive this COVID thing, if he went down with it, so it's best that he keeps his distance I'm afraid."

He felt like he was being told off, and he wasn't entirely sure what for, though he chose to ignore the reprimand, but found himself wondering who she could possibly be baking cakes for when all visitors were still banned from visiting. He thanked her sincerely for her time and for the information, but as they bid one another a good day, she did make one further offer, though quite what help it would be he wasn't yet sure. "If you find yourself in any further difficulties, please do call Mr. Mountford. Any time, day, or night I still have my husband's old shotgun that he used to use for the rabbits. Not sure if it would be of any use with dealing with your intruders, but if you need it, I know how to use it."

It was a frightening offer – the thought of a rampaging widow and a double-barrelled shotgun – but it was not unwelcome, and he wasn't about to turn it down out of hand. "I really do appreciate that Mrs Illsley," he said, as a squadron of meaty flies scrambled around his head "and I will, if I have any 'intruders' again."

It seemed a strange word to choose, one that lacked a common definition in the circumstances, but she gave no hint of its meaning and so he didn't pursue it. He thought about looking up its official meaning in an old university dictionary that they still had lying about somewhere in the house, but he couldn't be bothered to go hunting for it and he quickly forgot about it, his mind returning to his plans for the rest of the day.

As he went about his chores, he wasn't sure if she had believed him at all, her final offer seeming to suggest that she thought that their visitations were more likely to have an earthly origin, but whether natural or unnatural, there was something to be said for having a twelve-bore rifle to hand. Even if it only served to induce some sense of protection that might help him sleep at nights, it was better than nothing, and he found himself wondering how someone like him might go about applying for a firearm licence.

"You wouldn't get one." said his wife when he called her later. "And in any case, all guns have to be stored in the local gun club these days don't they.

Ever since Dunblane. I'm not sure I'd feel comfortable there being a gun about the place anyway, not with the kids. What were you thinking?"

He was making a habit of saying the wrong thing lately and so, not wanting to end up in another disagreement, he kept their evening call short. He promised to Facetime again before bedtime, when he hoped he would have more information to share.

He didn't bargain on the landslide that was waiting to bury him alive.

CHAPTER 15

"Mr Mountford? Hi, my name is Humphreys, I hear that you're interested in knowing about the old court rooms?" He sounded posh, like proper posh; 'old money' as they still say in some circles of British society.

News travelled fast in a small village, and it seemed that despite the lockdown, villagers remained primed and ready to be distracted from their enforced boredom at the drop of a hat. Just a few hours had passed since the conversation between landlord and housekeeper had run aground, and Tony had barely had time to get a few small maintenance jobs done, when the quick call-back had pulled him up short.

"Yes, thank you for calling me back," said Tony appreciatively, "and please, do call me Tony."

"Well, my name is Francis," his well-spoken neighbour replied, "delighted to meet you, though it would've been much nicer over a cup of tea and a piece of cake at the village tearooms."

There was no arguing with that, and they spent a good while discussing the craziness of the pandemic and the government's reaction to it. Neither of them was all that impressed by the recent policy decisions and bemoaned the inaction that had seemingly allowed the virus to gain a foothold on Britain's shores but were agreed that they wished the Prime Minister a full and speedy recovery. As they talked, Tony realised how much he was missing such casual conversation and so wasn't tempted to call time on their inconsequential chinwag despite the lateness of the hour. Passing the time of day with a fellow human being no longer seemed to be the waste of time and effort that he had once believed it to be.

Now it was close to becoming a craving and after all, time was no longer money, at least not for him.

As their discussion returned to the topic at hand, Tony felt a stab of alarm, as if the global crisis was less of a worry than his domestic situation, and he was suddenly reluctant to stir the hornet's nest that was sure to be waiting for him. He felt certain that this time he was going to get stung.

"So Tony, you were asking about the history of your house I understand?" said Mr Humphreys, filling the temporary silence, and keen to find out what was at the heart of the matter. He had his suspicions. He'd heard the rumours and had listened to the stories over the years and so he was not surprised to learn that the pot of troubles at the house may have finally reached boiling point.

"Yes," Tony replied somewhat sheepishly, giving in to the urge to downplay the recent goings-on so as not to feed the local rumour mill any more than he had to. "Just curious really, we've never really looked into it too much and as I've got some time on my hands, I thought it would prove to be an interesting distraction." He wasn't sure how much Mrs Illsley had told him, nor how much she had talked-it-up, but whilst Tony didn't want to spook him with tales of the supernatural, most of all he didn't want to sound like a fool.

"Well," started Francis Humphreys, clearing his throat, "the former house was used as the local courthouse for many years, right up until it was burnt to the ground around 1680. There are some old documents in the county library, but none of them have been – what do you call it – 'digitalised' yet."

"That's a shame," said Tony, "so they're not available online yet then?"

"No, not yet, not as far as I know anyway. I did browse through the file a few years ago, but I have to say it was all quite unremarkable really," he recounted. "Mostly land disputes over the top acre field between local smallholders, one or two libel cases where one villager had accused another of something preposterous, you know the sort of thing."

"How far back to the records go?" asked Tony, skirting the burning issue.

"Fifteen hundred or so," Francis recalled, "can't think that there would have been much of a village to speak of before then. The earliest recorded hamlet around here was just a smattering of farm cottages at the main crossroads, where the pub and the post office are now. The houses there aren't even original, the hovels that were once there were demolished at the turn of the last century, there's a photo in the Kings Head that shows how it all used to look before the first war."

"Fascinating. I'll have to have a look when they're next open."

"Yes indeed, whenever that might be," bemoaned Francis, "but let's not get started on all that again, eh? I just hate being told what I can or can't do don't you? Anyway, enough of that, so yes, your house was the courthouse used mainly for cases that were then referred to the quarter sessions in the county town if they couldn't easily resolve them, but any serious stuff would have been heard at the Assizes as they used to call them back in the day."

"You mean murders and suchlike?"

"Yes," said Francis, "if there ever were any that is. I mean this is a peaceful part of the world. I can't imagine anyone getting that heated up over anything to be honest with you, not enough to commit a crime of that magnitude. But you never know, there's 'nowt so queer as folk' as they say."

"What about witchcraft?" It was a question that he had hoped not to have to ask directly, but he felt that Mr Humphreys was also avoiding mentioning it. He needed him to open up if he knew anything at all, and they were fast running out of time. The subsequent pause suggested that there was something, but his informant seemed to be intent on playing his cards close to his chest.

"Witches?" he answered, as if the question was an absurd one, but there was something in his tone that suggested it was not entirely unexpected.

"Yes," probed Tony. "Mrs Illsley said that there used to be a dunking stool at the pond, near to where the old stocks are."

"Indeed, there was," Francis confirmed, "but as you probably know, even those that were condemned as witches were never really into the occult or anything like that. They were usually just unfortunate old ladies, who lived alone and so were easily accused whenever there was an outbreak of disease or a bad harvest. Yes, we too had a 'cucking' stool, as they were called, though it has long since gone and I don't know of anyone living who would even remember exactly where it was, but like most English villages we had one, yes indeed."

"And was it ever used?" asked Tony, "for determining if someone was a witch or not?"

"I think so," admitted Francis finally. "There are some records of witch trials in the local area in the time of King James the First. It was quite a popular public pastime back then I think you can call it. There was so much political and religious turmoil back then, that to accuse someone of witchcraft was a sure-fire way of causing serious harm to a person's reputation. And if they happened to be a bit peculiar, or look a bit strange, or maybe had some nervous disposition or mental illness, then their chances of them getting off were not too good."

"You mean that once they were accused then their fate was sealed?"

"Pretty much," said Francis, "especially if their accuser happened to come from a landed family or from the local gentry. A lot of innocent people lost their lives in those days before and after the civil war, even King James himself got in on the act. In fact, you could possibly say that he was the instigator of it all, at least on our shores."

"What do you mean?" asked Tony, not being all that well clued up on British political history.

"Have you never heard of his book on Demonology?"

"Nope, that's a new one on me."

"Well, as King James VI of Scotland he first published it towards the end of the sixteenth century and once he acceded to the English throne, he was determined to have it made widely available south of the border too. Caused quite a stir in fact, they say that it even inspired Shakespeare to write the witches scene in Macbeth."

"Well," gasped Tony. "I never. You learn something every day. At least our King only gets involved in horticulture and global warming."

"Why do you want to know?" It was Tony's turn to stay silent this time and Francis didn't wait long to break its hold. "About witches I mean, not the King. Seems like a strange question to ask?"

For a moment Tony considered making something up, but it would only sound even more ridiculous to his new-found friend, and so he opted for the truth. After all, how bad could it be? Francis would either think him a fraud or a fool and as he clearly had nothing to gain from making the whole thing up, the worst-case scenario was that he would think him gullible and naïve, a little wet behind the ears as they used to say in these parts.

Jumping in with both feet was the only reasonable option open to him.

"We've been having some, what you might call 'disturbances' of late," he began, unsure of how much to tell. "It seems that some of our guests were messing about with a Ouija board a few months ago, and it may have stirred something up. Since then, we've had quite a few incidents that are not easily explained, and so I'm wondering if we have to face facts that it might be, you know, paranormal."

"Oh." said Francis, a little unnerved himself by what he had already heard. "You don't want to be messing with those things. But haven't you always had some strange goings on there? I've heard stories about your house for years, the previous owners were village people right up until they died, and the old man always said that it was haunted. Though they weren't too bothered by it as I recall."

"Yes, that's true," said Tony, fearful that things were already moving too fast, but he was curious and so he wanted to know more. They had bought the cottage as a vacant possession after the previous owner had died leaving no next of kin and so the sale had gone through probate, leaving no quarter for hand-me-down tales of things that went bump in the night.

"We had already experienced a few things over the years, and some of our guests have reported strange goings-on, but until recently it's just been odd stuff, you know the kinds of things. Lights going on or off, things being moved about or disappearing, seeing stuff out of the corner of your eye – movements or shadows – but nothing all that unsettling. I've never minded being here on my own, not before this anyway."

"But I don't get the witch thing?" quizzed Francis. "Where does that come in?"

With a heavy heart, Tony opted to tell him the whole story, all about the Watsons and the misspelt Ouija board message, the strange dark shadows that his family had witnessed and his son's late-night visitor. It made for a scary tale and Tony had no doubt whatsoever that as soon as their call was over, his little cottage would once again be the talk of the town. After all, it would make a wonderful diversion to the current obsession with coronavirus, which was the dominant story on every news broadcast and every channel.

"All sounds very peculiar to me," said Francis when Tony had finished with the retelling. "Our very own 'wonderful discovery of witches' as they used to say. And you say that you're there on your own now, your family have returned to London, have they?" Tony hadn't said, but Mrs Illsley clearly had, and he was in no position to be offhand and so he just substantiated the rumour that was obviously doing the rounds.

"It's just me and one large and slightly paranoid dog." said Tony. "Though I'm not sure for how much longer I'll be able to stick it out. One more fright and I think I'll be heading back to London on the train. There's only so much one man and his dog can take."

"Well listen," said Francis, "I'll see what I can do to help you out. Like all the counties in England, ours had its fair share of disturbances in the years following the Pendle witch trials in Lancashire. I'm not sure whether there was anything that was associated with your house though, but I do know a lot of people from the local history society, so we'll put our heads together and see what we can find. I've also got some local research papers of my own in the loft, so I'll get them out and see what I can see, you never know, I may have overlooked something in the small print.

"That would be amazing" said Tony, genuinely grateful, his mood revitalised at some prospect of progress, however small.

"Oh, I do have one thing that might be of interest, thinking about it, I have never read it cover to cover myself," said Francis, almost as an afterthought. A Puritan minister called Richard Bernard, who presided over the local parish church in the village of Batcombe, which isn't too far away from here in Dorsetshire, wrote an infamous guide back in the 1620s called '*A guide to the grand jury men*'. It was issued to all the Western Circuit judges at the time and was used as the main reference point in witch trials for the rest of the century. I have a copy of that if you'd like to see it, for context I mean?"

"Again, that sounds great." said Tony, unsure that it would be of any help but keen to amass as much knowledge on the subject as possible, especially if it was locally relevant.

"My copy is an original, so I'd ask you to take great care of it please," said Francis, as he shuffled off to retrieve it from his library, returning a moment later with the dusty volume in his hands. "I got it at auction a few years ago, cost me twenty pounds or thereabouts, and it is the most curious of books. Quite readable though, but it relies heavily on the Bible for its teachings on the subject and is heavily influenced by both the King James script and the goings on in Pendle, but it's basically a 'do's and don'ts' for those who sat in judgement over cases brought before them – not just how to identify a witch, but also to rule out cases of fraud or local vendettas against innocent people, of which they were only too aware. It might have been considered a balanced assessment back then, though these days it reads like it's been written by someone who was destined for the funny farm."

"Well, it'll give me a start anyway," said Tony. "Shall I come around to fetch it?"

"No, no." said Francis, startled at the very suggestion, his fingers flicking through the pages as he searched for one particular chapter and a verse that he seemed intent on sharing. "No need for that, I need to avoid contact with people as much as possible, doctor's orders I'm afraid. I'll give it to Mrs Illsley when I next see her, and she can pop it round to you, that'll be best."

"That's really most generous of you, I'll take good care of it and have it back to you as soon as I'm done," Tony assured him.

"You're most welcome," said the old gentlemen, his manners harking back to a former age when politeness was a given. "And be careful," he added with all the air of someone who knew more than he'd said. "I don't believe in spooks and all that myself, but there's folks that do, and it wouldn't be the first time that I was wrong. At times like this our minds can play tricks on us, especially when we've no one to keep us company at nights."

He spoke like a man who'd had experience of being alone and Tony assured him that he would heed the well-intentioned advice. It was a warning of sorts, one that had held little fear in the moment but as the day wore on and the words had had time to churn over the mill in his head, it began to curdle into a potent mixture of foreboding and dread.

Particularly the words of that long dead minister, resurrected verbatim by Mr. Francis Humphreys in the course of their conversation, who claimed most vehemently in the second part of his guide first published in 1627 that *"though some have gone about to prove that there are no witches; yet the contrary tenant is undeniably true, that there are witches."*

There are witches.

CHAPTER 16

For the first time since his self-imposed isolation, his sense of abandonment was suddenly overwhelming. The evening had already given way to darkness and the prospect of another night alone in their creepy cottage was something that he was not relishing. For a minute or two he seriously considered calling a taxi and making a run for it, but then reality struck, as he knew that he'd be unlikely to get one to take him and his dog the twenty-minute trip to the train station. Truth be told, he wasn't a quitter, and he wasn't about to start now, but that did nothing to mask the primal urge to flee. The only alternative was, of course, to fight.

Decision made. He was stuck. He just needed to find something to take his mind off it.

He fixed himself some leftover cheese and stale crackers and retrieved his laptop from the conservatory, where it had become a permanent fixture these last few days. Returning to the snug, he added more fuel to the fading fire; just a couple of kiln-dried logs which soon restored the burner to full efficiency. Then, after making short work of his snack and after clearing a few more emails, he settled down to his research. Bruce followed his lead, curling up in his favoured spot on the rug, seemingly now at peace with the world despite the loss of his human pack. Together they would while away what little was left of the evening, and whilst Tony was hoping for an uneventful one, there was something in the atmosphere that suggested otherwise.

He'd known the close compressed feeling as a child, but rarely as an adult, a subtle yet crushing quality that is deeply imbued in solitude. Akin to a soft and cushioned closeness, crowding in on his senses, muffling his mind with a numbing caress as if another more oppressive dimension was now far too close for comfort. It had always been a disturbing feeling and one that he'd never been able to shake off once it had taken hold, so as soon as it began to wrap its tendrils around him, it would always be too late to break free. He was enveloped in it. Smothered by it. Lost in an unfriendly hug. Like a drowning man, he could still make out the starlit surface high above his head, but he would soon sink like the condemned into its depths and surrender to the claustrophobic crush as it caved in around him.

He had tried to explain the feeling to Charlie before, but he could never do it justice, yet it was his wife who had recognised it for what it was. It wasn't supernatural, at least not in the normal sense of the world, but it was like some genetic terror that had been passed down through the generations and one that was a prelude to something worse. Charlie thought it always came on prior to a period of immense sadness or at worst, to a bout of depression, but it was hard to be sure and even harder to see it coming.

Anxiety had crept up on him over a period of days. He had always been prone to such feelings, but he had learned how to manage them by recognising its early warning signs before it got a grip. Self-taught techniques that he had first deployed as a teenager, whenever the stifling sensation had begun to take hold. In those days the antidote had always been to throw himself into work, to drive himself on towards ever more success and the rewards that came with it. But all that was now behind him and there was little left in the locker that could hold back the rising tide of despair.

His work had always provided him with a lifeline, and by and large, it had never failed. Indeed, the very fear of failure had driven him forward and even in moments when the challenge before him had seemed too daunting to deal with, through sheer hard work and determination, even the most insurmountable problems had been overcome and the bank balance had ticked ever upwards.

Now, with his business failing in the face of an unseen enemy, his hard-earned bank balance was under serious threat of falling under its spell too, a curse for which there might be no known antidote.

He knew that he was not alone. He kept on reminding himself that there were many people out there that were much worse off than him, but in his darkest moments such thoughts beckoned the naysayers to his door and then the voices of reason would be drowned out. He knew that he would eventually succumb to the hammering in his head and fall foul of their slurs to sink into a deep depressive state that he had not known for years. Not since before Charlie had come into his life. And in some ways, he welcomed it.

He poured himself a generous measure of whisky, a more than handsome portion that he knew would leave him feeling sluggish in the morning, and though he told himself that he needed it, he knew that he was now at the top of a very slippery slope. A lump or two of ice clung to each other like dance partners, as he slipped them into the mix, floating an inch above the base as if to reinforce the fact that this was no 'wee dram', but his wife was not around to admonish him for it.

"Here's to you Bruce." he said, raising the glass high in the air in the direction of the dog who was laid out on the floor, legs outstretched in a posture that said he was in no mood to be disturbed. Though his tail betrayed him, beating out a different tune, to which only his master knew the words.

"At least you've not deserted me old boy." he added, as his mood took a nosedive towards oblivion, and the dog raised his head in acknowledgment before snorting in reply and laying his head back down to sleep.

As a floorboard croaked just inches above his head, he took another salutary swig and raised his glass towards the sound, refusing to accredit it to anything other than the easing timbers of an old house. "Cheers to you, too." he hailed up towards the low ceiling, "whoever you are. Whatever you are."

Old houses do that. They breathe in tune with the elements like a tall ship. Or with its crew.

After all, the heavy wooden beams were once living breathing things, until some medieval carpenters had cut them down in their prime. Then as seasoned joists they'd been hoisted up to hang from finely crafted oak A-frames, each chiselled peg dovetailed into carved sockets like ancient teeth in an angled jawbone. Dead men, whose hands had once lovingly laboured to shape each broad blade that would one day bear a tonne or two of hand-hewn reeds. The same dead men that now lay their heads further up the lane; a yew-lined route that leads to a secluded graveyard which had long since laid its single tracked secrets to rest.

Hand-made bricks from a bygone age recalled the imprecision of mudded men with wooden pallets, as they shaped and sheared off blocks of sandy slime into timber moulds until in searing kilns each one clinked against the other as the alchemy was completed. From thence loaded onto horse drawn carts and pulled down rutted lanes and along freshly cut canals, they had been tossed into the waiting hands of burly bricklayers in whose care the curling chimneys had climbed skyward like rising arteries. Each brick balanced on the next, butted in regimented lines of headers and stretchers and bonded in intricate orders of English and Flemish bond, to raise the channels through which small boys would one day clamber like vertical miners employed to sweep the soot from these shafts.

Roughly shaped flag stones concealed uneven floors of dirt and lime sand, that now lie forgotten beneath machine-woven carpets that have kept their lines hidden for centuries, to bury the coldness of the dank earth suffocated under unslippered soles. Behind the re-plastered walls, bars of timbered lath still lie in regimented tracks across the stone walls, each furrow firmly packed with a rugged mix of horsehair and lime, which has already crumbled into dust as every hung portrait strikes another nail into its bowed breast.

Tony had sat in silent contemplation far longer than he had intended, only occasionally shifting his position to sink another shot. He had turned on every lamp in the old part of the house, determined to keep the shadows at bay, like some homo-erectus hunter that has found himself stranded at dusk, and so he stokes a fierce fire to strike fear into the hearts of every potential predator. He reached across and loaded a couple more logs into the burner, opening the vents wide to fan the flames in a timely demonstration of man's mastery over fire.

The flames were enticing; they were calling to him, beckoning him to come closer. To make their acquaintance.

He found himself staring at the metal backplate behind the stove, an antique and complex etching of interwoven circles that swirled across its surface. They had studied it before but neither he nor Charlie had been able to reach any conclusion as to its meaning; at the pattern's centre, the positioning of each interlocking circle gave rise to flat flower-like symbols resembling daisies on a continuous and interlocking chain. Though the lines had faded with time, the image remained and as each indent was caught in the lamplight, he found himself wondering again as to its origins.

Why had an unknown artisan gone to such pains to leave such an intricate imprint for eternity.

The clock in the hall beat out its hourly chime, and Tony counted them out as the metallic melody called time at eleven o'clock. Though the laptop was balanced carefully on his lap, he realised that he had been sat there for over an hour already and had yet to even begin, but he no longer had the same urge to seek out stories of witchcraft and decided instead to wait on Francis Humphreys to come up with the answer from his local network. It might mean that he had days, maybe even weeks, to wait for an answer, but time no longer seemed to be of the essence. He had time to burn.

Another step on an upstairs floorboard. Bruce's ears stood to attention, though he didn't move his head from the rug. When the next conspicuous movement made landfall though, followed sequentially by another, his whole head darted to attention and his eyes turned towards his master for a reassuring word that never came. A low growl began to emanate from him then, as a fourth, fifth and sixth step landed on the floor above their heads and with every subsequent step, there could be no doubt that someone or something was walking the boards above their heads.

A Seventh.

Eight. Nine. Ten. Then it stopped.

Slowly, the fearless German Shepherd raised himself up and turned to face the unseen foe, his ears still on high alert, but his body rigid. Listening. Waiting. Anticipating the next movement that they each knew was but a moment away.

When it came it sounded like a stampede in the silence and it sent shockwaves through the house. It was no longer walking. It was running. Bruce went into overdrive, scaling the stairs like a cat, his teeth bared ready for the fight. If there were a human up there alone in the dark, then they would have been advised to seek sanctuary, but as Tony made chase up the stairs and flicked on the lights to illuminate the landing, he could see that the front bedroom was just as he had left it.

Bruce was already surveying, drinking in the smells from every crevice and leaving no stone unturned. It was cold up there, colder than it should have been, with the heat from the chimney acting as an additional radiator, but there was a chill about the place and Tony shivered as his eyes caught a glimpse of rapid movement to his right.

He turned to face the door through which he and Bruce had just entered, but there was nothing there and the lights were still blazing. Bruce charged off into the hallway and then in and out of each-and-every-room, as if he too had seen something and was determined to flush it out, but he came back within seconds, his efforts unrewarded and wearing a canine expression that was not unlike the look on his master's face.

It was one of bewilderment. There should have been someone there. There should have been something to find. It was impossible that there was nothing, but that's exactly what there was. Nothing. Nothing at all.

After a few more minutes they returned to the snug, Tony sank back into the worn leather armchair, but Bruce remained on edge, circling the room in an agitated state that all dog-owners know only too well. It was a full ten minutes before he returned to his place on the rug, but he remained on his guard, his head more up than down and his ears pricked so that every sound would be caught in his radar-like hearing.

As they sat there in silence just waiting for the next inexplicable sound, a plan began to hatch in Tony's mind, one that would require a more patient and less immediate response. He checked the charge on his phone and was pleased to see that it was almost at 100% - he would need it to be fully charged, as he knew from his limited research into the paranormal that it was common for batteries to be drained within minutes of an encounter. It was as if the ghost, or whatever it was, was able to feed upon the electrical charge as it manifested and so Tony reached for his back-up power source, just in case – a handy little device that provided a minimum of two recharges should one of them fail.

He had left the landing light on – in fact he had no intention of turning any of them off now until morning – and so from where he was sat, he could see his way up the turn in the staircase to the landing itself, where two of the bedroom doors were in full view. He sat silently and watched as one of them began to close, silently and gradually, so much so that Bruce did not stir. It was a new twin panelled oak door, and it had been fitted perfectly into its frame, it brass hinges well-oiled and the wood pre-treated to ensure that it would not warp in the heat of a modern home.

Only as it clicked itself shut, a task that normally required it to be pulled into place by one dull round handle, did Bruce spring to attention, his teeth bared and a low growl building once more. In contrast, Tony felt calmer than he had any right to be – maybe it was the technology that had lent him a strange sense of control, a temporary mastery over his environment that wouldn't last more than another minute. Or maybe it was just the thrill of the chase, the rush of adrenaline. Stupidity.

Tony readied himself but did not move. Instead, he clicked on his mobile phone and opened the Facebook app, determined to share this upcoming adventure with the world. He clicked on the Live option and as the counter began to tick on, he raised himself up on his heels and began his commentary. "Okay so as some of you will know, I'm at our holiday place now. Charlie and the kids are at home and so I'm here all alone with only Bruce for company and we are experiencing a few, what you might call, issues." As he spoke, he slammed his free hand against the wall in a direct hit that left an unsightly smudge of black and red across the painted plasterwork. "Including a bloody infestation of sodding flies."

He noticed that there were already three people watching, two of their close friends and Charlie herself who had already messaged him. He didn't know if she was warning him or telling him to stop; after all, they didn't want to scare off any future holidaymakers, but he no longer cared about the profits. He was more concerned to banish the feeling that he was alone and the thought that he'd be able to deal with the threat - if indeed he was being threatened - if he had some virtual friends to combat the spiritual ones.

"Don't worry Charlie, I'm fine. I've got Bruce." and he scanned his camera over towards the dog, who was suitably in-character, edging his way towards the stairs like a lion in pursuit of fresh meat. "A few minutes ago, we heard someone walking about upstairs, but we went straight up and had a scout about and there was no one. Now I've seen one of the bedroom doors close by itself so we're going up to investigate."

There were ten watchers now, eleven, twelve. He was attracting quite an audience and as he glanced at the screen, he saw a couple of messages from concerned friends and one or two sceptical strangers.

Be careful Tone.

Watch out for the spooks.

Ooh how exciting.

Rather you than me mate.

"What was that?" he asked of everyone and no one. He stayed silent as the footsteps began, hoping that the camera was picking up the faint sounds from the same room as before. "Can you all hear that?" he said, holding up the phone so that the stairs were in full view, just as Bruce began his ascent.

"The light has gone off.," he said in a sudden panic. "When did the landing light go off?" He hadn't noticed, he'd been looking at his camera, but as he glanced down again several people had replied to say that they'd just witnessed it. One person even thought that they'd heard the click of the switch.

Bruce was now at the top of the stairs and was advancing slowly on the front bedroom. Tony was bringing up the rear again and as he stepped onto the final tread, he wasted no time in reaching for the switch on the wall to pour some light onto proceedings once more. He turned the camera onto himself, speaking to his audience of twenty plus, who were all clearly gripped by this unexpected and rather personal entertainment. After all, they probably had little else to do.

"Okay so it's gone very quiet again now.," he said a little disappointed despite his now heavy heartbeat, his swagger now a thing of the past. "I'm not going to open the door until I hear something, I'm going to open it as soon as I hear the footsteps behind the door, so if there is something there it's got no chance at all of hiding."

He gulped at the air in anticipation. His mouth had gone dry. The silence was overbearing, only broken by the occasional loud snort from his left as Bruce sniffed greedily at the thin gap between carpet and door. Tony was looking at his own recorded image in the camera and was about to turn its viewfinder once more to the front when he noticed that the door to his rear was wide open.

"What." he said, almost in annoyance that he'd missed it and addressing nothing or no one in particular. "When did that get opened again?"

It's been open all the time mate.

Was always open Tone.

"But I watched it close." he said mystified. "Before we came up here, I watched it close by itself from the bottom of the stairs. It was pulled completely shut by itself."

Yeh whatever.

Get on with it.

Bored now.

He was starting to feel like a fraud when a loud bang from inside the closed room caught everyone's attention and in the same moment the bedroom door was flung open to smash back against the wall to the left like a garden gate on a windy night.

"What the fuck."

The camera had been fixed on Bruce as Tony verbalised his fear in a way that only those living in the early decades of the twenty first century would do, causing some members of the watching audience to laugh out loud as a movement in the dog's mouth synchronised perfectly with the unexpected expletive.

He hadn't filmed the incident in question. He found himself cursing his luck as the thirty or so that were now watching from all around the world were left disorientated and confused by his unsteady hand and the clattering of footsteps. He steadied himself as he followed Bruce into the room, swinging the phone around as he did so to ensure that he filmed every wall, behind the door and into every corner to prove beyond all reasonable doubt that it was just one man and his dog.

A book was hurled from the shelf to his right. It flashed across the camera in a blur of flapping pages and a thump as it hit the side of the bed and clattered to the ground. An unmistakeable sound from the ensuite bathroom alerted him to the fact that the taps had been switched on full force and the lights went off and on again, all as Bruce went berserk, barking and baying in a rabid cacophony of fear induced noise.

The whole thing may only have lasted for less than a minute, but it had seemed longer, and in his terror, Tony was completely unaware of the direction in which his camera had been pointed. He'd been looking one way as it filmed the scene behind him or pointed it at the floor as he was swept around to face the sounds that poured out from the bathroom, but as the rumpus began to fade a final loud slam from the bedroom opposite brought the incident to a close and Tony slumped down on the bed as Bruce continued to bark furiously at its foot.

"Shit." he said, relieved that whatever it was seemed to be at an end but at the same time fearful that it had only just begun. He looked down at the phone as he reached out to pat his trusted pet, and he was aghast to see the pandemonium that had broken out on his Facebook feed.

Did you see it?

See what?

Did you see what I saw.

That was freaky.

Shitting myself.

Tony ru ok

"What?" he asked of the assembled voyeurs. "I didn't see anything, what did you see?"

At first, he though it must just be some kind of mass hysteria for he was sure that, other than the book being thrown and the faucets coming on, there had been nothing to see, only a few loud bangs and strange movements. But as he read the stream of comments that was now pouring forth from his audience, he was left in no doubt at all.

Fucking weird shadow.

A shadow man, by the bed.

A black thing.

Unmistakable person shape.

Black thing with head cocked to the side on the bed.

Tony instinctively stood up, turning on his heels to survey the scene again. A crumpled duvet and scattered pillows – had he done that? The bed had been perfectly made before. Of that, he was sure. He always made the bed. Always. Without fail.

"Are you sure that's what you saw guys?" Tony asked nervously, hoping against hope that they were winding him up. "Are you all shitting me now?"

The common consensus was that they were not. They had seen what they had seen, at least ten of them were reporting the same thing, but several had already dropped off, unnerved by the experience, or rejecting it all as some elaborate hoax. Charlie was prominent amongst the remaining few and she was joining in the calls that he should watch it back and call her as soon as he had done so.

Tony ended the call and returned to the snug, all lights blazing and his trusted hound at his heel, visibly cowering in his wake, his ears flat and his tail bowed beneath him. Tony fell back into the armchair, his senses spinning and his heart thumping in his chest, so much so that he could even feel the pounding in his throat and in his ears. In that moment he needed a drink more that he had ever done in his life, but he could not bring himself to fetch the bottle from the kitchen where it had sat since his last indulgence.

He turned sharply to his left, as he thought he caught sight of something small and black moving on his arm. Then to his right, as the same thing seemed to crawl from the furthest corner of his eye, but as he turned his head there was nothing to be seen. Again, to his left, a tiny black dot that left a psychedelic trail of colour in its wake, like the multicoloured lights of a nineteen seventies single from an era of disco or glam rock.

"This shit is just fucking weird." he said out loud and that's when he heard it again.

A snigger. A light yet guttural sound that seemed to be at his expense.

He sensed movement again and this time he saw it. A fly. A large black abomination. A winged mini beast that feasts on the rotting flesh and putrid faeces of all other creatures.

A parasite. A portent of doom.

Or maybe it was just a fly. Another fly.

"It's just a fly," muttered Tony at which Bruce laid his head on his master's lap, sensing that something was badly wrong. "Just a fly old boy, nothing to worry about. Just a fly that's all."

CHAPTER 17

The social media site was taking a while to do its thing.

Formatting the live broadcast as it managed the information across its servers around the world, he left it to its machinations and still shaking, plucked up the courage to make his way into the kitchen, but this time he ignored the spirits and instead fixed himself a double shot of espresso coffee from his expensive machine.

On his return he was left cursing as he was met with a blank screen. The battery had been drained of power, a consequence of its recent use, however unlikely that seemed. Fumbling in his pocket he pulled out the recharge unit, but it too had been sapped of power and he was forced to reconnect the phone to the mains before it flickered back into life. It was a full two minutes before he was able to relaunch the app to check if his attempt to capture a live paranormal event had been successful or not.

To his relief, the recording was still being processed and he saw that he would need to be patient for a few minutes more. In the end it took a full ten minutes before it was ready to be published on his page; as he began to watch it back, he was soon horrified by what he had failed to notice at the time. There in front of the watching eyes of his friends and family, an undeniable outline of a human form was preserved in all its digital glory. It was present as his camera swept past the bed, still and unmoved with its back towards him, as if it had just risen from its resting place, but as the viewfinder swept back the other way, the new angle also revealed its edge reflected in the tall mirror that backed onto the bed. It had been there, and it had been real enough to have a reflection all of its own.

An arm, the dark shape of a leg and the side of a featureless face that was without form.

He jumped as his wife's familiar ringtone blarted out its tune, and he did not hesitate to answer though he had given no thought as to what he was about to say. But he needn't have worried; it was Charlie that did the talking.

"Tony, thank God you're okay." she sobbed, "what in God's name was that? You need to get out of there, right now."

"Hold on," he replied, far more bravely than he had any right to be. "I'm okay, we're okay. I've only just watched it back, it seems impossible, but I've been hearing noises all evening, so at least I know now what's behind it."

Right on cue, hurried footsteps scuttled across the floor above his head. He ignored them as best he could. Even Bruce did not move from his spot, though he was listening intently.

"You can't be seriously considering staying?" she asked. "Not after that."

"Look," he reasoned, "if that's all it's got, noises and a few books being thrown about and a black blob on the bed, then it's not going to harm me, is it?" Another noise from upstairs. It sounded like another volume of National Geographic had lost its footing on the bookshelf and tumbled to the floor. "I'm not going to be scared away Charlie, and in any case, where do I go?"

"You could come home?" she suggested, but it sounded more like an instruction. "We could tackle this together, once all this COVID drama is over. Let it lie for a while. I don't like you being down there on your own. I don't like being here on my own for that matter."

"Has anything else happened there?" asked Tony, remembering their dramatic video call.

150

"No, nothing," she answered, "it's been quiet. A bit too quiet for my liking, but the kids are missing you and Bruce. They keep on asking when you're coming home."

"But what if it follows me?" asked Tony. It was something that he hadn't even considered up until that point, but he was suddenly convinced that whatever had latched onto them was not necessarily only clinging onto the bricks and mortar of their cottage. "What if it's somehow linked to me? To us. What if I bring it home with me? Like the Watsons may have done."

It was a terrifying thought and Charlie was not at all willing to give it airtime. "Don't be so ridiculous." she scolded, "I've never heard such rubbish, you're just getting yourself all worked up over nothing. Where'd you get an idea like that from? The Watsons had an accident that's all, you said it, an accident."

"I know, I know, but I read something online earlier," he admitted, "probably nothing, but I read that these entities can sometimes attach themselves to a person and not just to a place. What if this thing does that? What if it did attach itself to one of the Watson family and what if it did travel back with them? What if it somehow caused their accident?"

"Stop."

"I can't."

"Stop it.," said Charlie, more insistent this time. "They had an accident that's all. It was late. Mr. Watson was tired, they'd had a long journey. It was an unfortunate accident. I want you to come home. Tomorrow."

"Okay?"

"Okay." he mimicked.

"I mean it Tony, I want you to get a lift to the station in the morning and get on the first train home, I'll pick you up from the station early afternoon. I'll bring the kids with me. There are some trains running now, they said on the news. They have to run so that NHS staff can get to the hospitals."

"Okay," he agreed, against his better judgement. "I'll do it. Tonight, I'll sleep in one of the kids' rooms, I'm not sleeping in the old part of the house anymore."

"That sounds sensible to me." she agreed. "Keep the phone handy, just in case."

He said he would and after telling her more about the conversation he'd had with the self-appointed village historian, she proceeded to tell him more about the house and the information that she'd gleaned from two centuries of census data. None of it seemed all that pertinent to their dilemma and as suspected, the row of two room hovels had mainly been occupied by local farm hands going back in perpetuity. Even the census of 1911, the last one that was publicly available, had failed to reveal anything more interesting, as each Head of the household was recorded as an Agricultural Labourer, with wives and a succession of children in various stages of education. Only the eldest were ever listed as being employed, most likely on the nearest farm which was shown to be under the oversight of a tenant farmer of 33 acres called Hunt.

Nothing of any note that would explain their disturbances.

Even though it was nearly midnight, Tony wasn't yet ready for bed. He knew that there was no way he was going to get any sleep after tonight's scare, and so there was little point in trying. Instead, he hunkered down in the snug and continued to search for clues on the internet, but his thoughts kept straying back to what he'd seen, and he must have watched the recording another five times before the clock in the hall finally struck the witching hour. His signal to call it a night? Perhaps, but he wasn't yet ready to oblige.

What was that thing? He asked himself the same question, repeatedly. A ghost? Maybe, but of what? It was impossible to determine how old it was or even if it were male or female. It was just a shape. A human shape of sorts, but there was nothing else to go on, other than its dark shadowlike form. A shadow being. A shadow person.

On a whim he entered 'shadow people' into the search engine and he was shocked at the number of hits that it generated.

There were several published works on the subject and even a recent enough film by the same name. He'd had no idea that it was even a thing, and the movie had passed him by, though judging by its date it was around the time when the kids had been very little and so anything that wasn't animated or didn't involve cuddly bears or rabbits would not have made the cut back then. The list was endless and the most popular channel for uploading video content was full to bursting with clips and home-made films of sightings from around the world. He was shocked to see that some of them had been viewed hundreds of thousands of times and the fact that they seemed so popular gave him an idea.

Safety in numbers.

He immediately returned to his Facebook page and set about working out how to download his recently posted video, a task which required some additional study on his part. It wasn't long before he'd figured it out though, and within fifteen minutes he was downloading the newly created content and uploading it to his online video account. He tagged it a few times with prominent words and phrases that would make it easier to find for anyone out there who was inclined to search for such things, before returning to his Facebook account to deal with the rising tide of questions and comments from his own contacts.

In the morning he would return to see what kind of response his uploaded video had received from what was now a global paranormal community, the like of which he'd had no idea even existed until the events of this evening. He wasn't expecting much but judging by the general reaction of his own friends and family, he was likely to face a good deal of scepticism. Even those that knew him had mostly assumed it to be a set-up, a mistimed Halloween-style stunt, but whilst some were shocked by its content, one or two accused him of staging an outright hoax.

To his relief, it seemed that everyone was up late as some of those who had watched it live had been quick to come to his defence, confirming that they had witnessed the whole thing and stating that if it was a set-up, it was a bloody good one. Even Charlie had chipped in, relaying to his followers and some of hers that she was really concerned for her husband's wellbeing and hinting at earlier scares that had led him to take such an unprecedented course of action.

He had never posted a live video before, and it was testament to its ease of use that he had been able to do so without messing it up. He had never been the most technically gifted end-user and like most men of his generation, never ever read the instructions, but as he perused the comments, he found himself duty-bound to reply to some of the more concerned ones and to rebuff any that he felt were a blatant affront to his integrity.

I'm fine thanks Cindy.

My thoughts exactly mate. Freaky as hell.

Not sure what it was.

Yes, Charlie and I saw some something similar on Zoom the other night.

You'd be very welcome Tim and yes – bring your chainsaw with you.

No way Melissa – I don't have time for hoaxes. This is 100% for real.

It was really late now, or early depending on your way of looking at things, and so there were very few reactions to his answers. Most of his earlier audience now appeared to be offline, though some of them were obviously not sleeping too easily after what they'd witnessed. He was just about to do the same, realising that it was fast approaching one in the morning, and he was beginning to think that, as the noises in the room above his head had now abated, he might be able to get to sleep after all, when the screen lit up and the familiar three-dots began to flash at the bottom of his post.

Someone was about to add their thoughts to the debate.

Mustn't Leave.

The scribe was listed as Anonymous. He had never seen such a thing before and until that moment, he didn't even think it was even possible to post on Facebook without an approved account. Maybe there was something in the settings that allowed a user to put up some sort of privacy block that prevented a contact from seeing their identity when posting on their page, but he didn't think so. After a momentary pause, the same indicator flashed to tell him that there was more on its way.

For our sake.

He quickly typed an answer, as the touch of an ice-cold finger traced a trail of terror down his spine. He spun around in his chair, but there was nothing to see, other than the uneven plaster to his rear. If it was his imagination, it was only to be expected. Just his overactive imagination, or a bead of his own sweat plunging down from his neckline.

'Who said that?' he typed at speed, but the comments had already gone from the screen.

Sunday 29th March 2020

DAY 7 OF UK LOCKDOWN

531 deaths reported in the UK – the total number of deaths due to COVID19 now stands at 3,232 with 25,596 people testing positive for the disease.

CHAPTER 18

There were three loud knocks; a furious fist that beat to time on the timber.

Then silence.

Another three followed, the same pace, the same sound. Heavy, insistent, and point-blank refusing to be ignored. The sound raised Bruce from an uneasy doze on the landing – his new favourite spot - and Tony heard him shuffle down the stairs ahead of him to confront any would-be intruders.

Tony groaned as he sat up in bed. As he struggled to his feet, he caught sight of his reflection in the full-length mirror by the door and found himself wishing that he'd remembered to pack his dressing gown. "Okay, I'm coming, give it a rest." he yelled, as the third and final trio of thuds echoed around the solid stone cottage, and grabbing a hoodie, he attempted to make himself look presentable. He let the dog out of the back door, before proceeding to the front and his first ever caution.

"Mr. Mountford?" asked the tall fair-haired officer.

Tony nodded, a little shocked to see a police car parked out front.

"May we come inside Sir?" she asked, "better to speak indoors, more private that way." It would have been obvious to anyone that he had only just woken up, his unkempt hair and unshaven state giving the game away before he'd even had chance to object.

"Yes, please come in," stammered Tony, waving them inside, but as his brain scrambled to find a reason for their visit his thoughts immediately strayed to his family and panic set in. "Is everything okay?" he asked. "It's not about Charlie is it, or the kids?"

"No, no, nothing like that Mr Mountford.," she said, not wanting to worry him unduly. "I'm WPC Carter, this is PC Mills, it's a civilian matter that we were wanting to discuss with you."

He couldn't hide his sense of relief and as he glanced across at the clock, he realised that he'd slept in for far longer than he'd intended. Eleven o'clock had come and gone and he felt a sudden rush of embarrassment to still be in his pyjamas. It was almost noon and he had slept the sleep of the dead. Even Bruce had not roused him for his morning walk.

"Can I get you a cup of tea or coffee?" he offered, remembering his manners, and apologising for his tardiness. "I'm usually up with the larks." he lied, "but last night was a bit"- his mind went blank as he tried to think of a word that might best describe it, but none was forthcoming - "anyway, it took me a long time to get to sleep. It wasn't a restful night."

"I'm sorry to hear that sir, but we won't take up much of your time." It was the male police officer this time and he wanted answers. "Are you the owner occupier sir?"

"Yes," said Tony, rubbing his stubble as he remembered that he hadn't shaved in hours.

"So, it's your primary residence is it sir?"

The penny dropped then, and Tony looked down, finally realising their purpose and a little embarrassed at being caught out like this. "Well, no," he said, "no, this is our second home. We've, rather I've, just come down to get some work done during lockdown, you know, trying to make the best of it. Stiff upper lip, blitz spirit and all that."

He smiled and feigned to laugh, but the friendly neighbourhood police didn't seem to be in the mood to reciprocate.

Above their heads, a floorboard creaked. Then another. All three of them looked up at the same moment and it wasn't long before another question came his way.

"Are you alone here sir?"

"Yes, just me and the dog," he said truthfully, beginning to wonder what might happen next and if it did, how he was going to even start to explain it. Please no, he thought, though it was closer to a prayer.

"You do know about the lockdown rules?" asked WPC Carter, "the travel restrictions? Essential journeys only? No house guests?"

"Yes, I'm aware of those," Tony replied, trying to remember the excuse that he and Charlie had agreed upon for exactly this scenario. "I came down the day before lockdown," he lied, "the rumour-mill was already suggesting it was likely so, as I was out of work for the foreseeable, I thought I'd just go for it."

The unmistakeable sound of footsteps gradually tapped their way across the ceiling, like a slow handclap from an absent audience. It was a poor excuse.

"Are you sure that there's no one else here with you Mr Mountford? Only, we were told that you came here with your family, just over a week ago." The pair had been well informed, but quite who their informant had been, was yet to be made clear. Tony immediately had his suspicions, but that would have to wait. "Can we take a look upstairs sir?"

"Yes, please do." said Tony, and PC Mills wasted no time in taking up the invitation as he strode up the stairs, like a man on a mission.

"If you do manage to find someone, I'll be delighted I can tell you," Tony shouted after him. The irony of his predicament was not lost on him, but he felt that he needed to come clean, before he got himself in any deeper. He was up to his neck in it already. "Look, we did come down together about a week ago, but the kids were kicking off. They were bored and between them they were driving us crackers, so my wife decided to take them home. Left me down here to sort things out."

"You do know that you've broken the law don't you sir?" The WPC had the look of someone who was only doing their job, and who was not particularly impressed with the role that she was now expected to play. "I should really be issuing you with a fixed penalty fine you know?"

"Yes, I know, I am sorry," he said as submissively as he could manage, just as her partner came bounding down the stairs, his eyes wide and his face an ashen shade of grey.

"What happened to you?" said WPC Carter. "Who was up there? I hope Mr Mountford for your sake, that you've not been lying to us. We take a dim view of being misled."

PC Mills wasn't speaking. He just looked dumbstruck. He looked terrified.

"Gary," the WPC asked, taking him by the elbow. "What's wrong with you? Was there someone up there or not?"

"No." he stuttered, clearly frightened out of his wits. "No, there was nobody up there. Nobody at all."

"Listen," said Tony, feeling a little sorry for the police constable, but also keen to learn what it was that he'd seen. He didn't get any further than that first word, and as it turned out, it was quite an appropriate choice. They all listened intently as the noise from upstairs became undeniable. Even Bruce, who had returned from a brief sojourn around the garden, was engrossed by it once more, as he quickly disregarded any human threat to focus his senses elsewhere.

Footsteps. Heavy, purposeful, and clear. Bruce was snarling now. The humans were staring, speechless, at the stairs.

One. Two. Three. Four. Five. Six. Seven. Eight. Nine. Ten. Eleven. Twelve. Thirteen.

There was no mistaking it, the direction was clear. All three of them stared at the empty flight of stairs, but something had just stepped down every tread, stopping dead at the foot of the carpeted sweep, just inches from where they were now huddled. There was nothing to see, but there had been something all the same, and they had all been first hand witnesses to it, four of them if you counted the dog who was now cautiously sniffing at the empty space, his nose down low his demeanour close to a crawl.

"What the actual fuck?" said WPC Carter, forgetting herself for a moment, but her partner wasn't hanging around.

"Let's get out of here." he yelped, hauling open the front door and leaping out into the rising wind, with his partner in hot pursuit. Bruce followed close behind, remembering his primary duty before scratching at the grass and cocking his leg at the gate, to mark his territory against the unseen threat.

Tony too had felt the call of nature in that moment and would shortly be making his own much needed visit, ghost, or no ghost. But firstly, he found himself wondering what the two police officers would be including in their official version of events that morning. He had a feeling that it wouldn't be a full and frank account, as whatever it was that had just spooked them all, neither officer seemed in any mood to hang around. After the performance that had just played out before their eyes, Tony had no doubt that both would soon fall foul of a bout of collective amnesia, and when it came to their written report, it would make for short reading.

Whatever their decision, they now had time to get their story straight on the way back to the station, but Tony was left feeling strangely comforted by his first face-to-face human interaction of a long and trying week. For he now knew, for sure, that he wasn't going mad, and he knew that he definitely wasn't imagining it. Any of it.

"C'mon you." he shouted to the dog on his return from the bathroom. "Let's get out whilst this sunshine lasts. It feels like rain to me."

※

At what point does a haunting become the norm?

An everyday run-of-the-mill expectation of just 'how things are'. As Tony walked the fields, his hood raised against the wind, he tried once more to rationalise what had just happened and the events of the last 48 hours and found himself wondering what more was yet to come? He was unharmed. Other than the fear that the haunting had induced - because that's clearly what it was – he'd been in no real danger at any point. As he wandered on, he figured that if he could accept these occurrences as simply the manifestations of a classic haunting then surely, he could live with it. And so could Charlie. The kids though were another matter.

He had always been a very practical man. Down to earth, people might say, not someone that is scared of his own shadow or other people's shadows for that matter. Footsteps. Bangs. Doors opening. Doors closing. Things moving on shelves or falling off them. Yes, they might make him jump, they were often instantaneous and so that was only to be expected, but he hadn't come to any harm. They couldn't harm him, could they?

And as for apparitions. The shadow man, the woman that Bill had seen all those years ago, the man that his son had seen in his room, the dark shape in the picture, the approaching darkness on the zoom call – none had actually caused anyone any physical pain, unless you counted Bill's untimely bump to his head. So other than the Watsons' accident on their way home – which to all intents and purposes was just that, an accident – this haunting, this presence, this thing posed no danger to him or his family, it was simply trying to scare them. Or to get their attention.

Well, they'd managed to do that alright. "Okay, so now you've got my attention." shouted Tony into the wind. "Now, do you mind telling me what it is that you want?"

Bruce barked at him in the distance, but for once he wasn't talking to his dog.

"What is it that you want?" he asked out loud but more quietly this time as he turned back along the circular route towards the cottage with Bruce in hot pursuit.

CHAPTER 19

"So which sneak has shopped us then?" said Charlie, as he relayed the morning's events to her over the phone. "I can't believe that someone would do that. What's it to them, the bloody snitches."

"Probably one of the locals," reasoned her husband. "You know what they're like, they don't like 'comers-in' at the best of times, least of all now."

"Well, they blame us for everything don't they. What about the money that we bring in, never mind the fact that their houses are now worth ten times what they were twenty years ago."

"At the very least." agreed Tony, thinking that it might be a lot more than that after the COVID-inspired exodus from London. "So anyway, it means that I'm stuck here for a while yet."

"What?" Charlie hadn't even considered the implications, but she wasn't prepared to go down without a fight. "You mean you're staying after all?"

"I have to, don't I? The police were very clear about it." He wasn't exactly telling the truth, but he needed a reason, and he didn't want to tell her about last night's cryptic social media message. Not just yet. He was still trying to convince himself that he hadn't just imagined the whole thing, but the chilling sense of caution would not leave him, and he couldn't help but wonder if the Watsons had chosen to ignore something similar.

It was a chance that he didn't want to take.

Charlie was stumped, and for a few seconds she stayed silent, until she began bawling at the kids to stop arguing over whatever game it was that they were playing. "How much longer do you think things are going to be like this?" she asked, desperate for some hope to cling to.

"It's going to be this way for a few weeks yet, I think, maybe a couple of months." If the news was to be believed, there was little chance of a reprieve until the other side of summer. It was all looking bleak. "I'll spend some time straightening up the garden, it's long overdue and I may as well repaint the bedrooms while I'm at it."

"How?" asked Charlie. "The shops are all closed. Where are you going to get the paint?"

"Online deliveries are still available aren't they and I've got all the tools I need in the shed as well as some leftover paint. You can sort out the colours and have them sent to me, we can pay for them out of the business account, there's still some spare cash in there and in any case it can all be put against this year's tax bill if we get in quick." It seemed like a sensible course of action, and so with some reluctance, Charlie agreed to get onto it. But whilst it provided a nice diversion, it didn't help with the other problem, as she was quick to point out.

"I'm just going to have to face it out, aren't I?" said Tony, as a door slammed shut somewhere above his head. It was like it was listening to him.

Taunting him.

Laughing at him.

"What was that?" asked Charlie.

"Oh nothing, just the wind." She didn't believe him, and he didn't blame her. She knew full well that it hadn't been the wind.

In fact, it was now sunny but cool outside, the wind had dropped a notch or two and a pleasant afternoon was in the offing, one that he would spend on one of his least favourite chores. Gardening. Slash-and-burn was his favoured method, and on this occasion, it would do just fine for what he had in mind. The garden was overgrown and in places had become a forest of brambles and vines, after being left to its own devices for far too long.

Other than a cursory cut every couple of weeks by their paid gardener, who had yet to make an appearance this season, Tony could not recall the last time that he had personally spent any time on it. Even during the renovation, he had chosen to leave it for later, but he had never got around to it, other than the small courtyard that Charlie had lovingly manicured as a seating area for morning coffee or afternoon tea.

He went to work armed to the teeth with all manner of tools, whilst Bruce lay spread-eagled on the path, relaxing in the unseasonal sunshine as all dogs – and some humans - love to do. Though most of the garden equipment had been bought second hand, he'd had them sharpened and serviced recently and although the chainsaw needed an overhaul and the hedge trimmer was kaput, most were in good working order. All that was required was to pick out what was needed, leaving the rest where they were; a rake, a pick, an immaculate silver shovel that he couldn't remember buying, a couple of hand tools for digging out the beds, a garden fork, some twine, and a pair of shears that just needed a drop or two of oil, were all soon laid out on the patio ready for use.

Before too long a fire of green wood was belching out clouds of smoke and a further tangle of bushes and brambles was next in line, having already fallen foul of the executioner's axe. Tony was like a man possessed, tearing, and pulling, cutting, and ripping; occasionally a vicious piece of bramble or thorn would bite back, and he would curse aloud, beating it into submission with his shears or hatchet, before hurling it onto the monstrous mound of vegetation that was piled high in front of him.

His whole torso was now soaked in sweat, his shirt ringing wet as he hauled another trail of fanged creeper towards the flames, his thick padded gloves offering little protection against their shark-like teeth. Sometimes it was like they had a mind of their own, reaching out to ensnare his ankles, snagging the cloth of his trousers and forcing him to kick his way out of their clutches. A couple of rotten pallets emerged from the undergrowth but almost as soon as they saw the light they were again engulfed, as hundreds of termites hitched a ride to a fiery end and an old fence panel fell apart in protest.

The recent spell of relatively decent weather had lent a preparatory hand and the kindling was tinder dry, each parched load alight in a moment, as the pyre snapped and cracked, its flames reaching skyward in an all-consuming show of strength. Tony stood by entranced, staring into the burning heart of his own creation; from his lowly position a distant telegraph pole stood tall through the smoke, like a wooden stake rising from the inferno's heart. All that it lacked was a willing sacrifice, but for now there was no focus for the flames.

More wood. It needed more wood.

Tony looked around the garden in a senseless panic, his eyes seeking out more timber to fuel the furnace. The first of the fauna was coming into bloom, in speckled shades of green that flashed far and wide. As his sight took in a glorious splash of yellow, where a buttery bed of daffodils had already sprung forth in their annual blaze of colour, he was pleased to see that the smoke had seemingly scared off the fury of flies that had been the bane of his life of late. He winced as his eyes settled on the rickety old shed, and a ragged looking magpie that regarded him with interest from across the lawn, drawn in by the unfolding drama and the prospect of a feeding frenzy as the bugs fled the scene as fast as their many legs could carry them.

One for sorrow.

One magpie. He looked around in case another was hiding somewhere nearby. An inquisitive mate or a territorial challenger, but there was none willing to accompany the first.

One for sorrow.

He knew it was lunacy, but he was determined to build the bonfire even higher. A towering firestorm that would blot out the sky.

The worn-out old shed had long since seen better days.

Today would be its last.

He yanked open the door and hastily tore his way into its depths for the sledgehammer that he knew was inside. As he pulled at a familiar hickory handle, he remembered that it was double ended, a heavy axe on one side to complement the square headed hammer on the other. Like some ancient Viking weapon for pillaging and plunder. He welcomed its considerable weight as he held it by the head in his hands, imagining himself to be some fair-haired northern invader with a lust for wreaking havoc.

He took a practice swing as he heard a dog barking in the background.

Then another.

The shed was shattered in three or four hefty swings, its frail lengths snapping under the brute force of the three-pound metal head. It gave him a deeply satisfying feeling as the roof crashed down on top of its remaining contents, and a few monstrous spiders fled the crumbling darkness as the glass window shattered on impact with the paving stones below. Even as he swung again, Tony knew that his actions were inexplicable, but he couldn't stop himself. It was insane, but he was being driven on by an overwhelming need to feed the flames.

His fire. The frustrations and fears of the last week or more were being released with every load that landed in the centre of the pyre, his pent-up anger released in a maelstrom of gut-wrenching rage. He collected up the splintered wood, a mighty haul that would stoke the white-hot wonder whose heat was now immense. Sweat was pouring from Tony's reddened back and he tore off his shirt and lobbed it into the bonfire, his arms scratched and bleeding from the many thorns that had gone unnoticed as they slit his ripe and roasting skin. He glanced up through the acrid smoke towards the house and was not at all surprised to see that he was being watched.

He had known it all along.

He had sensed it, even as he barrowed on the first bundle of garden refuse, he knew that someone was watching him. Urging him on. Willing him to burn it all.

A dog was barking.

In that moment, he felt sure that the shadow was that of a woman. A spirit who had no time for men. A festering hatred for men, like him and those who had gone before. How he knew all this he didn't know, he really didn't know anything, but he could feel her scorn and as he stepped closer to the flames and loaded the last of the former outbuilding onto the sacrificial mound, he knew that he was now as close as he could safely get.

But safety was the last thing that was on his mind.

One push and he would be overcome. Barking.

One more step and he would be part of it. Whining.

The heat had almost overpowered him, as the fire ate its fill, thick grey smoke engulfed him and he began to choke, coughing like a dying man whose lifelong addiction to tobacco has finally caught up with him. And still it watched him, no longer a shadow. No longer just a dark featureless shape. It had form, it had substance.

He thought he saw her shape turn and her head lower as she walked away, unable to stand witness to this most terrible of all ends, but the distant sight was soon lost in the smoke and his eyes were drawn back to the burning.

Just a push away. Whimpering.

A step away. Whining.

Best foot forward.

It was then that he felt a sharp pain in the back of his leg, a searing incision low down on his ankle that was painful enough to make him yelp out loud. He turned on his heels, and fell to his knees, the spell broken, scrambling away from the blaze that he had so recently stoked into life. The heat was suddenly unbearable, and he furiously patted himself down to put out the imaginary fire that seemed to be consuming him. He fancied that he could see a trail of smoke emerging from his trousers as he beat down on his legs and chest, but in that moment the fire caught on the breeze and the smoke sent him crawling like the rodents before him, coughing, and retching on his hands and knees.

It was only then that he noticed Bruce, cowering before his master with a confused look in his eyes, unsure if he was about to be fussed or scolded. The dog had bitten him. His dog had bitten him. Tony scampered further away from the flames and threw his arms around the relieved creature, in sudden realisation of what his faithful friend had done. He had saved him from a terrible fate, his body about to be burned to a crisp upon a bonfire of his own making. And were it not for the dog's ingenuity that afternoon's work would have seen him dead at his own hand, overcome by the fumes that were still rising above him in an acrid updraft of choking grey cloud.

"Good boy Brucie." cried Tony, his face smeared with soot and tears. "Good boy." He looked up and scanned the devastation around him, the desecrated shed, the torn-up trees, the hacked bushes and shrubs and he was angry. Angry at the unfathomable actions of an arsonist, and though he knew that he had been the architect of his own downfall, he could not begin to understand what had driven him to it.

He lay there for several minutes, ten, twenty, half an hour or more, he had no idea how long it was in the end, but it was only as the ferocity of the fire began to fade, that he clambered and staggered towards the house in a desperate search for sanctuary.

But he would find none there.

Monday 30th March 2020

DAY 8 OF UK LOCKDOWN

631 deaths reported in the UK – the total number of deaths due to COVID19 now stands at 3,863 with 29,110 people testing positive for the disease.

CHAPTER 20

"The blessed thing has been barking for hours," complained Mrs Illsley as she fidgeted at the door to The Cottage. She had taken a peek through the crack in the hastily closed curtains, but other than the constantly shifting shadow of the dog as he raced from front to back and back again, she could make out little of any substance within the dark interior.

"Have you tried knocking?" asked the burly gentleman, knowing full well that she probably had, but hoping against hope that she hadn't.

"Of course, I have Bill." she snapped, "do you think I'm a simpleton? It just makes him bark even more. He comes right up behind the door sniffing and whimpering, he probably needs to relieve himself, if he's been locked in there on his own all night."

"Well, I don't have a spare key anymore," said Bill regretfully. "I didn't want one after, well you know, I've never much cared for the place."

Mrs Illsley nodded knowingly and decided against probing any further on this occasion. She had known William for years. He had been a close friend of her late husband and had promised him that he'd be there for her in times of trouble. Though this wasn't exactly her trouble, she did need his help, and she didn't want him getting spooked again. Fortunately for them both, she was made of sterner stuff.

"Well, I do have one, thankfully." she announced retrieving the front door key from her housecoat pocket and letting it dangle from a length of worn pink ribbon that might once have been red. "But I'll be jiggered if I'm going in there on my own. That's why I called you and on this occasion it's most definitely 'gentlemen first'." She swung the key some more like a hypnotist's watch and although he stood and looked stupidly at it for a few more seconds, he knew that in the end he would have to summon up the courage to enter the house of his nightmares for the first time in several years.

"Alright then." he muttered, "but don't close the door. Is there something to wedge it open with? There." he pointed, "that'll do." He dragged the metal boot cleaner in front of the oak panelled frame and as he turned the key in the lock and the door fell inwards, he pushed the metal block hard with his foot and crammed it into the angle.

Bruce came bounding out between them, his tail between his legs and his tongue lolling excitedly from his jaws, still barking loudly but clearly ecstatic to be free from his overnight gaol. He raced into the garden and relieved himself, under the watchful eye of the two bewildered humans, who were soon to be the object of his undivided attention.

"Okay boy" said Mrs Illsley soothingly, stroking his fur as he leapt up at them, his large paws leaving dusty prints on their clothes. "It's only me, you know me, now whatever is the matter with you, eh? Calm down now, c'mon what's up?"

He barked in reply, still frantic, as if desperate to tell them something, darting back towards the open door and pointing with his snout, but stopping short of leading them back inside. He whimpered forlornly, his head lowered as he barked again and again, snarling as if at something unseen that was even now lurking inside.

"Well go on then." ordered Mrs Illsley, "I'll be right behind you."

At first Bill hoped that she was talking to the dog, but he knew that she wasn't and one glance in her direction told him that she wasn't going to wait much longer. He cursed out loud, and then still grumbling, he steeled himself to face whatever demons were waiting for him beneath those low ceilings on the other side of the threshold.

Mrs Illsley was true to her word and followed immediately behind, but Bruce stayed exactly where he was, his ears erect and his unkempt claws tapping out a tuneless serenade as he paced the flagstone floor outside.

It was the smell that was first to assault their senses, an odour that put them both in mind of the Victorian parlours and blackened kitchen ranges of their forefathers. An earthy acrid scent of hand-hewn coal on dampened down embers, ashes waiting in the grate for the scullery maid to rake away before being remade. By association their sight was first drawn to the fireplace where the fire irons stood unmoved and ready for service, but the darkness to the left of the brick and timber centre piece soon drew their eyes and then on instinct the two of them each covered their mouths with their hands, when they'd have been better advised to cover their eyes. For the smell would eventually leave them, but the sight of the blackened form in the soot encrusted fireside chair never would.

It was Tony. Or what was left of him.

Of that there could be no doubt, but he was unrecognisable. His shoes were still more or less intact, and his lower legs were still visible within the remains of his charred trousers, but his hollowed-out torso was like a blackened pit from whose depths, all but a couple of ribs were still protruding. As for the rest, all was dust, or rather, cold, and crumbled ashes. And in its centre, the unmistakeable oval shape of a human skull that had been toppled from its customary perch at the top of a partially incinerated spine.

Grey powder, almost how they both imagined the surface of the moon to look, or raw cement before the sand is added, but the other-worldly comparison that came into Bill's mind as his sight settled on the outline of a man that he had only this week been in conversation with, did not offer up the prospect of the same soft landing. He grabbed onto the housekeeper's arm as she in turn turned her face away, and with her chest heaving in horror, she buried her head in his arms.

Once back outside they called an ambulance, though they knew him to be dead, and the police came along for good measure. It was, after all, a suspicious death. Both witnesses were questioned at length, and each gave separate statements that were almost identical in every way, whilst the police began their door-to-door enquiries of the local area just in case the neighbours had seen or heard anything untoward in the preceding twenty-four hours.

It didn't take long. There weren't many people to question, but word soon got around and within an hour or two a steady stream of people seemed intent on taking their daily exercise on a route that passed right by that house - their eyes on stalks - and a rare crowd of concerned onlookers quickly gathered just beyond the hastily marked out yellow line of police tape.

"Nosey parkers." said Mrs Illsley, loud enough for the nearest of them to hear. She was holding onto a mug of hot sweet tea as if it was cold enough outside to freeze, but she was tired and determined to leave as soon as the police had finished with their questioning. Bill had already been collared by a couple of reporters and as a television crew began to weave its way up the lane towards the house, Mrs Illsley decided that she had had enough. She had never been one for public outpourings of emotion and she was not about to start now.

"Are we all done?" she asked curtly, tapping the police officer on the shoulder. "I want to go home. I've had quite a shock with all this business, and I need to have a lay down."

"Totally understandable madam," the handsome young officer agreed, "but before you go, could you clarify one thing for me?" A nod was all he needed as permission to proceed. "It looks like there has been a rather large bonfire recently, in the back garden. It must have been quite a blaze as the embers are still glowing. Do you know anything about that?"

"Yes," said Mrs Illsley, as if the answer should have been obvious to anyone. "Mr Mountford, Tony that is, was working in the garden yesterday - he had quite a clear out by all accounts. I could see the smoke from my house, so I had to take my washing in at one point as I thought the wind was changing, though in the end it didn't."

"What was he burning?"

"Just garden rubbish, I think," she said, trying to remember if he'd said anything else but she was certain he hadn't. "It smelt like wood and judging by the thick smoke most of it was probably freshly cut I'd say. It was long overdue; as you know, I keep house for them and a few of the recent families have complained that their children were unable to play out there, it was so overgrown."

"Okay, well that's everything for now then, I suggest you get some rest," he smiled. "You've had quite the ordeal."

"Has his wife been informed yet?" she asked quietly, almost whispering the question so that she could not be overheard. "And his poor children?"

"We're onto it," said the PC. "We have specially trained staff for just this sort of thing, and they're on their way now. Might even be there already."

"And what about Bruce?" she asked, looking across at the sad looking dog who many might have mistaken for a police dog, though if he was, he'd have been having an off-duty moment, stretched out in a patch of sunlight like he hadn't slept in hours. "Bill could always take him. Bill." she shrilled, over the heads of the growing crowd.

Bill ambled over immediately, clearly pleased to have an excuse to get away from the public interrogation to which he was now being subjected, and he immediately agreed to take the dog until other arrangements could be made. He wasted no time in calling the war-weary German Shepherd to him and without further ado, he and Mrs Illsley made their excuses and left, pushing their way out through the human scrum of onlookers and back towards their forever altered lives, with Bruce in close pursuit.

The house watched them go.

Bill could feel it watching him, its windows like eyes bearing down from beneath the hairline of immaculate thatch that he had once helped to restore. As they walked slowly away, the whole building seemed to be gloating at their expense, and he could not resist one last defiant look in return, his eyes immediately drawn to the upstairs window and to the pale grey shadow that he imagined to be staring back at him.

And he was smiling.

CHAPTER 21

The knock at the door came like a harbinger of doom. From the well-versed triple rap of bare knuckles on solid wood, it sounded to Charlie like it would be bad news even before she answered it, and when she did, she was left in no doubt. No doubt at all.

There had not been a word from Tony all morning and she was worried.

"Good afternoon," said the female police officer on the back of a well-trained smile. "Mrs Mountford, is it?"

At first the uninformed widow thought that, just like her husband before her, she was about to be cautioned for breaking curfew rules, but just as she was about to launch into the same well-rehearsed excuse, the uniformed woman took off her helmet to stop her in her tracks.

"May we come in?"

She was accompanied inside by a younger officer who seemed to Charlie to be not much more than a girl, most likely from the latest graduate intake or a cadet of some kind, if they still had those sorts of jobs after all the recent funding cuts. She also looked nervous and a little bit teary too, and as Mrs Mountford's mind began to process the situation that was unfolding before her, she quickly reached the only logical reason for their visit.

"It's Tony, isn't it?" she gasped. "Has he been in an accident? Is he okay?"

"Please, take a seat Mrs Mountford." said the older of the two women, as if it were her own home. Charlie didn't hesitate to comply, almost falling into the chair and motioning awkwardly that they should do the same and the news that she was dreading was not far behind. "I'm afraid there has been an accident, and I'm sorry to have to tell you, that we believe that it's your husband."

For a moment, there was silence, except for the faint sound of children playing in an upstairs bedroom and the pitter patter of impatient fingers, but it didn't last. "What kind of 'accident'? Is he, dead?"

"I'm afraid so madam," said the policewoman, "at the house, it seems that there was a fire and we have found a body, that we believe to be your husband."

"You believe it to be?" stuttered Charlie, hoping for a miracle. "What, you mean that you're not certain? It could turn out to be someone else?"

"It's unlikely that it's someone else, I'm afraid. We have been informed by your housekeeper, Mrs" and she paused to look closely at her notebook. "Mrs Illsley, she told us that he was the only one staying there, that you had come back here with the children only recently and had left him and your dog to," but she didn't get to finish her sentence.

"Bruce." sobbed Mrs Mountford, "is Bruce, okay?" It seemed strange to be so concerned for the family pet considering the headline news, but the policewoman hoped that one little piece of good news would be some small comfort in the distraught woman's hour of need.

"He's okay." the younger officer told her. "He's staying the night with a neighbour. I think his name is Bill."

"I have to tell the children," said Charlie, nodding in understanding, knowing full well that Bruce's wellbeing should not have been her prime concern. "How am I going to tell them?" she sobbed, "that their father is dead."

"We can help you with that," the younger officer advised, a little awkwardly. "If you want us to. I'm a trained grief counsellor and we have other resources available too if you need them. For now, just take your time, there's no rush, it sounds like they're happy enough upstairs. Shall I make us all a cup of tea?"

It was good advice, and that was exactly what she did do, following the homeowner's directions on where to find everything and as the older officer held onto Mrs Mountford's hand, helping her to take her first steps along grief's long and painful road, the younger officer took her time.

The kitchen was neat and tidy, though littered with children's hand paintings, family holiday snaps and magnetic alphabet letters that were spread across the surface of the family fridge like graffiti. A chain-link dog lead hung from a hook above a half-filled bowl of water and an empty metal dish, which she almost upended as she turned to reach for the milk.

As she closed the door to the fridge and her eyes settled on the silently sorted letters, she almost dropped the milk in shock.

DEAD

The first word that she saw.

FIRE

The second word.

HCTIW

The third.

There were others, but as she staggered backwards until her backside was nestled up against the cupboard on the opposite side of the room, she was unable to process the rest. She carefully placed the milk down onto the granite worktop, and reluctantly allowed herself to look at the last – a simple sentence that scared the life out of her.

I SEE THEE.

Somehow, she managed to complete her self-assigned task making three mugs of strong tea, though her hands continued to shake as she poured on the hot water and the tea began to infuse into the milk. But her mind was fully occupied, and she was unable to forget the hastily rearranged words that she knew had not been there when she had first gone into the kitchen. She didn't dare look back at it, just in case the letters had changed again, and instead she balanced all three cups in her hands, in time-honoured English pub fashion, and headed back to the lounge to deliver them to her unsuspecting audience.

"Are you okay?" her colleague mouthed at her, her voice barely audible in the room and though it was obvious that she was not, the officer nodded as she handed over two of the hot drinks, taking an immediate sip of her own to banish her keenly felt fear.

Mrs Mountford was oblivious to the unfolding drama, lost in her own thoughts and her own personal tragedy.

As they stood to take their leave a full hour later, the older police officer offered to stay longer to help with whatever might need doing, but Charlie was having none of it. She had already called her parents who were on their way and once they had arrived then she would impart the news that she so dreaded sharing. She had provided details of Tony's doctor and dentist, the very thought of which had brought home to her just how badly burned his body must have been and she had also given them 'chapter and verse' on their comings and goings over the last week.

She did not hold back and figured that a paltry fine for breaking curfew rules was now the least of her worries. In any case, she was sure that, in the circumstances, the police would not be in any mood to follow-up on such a minor misdemeanour. After all, her husband, and the father of her two children had paid the ultimate price for his transgression and that was more than enough of a punishment to be going on with.

As the police officers stood to go, the younger of the two gathered up the cups, intent on returning them to the kitchen. So intent, that she insisted on it, motioning to their host not to get up and already on her way even before her sentence was complete.

"What's going on?" her colleague mouthed, but she was already at the door.

The letters on the fridge were once again scattered in a flurry of meaningless combinations, as if stirred by an unseen hand after some kind of word game. She couldn't tell in that moment whether they were exactly as they had been on first entering the kitchen an hour earlier, but this time she refused to take her eyes off them and placing the empty cups on the drainer, she backed out of the room as if she'd come face-to-face with a rabid animal.

"What was that all about?" the superior officer demanded to know as the two of them settled back into the car for the return journey to their local station.

"I'd rather not say Sarge."

It wasn't a satisfactory answer, but they both knew that it would have to do.

"Do you think she'll be okay?" the new recruit asked her more experienced colleague after a mile or two of silent contemplation.

"One day," answered her sergeant, knowing that it might take years. "The initial shock of it all might go away in a few weeks and that's when it'll really sink in, and then she'll need all the help she can get."

"I'm worried for her," the younger one admitted, but she could not explain why. It was just a feeling that whatever it was that had brought this fate on that family, it was not done with them yet. Despite her recent and vigorous police training that had taught her the importance of focusing on the facts and only the facts, on keeping personal opinions and above all else, personal feelings, at bay at all times when dealing with members of the public and matters of the law, she was sure of what she'd seen and was not about to put it down to first day nerves or a momentary hallucination.

"Why?"

"I don't know, it's just a feeling, that's all."

"What happened to you in there?" the driver asked her fellow officer once more, as she turned the car onto the main road.

"There was a message, on the fridge," she confessed, her better judgement loosening her tongue. Best not to keep things to herself, not on her first proper day on the job.

"What kind of message? Like a written note?" the senior officer asked, suddenly in a panic that they had failed in their duty and not been as thorough as they should have been. "Do we need to go back; might it be considered as evidence?"

"No, it's gone now, it was only there for a few seconds as I made the tea." the young woman explained cryptically. "The kids' alphabet letters, they were rearranged into words, just for a minute, but when I went back in to put the cups back, they were all muddled up again. Like they were the first time, before I opened the fridge to get to the milk."

"Just put it in your notebook, officer." The order was clear and immediate, and it was the last word that passed between them on the subject.

There was nothing else to say.

Monday 15th June 2020

84 DAYS SINCE START OF UK LOCKDOWN

92 deaths reported in the UK – the total number of deaths due to COVID19 now stands at 47,456 with 234,578 people testing positive for the disease.

CHAPTER 22

The inquest had been a long time in coming, but when the day finally arrived it was subject to the same restrictions that all aspects of British society had become well used to in the intervening months. All interested parties had received their login details for the online meeting a week in advance and so were settled in their own homes to watch, and in some cases, to contribute to proceedings. Minimal human contact was assured.

This included muted members of the press who it seemed held a somewhat macabre interest in the case, despite the lack of public scrutiny in the weeks following lockdown. It had however, piqued the public interest on social media after failing to get any airtime at all on the more traditional channels of television and radio and so the journalists were there in force, in search of a much-needed scoop that was only loosely related to coronavirus.

S.H.C. was a rather uninspiring acronym, and for an unsuspecting public could have just as easily stood for a prominent US college or for an obscure condition of the heart, of little interest to any but the most dedicated academic or physician. Yet whenever the phrase *'spontaneous human combustion'* was mentioned, people tended to sit up and take notice.

"The first documented instance of this, the most curious of deaths are thought to have come to light in the first half of the twentieth century," explained the presiding judge, "though it has been suggested that it might go much further back than that, and whilst no known cause has ever been clinically proven, the existence of the phenomena would seem hard to refute."

If the inquest had been held in a public venue, it is almost certain that a murmuring wave of astonishment would have passed over the audience at that point, but in the virtual world of 2020, there was nothing but silence to greet this rather unusual introduction to court proceedings.

Sir Anthony Goldsmith-Brown O.B.E. was clearly in no mood for dilly dallying. He was well aware that this was a high-profile case and he clearly believed in getting the 'moose on the table' at the outset.

"But we are not here to speculate." he announced. "I will - as always - deal only in hard facts, to steer us right to the heart of the matter to aid our understanding of how and when the unfortunate Mister Mountford came to meet his end. For us to get to the bottom of this very unusual case, we will be calling upon a wide range of learned individuals from the fields of medicine and science, as well as the usual eye-witnesses - of which there are not too many - to give us a clear understanding of events as they unfolded."

"I would ask you all to stay on mute at all times unless you are called upon to give evidence." he ordered, enjoying the increased sense of control that this most modern of technologies had afforded him. "I have done a few of these ghastly things now, and I don't mind telling you that I won't stand for any background noise, so keep yourselves quiet at all times or else I will have the administrator remove you from the room without warning – and I'm assured that I can now do that at the touch of a button, which is just marvellous if you ask me." It was not intended as a joke, but it did cause a ripple of laughter all around the country to which he was, of course, completely oblivious.

"Proceedings are being recorded and so – especially for those of you who are here today representing the interests of the press – you will be able to watch it back later if there's anything you've missed. There's no excuse for getting your facts mixed up anymore is there, so I'd appreciate it if those amongst you who are of a more *sensationalist* persuasion could keep those tendencies in check. We don't want any scaremongering. Folk have enough to be scared about these days, what with this pandemic raging, so let's not give them anything else to worry about."

It was clearly a warning shot, and he wasn't about to wait for their agreement.

The first witness to be called was Mrs Dorothy Illsley, housekeeper to the Mountford family, and one of the first people on the scene that day. She relayed the events of that morning as accurately as she could remember, which she thought was pretty much perfectly. She described the scene that had confronted her and after choking back a slight sniffle with the aid of a generous sip of water, she explained how she was "quite unable to forget it."

"I'm sure it was a quite terrible ordeal Mrs Illsley," said the examining officer to put her at her ease. "Had you heard any noises the night before?"

"None at all, except for the barking of course?"

"And when did that start, exactly?"

"Well, I can't say for sure." she frowned. "It was late, I'd been asleep. It woke me up in the end but I've a feeling that he'd been going on for quite some time before I finally looked at the clock and saw that it was 3am."

"So could you put an estimate on how long it was before you looked at the clock, that the dog had started to bark?"

"An hour," she answered, uncertainly. "Two at most."

"So, you think it all started then in the early hours, during the first hour after midnight, between twelve and two o'clock in the morning?"

"Yes, I'd say so," she nodded.

"And did it go on all night?"

"No, he did quieten down, a bit," she admitted. "But he was on and off all night after that and then again in the morning, when I finally called Bill to come round."

Mister William Postlethwaite, or Bill to his friends, was next to take to the virtual stand and after confirming his name and address and being sworn in, he recounted his own version of events which - for the record - were almost identical in every detail to those of Mrs Illsley. In fact, he didn't deviate one iota from his own written statement that had already been submitted in evidence and so he had very little else to say that was of interest to the court.

"How did the dog seem to you, when you first opened the door?" asked the examiner. In hindsight, it seemed like an unusual question for a public enquiry, but in the absence of any other witnesses, of the human variety, Bill thought he could understand why they might have asked it.

"He was frantic." Bill recalled with a heavy heart.

"Scared?"

"Yes, I'd say so." said Bill, remembering how the dog had whimpered and refused to go back inside. "He was for a few days afterwards to be honest with you," said Bill. "Mrs Mountford couldn't collect him for a week or so, for obvious reasons, and he just wasn't 100% right for the whole time he was with us. Maybe he was missing the family, but he didn't want to be there, he was always at the door at all hours, as if just being inside freaked him out."

"If only animals could talk, eh?" interjected the coroner, at which Bill just nodded solemnly adding his own "if only" for good measure.

"He'd have a tale to tell, that's for sure."

Next up was the late Mr Anthony Mountford's wife, Charlotte and by her very demeanour, everyone watching on their monitors could see that she was dreading it. She was wearing dark glasses to cover her eyes and was heavily made up, which for those who knew her well, was not her usual look.

"Mrs Mountford," the coroner started in his most sympathetic tone. "Firstly, can I say how very sorry I am for your loss. I do appreciate your attendance here today at what must still be a very difficult time for you and your family."

Charlie nodded and offered a timid smile, but she said nothing, she wasn't of a mind to say very much at all if truth be told. In the end, she did open up a little, telling them some of the reasons for their midnight jaunt on the day that lockdown had first been announced and, feeling a little guilty, admitted that it had probably been a mistake but one that she would have to live with for the rest of her days.

"Can you explain to us, if you can, why your husband remained behind, when you decided to return to London?" her inquisitor asked. "All alone, in an empty cottage, without his family beside him?"

It seemed to be an overly dramatic statement, but she was in no mood to be put on the backfoot. "He wasn't alone." she snapped back. "He had Bruce for company. And for, protection." Looking back later, she wasn't sure why she'd added the last bit, but it resonated with the jury who were watching attentively from an undisclosed location.

"Yet you and the children departed for London almost as soon as you had arrived, did you not? What was the cause of this sudden change of heart?"

"The children didn't settle." she explained, telling only half of the story, and hoping that it would be enough. "They missed their things. They could never sleep in the cottage – they don't like the beds – and they wanted to go home.

Tony decided to stay behind for a few days to get a few jobs done that had needed doing for a while, and then he was going to come back on the train once they were up and running again."

"Which wasn't for a few weeks was it?"

"Well, no, but we didn't know that then, did we?" she explained irritably. "And if he had to travel back, then who's to say that it wasn't 'essential travel' for work or family reasons?"

"You ran your own events business didn't you Mrs Mountford" the coroner probed again as was his duty, "together with your late husband?" She nodded and so he continued. "It must have been a scary time for you?"

"Why do you say that?" she said, a little more brusquely than she'd intended, side-tracked into thinking that he knew more than he was letting on.

"Because work must have dried up overnight? All your bookings for the summer must have been cancelled, your livelihood must have been at stake?"

"Oh, yes." she admitted, visibly relieved. "It was, very 'scary'. We'd had a full itinerary for rest of the year and the cottage was always booked out for many months in advance. Years in fact."

"And all that was gone, as soon as the pandemic struck?"

"Of course, just like everyone else, we were facing an uphill struggle." she said, unsure where this line of questioning was leading but willing to go along with it for a while. "We were concerned, to say the least. We'd laid off our people and were hoping that the government would soon offer some help, which they did, eventually. But in those first few days we thought we would be better off in our 'bolt hole' and away from London where the pandemic was already out of control."

"Yes, well let's put that aside for now," said the coroner, "it's hardly relevant given the circumstances. What I'm trying to understand is whether your husband might have had any worries, any financial concerns, or personal issues, that might have driven him to do something, rash."

"What do you mean by that?" barked Charlie, in growing understanding of where his line of questioning was headed. "Are you saying that he might have killed himself? No way, not Tony. Never. He loved us too much for that, he wouldn't have, no. No way."

"People can be pushed into doing the most unlikely things when the balance of the mind is disturbed Mrs Mountford. Was there anything? Anything that he said, or did, or that he was going to do that might have hinted at a deterioration in his state of mind during your time at the cottage? Or once you had returned home?"

She thought for a moment, before shaking her head vigorously from side to side in clear denial of the very thought of it. "No. definitely not. He was quite sane. Quite calm and collected. Worried, yes, but not suicidal."

"And yet, there was some suggestion of strange goings on at The Cottage were there not Mrs Mountford?" It was the question that she was dreading but that the waiting public were anticipating most of all due to some sensationalist press coverage, one that she had hoped might have been kept out of it altogether. "There was a 'live broadcast' made by your husband on social media I believe, just a couple of nights before the tragic events of 14th June 2020, I believe?" and he directed the audience to the only notable piece of evidence that they had; a link to the brief five-minute video that he played in full, pausing it occasionally to emphasise a point or to ask his widow for her recollection of events.

When it was done there was a virtual silence as he let the visual evidence that her husband had not been alone in the house after all, sink in and so implying that he may not have been alone on the night of his death. He wasn't prepared to consider the supernatural possibilities of what they had seen. To him it was a flesh and blood intruder that was sat on the bed in that brief but most revealing short film, but he recognised only too well that identifying who it had been, was going to be a challenge.

"Do you have any idea as to who that figure might have been Mrs Mountford?" he asked, fully expecting her to deny all knowledge, but keen to ask the question just in case. "A friend, a neighbour maybe, or a girlfriend? A boyfriend even?"

It was not a particularly subtle suggestion and Charlie didn't hold back in her fury. "My husband was not having an affair and if you're suggesting that he was living a double life, then don't be so bloody ridiculous. I know my husband and he was not driven by his cock like some men are. He was loyal and loving and …" The tears had begun to flow now and even the magistrate had no doubt as to her credibility as a witness. "I loved him." she said, once she had got her emotions back under control. "Very much."

"Okay thank you Mrs Mountford, and may I apologise for having to put you through this," the coroner said serenely. "I have just a couple more questions if I may?" She said nothing and so he continued. "Was he a smoker or much of a drinker?"

"He liked a drink every now and again, who doesn't, but other than a slug of whisky before bed or a pint or two down the local, he wasn't a big drinker. And as for smoking, no not really, though he would have an occasional cigar at

Christmas or New Year," she recalled. "But I don't think there were any in the house, not that I was aware of anyway."

"And no, none were found, not that were contained in the official report anyway," he confirmed, and with his curiosity satisfied, he quickly moved onto what would be his penultimate question. "Did you and your husband have any life insurance?"

"Well, yes of course," she stammered. "We have a young family and a large mortgage and so of course we have life insurance, though it is yet to pay out. They are waiting on the result of this darn thing." She knew that she sounded desperate, but what was said was said and her choice of expletive was far more polite that she would have liked. "Any suggestion of suicide and I don't know what we will do."

"And how much is that for, please?"

She hesitated before answering, knowing the conclusions that those listening would be jumping to once they knew just how much she was set to gain from her husband's untimely death.

"One point five million pounds."

The cyber hush was palpable as even the coroner delayed his response, but he soon followed it up with another that was primarily intended to provoke a response. "I presume that will be sufficient to pay off your debts and to leave you and your family well provided for?"

"It should do, yes," Mrs Mountford answered defiantly, understanding that for many of those listening, it might seem motive enough for a murder. "For a while anyway. I haven't really given it any thought, none at all. I would give it all away to have my husband back" and at that, the tears began to flow, but the coroner was determined to have his say.

"And what about investments? Did your husband have much *'put away'* in that regard?"

"Yes, of course" she answered, choking back the tears again. "His pension was almost *'maxed out'*, he often said so anyway, though I never really understood it. I've never paid much attention to that side of things, but he always tried to ensure that he saved the maximum permitted each year. I haven't checked lately, our financial adviser does that for us, for me I mean, and he did say last time we spoke that we have *'nothing to worry about'*."

"Well, that's good to hear Mrs Mountford, with two young children it's very important that you will have nothing to concern you in the future, from a financial standpoint that is."

She wasn't sure if he was being sarcastic or not, but just as her lips began to form a reply, he stopped her dead in her tracks with the question that was on everyone's lips and which he had to ask, whether he wanted to or not.

"Did you consider your cottage in the country to be haunted, Mrs Mountford and if so, when did you first become aware that it had a 'ghost'?"

"If you've read the particulars from the letting agent – which I'm sure you have – you will know the answer to that question, but if you're asking me if I really believed it to be haunted, then yes there were some peculiar goings on there over the years. Until recently though, I never felt threatened by it. It always seemed like a friendly presence to me, like it belonged there and was simply watching over the place, and maybe us too."

"And when did that change Mrs Mountford? Can you say exactly?"

"The last time we were there was the first time we noticed any change in the atmosphere," she explained, praying that the deaths of the Watsons were not going to be dragged up for public consumption. If she ever wanted to sell the place and to move on from this terrible time in her life, then the last thing she needed was to have the idea that the house was somehow cursed doing the rounds. "It was like a different ghost had moved in, an evil spirit of some kind. Something that was intent on scaring us out of our wits and in the end that's why me and the kids finally went back to London. It was the last straw I suppose. Tony wanted to stay to sort it out though neither of us knew how, he was just going to give it a try, for all our sakes."

"Well, I am by no means an expert in the paranormal Mrs Mountford, but I do know that stress and pressure can play tricks on a person, but we will explore that theme a little later. For now, I have no further questions, and I think it's high time that we all took a lunch break" and so he thanked Charlotte for her staunch resolve and formally closed the session.

After lunch, it would be the turn of the scientific community to provide their much-anticipated input, a duty that was expected to take up the rest of that day and most of the next and the evidence on which the final verdict was most likely to turn.

She had been advised that there were a few possible outcomes including *Death by Misadventure* – if Tony had somehow been implicated in his own end – or *Accidental Death* if the cause was simply down to an electrical fault or some other such physical problem with the house or its contents. A full electrical survey of the house had been undertaken in the preceding weeks and that evidence had also been submitted, but she had heard from her representatives – expensive solicitors whom they had frequently used for business purposes over the years - that nothing of any note had come to light. Nothing that could have caused the kind of death that had befallen her unfortunate spouse at any rate.

On returning from a long-distance lunch break, it was the turn of the presiding medical examiner to deliver the results of her post-mortem, which she did in the minutest of detail. Dr. Riddhi Chowdhury provided chapter and verse over the course of several hours but was unable to determine with any degree of certainty whether the deceased was alive or dead when the fire had broken out.

"So, there was nothing in the toxicology report to prove it one way or another?" asked the coroner, more than a little disappointed to hear that the science in this case was proving to be so inconclusive. "Were you able to isolate any bodily fluids in order to complete the usual tests in these circumstances?"

"I'm afraid not," the doctor confessed, the intensity of the fire had completely destroyed the internal organs and so all traces of blood and urine were lost, though some trace levels of carbon monoxide and cyanide were present in the brain tissue, it was not enough to be certain that he had still been alive when the fire took hold."

"And from the x-rays of the body itself, was there anything there to indicate foul play?"

"Nothing at all, though relatively little skeletal evidence survived, there was enough of the upper vertebrae and all of the skull remaining to check for any foreign bodies, but there was no sign of any entry or exit wounds to the head and no surviving projectiles anywhere in the remains to suggest that the death had been anything other than a tragic accident."

"If it had been an execution-style killing, would you expect to be able to find the evidence in these circumstances?" the coroner asked, determined to exhaust this particular line of enquiry.

"Almost certainly," the doctor confirmed. "If he'd been shot at close range then we would have either found the bullet embedded within the crime scene somewhere, either still in the immediate vicinity of the body along with the bullet casing, or in the surrounding walls, floors or fittings."

"And there were no such findings?"

"None at all Sir."

"Well, that's something at least," the coroner concluded, making a few scribbled notes of his own on the desk pad in front of him before drawing the session to a close for the day.

Tuesday 16th June 2020

85 DAYS SINCE START OF UK LOCKDOWN

103 deaths reported in the UK – the total number of deaths due to COVID19 now stands at 47,559 with 235,574 people testing positive for the disease.

CHAPTER 23

The next day, it seemed that the evidence in favour of *spontaneous human combustion,* or SHC as it was referred to throughout the morning's session and a half, was rather more convincing than anyone had expected it to be. A veritable conveyor belt of scientists from all over the world were called upon to provide their remote evidence for the court's consideration and it soon became clear that there were recent cases from right across the globe. Latin America and Africa, Asia, and the United States; all had their own baffling examples of people who had simply gone up in flames, leaving just an ashy residue and causing little to no damage whatsoever to their surrounding environment.

Photographs were flashed into the homes of those watching, some from the latter years of the nineteenth century, others from the nineteen fifties - when an excessive build-up of sulphur in the atmosphere had often been blamed - and even one or two from the current century. Many of them bore an uncanny resemblance to the case before them, showing signs of scorch marks on the ceiling and floor, a gathering of soot around the body or on the chair and often with only the extremities remaining to suggest that a human body had once occupied that spot.

The hands. The feet. The head sometimes, as in this case, but nothing else.

"In these cases, there is rarely a clear source of ignition," explained an Italian professor in some highly specialist field, who had written a recent paper on the topic and so not surprisingly, was taking a very close interest in the case. "Though often they are found in close proximity to a source of heat, like an open fireplace or a radiator, it is as if the body has ignited from the inside and has burnt outwards, feeding off the fatty tissue like a chip-pan fire. The rate of consumption is rapid, the fire often burning out in mere minutes and the scorching heat at the heart of it is so intense that all bone is reduced to ash."

"There are examples from literature going back many centuries," explained another expert from one of the British colleges who had helped on several cases in the sixties and was now long since retired, but seemingly still in full command of his faculties.

"The cases that I presided over were often linked to a lit cigarette although the evidence for that was always circumstantial, though the victims were often heavy smokers and more often than not, heavy drinkers too. Cases in Russia are often cited as having a root cause in high-proof vodka which were thought to have internally ignited and caused a furnace in the stomach or bladder, but it doesn't help to explain why the fires always seem to burn themselves out before they can spread to the surrounding area. It's a mystery, though as a global phenomenon, it's one that cannot easily be refuted."

Attention returned once more to the bonfire in the garden and questions were asked of the fire investigation team who confirmed that they could find no evidence of any kind of accelerant being used, either in the garden or on the remains. "Fires tend to burn up, and not across," explained the Chief Investigator, who said that he had also seen several such cases in his years on the job and was not surprised to observe that the fire had not spread beyond the chair in which Mr Mountford was apparently sitting. "The speed at which the body was consumed would have been rapid and so the fire wouldn't have been able to spread to the rest of the furniture and would not have been sustained for long enough to set the ceiling alight. Though the ceiling was black with soot, that is only to be expected, but the chair itself survived, with some damage to the seat and back. Have you ever seen magnesium burn? It implodes, and that's what seems to happen in these cases. The fire burns inwards you see, it's all consuming and just as it begins to take hold, its superheated source burns itself out. And so, it stops."

They were even joined by an historian from a Liverpool university who looked like a sixties' comedian with unkempt hair and large, black-rimmed glasses, so much so that few people were unable to take him seriously, despite his subject of expertise. He explained how The Royal Society had first put forward the SHC theory as far back as 1746, citing examples from the slums surrounding the gin palaces of Holborn's London and espousing the part played by hard liquor, polluted air, and naked flames, none of which were pertinent to this case. Even the *British Medical Journal* had taken up the case just before the onset of the second world war when an LA Parry delved into the history books himself going back to the 1820's to find evidence to support his theory.

Finally, the police officers who had attended the cottage on Sunday 29th March were asked to give their version of events on that fateful day and although both accounts were almost identical, almost clinical in their retelling, both officers appeared nervous, as if it were their first time in court or as if the trauma of the day was too painful to recall. They were each quizzed for fifteen minutes or more, but neither of them mentioned the ghostly footsteps that they'd heard pacing the boards above their heads, nor the ominous sound of disembodied feet that had hammered down the stairs and out into the lane. Their official notes were provided as evidence, and both contained no written record of anything untoward having taken place, with each of them describing the deceased as being 'calm and unruffled'. It was a strange turn of phrase to have been used by them both, but neither of them offered anything more and so were stood down, each visibly relieved to be able to finally put the whole experience behind them.

But in the end, the coroner could not bring himself to embrace the pseudoscientific mumbo-jumbo on which the case relied, which he saw as more in keeping with the realms of science fiction than science fact and as a result, he settled on an Open verdict. It was not a verdict that anyone wanted, for it left his widow in limbo and left open the suggestion that Mr Mountford could well have taken his own life. It also left everyone in no doubt at all that the death was thought to be suspicious, even if it couldn't be proven one way or the other. He felt unable to rule it an accident or the result of misadventure as the medical experts had not been able to provide any evidence to show that there were drugs involved, and nothing had been turned up in the house to support a theory of foul play by person or persons unknown, other than the mysterious visitation that simply defied logic.

It was hard to prove suicide when the method was so ambiguous, as setting oneself alight without the presence of any kind of flammable substance was impossible, whilst to call it 'natural causes' would have been to invite ridicule. Unlawful killing also did not fit the bill as there was no evidence of assault or of a break-in, never mind murder, for which there was a complete lack of motive and no prime suspect.

It was indeed a mystery and although a precedent had been set in a similar case in Ireland, just a few years earlier, where the cause of death had been cited to be SHC itself, Sir Anthony Goldsmith-Brown could not bring himself to reach that conclusion. Not without specific incriminating and undeniable evidence, of which there was little of any note.

He was certain however that the deceased's state of mind was unbalanced at the time of his death and that the loss of his business and the fact that his finances were spiralling out of control - as illustrated by his business accounts and personal finances which were both submitted as evidence - must have had a negative and destabilising effect. The charred remnants of his notepad had been found amongst his remains, the assumption being that he must have been reading them or adding to them at the moment of ignition, but not enough of them had survived to provide any clear substance to his state of mind at the time. Of more value was the search history from his laptop, which had given clear credence to the supernatural angle, but whilst it was clear that he was pursuing that line of enquiry himself it did not make it real or provide any added weight to the argument that an evil spirit from beyond the grave was somehow at the heart of what was clearly a harrowing tragedy for everyone involved.

"I'm very sorry Mrs Mountford," the coroner explained afterwards in a private call to the widow and her advisers. "But I could see no other route open to me, and though I realise that this won't help you to bring probate to a timely conclusion, it would not have been helpful to anyone for me to have come down on the side of fantasy."

"Well at least now that the cottage is no longer a crime-scene, I can pay someone to get it tidied up and put it on the market – perhaps I can take full advantage of the London exodus.," she admitted sadly. "I've no intention of ever going back there again, so once the publicity dies down a bit, I'd still be hopeful that I'll be able to get a good price for it."

"It's in a great location," her solicitor agreed, "I'm sure it'll be snapped up in no time."

And it was.

Less than six months later, after a hasty redecoration by a local firm of painters and decorators and a complete overhaul of the gardens front and back, it was sold within thirty-six hours of going on the market to a professional couple from the City of London, who wanted nothing more than to retire to the country.

Tired of the rat-race, ready to settle down to a life of garden parties and country walks, the idyllic country cottage on the inter-section of three English counties seemed like the perfect escape from the daily grind that they had longed to be able to leave behind.

COVID had been the catalyst for these two fifty-something friends, and though they knew nothing of the history of the house - having failed, like so many others at the time, to do any research when making their snap decision to buy - it had not felt like a gamble.

It felt like destiny.

WEDNESDAY 2ND SEPTEMBER 2020

163 DAYS SINCE START OF UK LOCKDOWN

13 deaths reported in the UK – the total number of deaths due to COVID19 now stands at 50,149 with 299,864 people testing positive for the disease.

CHAPTER 24

"Well, you know what they say?" said Gavin, slamming the garden fork into the stubborn earth as he stopped to admire the blaze of crimson that was seeping across the sky like dye.

It was a rhetorical question, but Simon answered it anyway. "Red sky at night - shepherds' delight. It's a shame we're not bloody shepherds then, isn't it?"

The two of them had been hard at work ever since moving into the cottage, Simon focusing his attentions on the interior, planning, and readying the rooms for the changes that they wanted to make, both structurally and aesthetically. Gavin on the other hand was entrenched in the rear garden, busy readying it for the winter and its rebirth as an outside entertainment space – something that had been denied them in their old Tower Hamlets flat. And so far, the weather had been on their side; cloudy overall, but the temperature had been perfect, with just a light breeze for company.

COVID had been the final straw. Almost three months spent cooped up in a cramped two-bedroom apartment, with nothing to look at but the docklands skyline around Canary Wharf, had almost sent them their separate ways, but instead they had resolved their differences and agreed to get the hell out of there at the next available opportunity. They had dreamed of quitting the City for a while, but somehow the time had never been right. Then, after hearing about friends and family who were 'dropping like flies' and of several others who had failed to recover from Trump's dubiously dubbed *'China-virus'*, the whole experience had proved to be a catalyst for change.

Chief amongst those victims had been Gavin's own mother. She had been in poor health for a while, but when a COVID outbreak was confirmed in her Swansea care home, he had feared the worse. The fact that he'd been unable to be with her at the end was something that he had not yet come to terms with; he doubted that he ever would. His mother had been his world growing up, his father having taken his own life when Gavin was just fifteen and that had kept them close, even though he rarely got to see her more than a twice a year these days. It seemed certain to him now that she had known that he was gay, long before he had.

She had always been his staunchest ally in the face of the small-town prejudice that he had endured growing up, and countless times since. Her passing had left a void that he knew would never be filled; she was irreplaceable, the gap unbreachable, but she had never stood for any moping, and he could hear her now, berating him whenever he was sat about feeling sorry for himself because of one cross word or another.

"It's no good wallowing about it love," she'd scold. "C'mon now, get over yourself now, *repay evil with good and hell will not claim you.*" That was always one of her favourites. And when she wanted his help with the housework or the shopping – "*the seed of all evil is laziness.*" He was never, ever, allowed to be lazy.

His biggest regret was not moving closer when he'd had the chance and her sudden death had spurred him on to finally make the change, even though it was too late for the two of them. Stuck indoors for weeks on end, feelings of regret had slowly eaten away at him like a parasite feasting on his soul, but even more than that he was angry. Angry at the government for letting this happen, for stopping him from being with her when she most needed him, for seeing to it that she died alone and, he was sad to say, angry at his partner too; for putting the brakes on a potential move to Bristol when his every instinct had told him to take the job that he'd been offered. In the end, money had been the deciding factor then – the hefty anchor that had kept them moored exactly where they were for far too long.

They weren't alone though and thousands upon thousands were thought to have fled the capital already, finally deciding to make the change they'd been contemplating for years, as the new plague forced them to re-evaluate their lives. Even before they'd started looking, they heard that properties in the South-West were changing hands at an unprecedented rate, and by the time they finally decided to jump on that bandwagon, new instructions were being snapped up in a matter of hours.

The thought of buying 'off-spec' was not something that either of them had ever imagined themselves doing, as they were both very risk-averse by nature, but they soon realised that it was the only way they were ever going to make their dream become reality, and having missed out on two properties already, they were determined not to be pipped at the post for a third time. Even when their above-asking-price offer for the cottage had been accepted, they were so concerned that they were going to be gazumped that they took the perilous decision to skip the full structural survey and so proceeded to completion based on valuation only.

They did do some due diligence of their own before jumping off the deep end though; checking the sale history of the property over the last twenty years and looking into the local planning office records to see what work had been done by current and previous owners and when all of that seemed fine, they had finally taken the plunge. They'd also discovered, through some online sleuthing, that the property had been made available to rent for many years and that had given some reassurance that it must be of a sufficiently high standard to command the 'gold-star' status that several of the letting agencies had given it.

They were even able to read some of the reviews and were not put off by its apparent 'resident ghost', which had seemingly not been a deterrent for others either, with several guests loving it so much that they claimed to have returned 'year after year'. In fact, one such website had given it a 97% 'occupancy rate' suggesting that it had enjoyed an almost perfect booking history in its time as a holiday let.

"It doesn't *feel* haunted, does it Gav?" Simon asked on his way back indoors, taking a gulp of the refreshingly cold Sauvignon Blanc, that his partner had just handed to him.

"No, not a bit," his husband of ten years standing agreed, "I think it's got a nice vibe to it. Once we've knocked it into shape it's going to be perfect. You happy with it?"

"Ecstatic." proclaimed Gavin, taking the opportunity to sneak a quick kiss, as he threw his dirty clothes onto the floor of the utility room and headed upstairs to take a shower. "Shame the pub's still closed, it's a fab evening out there, I would have loved a pint or two down by the river."

"Never mind, there'll be plenty of time for that. I'll fix us some dinner and we can finish off that bottle in the garden," said Simon. "Maybe even open another, we've got another cold one left, I think."

It was then that the doorbell rang, and a recently installed innovation allowed them a sneak preview of whoever was loitering outside, without them having to open the door. *"An ideal gadget for those of an unsociable persuasion, like us,"* Gavin had christened it - a small tablet-sized screen mounted on the work-surface revealed the form of an old lady who appeared to be brandishing a rather appetising tray of muffins. "I hope those are chocolate ones." a near naked Gavin said as he disappeared around the corner of the stairs.

"I'm betting blueberry." was Simon's shout, as he reached for the door handle and smiled his most welcoming of cheesy grins.

"It is blueberry actually," said Mrs Illsley, introducing herself as 'the lady from up the lane'. They didn't shake hands, but kind of waved elbows at each other in a move that resembled a South Pacific seabird's mating ritual, and that was all that they needed to break the ice.

"Thank you, that's lovely." said Simon, a little more camp than he ever was in private, which left the former housekeeper in no doubt at all as to the nature of her new neighbours' 'arrangement'; something that she would have relayed to the rest of the village before the day was out. "You shouldn't have but do come on in and have a cup of tea. Gavin's just taking a shower, he looked like a navvy, so you timed it well."

"It looks like you've been very busy already," remarked Mrs Illsley, quickly surveying the room, and making a mental note of everything that had changed, or which looked like it might be about to. "My name's Dorothy, but you can call me Dot," she told him with a squeeze of his arm, and as he squeezed hers back, he got the strong sense that they were going to get along like the proverbial 'house on fire'.

"I'm Simon, Si to my friends," and with the pleasantries complete, he poured them both a very large dry sherry, on ice.

"Oh no, I couldn't possibly." objected Mrs Illsley rather unconvincingly, but Simon knew how to charm ladies of a certain age and he wasn't about to waste an opportunity like this. After all, information was power.

"Oh, go on." he teased, "you look like a sherry kind of girl to me." and that's all it took. Her defences were breached and by the time Gavin had come down to join them, just twenty minutes later, the two of them were well on the way down their second glass and doing a passing resemblance of old friends catching up on lost time. "Let me introduce you to my husband, Gavin." Simon even stood up and waved him closer, as if he was introducing a local celebrity or a member of the royal family.

"Hi, I'm Gav." he said instinctively reaching out his hand and then when she hesitated to do the same, he thumbed his nose at her as if that were the 'new normal'. "Sorry, old habits die hard don't they. Nice to meet you neighbour. I can't stand all this elbow tapping nonsense so if we can't shake hands or better still kiss, let's just pull faces at each other and be done with it."

"So, you are actually *married* then?" she said with a cheeky wink, at which both men winked back knowing that she had just revealed the main purpose behind her neighbourly concern. It wasn't the first time, and it wouldn't be the last, but she was harmless enough.

"Oh yes." said Gavin, "we are most definitely, married."

"Yes," said Simon, "it's all official, my mother wouldn't have us *'living in sin'* you know".

At that Mrs Illsley almost wet herself. It was the kind of laugh that should never be heard emanating from an old lady. A snorting, guffawing kind of sound, and a noise of such proportions that she found herself apologising as she covered her mouth, unsure if it was going to happen again or if it had been a prelude to something worse. "I'm so sorry, I didn't mean to say. That was so funny."

Her laugh was infectious. She stayed almost an hour and a half. The muffins were so delicious that they devoured all six in one sitting, washed down with a combination of hot tea and sherry, and topped off with the rest of the wine. Finally, just when they thought that they might have to make her a bed up in one of the spare rooms, she made her excuses and staggered to her feet. "It's been an absolute delight to meet you both," she giggled, "I think we're all going to get along quite famously." COVID or no COVID, she then kissed them both goodbye on both cheeks – each - and, using the frame of the door for support, leveraged herself out into the now cooler evening air, before heading off up the lane in the vague direction of her own home.

"Should one of us go with her do you think?" Simon asked, a little bemused.

"I think she must know the way by now, after all she was the *'housekeeper here for seventeen years'* you know."

"If she said that once, she must have said it seventeen times."

"Let's just watch her from here." and they did, as she meandered up the unmade road and around the bend about a hundred yards away, finally turning into a gated garden that they later discovered led right to her door.

It was just then that they heard a woman scream. And it wasn't Mrs Illsley.

CHAPTER 25

"What the hell was that?"

The two men stared at each other for no more than a few seconds, before the sound came again and this time there was no doubt at all as to its source. It was coming from inside the house.

Their house.

Later that night, as they reflected on the events of the day over a night-cap, they were adamant that neither of them had felt in the slightest bit afraid in the moment. The sound had been so clear, its point of origin so certain, that they had simply raced indoors and climbed the staircase almost in tandem as the scream sounded for a third time. A gut-wrenching, earth-shaking, soul-splitting scream that begged for mercy and pleaded for deliverance in any language that you might care to hear it in.

The desperate cry of a woman for whom all hope was lost.

As they navigated the turn in the stairs and stepped up into the narrow space of the landing, they each watched as the bedroom door was pulled shut with a clinical thump, but somehow it failed to stop them from charging towards it, certain that a living, breathing, screaming human being was shut up inside. Then almost in sync with each other, they reached for the solid brass handle and burst into the dark room.

Never in their wildest imaginings did they think that it was going to be empty, but as Simon found the light switch, feeling his way around the edge of the frame until his hands closed on the familiar square of plastic, each of them emitted the same shocked gasp as the vacant room stared back at them. There was nothing to see. There was nowhere to hide. The room was exactly as they had left it, sparse in every way. No bed, no furniture. Plain walls, simply painted on all four sides in some exotically named variation of beige and an unremarkable cut pile carpet, above which a plain white ceiling rose pendant swung back and forth, its prominent bulb screwed snugly within, like a malformed head wedged inside a noose.

"Let's not go jumping to conclusions Si." said Gavin on returning to the lounge.

"I'm not." Simon replied, "I'm being perfectly rational. We both know what we heard. We both know what we saw."

"Yes, we heard *something*, but we saw *nothing*."

"I wouldn't call that lightbulb swinging like that, nothing. There was no breeze. No windows were open."

"What about the draught from the door?" Gavin countered, "when we swung it open, maybe that caused it to sway?"

"Sway." Simon was incandescent now. "It was swinging, not swaying, and let's not forget that the door slammed shut first, before we got to it."

"Well, yes, it was closed, but it didn't slam."

"Closed by what exactly?" Simon was in no mood to rationalise their experience into a trick of the wind. "Closed by what?"

"I don't know."

"No, neither do I, so at least we agree on something then."

It wasn't quite an argument; they didn't have those. Nor was it really a disagreement, they didn't disagree about the events that had just taken place. It was just that when it came to the paranormal, Gavin's feet were always much more firmly rooted in bricks and mortar.

"We knew it was haunted, didn't we?" said Simon, sensing his partner's concern. "We just didn't know by what or how badly."

"No, and we still don't, other than it seems to be of the female variety."

"Well at least a girl ghost is less likely to leave bad smells in the bathroom." Simon had always been one to use humour to defuse a potentially explosive situation and this was to be no exception. They both smiled then, relieved to find a funny side to all of this, and both agreed to put the inquisition on the back burner until the morning.

"I prefer if we could put it on ice." suggested Gavin, "the thought of all those Spanish conquistadors burning people at the stake for refusing to say their *'hail Marys'* and *'our fathers'* seems a bit insensitive, given what our visitor had to say earlier. Once you'd oiled her tongue that is."

In all the excitement, Simon had forgotten all about the story of the previous owner who it seemed had met an unfortunate end in the very room in which they were now seated. Mrs Illsley had been quite clear that she really couldn't and probably shouldn't tell them about it, so soon after moving in and all, but tell them she did, and even during the retelling they both wished that she hadn't told them quite as much as she did. In the end she told them everything she knew, and it took quite some time in the retelling.

"I'm surprised it didn't come up in the searches," said Gavin, wondering to himself if their extortionately priced solicitor had done his job effectively. "I'm going to check with him in the morning."

"Do they include hauntings and unfortunate deaths in the searches? If we had known, would it have stopped us from buying the place?"

"No, probably not," reasoned Gavin, "but I would still like to have known that a man had been burnt to a crisp in our lounge without any satisfactory explanation as to the cause. At least I'm going to investigate," he insisted. "There must have been a lot of press coverage and there must have been an inquest and a coroner's report."

"Well, if it'll put your mind at rest, then yeh, why not," agreed Simon, though he knew that it would most likely come to nothing. "I'm going up, you?"

They lay awake for a while, listening to the silence. It was pitch black – unnervingly so, and something that would take some time to get used to after the bright lights of London, but it wasn't long before the drink did its job and carried the two of them off to sleep almost simultaneously.

Unbeknownst to them, another presence watched them silently from the doorway, until the dawn, when it evaporated silently with the morning mist outside.

Thursday 3rd September 2020

164 DAYS SINCE START OF UK LOCKDOWN

6 deaths reported in the UK – the total number of deaths due to COVID19 now stands at 50,155 with 302,580 people testing positive for the disease.

CHAPTER 26

"Does that mean that we're out of the woods now?" Gavin asked as he walked into the kitchen to make his morning coffee. "They just said on the news that restrictions are expected to be reduced in the coming weeks."

"No, that would be wishful thinking." Simon had no intention of allowing normal service to be resumed, not until he'd been fully vaccinated and any prospect of that was still six or more months away. "We've all proven that we are perfectly capable of working remotely over the last six months and as far as I'm concerned, I'm not putting myself back into the line of fire until it's been clinically proven that I'm not at any risk."

"Well, I don't see why you need to jump back into the rat-race if that's what you mean," his partner agreed. "You've served your time and we haven't moved all the way down here to have you spend six hours a day commuting to London and back at £250 a pop."

As a freelance consultant Simon had already broken with convention once, quitting the daily grind and the laws laid down by the Gods of Finance, for what he'd hoped would be a more sedate existence as his 'own boss'. It hadn't quite worked out that way though, and ever since remote working had become the norm, his firm had been so inundated with work that he'd had to sub-contract some of it to other designers. He hated to do it, but there were only twenty-four hours in any given day and so despite his workaholic nature, he had been forced to share his leads around – for a small introductory fee of course, keeping only the choicest contracts for himself.

He designed online content for learning-management-systems; whizzy little training packages that had come on in leaps and bounds over the last decade, to such an extent that face-to-face learning was now considered to be inefficient and expensive. Even the old dinosaurs in the City of London were starting to crack under the pressure of this more cost-effective way to deliver learning, but there were still many who were clinging onto the old ways by their fingertips and refusing to adopt his state-of-the-art software.

And then along came COVID19 and his phone had not stopped ringing. It was money-for-old-rope as his old grandad used to say. Charge a firm £50,000 to build them a 'bespoke' learning catalogue on the perils of cyber security or money laundering and then simply rebadge it for the next firm in the queue and charge them pretty much the same, and again and again until the market was saturated. The only thing was that it never was *saturated* – there was always the next thing, be it data security or discrimination risk or interviewing skills training. He was the 'genius' that knew what made the software tick and without him, they had no way to package up their self-styled training and no way to prove compliance when the regulator came calling.

And the beauty of it all was that the market was a global one. Okay so there were language barriers to be tackled – sometimes – but for most global businesses, the business language was English and so there was no need for translated versions, though when a firm just couldn't see a clear way forward without translating the content into thirty-six languages, then guess what? He just happened to know of a couple of reliable – and cheap - translation agencies in India and the Philippines, who could do all the laborious leg work for him. All he had to do was to import the new text or voice-over into his software when it was ready and hey-presto. That'll be £50,000 please, though he always gave a discount for multi-country assignments, albeit a small one.

In the last six months he had turned over a whopping £450,000 and he was on track to break the one-million-pound barrier for the first time in the current tax year. Of course, the tax man would get his hands on almost half of that –

having already benefited from VAT at 20% on top – but he didn't begrudge them that. So long as they spent it in the right places, like on the NHS who were now proving to anyone who ever doubted it that they were worth far more than even the most critical of 'keyworkers'. He had always paid his taxes – it was his socialist upbringing in a depressed South Wales mining town he supposed. His only wish was that everyone else would be minded to do the same.

And so, they had been able to pay cash for their early retirement crash-pad and still had more than enough set by - and yet more to come in - to turn it into everything they had ever dreamed of. No expense was going to be spared and there was absolutely no way in a million years that any spectres, ghouls, or headless bloody horsemen driving a carriage-and-four through the middle of their lounge was going to get in the way of their best-laid-plans.

"The only reason that you got to retire five years early is that you managed to get that excuse-for-a-bank to make you an offer that you couldn't refuse."

"I earned every penny of it." said Gavin with a rueful smile. "They had it coming in any case. I just helped them to see that one way or other, I was getting a six figure pay-off. Either we were going to come to an agreement with their reputation as an *equal opportunity employer* intact, or we weren't - they were sensible enough to come around to my way of thinking before I instructed my lawyers to go in for the kill. That's all."

A drumming sound like rain on a pane of glass, came in short sharp bursts, regular and rhythmic. It had been raining on and off all day, a light drizzle that was wet enough to soak you right through to the bone, yet quiet enough to go unnoticed in the confines of the cottage.

"Well, I've just had the plans through and judging by the initial estimates we are going to need all of that blood-money to knock this place into shape, and more. Take a gander at that." Simon pushed his tablet across the breakfast bar and as Gavin's eyes settled on the numbers at the bottom of the open email, he let out an involuntarily yelp.

"That's rather a lot more than I thought." he said grimacing but sensing that his partner was having second thoughts already, Gavin was determined that they wouldn't fall at the first hurdle. "It's only his best estimate and he hasn't even seen the place, has he? He's used to London prices. I reckon we'll get a much better deal down here. I'll get onto a few local firms today and get some more quotes, I'm sure it'll come in closer to our budget in the end. If not then we will just have to make a few modifications, that's all. Don't worry about it Si, you just focus on bringing home the bacon."

Neither of them had much liked the quaint *'olde-worlde'* style of the cottage, but they shared a common vision of how it could look – a fusion of old and new, with a wrought iron staircase at the heart of an open plan lounge. The fireplace would require a matching bespoke surround that would set off a double-breasted log-burner in steel and glass, a sharp contrast to a new tiled floor in grey slate smothered with a centre-piece designer rug. A hidden lintel would be needed to liberate the adjoining kitchen from its cramped corner and to show it off in all its splendour. A brand spanking new range in scarlet red with silver fittings; a double butler sink served by sharp faucets within a central island; sleek lines of silver and black base units shouldering the weight of solid granite worktops on three sides of the square. And to the rear, a most ornate conservatory would lord it over the whole lot, its double door exit, offering an escape to the hidden beauty of a revitalised Victorian pot garden, complete with an elaborate arbour.

And that was just the downstairs. Upstairs, the bathroom was also primed for a revamp, a complete refit was on the cards with nothing of the existing fittings expected to survive the cull. They would strip the rooms back to the bare brick, ridding it of layers of wallpaper, plaster, horsehair, and lath until all that was left was its shell.

And then they would begin again. A completely new look. A completely new personality. A new home with a new heart. After all, every home had one.

The details for each of the bedrooms and bathroom had yet to be worked out, but a small extension on the side of the house would create the space for a hi-spec ensuite next to the master bedroom as well as spacious walk-in wardrobes for each of them. It had been the one bone of contention between them over the years; the one thing that was always guaranteed to lead to an argument and then to the silent treatment from one or the other of them. They both loved their clothes, and they hated tripping over each other in the morning when getting dressed for work or in the evening, if getting ready to go out. They liked their own space, and they hated it whenever they got in each other's way.

"It's going to be fabulous when it's done" declared Gavin.

"It's going to be bloody expensive." said Simon. "Do you think there'll be any problems getting planning permission? It's listed after all."

"The architect doesn't think so, he's planning on leaving the original features and beams on show," said Gavin, "but as far as he's concerned, if we're in any doubt at all, we should seek forgiveness and not permission. In any case, the last people changed a lot already, so there's not much that's original left, or so he thinks from the video we sent him."

"Where's that bloody noise coming from?"

"What noise?"

"That tapping," said Simon, "Like a rapping sound. Drumming." And he demonstrated it almost perfectly with his own hand on the breakfast bar, a three fingered drum roll. Like an impatient customer waiting for his bill. "I thought it was the rain, but the sun's come out now and I can still hear it."

"Oh, that." replied Gavin. "I thought it was you. Wasn't it you then? I thought I could hear it earlier."

"No, it wasn't me." said Simon, turning his head towards the source of the sound. "Has it stopped now? I don't hear it anymore."

They both listened to the quiet. It was still. It was silent.

"It's stopped."

Or at least they thought it had, but it hadn't. It was the heartbeat of the house and it had been beating for hundreds of years. Sometimes it was audible above the interference of millions of spent minutes since the percussionist first played that muted tune, but for most of the time it was just a hushed tone, hidden behind a veil of silence that often lay out of reach to the modern world.

But not now, for it had been disturbed.

It had been shaken from its slumber by a Victorian parlour game, restored to life after centuries of silence.

It was audible again.

Thursday 19th November 2020

241 Days Since Start of UK Lockdown

407 deaths reported in the UK – the total number of deaths due to COVID19 now stands at 61,873 with 1,309,528 people testing positive for the disease.

CHAPTER 27

The first wave had turned out to be just a ripple and as the second heralded a return to lock down for the nation, Gavin and Simon handed the keys over to their appointed builders and moved into some relatively modest rented accommodation in the village for the length of the renovation. Most of their belongings remained in storage where they had been since leaving London and so, the long wait began.

In some ways, moving out had come as a bit of a relief, a break from the daily disturbances that had gone beyond the intriguing to the downright annoying. They had continued to hear the knocking, but not every day, sometimes not even every week, but whenever they had begun to think it had stopped, it would start up again. It was almost as if the house was trying to provoke them, waiting for one of them to comment on it over breakfast or when watching television in the evening.

"I haven't heard the tapping for a while Gav," Simon would announce, and almost before Gavin could answer the same three fingered beat would start again, louder than ever, as if it was taunting them, mocking them, reminding them that they would never be alone in their house. That the house would never truly belong to them, however much they tried to make it their own, it would only ever be a mask to be worn by someone else.

So, they had agreed not to mention it at all. Almost like some childish game where the protagonists each dares the other not to blink first – a staring contest, only the person on the other side of the table was invisible. To them at least, but it had worked, for a while. Then, on the day that they moved out, it was as if the house was having a monumental temper tantrum. The whole fabric of the building reverberated with it, like some demonic drum soloist beating out the same three notes on every surface, particularly in the snug where two clutches of glass bottles – left behind by the previous owners – ended up huddled closer together, as if for warmth against a coming storm.

It put Gavin in mind of a traditional song that he'd grown up singing along to, except that instead of ten artifacts there were, in fact, eleven:

> *Eleven green bottles standing on a wall.*
> *Eleven green bottles standing on a wall.*
> *And if one green bottle should accidentally fall.*
> *There'd be ten green bottles standing on a wall.*

He found that the tune was no longer just in his head. He was singing it aloud, as he watched in wonder as each glass skittle vibrated against the next, their marble stoppers firmly wedged like an Adam's apple in their necks. But as he reached the end, it was the one that was furthest away from him that was nudged from its resting place and as it overbalanced, he lurched forwards, just as it toppled over.

It seemed intent on destroying itself as it tumbled towards the stone slab beneath and though Gavin's fingers were only a fraction away from breaking its fall, he was too late. As he reached out his left hand to steady himself against the fireplace, a spray of thick discoloured fragments exploded up from the floor, shattering in spectacular fashion.

"Oh bollocks."

It was Simon who had reacted first, but Gavin was quick to have his say just a second or two later. "It's stopped." he said, standing up to listen, shushing Simon before he could say anything more. It was as if the tension had been released with the stopper, and as Gavin retrieved the dustpan from the kitchen and began to mop up the four-hundred years old remains, he picked up the discoloured glass ball and put it back on the shelf with the others.

"And then there were ten." said Gavin, as he watched the marble settle down on the uneven stone nook. It felt significant, but neither of them knew why, but they continued to ponder the possibilities as they prepared to leave.

"Either it was telling us not to go, or it was telling us not to come back." reasoned Simon, a little shaken by the whole experience despite his staunch determination that the house would not win. It would, eventually, be brought under their control, no matter how hard it pushed them in the other direction. "It's like a child," he continued, as he related his theory whilst they made to leave. "It wants its own way but it's not going to get it. All of the disturbances of late; the missing items, the breakages, the shadows that we've seen, none of it has caused us any *physical* harm, has it?"

"No," said Gavin, "but, it's scared the shit out of us once or twice."

It had. There was no denying it. "Yes, but there's no way I'm going to let it win," said Simon, with his usual stoic resolve. "I'm not gonna lie though, it's going to be nice to get away from it for a while, though I do wonder what the builders are going to make of it. I'm expecting some complaints, I just hope it doesn't drive them away, we weren't exactly blessed with many offers, were we?"

It seemed that the construction industry had never had it so good and that, despite a nationwide shortage of raw materials as demand for just about everything imaginable had outstripped supply, most builders were enjoying an extended golden summer. So much so that prices had risen across the board and what they had both thought to be a conservative budget had proven to be anything but. Fortunately, Simon's orders had also reached unprecedented levels, and so he had been working around the clock to keep up, raising his own rates into the bargain.

In the end, the local building firm that had won the bid – it was the only bid – had some experience of the house, and so they had been able to have a full and frank conversation about it before either side had put pen to paper. They had been surprised at just how nervous the lead contractor had been and he in turn had expressed surprise at just how nonchalant they were at the prospect of making the cottage their permanent home.

"I know what I'm letting myself in for." said Bill of Postlethwaite Construction Ltd. "But I'm charging you extra for it. You can call it 'danger money' if you like, or a 'sleep deprivation bonus', though it won't be me who'll be doing most of the work and I won't be mentioning any of the goings-on to any of the subbies that I bring on board. What they don't know won't hurt 'em."

♪

Preparations started shortly thereafter, and several skips had already been delivered, filled, and returned, ferrying a tonne of dusty and broken detritus to the local tip, from whence most of it would end up in landfill or as hardcore for other projects. Even from the street, the dust that spilled out from almost half a millennium of history seemed like smoke from a flameless fire, billowing up and out as the floorboards screeched and the doorframes snapped like succulent ribs or the meaty claws of a crab. Even the reclaimed window-frames, installed by the former owners, didn't survive the gutting, as despite their Victorian vintage they were not original to the building and so their tethered sash lines were torn asunder, to flap like sinews as the glass was shattered and each timber frame split apart.

And now the dust had settled on phase one, and the building was being made ready for its 'first fix' for the second time in the new century, it was clear that the last renovation had barely scratched the surface by comparison. Bare walls of crudely made brick were braced together by ancient oak timbers, that had now been treated for any earthly infestation; floorboards had been lifted and stacked neatly under cover outside, where they would stay until treated with the same noxious spray, ready for re-instalment before the weather turned; the modern staircase, torn apart for kindling was piled up in pieces in the garden to the rear, its short lifespan sacrificed to the God of progress.

"Morning gentlemen," said Bill, hailing the owners as they turned onto the path after a short walk from their digs. It wasn't exactly chilly outside, but the weather had certainly taken a turn towards winter over the preceding week and although the sun was doing its best to break through the cloud cover, all of them had donned their winter coats earlier than expected. "You're up and about bright and early."

"Well, you know what they say about that." replied Simon with a wink and a smile.

"The less we say about that the better." laughed Bill, as he threw a hard hat at each of them in turn before beckoning them inside. "Come on in, there's something that I want to show you, it's intriguing, some might say disturbing, but I didn't want anyone messing with it until you'd both had chance to take a look."

"Oh, that's all 'very mysterious." scoffed Gavin, as they stepped down into the hollowed-out floor and made their way across the debris field that was once their lounge, to where the old kitchen had been.

"Now I can't say it's the first time that I've come across one of these in an old house," explained Bill "but never one so deep as this one, and from what I can tell, it's still functional. It's quite a wide one too, bigger than your conventional manhole cover and big enough to climb down, should you be so minded. I don't advise that, by the way, just in case you were feeling adventurous?"

He reached down to lift a square wooden panel, and revealed a circular brick hole, with the outside of the top two or three courses visible above the dark earth beneath. Then he flashed a torch down inside and threw in a pebble, a faint 'plop' echoing back up towards them a few seconds later.

"How deep, do you reckon?" asked Simon.

"Twenty or thirty feet to the bottom I'd say," Bill estimated.

"And not unusual you say?"

"No, not at all. Most houses of the yeomanry would have had these back in the day."

"Yeomanry?" prompted Gavin. "What's that?"

"They were tenant farmers, not the landowners or the landed gentry themselves," said Bill. "And not the agricultural labourers who went from farm to farm to find work, but the families who more or less lived and died on the land, usually staying in the same place from birth until death."

"Is it going to be a problem?"

"I wouldn't have thought so." said Bill, "It's easily capped off, though some people like to make a feature out of them. A bit of a curiosity to show off to their friends, you know, a dinner-party conversation starter."

"That's an interesting thought," said Simon, "how difficult would that be to do?"

"Not difficult at all. We could just have a circular hole in the floor, cap it off with reinforced glass and hey presto."

"Do it." said Simon decisively. "Sounds like a 'feature' to me, and one that the planning officer might be quite pleased to see that we have 'preserved'. Might win us some brownie points when we show him what we've done to the ex-fireplaces upstairs."

"They also found another one of these," said Bill, reaching into his pocket to receive a small green vial the size of a nail varnish bottle. "We found quite a few of these, last time."

Gavin felt an unfounded sense of relief wash over him. "That's perfect," he beamed. "That'll replace the one that got broken. Do you know what they are?"

"I'm told that they are witches bottles.," said Bill with an involuntary cough. "Meant to ward off evil spirits, quite common back in the day, especially in the seventeenth century when people believed in such things. We found twelve, one got broken, so this would have made it thirteen in all then."

Simon looked at Gavin as if to share a superstitious thought, but he said nothing. The message was received loud-and-clear though, and a much-maligned unlucky number with a reputation for ill fortune that dates back to the days of the Knights Templar was not something that either of them wanted to dwell on for long. "I think you'll find it's two now; we also broke one of them on the day that we moved in."

"There is another thing." said Bill, a little more sheepishly.

His clients both looked at him quizzically, sensing the change of mood and knowing that something more disturbing lay at the root of it.

"The blokes have been reporting some tapping noises for a few weeks now" Bill explained. "Usually, the noise of the machinery and the hammering drowns it out, but in the quiet periods, at the start and the end of the day and when they break for lunch. It's been happening so much that they've even given him a name."

"Him?" both men asked at once.

"Thor. You know, because of all the hammering."

There was a respectful silence for a moment or two, but Simon sensed that there was more to the story and so he prompted their main contractor to continue with his tale.

"Well to begin with they said it was coming from all over. In the walls, from beneath the floors, but as they got the building clear of all of that, it continued, which seemed to rule out any possibility of it being rats or mice." Bill cleared his throat of the dust that their boots had kicked up, his mouth suddenly feeling very dry. "But they reckon from then on, it started to come only from one place, which was beneath the fireplace over there."

The men's eyes followed Bill's outstretched finger, though of course they needed no directing, and settled on the bare wall of the chimney breast, now clear of the imitation wooden surround. The mysterious backplate was still preserved, its circular patterns still a mystery to everyone, but that's not where they were being directed to look. Where the former flagstones had been laid, a plastic milkcrate was now balanced on top of a battered length of timber and even from where they were stood, they could both see that there was a hole beneath.

"They had a little dig, just for exploratory purposes," continued Bill, "in case of subsidence risk or anything like that, and they've found a cavity of some kind. I was concerned that we might need to backfill it with concrete or hard core, just to ensure that the building's integrity isn't compromised but when I took another peek inside it, well."

"Well, what?" asked Simon, "I assume it's not another well?"

"No, it's not. It's much more unusual than that," said Bill, tipping back his hard hat to scratch his head. "The first few layers were rubble, as if it had once been backfilled a long time ago. Pieces of old brick and broken stone mixed in with sand and shingle, but nothing dateable. At least not to the untrained eye. And then when they had excavated to about a six-foot depth, they came across something very intriguing, something that shouldn't really be there, at least not in a residential property like this one I would say. Why don't you take a look, tell me what you think?"

"Okay." said Gavin, grabbing the torch from Bill's hand and stepping forward into the opening of their soon-to-be feature fireplace. He knelt in the space that was once a grate and which would soon be again, and peered into the hole, the torchlight flashing in front of him as he delved deeper and saw the last thing on earth that he had expected to see.

"Fucking hell."

"What?" said Simon excitedly. "What is it Gav?"

"It's a fucking door." He was back on his feet now and dusting himself down, and the look on his face was more of wonder than of fear. "Take a look," he said, handing the torch to his partner. "It's still fixed in place; you can see the hinges and there appears to be a metal grille right in the middle of it."

"We didn't come across it last time we worked here, as we never disturbed the ground, just put in the new floorboards and that was it," Bill explained answering the question that he knew would come. "Although we had the floors up in here, we never dug down, never had any reason to at the time. So, we just replaced the old with the new and thought nothing more of it."

"That's not a grille." said Simon interrupting Bill in mid-sentence, his voice muffled by the hole in which his head and shoulders were now immersed. "Those are bars mate. That's a cell of some kind, that's what that is. Whoever or whatever was kept in there, it was not meant to get out."

CHAPTER 28

"I'm afraid that we'll have to report this one to the planning office guys." said Bill, "it's too rare a find and I'll be shot if it gets out that we found something of significant historical interest and the local archaeology department didn't get to document it."

The builders were eating their sandwiches now, perched around the edge of the room on various improvised chairs, as they considered their next move. It had just started to rain outside, but they had hardly noticed, so engrossed were they in the find of their lives.

"Problem is, they're on a bit of a go-slow at the moment, due to the pandemic, people off sick and what-not," sighed Bill. "Getting them down here might take a while, there's no one in the offices and the usual channels are clogged up as well. I might have to try a few of my contacts on the 'dark side', see if we can jump the queue, if not it could be weeks at best."

"And at worst?" asked Gavin, dreading the answer.

"Months."

"Shit."

"Well do your best Bill." said Simon, looking on the bright side as usual. "I know you will. In the meantime, what do we do? Is it worth opening it all up so we can at least get down there to see what we're dealing with? Maybe it's blocked off and there's nothing behind it but a wall of earth."

"And maybe it isn't." said Gavin. "I thought I could see a space through the bars, but the angle's tight so it's hard to say for sure. But I do agree, it's better that we know, and we can't get into any trouble for just making it accessible, can we?"

"I wouldn't have thought so, no." said Bill, "but I don't mind saying, I'm not going to open it on my own."

"Wouldn't dream of letting you." said Simon, "though I do have to dash, I've got something urgent to attend to. But I'll leave my man here to oversee things."

"Thanks pal." quipped Gavin, giving his partner a playful shove as they watched him go. "We'll be right behind you Bill, some nearer than others mind."

The two of them laughed out loud at that, just as the drumming started up again and it acted like a starting pistol. Bill called over a couple of labourers who armed with picks and shovels began to dig out the area in front of the fireplace and it wasn't long before they hit pay dirt. Gavin crowded closer to the much-expanded hole, straining to see what had been unearthed, but there was no doubt at all in their minds as to what it was.

Steps.

The first four in any case, and after a quick inspection, Bill gave the two wiry teenagers the go-ahead to finish the job. Within an hour the whole flight of stone steps had been exposed and the bottom had been levelled out enough to scrape away the dirt and stone from the base of the heavy timbered door. Its metal clasps were still in place, black and gnarled, with rusted rivets prominent across each sharply pointed length. The door itself was short, no more than five feet in height, so when they finally did manage to prise it open, they would have to duck down to get inside, assuming that there was something there to see. The moment of truth had arrived.

"Over to you Bill," said the taller of the two shirtless excavators as he stepped out of the hole and Gavin couldn't help but notice that his muscled torso was thick with dirt and sweat. Even his face and brow were blackened by the scorched earth beneath the fireplace, as if he was an ancient warrior emerging from the past, warpaint smeared across his chest and cheeks in readiness for battle.

"Gav." shouted Bill, breaking him from his trance. "Are we going in?"

"Yes, Bill." Gavin obeyed, stepping up to the plate to dutifully follow their builder down into the abyss. Once below, they each sidled up to the door, crouching to peer behind the metal grille that was now fully at their disposal.

"Dark in there isn't it?" said Gavin, as the silence got the better of him.

"Damn it." Where's my torch gone." cursed Bill, signalling to his crew above that he had mysteriously misplaced his own. A few seconds went by as another smaller one was lobbed down to them, but it would prove to be just as effective, as Bill slid the switch into the on position and shone its beam into the void beyond the closed door. There was only room enough for two down there at the foot of the stairs, but they could both peer inside without too much effort, though at first neither of them could find the words to describe what their eyes were seeing.

It was a room. A small, square space, complete with a wooden frame in the far corner and a rough wooden chair to the right with something square or rectangular set beneath. A length of chain was fixed to the wall at the other end from which, what could only be described as a metal collar, was dangling like a pendulum.

"Oh my God." said Gavin.

"Good heavens." echoed Bill. "What in God's name have we found?"

"I don't know," admitted Gavin, "but I doubt that it's got anything to do with God."

❦

Simon laughed out loud when Gavin told him all about it later that day.

Having grown up in a staunchly non-conformist household where he'd been expected to marry a nice local protestant girl by twenty-one or face the consequences, he had long since fallen out of love with religion. The fact that he had gone along with his parent's expectations, getting hitched to a very pleasant girl with whom he was still close friends, was the most stupid thing he had ever done. Their sudden divorce just two years later had caused a bit of a scandal in village, and though the two of them were in no doubt that their reasons were solid and their friendship untainted, his own father had turned his back on him the second the news of their separation became known. He hadn't spoken to him since and though his mother's stance had mellowed somewhat in the intervening years he and his father were still what they used to call *estranged*. The fact that his sisters had not disowned him was a blessing, but he would not have expected anything else from them, and for that alone, he loved them more than they could know.

As for his father, he could go to hell.

"It seems like we've stumbled on the explanation for our *little local difficulties*," said Simon, pushing thoughts of his family troubles to the back of his mind for another day. "Whoever was kept holed up down there, it must have been as a prelude to something else I'd say."

"Yes, didn't Mrs Illsley say the house was once a Courthouse?" asked Gavin intrigued.

"She did, so could this have been a holding pen of some kind?," he reasoned. "A staging post, a temporary place to keep them until they could be transported elsewhere, for further trial maybe, or for execution?"

THURSDAY 17ᵀᴴ DECEMBER 2020

269 DAYS SINCE START OF UK LOCKDOWN

463 deaths reported in the UK – the total number of deaths due to COVID19 now stands at 73,099 with 1,541,181 people testing positive for the disease.

CHAPTER 29

It would take four weeks for Bill's inside contacts at the local council offices to bear fruit, by which time the contractors had completed much of the first fix. Electrics were all in place, a complete rewiring effort from top to bottom and the hidden plumbing work was also more or less finished. Even the shell of the side extension, which was no longer open to the skies and so fully protected from the onset of winter, was now fully fitted out.

Christmas had now been officially cancelled, the government confirming that the long-awaited reprieve for the festivities was a risk-too-far for the NHS, and so for many families, including what was left of Gavin's and Simon's sisters, there would be no celebratory get-togethers this December. The two of them would spend their time in each other's company around the corner from what they hoped would eventually become their 'forever home' and Simon would spend most of his time working on completing a suite of virtual training for a global insurance firm who were desperate for it to be delivered in time for year end. There was a completion bonus in it for him, should he manage to do so, and as he had already earmarked it for a new top-of-the-range surround sound system that would be able to pipe music from any format all over the house, he was keen to get on with it.

Gavin on the other hand, would be engrossed in a far more original pursuit.

Since the discovery of the door, he had spent much of his time online and on the telephone chasing down leads. He had been determined to find some trace of the house's history and although he was still unable to visit the many local libraries and museums, he had hoped that there would be enough of southwest England's history on the world-wide-web to give him some answers. Then when the country finally opened for business again, he would have a readymade research plan on which to base any face-to-face investigations that were needed.

He still made a point of visiting the house on at least a daily basis, to check up on progress and to peek inside the 'cell', as they had started to refer to the room beneath the fireplace. After all, realistically it couldn't have been anything else and though they did not yet know who or what had been kept locked up in there, it was the opinion of the ailing local historian, who was himself now battling a bout of coronavirus, that it must have been used as a holding facility of some sort; a gaol for local felons who had not yet been transferred to the county town for trial and sentencing.

The conservation lady from the local council - whose name had slipped from his memory almost as soon as she was introduced on her one and only visit to date - had informed them that it was not unusual for such places of restraint to be incorporated in the home of a local alderman, back in the days before the police force had even been thought of.

"Were there no prisons then?" Gavin had asked her rather stupidly.

"Yes of course," she told him with a patronising smirk. "But not in a small village like this. Even in the closest towns, there were only ever overnight lockups, places where drunks would be forced to spend the night after disturbing the peace, until the local magistrate could be called upon to determine their punishment. This looks very much like one of those to me, though we have no record of it that I could find, so it's wonderful that it's been preserved and that we can now photograph it for posterity."

Jim, the archive photographer, had been all over it. His digital SLR camera capturing snaps from all angles, and though they had done their best to force open the substantial door, it remained jammed shut and wouldn't budge however hard they tried.

"It's most probably locked," she'd said and although Gavin knew exactly what he wanted to say in that very moment, he had thought better of it. They needed to keep the local council onside so his standard *'no shit Sherlock'* response for such moments might not have served him quite so well as it had done in more familiar company.

"What kind of key would have turned a lock like this?" asked Bill, peering closely at the solid metal lock plate with its traditional looking keyhole.

"A large one," said the visiting historian. "At least six inches long and half an inch or so in thickness, not very complex in design, but very sturdy, though if you do happen to find it, I wouldn't be at all surprised to find that it snaps apart in the lock. Either the key itself will have corroded over time and will be unable to take the pressure, or the internal mechanism within the lock itself will be all rusted up. So, if you do find it, be sure to call us."

"Well at least we know what we're looking for," said Gavin with a smile and that was that as far as their interest went. Catalogued, photographed, and assured that it would be preserved, either with access or not - that didn't seem important to them - so long as it wasn't removed, replaced, or converted into a subterranean toilet, it seemed that they were happy with it so long as it wasn't disturbed or filled in. A return visit was not on the cards, unless they did manage to find the key, in which case they expected to be called in without delay.

As they climbed back up the stone stairwell, the archivist cast her eye over the fireplace itself as it came back into view. "Oh, now that is interesting." she muttered under her breath, shining her torch into the opening to the chimney breast, "that's a turn up for the books. How did I miss that?"

"What is it?" asked Gavin, following her line of sight into the cavity of fireplace itself. "Oh, you mean the backplate. Yeh, we weren't sure what that was either, no one seems to know too much about it, but we assume that it's an original."

"Oh, it will be, you can be sure of that," purred the historian. "It might just look like a swirling daub of circles to the untrained eye, but that's classic Jacobean graffiti, that's what that is."

"What was that?" asked Gavin, more confused than ever.

"A common-all-garden inscription to ward off evil spirits in the days when belief in the Devil and his minions was at an all-time high." Her demeanour was now bordering on smugness, and it was not a quality that she was wearing at all well. "It's equally important to the planning office that this is preserved, preferably after some professional restoration work, but at the very least left untouched and untampered with. Can you get some up-close snaps of that too Jim?"

Mrs Illsley had come around to inspect their subterranean find almost within minutes of hearing about it, alerted to it by Bill who had reported back within a couple of days of completing the excavations. She had timed her arrival to the second, waiting for a break in the constant showers that had plagued them all week, but was very excited to see it and vowed to let them both know if anyone in her wide network of county friends could offer them anything by way of local information. They'd had high hopes for some local intelligence on the matter, but in the end, nothing was forthcoming and before too much longer, all external interest in it simply dried up.

So as a quiet New Year's Eve came and went, the two of them had simply got on with it, instructing Bill to install a trap door in their new oak panelled flooring in front of the hearth, that would be covered by an inch deep rug. Unless they wanted to show off their unique find to friends, that is. It was after all, a feature to end all features, and one that they were quite pleased with despite its connotations, but it would be many months before either of them would venture into its depths again.

The phrase 'feature fireplace' had never been more appropriate. But for now, it was very much a case of 'out of sight and out of mind', and there it would remain, until the renovation work was complete.

As for the key, unbeknownst to the current owners, it had already been found.

Thursday 11th February 2021

325 DAYS SINCE START OF UK LOCKDOWN

590 deaths reported in the UK – the total number of deaths due to COVID19 now stands at 121,290 with 3,597,890 people testing positive for the disease.

CHAPTER 30

Progress on the house had been slow, though in the time that had elapsed since their dark discovery, the building's transformed character had started to reveal itself.

An extortionately expensive steel beam had been raised into place, allowing a supporting wall to be demolished, and the surrounding walls and ceilings had been lathed and replastered throughout, ready for the second fix of electrics. It had been a horribly dirty job and great gobs of plaster had been deposited all over the dirt floor where they would most likely remain for another four centuries, buried beneath newly sprung floorboards.

Thousands upon thousands of yards of plastic pipework had been laid for the underfloor heating, snaking along the suspended wooden joists that criss-crossed the self-levelling screeding; it was all now hidden from view beneath a baker's dozen lengths of wide and weathered oak flooring that had been nail-gunned into place. The carpenters had been busy for weeks; the planning office had required the new owners to replace the extensively rotten floorboards on a like-for-like basis, meaning that expensive hardwood remained their only option even though it would eventually be carpeted throughout. Downstairs they had decided against extending the slate tiled floor from the kitchen, in favour of a contrasting wooden look in the lounge, but again that meant English oak and even more expense.

The fireplace was also starting to take on a fresh identity, but as the old one wasn't original, they'd been granted some leeway by the Preservation Standards Officers, and Simon had been clear on what he'd wanted from the outset and so it was out with the old and in with the new. A tall and angular stone surround with the preserved backplate retained to the rear and the two largest original flagstones re-laid, from where a stylish log-burner would keep them snug as bugs in the depths of winter.

In moving the stone slabs, another curious discovery was made although at first the builders thought nothing of it and it was Gavin who picked up on the anomaly, as he and Simon were taking stock over the weekend and making notes on what was still to be done.

They were measuring up the fireplace for the new log-burning stove, checking its dimensions as well as the depth into the recess of the chimney when something etched into the underside of the foremost slab caught his eye. He dropped the end of the tape that he was holding and, negotiating his way through the debris of dusty mortar boards and off-cuts of timber, he retrieved a discarded brush and cleared the dirt from the stone.

"I thought so, look at this Si," he called across to his partner who was more than a little irritated that he'd been left with the responsibility of working out the measurements for himself.

"What?" he asked, keen to get the job done and to get to the pub for the afternoon's rugby international before all the socially distanced seats were taken.

"There's a letter scratched onto the stone here" and pulling back the first slab to reveal the second that was leant up against the wall beneath it, he was taken aback to see the same thing repeated. "It's on the other one too."

"What is?"

"It's the letter 'W' I think, but it's more like two 'V's overlapping." He dusted down the second one just to be sure before putting them both back in its former resting place to examine the first one again. "It's not just a scratch either, it's a proper indentation, like they really meant for it to stand the test of time."

"Probably just the stonemason's mark, isn't it?," suggested Simon, a quite reasonable assumption in the circumstances and one that Gavin didn't immediately disagree with.

"Yeh, you're probably right." But it didn't seem right. It didn't seem right at all, and for weeks afterwards, Gavin continued to be troubled by it. Was it a monogram he wondered – a WW. Someone's initials maybe? The carvings had seemed purposeful, but he didn't want to bother anyone unduly with it, after all, it was probably nothing and though he did discuss it with the builders and took some photographs too, there were more important things for them to be getting on with.

Whilst Gavin was delighted at the prospect of an Easter moving-in date, he'd also been able to make significant progress with the house's history and through the online treasure trove that he'd unearthed, had uncovered evidence that a former house had indeed been present on their patch of land since Tudor times. It was of course impossible to tell with any certainty whether it was the exact same building but there was no doubt that the residents had been of some prominence in the local parish as documentation was plentiful.

Alderman Oliver Hunt, assumed to be a brother or cousin of the staunch Parliamentarian and Justice of the Peace, Robert Hunt, had lived on this spot for several decades and although it seemed likely that his house had been much grander then, tithe records had proved beyond all doubt that his acreage had accounted for much of the ancient lane itself and for the surrounding estate.

Gavin had unearthed a record of 'enclosures' from the seventeenth century, a movement that had revolutionised the English farming system and led to the displacement of thousands of agricultural labouring families. An Obadiah Hunt was listed as the agent for several land enclosures in the early part of the century; parcels of formerly common pasture that were partitioned off under the new regime enabling landowners to grow rich at the expense of their poor tenants. At the start of what would one day be coined the 'agricultural revolution' in England, improved farming techniques had increased the yield of arable lands like these dramatically, pushing up prices as they sought to feed the growing populations of nearby Dorchester, Salisbury and Exeter, and the Hunts had been perfectly placed to take full advantage.

But farming had not been their only pursuit.

"So, what are you saying Gav?" asked Simon nursing a mouthful of Chardonnay as if it was to be his last. "That our house is somehow linked to witch-hunting?"

"I'm not sure yet," said Gavin, "but it seems a bit of a coincidence to me that a sizeable property that stood on the site where our house now stands once belonged to this chap Oliver Hunt, and that a local man called Robert Hunt was a leading judge and probable persecutor of witches."

"When was this?"

"Middle of the seventeenth century," said Gavin with more conviction than he'd intended, but he'd been deep in the subject for a few weeks now and he felt as if he'd become a bit of an authority on it. "The civil war came to a head in the 1640s so these would be the commonwealth years, you know, before the Restoration."

"Restoration?" said Simon. "I never paid any attention in school, what was that then? Isn't that something to do with the Catholic church?"

"Well sort of," answered Gavin not wanting to be too patronising and suspecting that his partner knew all about it anyway and was just being facetious. "But, no not really, you're thinking of the Reformation. Cromwell was in charge of the Roundheads and had deposed the first King Charles and chopped his block off, but his Parliamentarians didn't last very long and by the 1660's they had agreed to put Charles the Second on the throne, but with much reduced power."

"Yes, but wasn't he a Catholic?" asked Simon, clearly in an argumentative mood.

"Yes, but that's not the point."

"Well, what is your point then?"

He was winding him up and Gavin knew it. "Will you just drink your bloody wine and listen for a minute," and he leant over to refill both of their glasses to the brim before continuing. "The witch-hunting craze had started on the continent years before, but it only really kicked off in England once James the First of England – the Sixth of Scotland – had succeeded to the throne and decided to have a book published on the subject."

"When was that then?"

"1604 to be precise, earlier in Scotland," said Gavin, "and from then on there were loads of instances of witches being tried and executed throughout the country and it went on throughout the century until a law was finally passed to stop it, but for one hundred years anyone who was a bit odd, or who looked a bit funny at some local squire or lady of the manor, was liable to be accused of being a witch."

"Right," said Simon trying his best not to be too dismissive of his husband's new-found obsession. "So, these witches weren't really *witches* at all then, they were just poor unfortunates, like in that play by whatshisname, the bloke that married Marilyn?"

"Yes, *the Crucible*, by Arthur Miller," said Gavin, "and just like in Salem, it was usually a local busybody who starting things off by accusing someone that couldn't defend themselves – because they were poor, simple or just defenceless – and before you knew it, they were up in court and off to pay the hangman."

"Not burned?" Simon asked, "at the stake?"

"Apparently not" replied Gavin. "Not in England anyway. "We preferred to hang ours, not that that was any more pleasant, though it was supposedly quicker. Usually."

"Isn't it possible that some of them *were* witches though?"

"Only if you believe in black magic, which I don't by the way, so I'd say not." said Gavin, though some may have been herbalists or local healers who knew how to use natural remedies to cure common ailments."

"Or natural poisons to have the opposite effect?"

"Well possibly," agreed Gavin, "but that would be simple poisoning wouldn't it, though back then they might have called it witchcraft. But you're getting me off the point."

"What is your point Gav?" said Simon with another smirk, taking a slurp from his freshly filled glass.

"My point is that the bloke that owned our house, I mean a house on our land, may have been involved in all these, goings on," continued Gavin. "The name

Hunt is common enough, but this magistrate Robert Hunt was said to have been a bit of a religious zealot and belief in witchcraft, at least publicly, was commonplace - the Bible was very clear on it."

"Thou shalt not suffer a witch to live" said Simon, jumping in.

"How do you know that? I never took you for a biblical man."

"Sunday school, South Wales, circa 1980," said Simon. "I never missed you know." He was doing a passable attempt at a Welsh accent now though he'd been out of the valleys for so long that his Welsh language skills were very much a thing of the past. "My parents were staunch non-conformists I'll have you know, Baptists no less."

"Funny you should say that." said Gavin, "but back in the mid sixteen-hundreds, the Bible had only been available in English for a hundred or so years and that had led to the rise of dissenters, people who were opposed to the teachings of the Catholic church once they discovered that most of their sacred rites are nowhere to be found in the Bible."

"So, they went back to basics," said Simon. "Yes, I know all that from my schooldays, but what's that got to do with our predicament?"

"Denying that witchcraft existed, in itself, was seen as tantamount to heresy." said Gavin. "If you didn't take an accusation seriously, then you too could stand accused of being a non-believer and that's why so many people got on the bandwagon and why so few people were brave enough to oppose it, when it was probably obvious to everyone what was going on most of the time."

"Oh, I see," but it had been a long day and Simon's concentration was on the wane and though he had been doing his best to keep up, it was obvious that he wasn't going to be able to continue with it for much longer. History was not his bag.

"Look here," said Gavin, reaching down to the side of his chair to retrieve a battered old book, which he passed across to his partner. "I sent for this online, it's a copy of a book by a chap called Joseph Glanvill, written in 1681."

"*Saducismus Triumphatus,*" Simon read aloud, opening the cover to reveal the reproduction copy in all its glory. "*Or full and plan evidence concerning witches and apparitions, in two parts, the first treating – dealing with in other words I suppose - of their possibility, the second of their real existence.*"

"Yes, and edited by Henry More no less," said Gavin, "he was very high up, physician to the King and everything, so his opinion counted. Anyway, this book laid out all the reasons why people should believe in this stuff, and," he paused there for full effect, "the whole thing was addressed to Robert Hunt."

"This Hunt fella?" asked Simon, "So he's the one who was sending them down, as witches?"

"It would seem so, yes," said Gavin triumphantly. "At least he was one of them anyway. He was a judge on the Western Circuit. He wasn't alone, there were a fair few of them who seemed to take a very personal interest in finding and sentencing these poor wretches to hang, but Hunt was one of the active ones in this area, and if I can find evidence that links him to an Oliver of the same name, then I might even be onto something, maybe even the reason why we have a prison cell in our basement."

"You mean you don't even know if they're related," scoffed Simon. "After all that, they might just have the same surname?"

"Don't be an arse Si." said Gavin, feeling a little crestfallen. "There's every possibility if you ask me. I'm just going to do some digging in the parish records and see what I can find out."

"How much did this cost you?" Simon asked, waving the reproduction pamphlet in the air like a political manifesto in the Houses of Parliament.

"Not much," said Gavin. "Got it on eBay, fifteen quid or thereabouts."

It seemed like a good place to stop the debate.

"I'm only teasing Gav," said Si, a few minutes later, conscious that he may have gone a little over the top. "It's just that I don't think it's a very good idea for us to go delving into all this dodgy black arts stuff, not when we already seem to have a resident ghost."

For a minute or two Gavin stayed quiet, pondering the point, and stopping just short of an outright sulk. It was a good one, but he had no intention of meddling in anything. It was just that if the house, or the land, had a history then he wanted to know about it. All about it.

"I just want to get to the bottom of things Si," he said defensively. "I don't like all this hocus pocus stuff anymore than you do, but you have to admit that we've got a problem back there," he said waving a finger in the general direction of their house, "and we need to find a way of making it stop. Preferably before we move back in. I know you said that it can't hurt us, but you don't know that. Look what happened to the last guy, what was his name, Mountford?"

At the very mention of the name, Simon jumped up in his chair and spilled his wine over the not-so-plush sofa that had already seen better days. "Oh shit, oh stuff it, I forgot."

"Forgot what?"

"We had a phone call" he spluttered. "The day that I went to have my second COVID jab. From a Mrs Mountford, Charlotte, I think she said her name was. Said she wanted to speak to us, urgently. Something about the house."

"And you forgot?"

"Sorry Gav." said Simon sheepishly. "Slipped my mind, lots on my plate at the moment."

"And no idea what she might have wanted?" Simon shook his head. "No hint in her tone? How did she sound; anxious, scared? Angry?"

"No, don't think so. Maybe a bit impatient?" Simon guessed, wanting to offer something in recompense for his oversight. "A bit miffed that no one was there to pick up, maybe."

"Well, she'll be even more *miffed* now won't she." Gavin shook his head, annoyed that they could have lost valuable time or even a valuable contact. "Did she leave a number? Tell me that she left a number."

"Well of course she left a number." A scrap of paper torn from the corner of a newspaper passed between them; an almost illegible series of numbers was scratched upon its flimsy surface like a coded message in some fifties gangster flick. "It's all I had to hand." Simon protested, as Gavin shot him a barbed look that could have split his lip. "It was that or nothing, I didn't want to miss it and at least I haven't lost it."

"It's a good job that one of us is taking this seriously Si, because if this whole move had been left to you, God knows where we'd be."

It could have turned into a full-blown argument, but neither of them had the energy for it, least of all Gavin, whose only concern now was to get in touch with the former lady of their house, and to hear her story, though his intuition was already telling him that her tale might not be for the faint hearted.

The morning could not come soon enough.

Friday 12th February 2021

326 DAYS SINCE START OF UK LOCKDOWN

546 deaths reported in the UK – the total number of deaths due to COVID19 now stands at 121,836 with 3,608,876 people testing positive for the disease.

CHAPTER 31

Charlotte Mountford looked every inch the widow.

She was sporting a pair of charcoal jeans and a long black coat with an expensive lamb's wool scarf drawn up around her neck, and the dark glasses, that had become an almost permanent fixture of late, did nothing to mask her tired and pale complexion. It wasn't the season for sunglasses, and though it was bright outside, the temperature was only a couple of degrees above zero, with the windchill doing its level best to take it below freezing. It had been almost a year since her husband had passed. Almost a year since her world had been turned upside down, along with the rest of the world, and now here she was again, back where it had all begun.

As she stepped from her car and stared up at the very house where her beloved husband had met his end, she was surprised at how little it seemed to have changed, at least from the outside. In that moment she didn't feel scared to be back, nor was she in the slightest bit unnerved at the prospect of going back inside; in fact, all that she felt was anger. A simmering hostility in her gut between the life that had been rightfully hers – a bright future with her children and their father – and the one that remained.

"Hello."

As the two men approached, she wasn't sure which one had greeted her, but it didn't really matter; she wasn't planning on staying for long.

"Hi," she said in return. "Which one of you is Simon?"

"That'll be me," said the taller man, raising his hand in a form of salute.

"And I'm Gavin."

"Yes, we spoke on the phone, didn't we? Well, it's very nice to finally meet you both," she said with little sincerity. "I'm sorry that we never met over the sale, but I was in no fit state to see anyone then," though both Gavin and Simon later agreed that any improvement since must have been slight. She clearly didn't enjoy meeting up with anyone these days and it was written all over her pale and unmade face. She clearly no longer cared all that much for how she looked to the outside world.

"I'm sorry about your husband," said Gavin, trying to find the right words to say. "It must have come as a terrible shock."

"It did," said Charlie, still tearing up behind her shades after months of grief. Even after a year, she still found it hard to talk about him. A year of almost continuous confinement due to the pandemic that had done nothing to hasten her recovery. A year in which time's reputation as the ultimate healer had failed to deliver on its much-touted promise.

"Do you want to have a look around?" asked Simon, "you can see what a mess we've made of the place. Might make you glad to be rid of it."

It wasn't one of his most subtle statements and it took Gavin all his resolve to refrain from elbowing him in his side. "You must have been driving for hours, do you want a cup of tea?" said Gavin in an attempt to smooth any frayed relations. "The builders have got a tea making station set-up in there, so I'm sure we can cobble something together."

She conceded to a quick cuppa and as they squeezed their way inside, a couple of cheery tradesmen greeted them on their way to what passed for the kitchen.

"It's starting to take shape," Simon said, genuinely pleased at the visible progress that had now been made. There were still electric cables hanging down everywhere and various hand tools propped up in corners and against

263

walls, but the walls were all plastered now, and the coving and skirting boards were in the process of being fitted. "A couple more months I reckon, and we should be in, I can't wait to be honest, it's been a long wait."

"It looks so different," said Charlie, struggling to locate the spot of her husband's 'accident'. "It's so open now, I can't get my head around it."

"That was what we wanted really," explained Gavin, choosing his words very carefully. "We wanted to stamp our own personalities on the place, make it a bit more of 'us'."

"Well, you've certainly managed that," said Charlie, giving off vibes that the two boys found hard to interpret positively or negatively. Not that it mattered. It wasn't her house anymore, and neither she nor they cared whether their tastes were mutual or not. "Didn't the planning officer object to any of your modernisations – it's Grade II listed after all?"

"Here and there." said Gavin, "but we kept on the right side of them, just. Milk?"

"Yes please," said Charlie, more brightly than she felt, "no sugar."

As Gavin stirred the drinks into life and did his best to shield them from the dust that was still swirling about the place, his partner decided to bring the conversation up to date.

"Gavin said that you had something that you wanted to tell us Mrs Mountford?"

"Please, call me Charlie."

Simon smiled as formalities ceased, but though she smiled briefly back, he couldn't tell if it had reached her eyes and somehow, he doubted that it had. "Was it something to do with the house, your husband maybe?"

"A bit of both really," she said, flustered that she was suddenly the focus of their undivided attention. "You know that he died in here?," she said clearing her throat. "And you know, *how* he died?"

They both nodded, choosing not to elaborate, as if to say more might throw her off her train of thought or cause her to regret her decision to come.

"It didn't stop, with his passing; I thought it would, but it didn't."

Simon looked at Gavin, then at Charlie, and back again to his partner, before motioning for them all to head out into the garden where it was quieter and less atmospheric. Something seemed amiss, standing there in the expanded space, looking at the place where her husband had lost his life. It seemed full of foreboding, like they were standing in the path of an oncoming train, whose brakes were already beginning to screech. "That's better," he said as they reached the garden at the rear, "there's more air out here. Not too cold, is it?"

It wasn't, and though the concern wasn't addressed at Gavin, he joined their visitor in agreeing that it was much better that they were now 'out of there', where they could talk more freely about recent events.

"Something followed me home," said Charlie with a shudder. "It didn't stay here, with the house. It followed me back to London." For a few seconds nothing more was said, and Charlie sensed that her revelations had failed to register with the new owners, so she decided to ram home the point. "It followed us. Like it had hitched a ride somehow, and not for the first time. I think it did it before too, to some of our former guests."

"When you say *something*," Gavin started to say but Simon jumped in.

"You mean whatever was bothering you when you lived here?" he asked her. "The ghost, the poltergeist, whatever it was?"

"Yes," she said on a deep intake of breath. "I know it sounds crazy, but something had changed in this house, since our previous visit. It was always haunted; I think you know that we never tried to hide it. It was in the bumph that we put out and if anyone ever asked us, we always told them straight. If you're scared of things that go bump in the night, then this place is probably not for you, but if you don't mind a few disembodied voices, a creak or two on the stairs and a few things moving about every now and again, you'll probably love it." There was a clear emphasis on the 'probably'.

"Was it ever seen?" asked Gavin, "whatever it was. Did anyone ever report anything?"

She hesitated at the question, as if thinking how best to answer it. "Some people are more *sensitive* to these things, or so they say, and so yes, one or two people claimed to have seen, *something*. But until the last time, not us, not really."

"And what was it?"

"What do you mean?"

"Girl or boy?" asked Simon. "Male or female?"

"It was a woman we think," said Charlie. "Or at least it always used to be, but as I say, the last time we came here it was different. Something had changed and not in a good way. The dog wasn't happy, the vibe was darker. Thicker. You could feel it, like a presence, as if someone else had moved in while we weren't looking."

It was then that she told them about the discovery of the Ouija board and the terrible fate of the family on the motorway, whose name she kept to herself. She told them all about what her children had seen and what she and Tony had experienced on their video call, and she told them about the noises. In fact, she told them most of what she could remember, and it was a lot. But she didn't tell them everything, to be honest, she lacked the strength, and chose instead to put the spotlight back on them.

"Are you scared of it?" she asked bluntly. "Are you scared to move back in?"

Both Gavin and Simon spoke at once, contradicting each other as if it was a well-rehearsed comic routine.

"Yes and no then." smiled Charlie, amused that the two of them were so obviously well matched. "Which is it?"

"A bit of both to be honest with you," said Simon, sensing an opportunity to lighten the mood. "Charlie, you said it had followed you home; what exactly has followed you and do you think it might have followed you back here again?"

This time she did laugh, admitting that she hoped it had and asking out loud if it wouldn't mind staying put now with these nice boys. "The noises, mainly. Sometimes I think I'm imagining it, that I'm just hearing it in my head, but the kids have heard it too. Separate to each other, at different times of the day and night, and that's why I know it's not my imagination and that I'm not just going through a mental breakdown. It's with us, I'm sure of it, but I wish it wasn't, I wish it had stayed put, I really do, I'm sorry." Her laughter turned to tears in that moment as the emotion of telling her tale got the best of her and it all came rushing back. She was done. She had nothing more to say.

"Why don't we bring you up to date then?" said Simon patting her on the shoulder when he'd rather have given her a hug, but COVID protocols reigned supreme. "Give your nerves a rest. It must be hard for you." He motioned to Simon that he should take the lead, which he did, and between the two of them, they told her of their experiences, but by comparison it seemed lame, and so it wasn't long before they decided that to *show* might be better than to *tell*, on this occasion.

"The builders have unearthed a couple of things that you probably didn't know were here," Simon told her, leading them back inside. "Firstly, did you know about the well?"

"A well?" she said intrigued. "Where?"

"Over there," said Gavin, pointing back inside towards the kitchen, and it wasn't long before they were gathered around it like a coven around a cauldron. "It's pretty deep, the conservationist guy from the council thinks it's been here for several hundred years."

"Wow." said Charlie, "we had no idea. We didn't take the floor up in here in the end. What will you do with it?"

"Make it a feature." beamed Gavin. "Put some lights under there and use it as a light tube in reverse. Should be a useful diversion when Simon's droning on to our dinner guests about work."

"But that's not the best bit." said Simon, ignoring the sideswipe and instead, he took up the tale leading her into what was once the lounge, stopping by the recently installed trap door and crouching to lift the lid. "Did you know that there was a hidden room, beneath the fireplace here, one that would seem to have been here for a long time? Maybe since the beginning."

"What?" she cried out eyes wide. "No, I didn't." and she looked suitably shocked as Simon reached for the circular brass handle and pulled hard to heave up the cover and to reveal a small flight of stone steps that led down into the ground.

"After you," he said, motioning for her to make the short descent, but she hesitated and so it was Gavin that took the lead, shuffling his way down into the void with Mrs Mountford in close pursuit. Simon stayed put, there was only room for two in the subterranean cavity and he didn't want to crowd her.

"Is it unlocked?" he heard her ask, to which Gavin made a muffled reply that it was not. Her disappointment was palpable, but it was a leading question that would soon be answered.

"It didn't come with a key unfortunately," Simon said, a little too loudly to travel the short distance down to them, but as they made their way back up to ground level, she said something that neither of them had expected to hear in a million years.

"I think I might have the key."

"What?" said the new owners in sync.

Stunned silence followed, but in that instant, neither of them could quite believe what had just been revealed and as Gavin stood enthralled by her unexpected response, it was Simon that found the words.

"How?" he spluttered, "I mean, how do you know it's the right one?"

"We found a key, behind the fireplace, when we first had the place fixed up," she explained. "An old key, a big chunky thing. It was obviously antique, so we kept it. We assumed that it must have belonged to the house at some point, but just figured that the lock that it had once fitted was long gone."

"Do you know where it is?" asked Gavin, hoping against hope that she had brought it with her.

"Yes," she said with mixed emotions at the prospect. "I know exactly where it is. It's in the bureau at home. When I get back, I'll send it to you, it's of no use to me now is it? May as well have it back where it belongs."

"I can't believe it," said Gavin.

"That's amazing" agreed Simon, "I can hardly wait. I think."

It seemed like the right moment to bring their illegal gathering to an end, but as they made their way back through the house and out into the lane, Simon remembered the one loose end that he wanted to tie up from their earlier conversation.

"The Ouija board session," he prompted, "that you mentioned earlier. Did it come up with anything, do you know? Were there any messages?"

"Well, I can't tell you anything about the family that brought it here, because it certainly wasn't us," she assured them. "And I wish that we had never seen it quite frankly, but we were told about one thing that had happened to some of our guests who used it; five letters that didn't really make any sense, at least not in the order that they were given."

"That's all very cryptic," said Gavin.

"Quite." she agreed, "at first, we didn't get it either and even now I still think that it might just be a tall tale, but if you assume that the letters were given in reverse, then it spelt out 'WITCH'."

Simon looked at Gavin with an expression that said it was no coincidence. Gavin was beaming as if he'd just scratched the foil off a winning lottery ticket. "I knew it." he said, almost punching the air with delight, he was doing a jig on the spot though and that was enough to tell Charlie that her newly imparted tale had ticked somebody's box.

"I've been doing some research into the house," he told her, sensing her confusion. "It would seem that one of the earliest owners of a house on this plot may have had a keen interest in witchcraft, back in the days when being accused of being a witch would get you killed."

"You mean he was a witch?" asked Charlie.

"No, we think he was a witchfinder," said Gavin triumphantly. "Or at least his brother was. A bit like that Matthew Hopkins bloke up in the Fens, but this one was very well connected and keen as mustard on rooting out any local miscreants and bringing them to justice."

"But surely, they weren't really witches, were they?" asked Charlie, unconvinced even after all that she had been through that sorcery, spells, and suchlike, were anything but stuff and nonsense.

A loud bang from beneath their feet begged to differ, as if a subterranean door had been slammed, but they could see that the one they knew of was still firmly secured.

"We don't know" said Simon, not for the first time choosing to ignore the intrusion on their conversation. It wouldn't be the last either, but he knew that what he'd just heard had shaken the ground beneath their feet and whilst the bottles had been removed for safekeeping, he thought he could still hear them rattling all the same. "But if you can get us that key, maybe we'll be able to find out and maybe then, whatever has attached itself to your family, might be ready to let go?"

It was only a hunch, but it seemed a good one, and Charlie couldn't wait to test it out.

SUNDAY 14TH FEBRUARY 2021

328 DAYS SINCE START OF UK LOCKDOWN

520 deaths reported in the UK – the total number of deaths due to COVID19 now stands at 122,868 with 3,624,681 people testing positive for the disease.

CHAPTER 32

It was Valentine's Day, but neither of them felt much like celebrating.

Gavin had hoped to spend the day obsessing over his research project, but after visiting the local clinic in the morning - where he joined the ranks of the 'fully vaccinated' - he found that he just couldn't settle to it. His thoughts kept on drifting back to the cell door and the tantalising prospect that they might soon be able to step inside. It was proving to be a strange feeling and not an altogether welcome one, as the prospect of breaking-and-entering - even with the original key in hand - felt like an invasion of privacy.

He hadn't shared these feelings with Simon, but by the time the delivery man finally rapped on the door, it was already well after noon, and he was already feeling groggy from the after-effects of the jab. Despite his flu-like symptoms, it was Gavin that jumped up from the sofa to accept the small parcel and like an excited child on Christmas morning, he simply couldn't wait to open it.

"It doesn't look much does it, Gav?" said Simon, as the two of them sat staring at the pencil length metal object on the table.

"Doesn't look that old either." said Gavin, wondering to himself if there had been some mistake. "There's only one way to find out though isn't there?"

It was fast approaching one o'clock and the light outside was already beginning to lose some of its lustre, but as much as Gavin wanted to get right to it, it was Simon that put on the brakes.

"I've got to finish that report," Simon said, refusing to contemplate heading over to the house for at least another couple of hours. "They're expecting it today. There's a meeting tomorrow and the big boss wants to share this with the world, so I must get it over to her by four at the latest. After that, I'm all yours."

"Yeh, where have I heard that before?" said Gavin, more than a little disappointed to have to defer what they had already christened as *'the grand opening'*. He was on tenterhooks and the thought of any further delay only added to his growing sense of agitation. He wanted to open it. He needed to open it.

"Anyway, didn't that planning guy say that we had to wait on them before we opened it?"

"Yes." Gavin snapped back, "but imagine what idiots we'd look if we dragged them all the way out here only to find that it was the wrong key. Surely, we have to try it ourselves first, just to be sure. After all, it belongs to us now, doesn't it?"

It was then that an idea came to him, a spark out of nowhere and the more he turned it over in his head, the more he liked it and the more he liked it, the more convinced he became that it might just turn out to be one of his best ever. Fluey feelings or not, in that instant his mind was made up.

"What are you grinning at?" said Simon, bemused by his partner's sudden upturn in mood. "You've been like a bear with a sore head all morning, now you look like the cat that's got the cream. What is it?"

"Nothing." lied Gavin, but the glint in his eye told a different story. He was planning something, but he wasn't about to lose the element of surprise. "Rendezvous at five pm, the house, and don't be late."

"Oh no, what are you cooking up now?" groaned Simon, convinced that it wasn't going to be to his liking.

"Never mind, it's gonna be great." said Gavin, "just be there, on the dot, not a second later, or you'll spoil it."

Ten minutes later and Gavin was gone, slamming the door to their rental property firmly behind him as he stepped out into the mid-afternoon air, his mind set, and his fears banished, at least for a few hours more.

※

So now Gavin found himself with a couple of hours to kill and some headspace to think through all that he had learned so far about the cottage and its chequered past. He hadn't noticed it at the time, but since they'd been out from under its thatched roof and claustrophobically low ceilings, the brain fog that so many had begun to report feeling since the onset of the pandemic had lifted and so, whilst Simon filled his days with tedious analysis, he had been free to plunder the riches of the internet.

What he had found was a veritable treasure trove of long forgotten documents and whilst not all were yet digitised, it made for a very pleasing and very long TBR list. From what was available to read immediately, it became quickly apparent that their newly adopted county had seen more than its fair share of witchcraft depositions and indictments during the second half of the seventeenth century.

Most of the documented cases seem to have fallen to the north, in the villages surrounding Frome and Shepton Mallett, but Wincanton and Brewham, as well as the smattering of tiny hamlets on the borders with Dorset had not been immune to the craze that pitted neighbour against neighbour and tore families asunder. The more he'd read, the more he found himself immersed in the whole dreadful business that defied rational explanation, at least by twenty-first century standards.

It was a time of religious strife, as the rise of Protestantism challenged the very fabric of the English order. The Jacobite King James had returned the State to a Catholic footing at the start of the century, only to find itself pitched into a bloody civil war just a few decades later. However, Cromwell's short-lived Protectorate didn't last, and as the Restoration of the mid 1660s hailed the arrival of yet another Catholic monarch in Charles II, an avalanche of dissenting voices would continue to shake the foundations of church and state. Added to that, the ever-present threat of an unforgiving plague and Gavin found himself beginning to understand why people had been on the lookout for a scapegoat. Someone had to shoulder the blame for all the upheaval and uncertainty and in a period that had seen so much death and destruction, the populous could be forgiven for thinking that the Devil himself was at large throughout the sleepy shires of England.

The National Archives at Kew remained closed to visitors and so any desire that Gavin may have had to see any original documents was quashed before he'd even begun. Instead, he'd had to make do with secondary sources and the results of other people's academic research, most of which he was pleased to say was free to view online.

That Robert Hunt had played a more than significant part in the examinations and trials of accused witches in the villages and hamlets of Somerset seemed an undeniable truth, as various documents attested, some even written by his own hand. The full extent of his involvement was, however, something of a grey area with various commentators unsure of just how far his interventions went, or if he was merely responding to local disturbances reported by townspeople and villagers across the counties of his circuit.

Did he simply fan the flames of the devilish outcry, or did he start the fires himself? From the surviving record it was hard to say one way or another.

What was clear though was that he was sympathetic to such evil claims and, as has been the defence of hundreds of officials over the centuries when accused of unjust dealings, he may have wanted to be seen to be 'doing his job' as a leading local magistrate and Justice of the Peace.

Whether from his family seat in Compton Pauncefoot or his parliamentary office in Westminster, the much-travelled and one-time Member-of-Parliament for Illchester, would have been acting on leads provided by informants and dealing with cases as they came before him at the Quarter Sessions. If upheld, they would then be referred to the higher Assizes court, which were required to hear the most serious cases of which accusations of witchcraft was seen to be one of the most heinous.

That much of those records had been lost to history following a night raid by the German Luftwaffe over Exeter during World War Two, left Gavin clutching at straws for an answer to the question that now vexed him most of all. What was left for future generations was a tantalising glimpse into a handful of cases that had come before the courts in the second half of the seventeenth century, all of which were most certainly presided over by the venerable Robert Hunt, whose own daughter had been the subject of a witch's ire.

According to one surviving document, written in his own hand and recently digitised for a new virtual audience, Gavin was stunned to read of a strange incident recorded for posterity in a letter from Robert Hunt to his brother-in-law William Bull in December of 1667:

> *"My daughter Brodrepp I thanke God came hither well on Saturday after the three weekes or more, greate torments shee had indured, one whiles in her throate, another tyme at her hearte, some tymes in her belly and at other tymes in her backe. Such strange paines as if shee was thrust with nayles or needles, and at two of the clocke*

every morninge the torment enforced her to ryse and found noe ease in any place. On Sunday last, at about two of the clock, she had a violent fitt and some tyme dead and about four of the clocke shee was assaulted more violently: her eyes stretcht and swollen out her teeth clencht, her lipps open, her chin gatherd upp like a button, her hands and armes turned backwards, and leggs and arms soe stiff and distorted that they could not bee bowed. For an hower shee remayned as dead, and lookt most gastly, but in this fit she groaned only once, 'Alice Knight has made mee giddy.' upon this they sent for Alice Knight whoe, thoe very unwillinge, yet came to the house but when she came neare the house she fell a trembling as soone as she came in she prest to see my daughter and the childe, but instead of that, they after much adoe, drewe some bloud from her arme by a bramble and then made her kneele and pray that neyther the divell nor any of his instruments might doe her any more hurte, but this she was unwillinge to do, but at last did. As soone as the bloud came, my daughter had ease, and fell into a fyne sleepe and ever since has beene in ease and welle I thanke God. In her pillow several Knackes were found, made upp in feathers and bound with red silke. I have three of them hear two they burned. This Alice Knight, my daughter never suspected her, nor had seene her in three quarters of a year.

Reading the transcript in the afternoon light of a twenty first century winter, the burden of proof seemed flimsy at best, and though Gavin did his best to track down the fate of the accused Alice, the verdict remained lost in the mists of time. The evidence – if indeed that's what it was - seemed circumstantial at best, some might say construed and if that was 'all they had on her' - as today's crime novelists would no doubt put it - he was convinced that she should have walked free, though he feared that she had not.

The fact that Robert Hunt had been open to the idea that his own daughter had been attacked by demonic powers, was proof enough for Gavin that he'd been in it up to his neck. Whether for reasons of personal gain or political influence, there was no way of knowing either way, but the contents of this handwritten letter in itself demonstrated that the magistrate believed in witchcraft. Consequently, would not all such cases have been favourably received at his hearing and so, in all likelihood, would have been referred to the Assizes, where he himself would have sat in judgment over the fate of many an innocent victim, including the poor unfortunate Alice Knight.

Whatever Hunt's motivations were, one final tantalising glimpse was offered up more than once from the depths of the digital archives, but it wasn't until the afternoon light was beginning to fade, that Gavin had been able to track down the source.

Less than half a century after Hunt's exploits, a literary scholar had put pen to paper in *'an historical essay concerning witchcraft'* that was published in 1718, and who, Gavin figured, may have had access to information long since lost to us. In his tract, Francis Hutchinson stated that Robert Hunt's *"searches and discoveries were opposed and checked by a higher authority, by which means the poor people were saved and the consequence was that the country was quiet."*

As hard as Gavin might try, he failed in his efforts that afternoon to track down the identity of this 'higher authority', and so with the afternoon almost at an end, he was forced to call it a day, and instead to focus his attentions fully on his plans for the evening ahead.

CHAPTER 33

Gavin had found the candles in one of their carefully packed-up boxes, one of the few that they'd brought with them and one that had almost been sent into storage with the rest of their belongings. He'd had a feeling that they might come in handy, and so he knew exactly where to find them once the idea had come into his head.

A candlelit dinner for two, amongst the clutter and the dust, surrounded by bare plaster walls and unfurnished floors; it was somehow too good an opportunity to miss. He thought it would be a hoot and he was certain that Si would love it. The last year had been a drag and both of them had agreed that the continued restrictions on public places including restaurants and pubs, was an expensive price to pay, just to avoid a debilitating bug.

Of course, the electricity supply was still turned off, and so he wasn't about to prepare a five-course feast, but the local fish and chip shop had been doing a roaring trade throughout the pandemic and the two of them had yet to savour its delights.

In the refurbished conservatory, he positioned two trestle benches four feet apart and using some leftover hardwood that was being used to create their shelving, he set up a makeshift table at just the right height. Four discarded milk crates – that the builders had been using as improvised steps – made perfectly decent perches once he'd kicked them into place on opposing sides and placed on top of one another. Then he placed the six tapered candles into their holders and spread them out like the dots on some dice, before standing back to admire his handiwork.

The temperature had fallen since the onset of darkness and though the drizzle continued to tap out a tune on the conservatory roof, everything was just as he'd imagined it. He'd placed his order to collect at five-thirty and was delighted to find that it was ready right on time – *'cod and chips twice with a pickled onion and a large portion of mushy peas'*. Somehow it seemed highly appropriate for the setting – a dinner fit for a construction site - and as he rushed back from the chippy to make ready for his husband's arrival, he couldn't help congratulating himself on his ingenuity.

It would be a night to remember, one way or another, he was sure of it.

Simon arrived right on cue and followed the lights to the back of the house, clapping his hands together in delight when he saw what Gavin had done.

"That's brilliant mate." he roared, "you silly bugger."

"C'mon then, it's getting cold." ushered Gavin, showing his partner and best friend to his seat like a waiter in an expensive West End restaurant. "Would sir like to try the wine?" he asked, revealing a bottle of their favourite red from behind his back like a music hall conjuror in days of old.

"No, just pour me a large one, and be quick about it you fool." ordered Simon, already chomping on a hot chip, and dunking the remaining half in his peas, before devouring another.

"Did you get your report finished?"

"Yep, all done." said Simon. "Have you tried the key?"

"No of course not." said Gavin, "I wanted to wait for you."

"You mean you're scared?" teased Simon.

"Not at all," lied Gavin. "Just wanted to share the moment that's all. You know what they say, *'a terror shared is a terror halved'.*"

"That's a new one on me, I have to say," scoffed Simon, as he tucked into a large piece of battered cod like he hadn't eaten for a month. "This is delicious." he said, jabbing his fork at his take-away meal with one hand, whilst picking up another chip with the other. "I have to say Gav, you do have some madcap ideas from time to time, but this is one of your best," and he raised his glass in salute before necking half of its contents.

A breath of wind shuddered through the tidy array of candles, each flickering light sending a shadow dancing across the jagged profile of reflective clutter that had been left leaning this way and that around the room. They settled almost at once as if in sync, like a dance troupe or a well-choreographed ballet, in time with unheard music.

For a moment or two they sat in silence, chowing down their dinner in the semi-darkness, and watching like hawks as more dark shadows swayed in the garden outside. Somewhere upstairs, a floorboard creaked as the house settled into its new dimensions, which made Gavin think of a snake, shedding its skin, or a shape-shifting tadpole destined for bigger things.

"You know that pamphlet that Dot dropped off this week?" asked Gavin, deciding in that instant to take advantage of the moment by enlightening his husband on another bit of research. "The one by the Puritan minister. The one that was intended for Tony Mountford, but which never made it in time."

"Oh yes," said Simon, his facial expression eventually moving from one of *'what the hell are you talking about?'* to *'sorry, I forgot all about that.'*. "What of it?"

"Well, I finally got around to reading it and once I got into it – it's obviously written in an earlier form of English, like Shakespeare - it was, how should I put it, quite revealing."

"In what way?"

"Well, you know that it was written by a Puritan minister that lived around here somewhere?"

"Yes," said Simon, remembering what Dot had told them, having passed on the knowledge that she had been entrusted with by the now late Mr Humphreys. "Batcombe, wasn't it?"

"Yeh. Well, it was addressed to the Western Circuit magistrates, not to Robert Hunt, but to his predecessors in 1627," Gavin explained, a clear edge of excitement in his voice. "But it was used for years afterwards apparently, and according to what I've read, would have been applied by Hunt and the others in all of their dealings with witchcraft cases whenever and wherever they came up."

"Hence the title?" asked Simon for confirmation, munching on another chip. "A Guide to Grand Jury Men. So, what's so interesting about it then?"

"It really is a guide, but it starts off trying to disprove witchcraft by warning the judges to be careful of people who might be trying to pull the wool over their eyes."

"Oh." said Simon, "who would want to do that then?"

"People who have a grudge against those that they accuse I suppose?" said Gavin. "Spiteful people, family feuds, arguments between neighbours over land or animals. Protestants and Catholics, that kind of thing. But it goes on to point out that bad things happen to people, that don't necessarily involve witches or need to have a diabolical cause."

"Like, 'shit happens'?" asked Gavin with a smirk. "How very forward thinking."

"And as you might expect, it's very heavy on Bible verses. In fact, it's positively littered with them, at every turn, sometimes every paragraph, it draws its proofs from the Bible, both Old and New Testament, but the reader is left in no doubt whatsoever as to the existence of witches and in fact it concludes that to claim that witchcraft does not exist is heresy in itself."

Gavin pulled out his notebook and proceeded to read verbatim from his scribblings, the same words that the late Tony Mountford had heard in that very house, almost a year earlier:

"*'That there are witches.'* – that's the heading to Chapter 1 of the 2nd Book – *'Though some have gone about to prove that there are no witches: yet the contrary tenant is undeniably true, that there are witches'*, and he goes on to quote chapter and verse from the Bible to prove his point, beyond all reasonable doubt."

"Okay," said Simon, already starting to tire of the recital. "So, they were all convinced then, if only to save their own skins, what's it all got to do with our predicament?"

"Hang on, don't get all tetchy about it." Gavin cautioned, "I'm getting to that bit. In Chapter 2, which is entitled, *'what kinds and sorts of persons they bee which are most apt to become witches'*, and this is where I almost fell off my chair. Though he acknowledges that men can indeed also be in league with Lucifer, he says that *'witches there bee commonly more women than men'* again drawing his evidence from Bible verses including Adam and Eve, from 'experience', from 'stories and relations' – citing the Pendle witches as an example which he does a lot – and, and here's the best one because, 'they are commonly impatient and more superstitious, and being displeased, more malicious and so more apt to bitter cursing and far more revengeful than men and so herein more fit instruments of the Devil.'"

"That's astonishing." gasped Simon, "so he's providing a reason to accuse women – half of the population – of being witches, just because they are women?"

"There's more where that came from." said Gavin, delighted that his words were having the desired effect. "*They are more tongue ripe and less able to hide what they know from others, and therefore in this respect, are more ready to be teachers of witchcraft to others … and lastly, because where they think they can command, they are more proud in their rule and more busie in setting suche on worke whom they may command, then men. And therefore, the Devil laboureth most to make them witches.*"

"So, he's saying that because they are bossier when put in charge of things that the Devil prefers women over men as they are more likely to do his bidding and to force others to do the same?" asked Simon, checking his understanding.

"That's about the long and short of it, yes."

"What else does he have to say on the subject?" asked Simon, his interest finally piqued by the clear injustice of it all.

"Well, the Catholics don't come out of it that well either." admitted Gavin. "He calls them '*papists*' and says that they are '*superstitious and idolatrous*' and so more likely to fall foul of the Devil."

"Okay, so Catholic women would have been in big trouble then."

"You'd have thought so." said Gavin in full agreement. "And if you were poor as well then you really were fair game – listen to this. '*Of this sort are men, but very many women, younger and older, but almost all very miserably poore, the basest sort of people, both in birth and breeding*'. He claims that there are good witches as well as bad ones, but that these 'white' witches, or 'cunning folk' – healers by another name

– are just as bad as the bad ones, as the Bible did not distinguish between them and so should also be condemned to death".

"And on the basis of this book, the magistrates were asked to decide who was guilty and who was innocent?" Simon had stopped eating by this point, his mouth open in astonishment and his heart beating a little faster than before. "Unbelievable. Religion has a lot to answer for if you ask me."

"Correct." said Gavin, "and in the later chapters, he provides them with a long list of instructions on things to look out for in their *'examinations'*, so that when trying a witch and sentencing them to hang, they could do so with a clear conscience."

"What sort of things?"

"It's a very long list, but I made note of a few," said Gavin, and he started to reel them off, stopping only when his partner indicated that he'd heard enough for one sitting. "Cursing – that's you condemned for one – confessing to it, asking after the sick person, being named by the sick person, being seen by the sick person, being named by neighbours and relatives of the sick person, being named by another witch, having a witches mark about their person."

"But all of those are circumstantial or even contrived," said Simon, shocked by the apparent ease of conviction needed to send a person to the gallows for the crime of witchcraft. "How could it have been so easy?"

"Well according to Richard Bernard there was only one proof needed to convict," said Gavin quoting again from the original source that Hunt and every other magistrate on the Western Circuit had at his disposal; "and that was *'to prove a league made with the Devil. In this only act standeth the very reality of a witch;*

without which neither she nor he are not to be condemned for witches. Without this league they be free.'"

"Which begs the question," said Simon, "how on earth was it proven that the accused was in league with Lucifer? Don't tell me, Bernard had the answer to that little conundrum too."

"Of course, he did," said Gavin, rifling through his notes. "In spades ... Listen. *'this is the principal point to be inquired after in all enquires; this must be only aimed at; all presumptions must tend to prove this, and to discover this league; without which no word, no touching, no breathing, no giving, nor receiving are of force to bewitch any. If this be not proved, all the strange fits, apparitions, naming of the suspected in trances, sudden falling downe at the sight of the suspected, the ease which some receive when the suspected are executed, be no good grounds for to judge them guiltie of witchcraft'."*

"And yet," said Simon sadly, "so many were convicted and hanged. So how could it have been so easy, if this Bernard fella in his pamphlet claimed it was so hard?"

"I suspect because he spelled out exactly what to look for and the evidence required in order to bring a conviction under the law and guess what?" Gavin asked, not waiting for an answer. "The appointed magistrates of this 'green and pleasant land' of ours duly obliged, at least those of the Western Circuit whose crimes against humanity are now largely forgotten."

"Tell me." said Simon, now fully engrossed in the gruesome tale.

"Supposedly, they always had a familiar spirit, at least that's what Bernard says," said Gavin. "Like a toad, a cat, anything really, but always an animal, but that's only the start. They also have a witches' mark, and this is where it gets weird, because they really believed that the familiar would suckle on their blood wherever this mark was found. The Guide instructs the Jurymen to *'search diligently for it in every place, and lest one be deceived by a natural mark ... this is insensible, and being pricked will not bleede'."*

"So let me guess then." said Simon, his anger rising. "These supposed Godly men spent their time inspecting every crack and crevice of the female form in search of these 'marks' and then on finding them, they stuck pins in them to see if they a) hurt or b) bled. And what were these marks supposed to look like? Bloody perverts."

"Here, I've got that too, hang on" said Gavin, scrutinising his notes in the candlelight. "*It's sometimes like a little teate; sometimes but a blewish spot, sometimes red spots like a fleabiting, sometimes the flesh is sunken in and hollow'.*"

"How very handy then." scoffed Simon, "these marks could take just about any form and be found just about anywhere?"

"Exactly," said Gavin sadly, "but do you know what I found most disturbing of all? More than the fact that men were granted sole rights to examine the witches and to determine their fate, more than all the circumstantial and uncorroborated evidence on which they were instructed to rely, if no confession was forthcoming then two further steps were open to these learned men."

"Go on."

"Firstly," said Gavin, reading from his hastily assembled notes. "*'And whether she can be brought to shed teares or no; for it is avouched by learned men, upon experience in many trials of witches, that a witch indeede, will hardly or never shed a teare, except God worke the grace of true repentance, which will appear by a free confession'.*"

"So, if she confesses to being a witch, only then will her anguished tears count in her favour?"

"So, it would seem," said Gavin, but he wasn't yet done. "And *'if none of these will work to bring them to confesse, then such as have authority to examine should begin to use sharp speeches and to threaten them with imprisonment and death. And if the presumptions be strong, then if the Law will permit, to use torture or to make a show thereof at least, to make them confesse'*."

A silence fell between them at that, as each of them let the full meaning of what they had just read and heard settle into their consciousness. It needed no further explanation, but Simon could not resist having a go at making sense of the indefensible. "So if our innocent victims, who we can assume were holed up in our own house four hundred years ago, could not be proven to be witches through their words or deeds, through the accusations of others or at the hand of other convicted witches, or if no witnesses could be found to prove that they were in league with the Devil, then simply through the threat of torture or their refusal to confess, they could be convicted as a proven witch and hanged by the neck until they were dead."

"And all in the name of God." sighed Gavin, almost moved to tears himself. "And we have the official handbook to prove it. A manual for murder."

"I think I've eaten my fill already" said Simon, screwing up the greasy chip papers into the carrier bag and tying its plastic handles into a knot, before lobbing the resulting ball into the builders' open dustbin like a basketball.

"Shot." said Gavin, slow clapping the expertly executed basket in mock approval. He then took their newly acquired key from his pocket and ushered them towards the task at hand. "Shall we?" he asked somewhat ominously, rehearsing its rotation in an imaginary lock, so that the candlelight caught on its edges in a dull glint of rusted metal.

Gavin had had the foresight to bring a heavy-duty rubber torch with him, but Simon simply swiped up on his phone to activate its torch feature, and after extinguishing the candles in a single breath, as if it was the culmination of a six-year old's birthday party, they made their way towards the trap door and an experience that neither of them would forget in a hurry.

There was no need to lift the trap, it was already standing open.

"Did we leave that open yesterday?" asked Gavin, fully doubting that they had. "I could have sworn it was closed when we came in."

"I can't remember," said Simon, "I really can't say, and it was too dark to see when I came in. Tell you what, let's just agree that we did, there's a good chap."

"Good idea," agreed Gavin not wanting to spook themselves before the main event had begun, as they began their descent with Gavin in the lead and Simon in tow. "This torch is brilliant," he said, happy to have something to say. "It's so powerful, I don't think we need yours as well, do we?"

"Probably not," answered his unusually nervous partner-in-crime, "but I'll keep it on, just in case."

"Just in case of what?"

"In case you drop yours, or it goes out," jabbered Simon. "I don't know, I just feel better with it on that's all. Now let's just get on with this shall we, why did we have to do this in the dark anyway?"

"Dunno, but maybe we should have informed the planning office after all?" said Gavin, losing his nerve as the darkness deepened around them."

Simon gave a nonchalant shrug and wriggled the key into the large and rusted lock plate. "Too late for that now," and he turned his wrist to the left, expecting the spring-loaded mechanism to break, but when a loud and satisfying click told him that the lock had immediately released, he could hardly believe their luck. He left the key where it was and pulled on the wrought iron handle, testing it to see what give there was and then pulling harder as he sensed movement; but at first it didn't budge.

"What's wrong?" asked Gavin with a nervous glance to his rear. "Is it stuck?"

"A bit" said Simon, "but I think it'll come if I give it a really good yank. Stand back a bit, I don't want to land on top of you. I don't want to have to call an ambulance and be left to explain all this to some green gilled paramedic." He readied his stance, placing his sturdy boots a couple of feet apart and flexed his knees, placing both hands on the cast iron handle, as Simon placed his on his partner's back, just in case the door gave more easily than either of them were expecting.

It didn't, but it did move a little with the first tug, then it moved another few inches with the second and finally, on the third pull, it opened enough to allow them to get inside, though neither of them rushed forward into the shadows. Instead, Gavin reached out, holding the torch in front of him like a sword or a light sabre, pointing it into every corner and edging forward beyond the threshold. Then he peered inside, checking for spiders as much as anything else, but there was not a cobweb in sight; the small space was devoid of all life, as it had been for centuries. It was empty. Almost empty.

"Anything?" asked Simon, his view obstructed.

"Yes," answered Gavin, "but I'm not sure what it is," and with one surge of adrenalin he stepped inside, as if a moment longer spent thinking about it would have sent him running in the opposite direction. "It's a chest, it was underneath the chair. An old one, by the look of things," and he reached down to pick it up, blowing the dust of ages from its plain concave top. "But it is a chest, that's for sure."

Then all the lights went out.

CHAPTER 34

Back at their temporary residence they tried to rationalise what had just happened to them. They had made what could only be described as a 'mad dash' from the cell, scrambling their way up the stone steps in the pitch-black side-by-side and hauling each other through the trapdoor, from where they had bolted as if the Devil himself was on their heels. Each of them had fallen at different times, tripping over random items on the uneven surface only to be pulled back up by the other before snatching at the front door and clawing their way out of there. They hadn't stopped there either; in fact, they hadn't stopped running until they were back in their rented accommodation, and it was only then that they felt able to breathe more easily.

The whole scene would have seemed quite comical to an unwary passer-by, but no one else was there to witness their race up the lane to the village centre, and so they were hopeful that they'd got away with it, their reputations as fearless entrepreneurs still intact.

"How could both of our batteries have been drained in exactly the same moment, Gav?" panted Simon, not expecting his partner to have the answer, but asking him anyway. "That's just not possible. Something must have been feeding off the power, mine was fully charged when I arrived, it can't have gone down that quickly. Can it?"

"No, I put new ones in the torch before I went over there this afternoon," said Gavin, his heart beating hard in his chest. "Big chunky C-types, three of them. It was fine too, until I picked this up." He was cradling the metal casket in his lap, still unopened, its unsecured and rusted clasp still in place.

"We gonna take a look inside?" asked Simon, "it's what we went down there for isn't it? We were hoping to find something weren't we, and that is most definitely *something*."

Of that there was no doubt. It was expertly crafted. Metal plates on each side, riveted together with crusted metal bands around each edge and across the top, an indecipherable inscription was scratched into a dull tin plate. It wasn't particularly deep, but it was wider than a conventional casket, one that might have been used for jewellery or other valuables.

It was intriguing. It was inviting.

"Do you think we'll be able to read it when it's been cleaned up a bit?" asked Simon, picturing the surface of old limestone markers in the nearby churchyard whose testimonies had all too often crumbled into dust making them illegible to all but the most experienced taphophile.

"I'm not sure, the plate is well worn, looks like it might fade even more if we rub it too hard." said Gavin, putting paid to Simon's upbeat outlook. "Shall I open it then?"

"Too right." said Simon, "Get on with it, the suspense is killing me. If you don't open it soon, I'm gonna do it for you."

"What if there's something awful in there?"

"Like what?"

"I don't know," said Gavin, "an old skull or something?" The look on Simon's face was answer enough. "Okay, okay, I'm opening it."

He prized the clasp away from the body of the box, being extra careful not to break it, and ever so slowly began to lift the lid. What he expected to find, he truly had no idea, but what he did find was certainly unexpected.

"It's a book."

A leather-bound volume stared back up at him, with traces of what was once a plain red surface, but which had since been tarnished by the hands of time. Inlaid on the binding was a stitched pattern of four rectangular frames, one inside the other, and in each corner, a decorative floral pattern was repeated with stunning intricacy.

"Hand stitched, I'd say," said Gavin. "Shall I take it out?"

Simon didn't speak, he just nodded in awe, as Gavin lifted the ancient binding from its casket where it had lain undisturbed for centuries. The smell was familiar; the nostalgic scent of old books, a musty reminder of hours spent rifling through reams of academic research, or simply seeking an escape into another world from the mundane and daily grind of this one.

"The spine is incredible." remarked Gavin turning the volume gently in his hands. It was horizontally ribbed along its length in five separate places and in between the book was bowed, its colour draining from red to black even in the full glow of their LED floor lamp.

"It's a Bible, isn't it?" said Gavin knowing full what it was, "and an old one at that."

"Got to be a King James," said Simon, "but from when? Open it, it must say somewhere?"

Gently Gavin turned back the front cover, the metal clasps on either end audibly objecting as he did so, as an ornately laid out title page was revealed, painstakingly decorated with pivotal scenes from the four gospels.

"Newly translated out of the original Greek and with the former translations diligently compared and reissued by his Majesty's special commandment," read Gavin aloud. "This is incredible Si," but he couldn't help reading more. "Imprinted in London by Robert Barker and John Bill, printers to the King's Most Excellent Majesty. M.DC.XX."

"M.DC.XX" repeated Simon, that's hang on, 1620, bloody hell, that's 1620. That's four hundred years ago."

Gavin turned another page and gasped when he saw that something was handwritten on its surface in swirling black ink.

quia frater meus interfectorem maleficarum - RH

"What does that say?" said Gavin, squinting at the page, "I need my glasses to read that properly, but I think it's Latin. How's your Latin Si?"

"Appropriately rusty." he admitted, having last been in a Latin class in the 1970's. "Hang on, let me type that into my phone, there's a translation app that I sometimes use for my courses, just a minute." He tapped away, providing a running commentary as he typed. "q-u-i-a f-r-a-t-e-r, this app is really good, I sometimes spot-check the translations that I get from these agencies just to check that they know what they're doing. a-r-u-m. Finished."

He clicked on the translate button and waited a second for it to process, and once it had finally finished, he almost dropped his phone in shock.

"What does is say Simon?"

"It says," but he was forced to stop, just to clear his throat.

"It says, *'for my brother, killer of witches'*" and then for clarity, "or it could be 'because my brother is a slayer of witches', but let's not split hairs."

It wasn't quite silent in their small sitting room, but the clock on the wall suddenly seemed very loud indeed. It was the only sound. A strange scent of sulphur had permeated the room and it wasn't down to nerves. It was coming from the box, or from the book; or from both.

"And it's signed, RH" added Gavin.

"RH?" Simon had seemingly forgotten already, so Gavin didn't hesitate to remind him, and though it was still a question that needed answering beyond all reasonable doubt, it seemed too much of a coincidence to be anything else.

"Robert Hunt?" said Gavin with a shrug. "Perhaps, or is that too neat? It can't be that easy, can it?"

Outside it had started to rain.

"You said that Hunt was stopped, what was it again, by a higher authority?"

"Yes," said Gavin, remembering the reference that he'd found online.

"What did that mean exactly?" asked Simon, giving it due attention for the first time. "A higher legal authority or did he mean something more, spiritual?"

"I don't know. I didn't read it like that." admitted Gavin. "What are you getting at though? Do you mean that he was stopped in his tracks by divine intervention, like Saul before he became Paul?"

"No, nothing so dramatic." said Simon disparagingly. "Hunt died in 1680 or thereabouts, so did that fella simply mean that the magistrate was stopped in his tracks by nothing more than his own untimely death?"

"Oh." said Gavin, for once impressed by his partner's powers of deduction. "Maybe, I hadn't thought of it like that. No, I was thinking literally, actually. That someone at a higher level of authority, a more senior office or even the King himself decided that enough was enough and put a stop to his apparent one-man crusade. I'll keep digging – see what else I can find, but I reckon we're on the right track, don't you?"

Simon nodded, deep in thought, and for the first time in a while it was not his day job that was on his mind.

Tuesday 16th February 2021

330 DAYS SINCE START OF UK LOCKDOWN

501 deaths reported in the UK – the total number of deaths due to COVID19 now stands at 123,918 with 3,648,904 people testing positive for the disease.

CHAPTER 35

In the days that followed, Gavin returned to the works of Joseph Glanvill, and to his published record of Robert Hunt's lost *book of examinations*, reproduced in its entirety as proof-positive for the existence of witches.

On completing its second reading, with no help from his partner who was again hard at work on a new contract and so in no mood to be interrupted, Gavin was left in no doubt as to the role played by Robert Hunt in what was a fanatical pursuit of witches in the area that they now called home.

He had yet to prove a direct link between the witchfinder's activities and their own property, but the fact that so many of the recorded events had occurred in an inverted triangle of activity, which stretched from Wincanton, just a few miles to the south, to Frome and Shepton Mallett in the north, seemed to be a coincidence too far. Proving it would be an altogether more difficult task, but like so many researchers before him he would come to rely heavily on the same seventeenth century philosopher whose firm belief in witchcraft and the afterlife transcended the centuries that divided them.

Certain that there was something he had missed on their first reading, Gavin settled down with a hot drink and packet of his favourite biscuits and once more began to turn the pages on what - at face value - was nothing more than one man's obsession with the occult. And yet it hailed from a time when such beliefs were widespread, and Gavin felt himself wondering if, during the fast-approaching age of invention, we had been duped by the Devil himself into believing him to be a figment of our own fervent imaginations.

"Go on then." said Simon, unsure that the answer would be to his liking. "What's that you've got there?"

"You want the full title?"

As Simon nodded, Gavin gave a theatrical cough and began.

Extracts from Saducismus Triumphatus, or, Full and plain evidence concerning witches and apparitions, by Joseph Glanvill, late Chaplain in Ordinary to his Majesty and Fellow of the Royal Society – LONDON, printed for A.L. and Sold by Roger Tuckyr at the Golden Leg, the corner of Salisbury Street, in the Strand. MDCC."

"The year 1700?," said Simon, quizzically. "Isn't that too late?"

"It's a retrospective account," said Gavin, "a historical review from the end of the century. Want me to read it out loud?"

"If you must." said Simon, "so long as you don't expect me to do a quiz at the end. And quit with the old English, can you? It does my head in. Just use your super-powers to give me your best guess as to what it would sound like in the 21st century."

Gavin promised that there would be no test, and after reluctantly agreeing to Simon's demand, even though it would sound 'less atmospheric' as a result, Gavin reached for his reading glasses and began his recital.

"RELATION. III. – which I suspect means the first piece of evidence being presented or investigated," explained Gavin. "Which containeth – I mean contains, sorry - the Witchcrafts of Elizabeth Style of Bayford, Widow.

> *1. Exam. Rich. Hill of Stoke Trister, in the County of Somerset Yeoman, being examined upon Oath, Jan. 23. 1664. before Rob. Hunt, Esq one of His Majesties Justices for that County, concerning the bewitching of his Daughter by Eliz. Style, declared, That his Daughter Eliz. Hill, about the Age of 13 Years, had been for about two Months past, taken with very strange fits which have held her an hour, two, three and more; and that in those fits the Child has told her*

Father, the Examinant, and others, that one Eliz. Style of the same Parish appeared to her and is the Person that Torments her. She also in her fits usually tells what Clothes Eliz. Style has on at the time, which the informant and others have seen and found [to be] true.

He says further, that about a Fortnight before Christmas last, he told Style that his Daughter spoke much of her in her fits and did believe that she was bewitched by her. Whereupon Francis White, and Walter, and Robert Thick being present, willed her to complain to the Justice against him for accusing of her. But she having used several put-offs, said she would do worse than fetch a Warrant. After which the Girl grew worse than before, and at the end of a fit she tells the Examinant when she shall have another, which happens accordingly, and affirms, that Style tells her when the next fit shall come. He informs further, that Monday Night after Christmas day about Nine of the Clock, and four or five times since about the same hour of the Night, his Daughter has been more Tormented than before, and that though held in a Chair by four or five People, sometimes six, by the Arms, Legs, and Shoulders, she would rise out of her Chair, and raise her body about three or four foot high. And that after, in her fits, she would have holes made in her Handwrists, Face, Neck, and other parts of her Body, which the Informant and others that saw them conceived to be with Thorns. For they saw Thorns in her Flesh, and some they hooked out. That upon the Childs pointing with her Finger from place to place, the Thorns and Holes immediately appeared to the Informant and others looking on. And as soon as the Child can speak after the fit, she said that Widow Style did prick her with Thorns in those several places, which was horrible Torment, and she seemed to the Informant and others standing by, to be in extreme pain and torture. The Child hath been so tormented and pricked with Thorns for several Nights, at which times the Informant and many other People have seen the flesh rise up in little bunches in which Holes did appear. The Pricking held about a quarter of an hour at a time during each of the four fits, and the Informant hath seen the Child take out some of those Thorns.

"So, wait a minute Gav." interrupted Simon, "that's all a bit heavy, isn't it? Thorns. Are we supposed to believe that?"

"I thought you weren't going to ask any questions." said Gavin, looking over the top of his narrow-framed spectacles, like some schoolteacher from the 1940s.

"Well, I wasn't planning on it Gav. But I wasn't expecting that either was I?"

"Shall I continue?" asked Gavin, and as his partner gave a reluctant nod, he set to work.

The same Rich. Hill Examined Jan. 26. 1664. informs, that when he rode from the Justices house with a Warrant to bring Styles before him, his Horse suddenly sat down on his breech and he could not after ride him, but as soon as he attended to get up, his Horse would sit down paw with his feet before. He said further, that since Styles was Examined before the Justice and made her Confession to him, she had acknowledged to the Informant that she had hurt his Daughter, and that one Anne Bishop, and Alice Duke, did join in bewitching of her.

Taken upon Oath before me, Rob. Hunt.

2. Exam. William Parsons Rector of Stoke Trister, in the County of Somerset, Examined the 26. of Jan. 1664. before Rob. Hunt, Esq concerning the bewitching of Rich. Hill's Daughter said, That on Monday Night after Christmas day then last past, he came into the room when Eliz. Hill was in her fit, many of his Parishioners being present and looking on. He there saw the Child held in a Chair by main force by the People, plunging far beyond the strength of nature, foaming, and catching at her own Arms and Clothes with her Teeth. This fit he conceives held about half an hour. After some time, she pointed with her finger to the left side of her Head, next to her left Arm, and then to her left Hand and where she pointed, he perceived a red spot to arise with a small black [mark] in the midst of it like a small Thorn. She pointed also to her Toes one after another and expressed great sense of Torment. This latter fit he guesses continued about a quarter of an hour, during most or all of which time her stomach seemed to swell, and her head where she seemed to be pricked did so very much. She sat foaming much of the time, and the next day after her fit, she showed the Examinant the places where the Thorns were stuck in, and he saw the Thorns in those places.

Taken upon Oath before me Subscribed,

Rob. Hunt.

William Parsons Rector of Stoke Trister.

3. Exam. Nicholas Lambert of Bayford, in the County of Somerset Yeoman, Examined upon Oath before Rob. Hunt, Esq Jan. 30. 1664. concerning the bewitching of Rich. Hill's Daughter by Elizabeth Style, testified, That Monday after Christmas day last, being with others in the house of Rich. Hill, he saw his Daughter Elizabeth taken very ill, and in fits that were so strong that six Men could not hold her down in a Chair in which she was sat, but that she would raise the Chair up in spite of their utmost force. That in her fits being not able to speak, she would rest her body as one in great Torment, and point with her Finger to her Neck, Head, Hand-wrists, Arms and Toes. And he, with the rest looking on the places to which she pointed, saw suddenly little red spots arise with little black ones in the midst, as if Thorns were stuck in them, but the Child then only pointed without touching her flesh with her Finger.

Taken upon Oath before me

Rob. Hunt.

4. Exam. Richard Vining of Stoke Trister Butcher, Examined Jan. 26. 1664. before Rob. Hunt, Esq concerning the bewitching of his Wife by Eliz. Style, said, That about two or three days before St. James's day three years since or thereabout, his late Wife Agnes fell out with Eliz. Style, and within two or three days after she was taken with a grievous pricking in her Thigh, which pain continued for a long time, till after some – treatment - she was at some ease for three or four weeks. About the Christmas after the mentioned St. James's day, Style came to the Examinants house, and gave Agnes his Wife two Apples, one of them a very fair red Apple, which Style desired her to eat, which she did, and in a few hours was taken ill and worse than ever she had been before. Upon this, the Examinant went to one Mr. Compton, who lived in the Parish of Ditch-Eate, for – treatment - for his Wife. Compton told him he could do her no good, for that she was hurt by a near Neighbour, who would come into his house and up into the Chamber where his Wife was but would go out again without speaking. After Vining came home, being in the Chamber with his Wife, Style came up to them, but went out again without saying a word. Agnes the Wife continued in great pain till Easter Eve following, and then she died. Before her Death her Hip rotted and one of her Eyes swelled out, she declared to him then and at several times before, that she believed Eliz. Style had bewitched her, and that she was the cause of her Death.

Taken upon Oath before me,

Rob. Hunt.

Whilst the Justice was Examining Style at Wincanton, (which is not above a Mile and a half from Stoke Trister) upon the former evidence against her, he observed that, Rich. Vining looked very earnestly upon him. Whereupon he asked Vining if he had anything to say to him. He answered that Style had bewitched his Wife, and

> told the manner how, as is in his deposition related. The Woman Style upon this seemed appalled and concerned, and the Justice saying to her, You have been an old sinner. You deserve little mercy: she replied, I have asked God mercy for it. Mr. Hunt asked her, why then she would continue in such ill courses? she said the Devil tempted her: and then began to make some Confession of his – dealings - with her. Upon this the Justice sent her to the Constables house at Bayford, which is in the Parish of Stoke Trister, (the Constable was one Mr. Gapper) and the next Morning went thither himself, accompanied with two Persons of quality Mr Bull, and Mr Court, now Justices of the Peace in this County.

"Never mind, about this bit" said Gavin, turning a couple of pages at speed, "it all gets a bit repetitive there, hang on, yes here we are."

> 'I left Mr. Hunt, and the other two Gentlemen at the Constables house, where Style was, upon business of further Examination, where she enlarged upon the Confession she had before begun to make, and declared the whole matter at that and two other times after in the particulars that follow.
>
> 5. Exam. Elizabeth Styles her Confession of her Witchcrafts, Jan. 26. and 30. and Feb. 7. 1664. before Rob. Hunt Esq she then confessed, that the Devil about Ten years since, appeared to her in the shape of a handsome Man, and after of a black Dog. That he promised her money, and that she should live gallantly, and have the pleasure of the World for Twelve years, if she would with her Blood sign his Paper, which was to give her Soul to him, and observe his Laws, and that he might suck her Blood. This after four solicitations, the Examinant promised him to do. Upon which he pricked the fourth Finger of her right hand, between the middle and upper joint (where the sign at the Examination remained) and with a drop or two of her Blood, she signed the Paper with an [O]. Upon this the Devil gave her Sixpence and vanished with the Paper.

That since he hath appeared to her in the shape of a Man, and did so on Wednesday seven-night past, but more usually he appears in the likeness of a Dog, and Cat, and a Fly like a Millar, in which last, he usually sucks in the Poll about four of the Clock in the Morning and did so Jan. 27. and that it usually is pain to her to be so sucked. That when she hath a desire to do harm, she calls the Spirit by the name of Robin, to whom when he appears, she uses these words, 'O Satan give me my purpose'. She then tells him what she would have done. And that he should so appear to her, was part of her Contract with him. That about a Month ago he appearing, she desired him to torment one Elizabeth Hill, and to thrust Thorns into her flesh, which he promised to do, and the next time he appeared, he told her he had done it. That a little above a Month since this Examinant, Alice Duke, Anne Bishop, and Mary Penny, met about nine of the Clock in the Night, in the Common near Trister Gate, where they met a Man in black clothes with a little Band, to whom they did Courtesy and due observance, and the Examinant surely believes that this was the Devil. At that time Alice Duke brought a Picture in Wax, which was for Elizabeth Hill. The Man in black took it in his Arms, anointed its forehead, and said, I Baptize thee with this Oil, and used some other words. He was Godfather, and the Examinant and Anne Bishop Godmothers. They called it Elizabeth or Bess. Then the Man in Black, this Examinant, Anne Bishop, and Alice Duke stuck Thorns into several places of the Neck, Handwrists, Fingers, and other parts of the said Picture. After which they had Wine, Cakes, and Roast meat (all brought by the Man in black) which they did eat and drink. They danced and were merry, were bodily there, and in their Clothes.

"Now, whilst I hate to interrupt again." started Simon, looking confused, "but what the hell is going on now? What's a 'poll' for heaven's sake."

"I'm not sure," Gavin admitted, taking off his glasses for a moment to consider it. "It could mean her head I suppose, like a per-capita tax, Poll Tax by another name – you know, a tax on each head or person, but I'm not certain. What else could it mean?"

"Hang on, I'm having a look," said Simon, the Google app already open on his smart phone and his fingers tapping away. "It's not obvious, but it seems like you might be right. In middle English it may have been used to describe the back of the head, or the scalp."

"Satisfied?" asked Gavin, seeking permission to proceed, and with a nod from his partner, he put his glasses back on and was set to continue when he was interrupted once more.

"And what's with all these 'wax' things and 'pictures'? asked Simon, clearly irritated by his lack of understanding. "Do I take it that these are meant to be images of people that the so-called 'witches' want to hurt? Like dolls in voodoo rights?"

"I assume so." answered Gavin, though even he didn't know for sure. "Your guess is as good as mine really, but it seems that way, doesn't it to you?" Simon seemed to agree though he said nothing in reply. "Shall I continue, or have you had enough? Right, listen up then."

> *"She further said that the same persons met again, at or near the same place about a Month since, when Anne Bishop brought a Picture in Wax, which was Baptized John, in like manner as the other was, the Man in black was Godfather, and Alice Duke and this Examinant Godmothers. As soon as it was Baptized, Anne Bishop stuck two Thorns into the Arms of the Picture, which was for one Robert Newman's Child of Wincanton. After they had eaten, drank, danced, and made merry, they departed. That she with Anne Bishop, and Alice Duke met at another time in the Night, in a ground near Marnhul, where also met several other persons. The Devil then also there in the former shape, Baptized a Picture by the name of*

Anne or Rachel Hatcher. The Picture one Durnford's Wife brought, and stuck Thorns in it. Then they also made merry with Wine and Cakes, and so departed. She said, before they are carried to their meetings, they anoint their Foreheads, and Hand-wrists with an Oil the Spirit brings them (which smells raw) and then they are carried in a very short time, using these words as they pass, 'Thout, tout a tout, tout, throughout and about'. And when they go off from their Meetings, they say, 'Rentum Tormentum'. That at their first meeting, the Man in black bids them welcome, and they all make low obeyance to him, and he delivers some Wax Candles like little Torches, which they give back again at parting. When they anoint themselves, they use a long form of words, and when they stick in Thorns into the Picture of any, they would torment they say, 'A Pox on thee, I'll spite thee'. That at every meeting before the Spirit vanishes away, he appoints the next meeting place and time, and at his departure there is a foul smell. At their meeting they have usually Wine or good Beer, Cakes, Meat, or the like. They eat and drink really when they meet in their bodies, dance also and have Music. The Man in black sits at the higher end, and Anne Bishop usually next [to] him. He uses some words before meat, and none after, his voice is audible, but very low. That they are carried sometimes in their Bodies and their Clothes, sometimes without, and as the Examinant thinks their Bodies are sometimes left behind. When only their Spirits are present, yet they know one another.

When they would bewitch Man, Woman or Child, they do it sometimes by a Picture made in Wax, which the Devil formally Baptises. Sometimes they have an Apple, Dish, Spoon, or other thing, from their evil Spirit, which they give the party to whom they would do harm. Upon which they have power to hurt the person that eats or receives it. Sometimes they have power to do mischief by a touch or curse, by these they can mischief Cattle, and by cursing without touching; but neither without the Devils leave. That she hath been at several general meetings in the night at

High Common, and a Common near Motcombe, at a place near Marnhull, and at other places where have met John Combes, John Vining, Richard Dukes, Thomas Bolster, Thomas Dunning, James Bush a lame Man, Rachel King, Richard Lannen, a Woman called Durnford, Alice Duke, Anne Bishop, Mary Penny and Christopher Ellen, all which did obeyance to the Man in black, who was at every one of their meetings. Usually, they have at them some Picture Baptized. The Man in black, sometimes plays on a Pipe or Cittern, and the company dance. At last, the Devil vanishes, and all are carried to their several homes in a short space. At their parting they say, 'A Boy. merry meet, merry part.' That the reason why she caused Elizabeth Hill to be the more tormented was, because her Father had said, she was a Witch. That she has seen Alice Duke's Familiar suck her, in the shape of a Cat, and Anne Bishop's suck her in the shape of a Rat.

That she never heard the name of God or Jesus Christ mentioned at any of their meetings. That Anne Bishop, about five years and a half since, did bring a Picture in Wax to their meeting, which was Baptized by the Man in black, and called Peter. It was for Robert Newman's Child at Wincanton. That some two years ago, she gave two Apples to Agnes Vining, late Wife of Richard Vining, and that she had one of the Apples from the Devil, who then appeared to her and told, That Apples would do Vining's Wives business.

Taken in the presence of several grave and Orthodox Divines before me

Robert Hunt.

6. Exam. William Parsons Rector of Stoke Trister, Examined Feb. 7. 1664. before Rob. Hunt Esq concerning Elizabeth Style's confession, said, That he heard Style before the Justice of Peace, at the time of her Examination confess, as she has done also to the Examinant several times since, that she was in Covenant with the Devil, that she had signed it with her Blood, that she had been with the Devil at several meetings in the night, that at one time of those meetings, there was brought a Picture in blackish Wax, which the Devil in the shape of a Man in blackish Clothes, did Baptize by the name of Eliz. Hill, that she did stick in one Thorn into the Hand-wrists of the Picture, that Alice Duke stuck Thorns into the same, and that Anne Bishop and Mary Penny were present at that meeting with the Devil.

Taken upon Oath before me Subscribed,

Robert Hunt.

William Parsons Rector of Stoke Trister.

This Confession of Styles was free and unforced, without any torturing or watching, drawn from her by a gentle Examination, meeting with the Convictions of a guilty Conscience. She confesses that she desired the Devil to torment Eliz. Hill, by thrusting Thorns into her flesh, which he promised, and said he had done it. That a Picture was Baptized for her the said Elizabeth, and that She, the Familiar, and Alice Duke stuck Thorns into several places of the Neck, Hand-wrists, Fingers, and other parts thereof, which exactly agrees with the strange effects related, concerning the torments the Child suffered, and this mischief she confesses she did, because her Father said she was a Witch. She confesses she gave two Apples to Vining's Wife, one of which she had from the Devil, who said it would do the business, which — matches - also with the Testimony of Vining concerning his Wife.

She confesses further, That the Devil used to suck her in the Poll, about four a Clock in the Morning, in the Form of a Fly like a Millar, concerning which, let us hear Testimony.

7. Exam. Nicholas Lambert Examined again Jan. 26. 1664. before Rob. Hunt Esq concerning what happened after Styles confession, testifies, That Eliz. Style having been Examined before the Justice, made her Confession, and committed to the Officer, the Justice required this Examinant, William Thick and William Read of Bayford to watch her, which they did; and this Informant sitting near Style by the fire, and reading in the Practice of Piety, about Three of the Clock in the Morning, there came from her Head a glistering bright Fly, about an Inch in length, which pitched at first in the Chimney, and then vanished. In less than a quarter of an hour after, there appeared two Flies more of a less size, and another colour, which seemed to strike at the Examinants hand, in which he held his Book but missed it, the one going over, the other under at the same time. He looking steadfastly then on Style, perceived her countenance to change, and to become very black and ghastly, the fire also at the same time changing its colour; whereupon the Examinant, Thick and Read conceiving that her Familiar was then about her, looked to her Poll, and seeing her Hair shake very strangely took it up, and then a Fly like a great Millar flew out from the place, and pitched on the Table-board, and then vanished away. Upon this the Examinant, and the other two persons looking again in Styles Poll, found it very red and like raw Beef. The Examinant asked her what it was that went out of her Poll, she said it was a Butterfly, and asked them why they had not caught it. Lambert said, they could not. I think so too, answered she. A little while after, the Informant and the others looking again into her Poll, found the place to be of its former colour. The Examinant demanding again what the Fly was, she confessed it was her Familiar, and that she felt it tickle in her Poll, and that was the usual time when her Familiar came to her.

Taken upon Oath before me

Robert Hunt.

8. Exam. Eliz. Torwood of Bayford, Examined Feb. 7. 1664. before Rob. Hunt Esq concerning the mark found about Eliz. Style after her Confession, deposes that she together with Catharine White, Mary Day, Mary Bolster, and Bridget Prankard, did a little after Christmas last, search Eliz. Style, and that in her Poll they found a little rising which felt hard like a Kernel of Beef, whereupon they suspecting it to be an ill mark, thrust a Pin into it, and having drawn it out, thrust it in again the second time, leaving it sticking in the flesh for some time, that the other Women might also see it. Notwithstanding which, Style did neither at the first or second time make the least show that she felt anything. But after, when the Constable told her he would thrust in a Pin to the place, and made a show as if he did, O Lord, said she, do you prick me, when no one then touched her.

The Examinant further said that Style has since confessed to her, that her Familiar did use to suck her in the place mentioned, in the shape of a great Millar or Butterfly.

Taken upon Oath before me Rob. Hunt.

"A millar?" asked Simon, "what's a millar?" asked Simon, his concentration clearly on the wane.

"I did look that up," said Gavin, "as I had the same question. It seems that it was what we might called a bluebottle, or a horse fly. A big fat fly, the kind that makes a lot of noise and can give a nasty bite too. There's a lot more where that came from too. They were very thorough it seems, but much of the remainder is a variation on the same theme; other witnesses that more or less corroborate what the others have said."

"Anything that we haven't already heard?"

"Well, the fourth piece of evidence relates the examination and confession of Alice Duke who they call – *"another witch of Styles knot"* – there's nothing like a fair trial is there? That comes from early in 1664. Want to hear it?"

"Go on then." said Simon, "but make it the last, it's too heavy for me."

314

"She confessed that her Familiar doth commonly suck her right Breast about seven at night, in the shape of a little Cat of a dunnish colour, which is as smooth as a Want, and when she is sucked, she is in a kind of a Trance. That she hurt Thomas Garret's Cowes, because he refused to write a Petition for her. That she hurt Thomas Conway, by putting a Dish into his Hand, which Dish she had from the Devil, she gave it him to give his Daughter for good hansel. That she hurt Dorothy the Wife of George Vining, by giving an Iron slate to put into her steeling Box. That being angry with Edith Watts, the Daughter of Edmond Watts for treading on her Foot, she cursed Edith with a Pox on you, and after that touched her, which hath done the said Edith much harm, for which she is sorry. That being provoked by Swanton's first Wife, she did before her death curse her, with a Pox on you, believes she did thereby hurt her, but denies she did bewitch Mr. Swanton's Cattle. She said, That when the Devil does anything for her, she calls for him by the name of Robin, upon which he appears, and when in the shape of a Man, she can hear him speak, but his voice is very low. He promised her when she made her contract with him, that she should want nothing, but ever since she hath wanted all things.

Taken before me

Rob. Hunt.

1. Exam. Thomas Conway of Wincanton, in the County of Somerset, Examined Feb. 12. 1664. before Robert Hunt Esquire, concerning Alice Duke, informs, That about Twelve Months since Alice Duke alias Manning, brought a little Pewter Dish to this Informant, and told him it was good hansel for his Daughter. The Examinant willed the said Alice to carry it to her, she being within by the fire, but she forced the Dish into his hand and went away. Shortly after he was taken extremely ill in all his Limbs. Of which illness the Physicians, whom he applied himself to, could give no account. When she went from him, she was very angry and muttered much, because he would not sign a Petition on her behalf. She hath confessed to him since that she had the Dish from the Devil and gave it to him on purpose to hurt him. He hath been, and is since in great torment, and much weakened and wasted in his Body, which he imputes to the evil practices of Alice Duke.

Taken upon Oath before me

Rob. Hunt.

2. Exam. Mary the Wife of Tho. Conway, Examined March 6. 1664. before Rob. Hunt Esq concerning Alice Duke, said, That her Husband Tho. Conway about a year ago delivered her a little Pewter Dish, telling her he had it from Alice Duke for good hansel for his Daughter, who had lately lain in. In this Dish she warmed a little Deer-suet and Rosewater, anointing her Daughters Nipples with it, which put her to extreme pain. Upon which suspecting harm from the dish, she put it into the fire, which then presently vanished and nothing of it could afterwards be found. After, when she anointed her Daughters Nipples with the same Deer-suet and Rosewater, warmed in a spoon, she complained not of any pain. She further said that her Husband after he had received the dish from the hands of Alice Duke, was taken ill in all his Limbs, and held for a long time in a very strange manner.

Taken upon Oath before me

Rob. Hunt.

3. Exam. Edward Watts of Wincanton, in the County of Somerset, Examined Mar. 6. 1664: before Robert Hunt, Esq concerning Alice Duke, said, That he hath a Child called Edith, about Ten years of Age, who for the space of half a year hath languished and pined away, and that she told him that treading one day on the

> *Toe of Alice Duke, she in great anger cursed her with a Pox on thee, and that from that time the Child began to be ill and to pine away, which she hath done ever since.*
>
> *Taken upon Oath before me*
>
> *Rob. Hunt.*

He read the rest in one sitting, pausing occasionally to dunk another biscuit into his rapidly cooling tea, and at every pause he sensed that the room had edged just a degree or two colder.

"And so, what happened to them?" asked Simon, "these poor women, this Elizabeth Style and Alice Duke?"

"It says here that Style died in 'gaol', after being found guilty at the Taunton Assizes," and Gavin continued to read aloud from the document before him.

> *"This Elizabeth Style of Stoke Trister, in the County of Somerset, was accused by diverse – various - Persons of Credit upon Oath before Mr. Hunt, and particularly and largely confessed her guilt herself, which was found by the Jury at her Trial at Taunton; but she prevented Execution by dying in Gaol, a little before the expiring of the term her Confederate Daemon had set for her enjoyment of Diabolical pleasures in this life."*

"Stoke Trister?" said Simon, "I've seen that place, isn't that around here somewhere?"

"It's just along the A303, not far at all."

"So, this Hunt fella, was rounding them up, sending them to hang in trials that he would most likely be presiding over himself as one of the circuit judges," reasoned Simon.

"And most likely listening to evidence in other cases that his brother had procured for him through his own *examinations*" added Gavin. "This is likely to be just the tip of the iceberg, it's only a fraction of the Assizes records from just a couple of the years of his time in office."

"But the evidence is ridiculous." argued Simon, "it's obviously hearsay, targeted at people who are quite unable to defend themselves. She was a widow, so was most likely without family or anyone who would speak on her behalf. These *confessions* are obviously obtained under duress, they should have been thrown out as unsafe, you can't execute a person based on this. Testimonies from children for goodness sake and servants, who've clearly been told what to say as to do anything else would have cost them their livelihoods and reputations. It's scandalous."

"And they were all perverts too by the sound of it." added Gavin for good measure. "All that weird stuff about *anointing their daughters' nipples*."

"Not to mention their familiars suckling on their bodies. Given that they were all supposedly so religious it doesn't say much for their piety does it." Simon hated hypocrisy more than anything and so this account was really starting to press his buttons.

"I agree Si, though I don't doubt that the vast majority were good God-fearing Christian people, why is it always a few bad apples that have to go and ruin it for everyone else. And they always seem to be men."

"I know, there were some men accused of witchcraft too, but it was mainly women. And women accusing women too, that's what was going on here. It's people with grievances and no one being able to deny witchcraft 'cos if they did, they were branded a witch for doing so. So, what next?" asked Simon, "can't you find out anything more?"

"Well, I can only go by what's online at the moment," said Gavin ruefully. "The local libraries are still shut, but there might be more that I can find out. If not, then I'll just have to wait until I can get to the original record, but that's not going to be for a few weeks or more."

"And what do we do in the meantime?"

"We wait," said Gavin. "After all, whatever is haunting our house has likely been there for almost four hundred years. It can wait for another four weeks."

"Well, I'd say you need to give it a rest for a bit anyway." said Simon, shooting his partner a concerned look that was received and understood. "You look really tired again Gav, are you sure you're not overdoing it?"

"I'm okay, honest."

"You don't look like it to me. More tea, or something stronger?" asked Simon, as he planted a kiss squarely on his partner's forehead and made to leave the room.

"Something stronger?" said Gavin, but it wasn't an answer, it was a question, and it wasn't directed at Simon. "There's something else that I found out, that I've been meaning to tell you about. It wasn't water in those witches bottles you know, well not the kind that you get out of taps or streams. It was urine. Witch's urine: their fingernails or strands of their hair were pickled in it. Sometimes there are metal pins or nails in there too, as if by interring the pins that they might use to afflict others by sticking them into wax dolls and suchlike, they could contain them somehow. And though I hate to say it, sometimes thorns too, as it seems like in the case before us, it was quite common for victims to cite them as a symptom of bewitchment – maybe intended to ridicule the crown of thorns that was placed on the head of Christ at the crucifixion and the nails that were used in his hands and feet. They're not in the house to ward off evil spirits, they were left there to keep the witches quiet, to keep them from bothering the residents, to keep them from haunting us."

"And we've removed them."

"Worse than that." said Gavin with a shiver. "Two of them have been broken."

"Two?"

"Yeh, we broke one, but so did the Mountfords, remember?"

"So, there were originally thirteen in all then?" figured Simon, "assuming that all of them have now been found and as the house has now been gutted twice in its history, I can't imagine that there are any more hiding places to be had, do you?"

"No." agreed Gavin, but he looked puzzled. "Just a thought Si, but what if by breaking them their spirits have somehow been released?"

"What do you mean?"

"Well, Charlie Mountford said that they had always had a ghost, didn't she? And that they broke the first bottle during their renovations which would have been coming up twenty years ago. So, what if that ghost was the one that was haunting them before the incident with the Ouija board?"

"And you broke another" added Simon, "and something did change for us as well didn't it, after the second bottle got broke? The tapping, it seemed to get worse, and Charlie didn't mention that particular phenomena much, did she, though Bill says that it's been happening a lot lately."

"So, are we making it better?" asked Gavin, "or worse?"

There was no answer to that.

Friday 11th June 2021

445 Days Since Start of UK Lockdown

11 deaths reported in the UK – the total number of deaths due to COVID19 now stands at 133,116 with 4,073,710 people testing positive for the disease.

CHAPTER 36

When 'moving in' day finally arrived, it went without a hitch.

Even the British weather failed to spoil the day, staying dry throughout and deeming fit to throw in some sunshine when the moment came for them to celebrate. Bill was there to greet them with a bottle of finest champagne and even Mrs Illsley graced them with her presence, congratulating them both on the amazing transformation.

"It's not us who should be congratulated," said Gavin, "Bill and his team did all the work, we just paid for it."

"Which reminds me," said Bill with a chuckle, "my final invoice will be with you on Monday."

That caused a peel of laughter to roll around the small gathering as they all raised their flutes in the air to toast the end of a long and arduous project and what they hoped would soon be the end of the worst pandemic in a hundred years. There was still work to be done, and a 'snagging' list that was growing longer by the day, but everyone agreed that the décor was a triumph, and the fixtures and fittings pushed the property way into the luxury bracket, should they ever decide to rent it out again.

"I can't believe we're finally in." admitted Gavin when everyone had left. "It's everything I could have ever imagined it to be Si, thank you for making it happen."

"We did it together Gav," said Simon, as humble as ever, even though they both knew full well that it was his 'gravy train' of contract work that had paid for it. After all, as a project, it was way over budget by anyone's measure. "There was no point doing it if we weren't going to do it properly, was there?"

They had already been disturbed by movement upstairs and so were not unnerved when a familiar impatient rapping interrupted their train of thought. Immediately they put their latest plan into action, refusing to be startled or surprised and, if they could possibly avoid it, not allowing whatever it was to scare them into evasive action.

"Glad you like it." shouted Gavin.

"We love you too," said Simon, "but pipe down now will you, we've got things to discuss."

Incredibly it seemed to work, and in the subsequent calm the two men looked at each other in stunned contemplation, waiting on the next interruption, which never came.

In the preceding weeks, Gavin had continued with his research and as the libraries had now reopened, he was able to make a few trips to see what else he was able to find. The neighbourhood was still very rural and although many of the villages including their own had pushed their boundaries to the limit in recent years, with new housing estates springing up everywhere, there was still abundant countryside that hadn't changed for centuries.

Tiny hamlets made up of thatched cottages nestled around stone-built churches would have made up much of the old estate, with a local manor house lording it over them all. Some of the lost character of old England had survived the influx of urban migration, especially in the centres of the former villages. Many had grown into towns in the intervening years, with their narrow and cobbled streets that snaked away from the main thoroughfare in a ramshackle line of timber-framed nostalgia.

It was not impossible to imagine how, back then, it would have been quite impossible for a stranger's arrival to have gone unnoticed, or for a visiting relation to become the talk of the town. The poorest in society would have made easy targets for the elite to prey upon whenever the harvests failed, or if a family member came down with a mystery illness or met with an untimely death. Everyone would have known everyone else's business, and everyone would have been everyone else's business.

Gavin was able to trace the history of their village and the plot of land on which their house now stood with relative ease, but there was no record of an underground cell, nor that the building had ever been used in any way to enforce local laws. An old map of the oft absent Lord's landholdings had shown a scattering of properties dotted around the cross-roads at the heart of the village, where the thatched pub still stood. The town stocks were marked too, a regular place of humiliation for habitual drunks, serial debtors, and other petty criminals. But still no surviving record of witches.

He'd even been able to get his hands on a copy of the original deed for the former property from the early 1600s and was delighted to find the name of Oliver Hunt, scratched onto the vellum parchment in his own hand, dating from the middle years of that eventful century. But as to what had ultimately happened to the original building, he could find no record and as theirs dated from a later time, he had been unable to account for events in the intervening years. After weeks of searching, he had come to accept that he probably never would. He had reached a dead end.

Of Robert Hunt however, Gavin had enjoyed more success. Born in 1609 he'd lived a relatively long life for the times, 'departing this life' on 20th February 1680. He had been a follower of Cromwell during the civil war and as a Parliamentarian, had been fortunate to have come out on the winning side. His legal training at Cambridge and his time spent at the bar in London, had prepared him well to serve as a Justice of the Peace, and having been favoured by the victorious Roundheads, he had been in post at various times in the 1640s, fifties and then again in the sixties right up until his death.

Most importantly he had achieved a certain notoriety for having uncovered a "*hellish knot of witches*" in Somersetshire, and his service as a judge took him as far away as Cornwall on the Western Circuit, so witch-finders far and wide would have received a favourable ear - if not outright encouragement - in their pursuit of the Devil's disciples.

That he had employed his own team of local 'watchers' was hard to refute, as the circuit would only bring him back around to each town a couple of times a year, so he would have needed a dedicated troupe of informants to steer a steady stream of suspects towards the bench. The infamous and self-proclaimed *Witchfinder General*, Matthew Hopkins, had already set the benchmark for that self-styled profession, when he deployed his 'watchers' throughout the Fens of East Anglia during the 1640s. Having read all about his exploits, Gavin was left in no doubt that Robert Hunt may well have followed by example, and so it seemed logical to believe that his brother Oliver could well have been so employed, judging by the inscribed Bible that was now in their possession.

But proving it was going to be another matter.

The Somerset Heritage Centre was still closed to visitors and much of what Gavin was keen to see had not yet been digitised and it would be another eight weeks before he could hope to unearth more of the story. Not that he needed his new-found obsession to fill his time and as the first of their stored belongings from what felt like a former life began to arrive, he turned his attentions to the more mundane task of getting their house in order.

The wardrobes were first to be filled and even though they had both taken the opportunity to thin out their collection, it wasn't long before their dressing rooms were at capacity. Next came the kitchen, and although they had replaced much of their former gadgetry, it still took most of the day to fill the glinting cupboards with plates, glasses, mugs, and related paraphernalia.

Then onto the lounge, where their new furniture was already laid out in homage to their imposing wall-mounted flat screen television; a two-seater soft leather sofa with matching armchairs flanked an extortionately priced rug that Simon had picked out in a recent online sale. All eight square feet of it had seen its price tag slashed by a whopping fifty percent, but at five grand, it was hardly a bargain-bucket purchase. The fact that it complemented the ochre-red feature wall to perfection had gone a long way to persuading them both that it was 'money well spent'.

Around the rest of the house, boxes remained in various states of unpacking, but as the day drew to its close, Gavin was too bushed to care. Tomorrow was another day, and at ten minutes to midnight, it didn't take him long to decide that he would take care of what remained in the morning.

"I'm callin' it Si." he shouted from the top of the stairs, expecting to hear his partner respond from his well-appointed study where he had been hard at work since midday. "Simon, I'm going to bed, how late are you staying up?"

Still there was no answer, and with his back aching and his legs feeling like they had lead weights attached to them, Gavin made his way downstairs in a huff. As he turned the corner into the small, but perfectly formed room, he was surprised to find the chair empty and the computer in sleep mode, paperwork strewn across the L-shaped desk as if a meeting had been interrupted in full flow.

"Simon?" No answer. Gavin's heart was pounding in his chest, his pulse racing as a bead of sweat slipped from his brow and his voice caught in his throat as he called out again. "Si?" he shouted, visibly alarmed that his husband had seemingly vanished into thin air, as the newly installed mantlepiece clock chimed out the midnight hour. Immediately, he felt a stab of concern, and though his rational mind told him that a fifty-year-old man couldn't just disappear and that he was most likely in the garden with his earphones in, something else whispered in his ear to tell him to look elsewhere.

Steps.

Later, he wasn't sure that he had heard it or if he had just imagined it, but in the moment, he didn't hesitate to follow. He turned on his heels and strode across the lounge, lifting the rug and pulling up the trapdoor to reveal the stone stairwell, now illuminated by the fluorescent ceiling light above. He could see from where he was stood that the cell door was closed, and that a faint light was shining through the reconditioned metal grille.

"Simon." He was angry now. "Simon, what the fuck are you doing in there of all places?"

He thought he heard his voice then, just a croak or an attempt at a reply, as if he was unable to speak, or as if he was being restrained somehow.

"I'm coming down." he said, somehow plucking up the nerve to make the descent.

He counted the steps in his head, though he may have spoken the last three out loud as he reached out to open the ancient door, which had now been restored into a shining example of medieval carpentry, complete with gun metal rivets and smooth cast iron hinges. It belonged in a castle more than a country house, but as he took hold of the handle and pulled, his sight settled on just about the last thing on earth that he had expected to see.

Nothing.

And then the trapdoor fell above him with a sickening thud.

CHAPTER 37

"Gavin." Simon was starting to panic now, so he raised his voice to another level. "Gavin?"

He thought he heard a muffled reply coming from the lounge, so he raced back down the stairs and stopped by the hearth to listen again.

It was coming from beneath his feet.

Frantically he threw back the crumpled rug and pulled at the trapdoor handle, but it resisted him, and it took him a few more seconds to turn the circular latch that they'd had installed to keep the lid in place, should the wind cause it to rattle in its casement and loosen its grip. Or should anything ever want to get out.

"What in God's name are you doing down there?"

Almost as soon as Simon had lifted the wooden cover an inch, Gavin forced his way out like the undead from a grave and threw his arms around his husband's neck as a fearful sob escaped from somewhere high up in his chest. He had been locked down there in the pitch black.

"How long have you been down there?" screamed Simon rather louder than he had intended, "and how did you manage to pull the rug back?"

Gavin was so distressed that he seemed to be on the verge of a full-blown panic attack. "Where did you, go?" he stammered as if the surrounding air was light on oxygen, "where were you? I couldn't find you, anywhere."

"I heard a noise outside in the lane," explained Simon, "I went out to investigate. But you didn't answer my question – how did you get in there?"

"I thought that's where you were." yelled Gavin pointing frantically at his feet. "I went down because I saw a light on, inside the cell."

"But that's impossible Gav," said Simon. "There are no electrics down there, so how could there have been a light on?"

"I thought you must have been on your phone."

"And why would I have gone down there, at midnight, to look at my phone?" asked Simon, trying to make light of it. "I know I often use it in the bathroom Gav, but down there?"

"But there was a light." pleaded Gavin, "I saw it. There's no way on earth that I would have gone down there without a light. No way José."

"Didn't you have your phone?"

"No," said Gavin, "I was off to bed, I'd left it upstairs. I didn't know that I'd need to find my way out of the smallest room in the house buried underneath the fricking fireplace, did I?"

They both laughed then, but it was nervous laughter, neither of them was in any mood for joking around and it was about to get worse.

Three loud bangs resonated around the room and at first, they thought the sound was coming from the cell door beneath, but the second time it happened they realised that someone was paying them a late-night social call, one that they were not about to answer in a hurry.

One. Two. Three.

They didn't move.

One. Two. Three.

They edged a few feet closer to the door, Simon in the lead, Gavin holding onto his arm for dear life.

One. Two.

"Oh, bollocks to it." It was Simon. It was his house, and his mantra hadn't changed; nothing or no one, real or imagined, was going to scare him out of it. He reached out on the second booming knock and pulled open the front door as quickly as was humanly possible.

But there was no one there.

"What the hell?" It was Gavin this time. "That's just not possible, there's no way anyone could have moved that fast. There has to have been someone there. Doesn't there?"

"Yes," agreed Simon quietly, "but there isn't, is there?"

He pushed on the door and allowed it to slip slowly back on its hinges until it clicked shut with a reverberating clunk.

In that moment, a snippet from the theme tune from *Star Wars* was just about the last thing they expected to hear, but when it went off for the second time, it was Gavin who was the first to realise its significance. The motion detector on their new video doorbell, that he had only activated earlier that day, was going off and as the doorbell itself hadn't been pressed that could only mean one thing – someone *had* been knocking at the door. They rushed to the study to check the wall-mounted display.

"Normally we'd get notified on our phones," said Gavin, but I didn't get around to downloading the app, but this is just as good and as he pressed the on-screen play button to activate the flashing message; what they saw would keep them awake that night and for a few nights to come. In fact, it would never leave them. They would take it to their graves.

Though the picture was in black-and-white and rather low-resolution, there could be no doubt as to what it had captured. Still, it was so incredulous, that they would each press the replay button at least once more before Gavin clicked the pause button to freeze the frame on the screen.

A full body apparition of a man in Puritan clothing was waiting patiently for their answer, as if he had all the time in the world. On his head was a dark hat, his black coat was buttoned down the centre and splayed at the bottom, with neatly matching pockets. Around his neck and shoulders, was a light covered split collar and, in his hand, a long staff with which he was poised to strike the door for a third time. His lower body was less clearly defined, whether a limitation of the camera itself or a real likeness, they were unable to tell, but that was of no matter, for it was obvious to them both that whoever it was, he was not of this time.

"Look at his face." said Gavin, jabbing his finger towards the screen as if accusing it of some misdemeanour or other. "It doesn't seem to have one."

"Play it again," ordered Simon, his hands now at his side as he contemplated the impossible, whilst beginning to accept that what he was looking at, was more than likely, a ghost. Gavin pressed the replay button, and they watched in awe as the five second clip played for the fourth or fifth time in quick succession. Its facial features were vague at best, and although it wasn't exactly devoid of eyes, nose, and mouth, it was like a blank canvas, vaguely unfinished as if it was a painting to which the artist had yet to complete the most important piece. Without warts; without all.

Not that either of them needed to see its face to know its identity.

"Oliver Hunt, I presume?" said Gavin with a stutter, speaking his name on that spot for what was most likely to have been the first time in several centuries.

"Aye."

Whether the unsolicited answer had come from somewhere in between them, or from somewhere nearby, one thing was for sure; neither of them had spoken. They were stood just inches apart, looking straight at each other; their lips hadn't moved, and ventriloquism was not in either of their skill sets.

"What in God's name was that?" said Gavin, or it may have been Simon, for they both spoke and what they said was much of a muchness.

Later on, they could not even remember which of them had asked the question, but the sentiment was the same, and this time, no answer was forthcoming.

The accent had been local and unfamiliar, a whisper that hissed at them, but of a man that had once walked within their walls.

And to all intents and purposes, he hadn't left.

CHAPTER 38

"What are we going to do?"

It was Gavin and he had now passed beyond scared. He was terrified. No sooner had he been released from the darkness of an underground bunker, than he'd come face-to-face with a former occupant of the house, whose body had most likely been buried in the local churchyard more than three centuries before and was now just dust and bones.

Yet here he was, a walking talking Bible-bashing bogeyman.

"Nothing has changed" said Simon fearlessly, doing his best to bring some common sense to bear on the rapidly worsening situation. "All that's happened is that we've had a scare, that's all. It's upped its game and so we need to do the same."

"Upped its game." said Gavin choking back a half-hearted guffaw. "Upped its fucking game? It's done more than that mate; it's just scared me shitless. I thought I was going to die down there, I thought I was going to suffocate, if I didn't die of fright first. We're filling it in. I'm calling Bill in the morning, he's going to order half a hundredweight of ready-mixed concrete, which is being poured through that window and down that fucking hole until it's filled to the brim. Bastard thing."

"Okay, okay" said Simon soothingly, "if you want to do that then I'm not going to stand in your way, planning permission or no planning permission. But I'm more concerned to get to the bottom of this, this thing, because I don't want this freakish nightmare to carry on for any longer than it has to and filling up that hole does not solve our problem, does it?"

"That's easy for you to say," said Gavin, as he punched his partner's shoulder for emphasis. "You weren't down there, on your own. You'd gone galivanting down the road to investigate 'a noise' whilst I was frantically looking for you and getting myself banged up into the bargain."

"There *was* a noise," said Simon, "are you suggesting that I imagined it?"

"What noise?"

"A bang," said Simon, now firmly on the defensive. "A loud bang, outside, like two cars had been in a shunt or something. Or a firecracker had gone off."

"Well, I didn't hear it," said Gavin, "and I was just upstairs at the time, so maybe you did imagine it."

"Or maybe it wanted me out of the house, so that it could lure you down there?" said Simon, pointing towards the still open trapdoor.

"Don't say that." Gavin got up immediately and closed it, just in case.

"Where did you put that Bible, Gav?"

"Why? Are you thinking of rekindling your faith?"

"In the present circumstances," reasoned Simon, "it might not be the worst idea in the world, would it? But no, I want to take a closer look at it. We never really got beyond the first couple of pages, did we? Maybe we've missed something, maybe there's more to it than just an old family Bible?"

"A very old family Bible," said Gavin as he reached behind the sofa for the sealed chest and raised it into the light. "Gosh I forgot how heavy this was, there's some weight in this I can tell you. I had a quick search online to see what it's worth, surprisingly not that much, just a few thousand apparently."

"I don't think we should sell it," said Simon with rather more conviction than Gavin expected, in the circumstances. "It belongs here, doesn't it? I don't think the house would take kindly to it being sold to some collector in Japan, or America, do you?"

Two loud bangs sounded on the ceiling right above their heads.

"One for yes, two for no." said Gavin, a statement which also needed decoding. "That's what the ghost-hunters always say on those TV programmes when they're doing their 'calling out' or their 'lone vigils', don't they?"

"Okay so the house agrees," said Simon. "It's staying put. It's okay we're not going to sell it."

One loud bang sounded from the same spot, which Simon managed this time to ignore, as he settled the heavy-set book onto his lap. "Now, let's have a proper look at this thing."

He opened up the Bible for the second time and began to move through the well-preserved pages. He skipped the inscribed dedication from brother to brother, and the section marked 'translation to the reader' with its illustrated first letter 'Z' in the style of the old manuscripts of Lindisfarne and other English monasteries from an even older vintage, and on through *'the first booke of Moses, called Genesis'*. At the top of the page above the lavishly illustrated header, was the chapter heading, *'the creation of the world'*, which he reasoned in an age when few people could read ensured that those few who could, were easily able to read aloud in churches throughout the land, to the majority who could not.

He continued to leaf through page after page, on the lookout for annotations or personalisation, anything else that would link the edition to the man that they were seeking, but the Old Testament was clean. So, he next turned to the

New Testament, the centrepiece crafted in the shape of a heart around which the names of the disciples and the sons of Abraham were emblazoned in individually named squares, and the writers of the four gospels were pictured hard at work crafting the good book for the benefit of future generations of believers and sinners alike.

It wasn't until the very end that he found what he had hoped might be there. After Matthew, Mark, Luke and John, the book of the Acts and all the letters of Paul and John's final book of Revelation, came a revelation of their own. A long list of names, all of them women, all of them ascribed a year between 1640 and 1670 and there amongst them was the name of Elizabeth Styles, anno domini 1664.

"I recognise that name." said Gavin. "She was one of the women that was tried before Robert Hunt, for definite; she was in that book by Glanvill."

"The one that died in jail," echoed Simon, "waiting for her execution date."

One loud knock, like a carpenter's mallet on dense oak; yes, the house replied.

Saturday 12th June 2021

446 DAYS SINCE START OF UK LOCKDOWN

11 deaths reported in the UK – the total number of deaths due to COVID19 now stands at 133,127 with 4,079,132 people testing positive for the disease.

CHAPTER 39

"Other than the usual noises, or stuff moving about, did anything actually happen to you Bill, or to any of the other tradesmen, when you were here working?" It wasn't meant to be an interrogation, but Simon felt sure that their builder had been holding back, and now was the time for everyone's cards to be placed firmly on the table.

"Yes Gav," Bill said without hesitation, as if he too wanted to get something off his chest. "You know I never liked this place, and I liked it even less after what happened to the last bloke that lived here, but I always did my best to never be here alone, as you know."

"So why didn't you tell us everything?" asked Gavin, "didn't you think that we had a right to know? Instead of just leaving us to find out everything for ourselves, the hard way."

"Yes, of course you do guys, but mainly it was just the usual stuff" shrugged Bill, "and it happened so often, daily like, that I just didn't see the point of bothering you with all the details. You've had enough to deal with, living betwixt and between houses, without me adding to your woes."

"Do you want to tell us now then?" said Simon, sure that there was something important that he was keeping to himself. "You never know, it might even be the missing piece in the jigsaw?"

"What like?"

"Well," Simon started to say, but then he passed the baton to Gavin to continue. "Why don't you tell him what happened to you last night Gav?"

"I'd rather we talked about the snagging list" admitted Gavin, "but if you insist" and he told him all about his experience in the cell and their mysterious late-night caller. Once he'd finished, Bill seemed to be on the verge of an all-out confession, but then he hesitated, clamming up mid-sentence.

"What?" pressed Simon. "C'mon Bill, if you've got something on your mind?"

"There was one time," Bill started to say, "one of those building site pranks, you know what youngsters are like. One of the labourers was giving it large, telling everyone how he wasn't scared of anything. Tough guy act, you know the type?"

Neither of them took the bait, almost certain of what was to follow.

"We dared him to eat his lunch in the cell, with the trapdoor down," said Bill clearly ashamed of himself.

"Only not only did we put the lid down, but we locked it, and then we went down the pub and left him there."

"Shit."

"Oh Bill, that's…," said Gavin, unsure of what word to use to best describe his behaviour. "Mean." wasn't really the right choice, but it's the word that came out.

"I know," he confessed. "But he had it coming, he was such a macho man and he'd taken the piss out of some of the others who'd refused to be left alone on site in the past, so he had it coming. And we only stayed for one pint. Okay we had two, but we were quick, lockdown rules were still in force and so we were hanging about outside, and table service wasn't exactly quick."

"And when you got back?"

"A quivering wreck." said Bill. "Crying, sobbing actually. I did feel bad about it, we all did. He called in sick the next day and then, he never came back."

"What, not at all?" asked Simon.

"Not at all. Got a job on another site within a week," Bill recalled. "One of the plasterers saw him a few weeks later, said he looked so terrified when he asked him that he wouldn't even talk about it."

"Do you know what happened to him down there?" asked Gavin, wanting to compare notes.

"Some," said Bill, "but it's only hearsay, he never told me himself, so I can't vouch for it, though I did hear the same story from two separate sources."

"Go on," said Gavin, unimpressed in the extreme to hear what they had done. "And then you can tell us everything else that you've forgotten to mention."

"At first, nothing" said Bill, "he had his phone, but not surprisingly there's no way you can get a signal down there, but we thought he'd be able to use the torch or the backlight."

"You thought?"

"Yeh," said Bill meekly. "But we were wrong on that score as well."

"He said that his battery drained almost immediately that we shut the door, and it was pitch black. He shouted for us, but we didn't hear him, honestly, we didn't," Bill muttered, "we were already out of the gate and on our way to the pub. We didn't hang around."

"And then what happened?"

"He said that he could hear whispering," said Bill. "Voices, but indistinct, couldn't make out the words, but he was sure that they were female voices, very quiet, almost like they didn't want to be heard or at least not understood anyway."

"Poor bugger," said Gavin, reliving his own ordeal of just the night before.

"And then crying, which he said was the worst thing of all," Bill continued. "Sobbing, not gentle, but desperate, the kind that you only make when all hope is lost."

"For someone who didn't know too much, you certainly have quite the tale there, Bill." The man's reputation had come down a notch or two for Simon, and with every sentence, he was slipping further down his Christmas card list. "Anything else?"

"That was it," said Bill with a heavy heart. "He couldn't wait to get out of there."

"You should be ashamed of yourself."

"It was only a prank guys," said Bill, trying in vain to repair his dented integrity. "What can I do to make up for it?"

Both men had the same idea at the same time, and each looked at the other with a mischievous glint in their eyes.

"Do you want to tell him Gav?" said Simon, "or shall I?"

CHAPTER 40

"Five minutes." said Bill, "no more, okay?"

"That's all Bill," shouted Gavin from the top of the steps.

"Think of it as penance." said Simon, as he closed the lid on the darkening room in which Bill had somewhat incredulously agreed to be entombed.

"Five minutes." he said to himself out loud, "that's not long, anyone could manage five minutes" and he started to count off the seconds like a child playing blind man's bluff. What this little reprimand was supposed to achieve, he could not say, but the fact that it was intended as a punishment put him in mind of those that may have gone before him, and the very thought of those poor unfortunate wretches made him lose count immediately.

They had said to think of it as an experiment. On the previous occasions the victims had gone in there with their lights and torches blazing and they had drained almost as soon as the trapdoor had closed. Bill had been given the same heavy-duty black rubber torch that Gavin had been carrying, loaded with completely fresh batteries as they had stood on the threshold itself, out of the packet, just to prove to all that they were fully charged. His task, should he care to accept it, was to sit with the light off for as long as he could possibly stand it, and then – only when his nerves couldn't take it any longer – he was to push the on switch and call for them to let him out.

An endurance test, and at worst he was to turn on the light after five minutes, but he never made it to five. He wasn't sure if it was three, three-and-a-half or four, but the temperature was dropping faster than he could count and as his teeth had started to chatter, when he decided that he could take it no more. He flicked on the light. And saw that he was no longer alone.

CHAPTER 41

"Time's up Bill" called Simon, as he lifted the lid to allow a liberating cube of light to charge down the steps.

But Bill was yelling now, and already on his way out of the unlocked cage as if his tail was on fire. He almost ran them down halfway up the steps in his yearning to get above ground and once there, he fell like a falling star onto the waiting sofa.

At first, he couldn't get his words out fast enough and it was impossible for Gavin or Simon to make sense of what could only be described as an emotional breakdown. On the spur of the moment, one of them handed him a stiff drink, Bill had no idea which of them it was, but he took it and with one twist of his wrist it was gone. A delayed burning sensation warmed his throat as he handed back the heavy tumbler for another generous shot, just in case the first failed to have the desired effect.

"I saw them."

"Who?" asked Gavin impatient to know what it was that was holed up beneath their feet during the daytime and roaming through their house at night. "Who did you see?"

"Them?" asked Simon, for the first time feeling truly scared in his own home. "You mean to say there's more than one?"

At that Bill laughed out loud, and it was so unexpected that neither Gavin or Simon knew quite how to react, so they just stepped back and waited for him to reveal all. "Oh yes." he said. "There's most definitely more than one."

"How many more?"

"I counted nine, I think," said Bill, still shaking, despite the whisky. "But it could have been a few either way, I didn't really have much time to think about it."

"Nine?" said Gavin struggling to comprehend what he was being told. "How could nine people fit into such a small space as that. Are you sure about that?"

"There or thereabouts, yes," he stammered. "Though not all at the same time, and not, all of them, if you know what I mean. Sometimes, just their faces."

"And what did they look like?" asked Simon, not quite knowing what to expect in reply. He'd never come face to face with the undead in his life before and he wasn't all that keen to make their acquaintance now, but he wanted to know what to look out for.

"Sad," said Bill remembering their faces all too clearly. "Lonely, scared, desperate. Trapped."

It wasn't what they'd expected him to say, but it was Simon that asked the obvious question in reply. "Not frightening?"

"Not terrifying?" added Gavin for good measure.

"Look I'm not saying it didn't scare the pants off me for a minute there," Bill admitted, as the alcohol did its thing, "but that was just the shock of seeing them when the light went on, when up until that moment I only had a sense of it being very crowded down there, like at a football match in the old days, but I had just put that down to claustrophobia. Now, thinking about it, remembering their cold pale faces and how ashen grey their lips were, I just couldn't help but think about my own daughters and what I might have done had they been accused and locked up like that."

He was on the verge of tears.

"I'm going back down there." said Simon in a sudden rush of bravado, getting to his feet and snatching the torch from Bill's grasp. He was still holding onto it for dear life and so it took a couple of seconds to prise it free. "You coming with me?" he asked, challenging Gavin to join him, "or are you going to let this Hunt fella win? This is our chance to get to the bottom of this and I'm not sure that I'll ever feel up to facing it more than I do right now."

Gavin hesitated, unsure if he shared the same sense of 'derring-do' or not, but the prospect of being locked down there again proved too much and so he graciously declined, opting instead to hold the fort at the top. "I'll stay up here Si, just to make sure that there are no mishaps. I'll sit on the top step so the hatch can't close, whatever happens. Think of me as your insurance policy."

"My *'get out of jail free card'* eh?" said Simon, trying to see the funny side of things as usual. "Well, I guess it's my turn then isn't it, best get this over with, so here goes nothing."

"Tell me again why you're doing this Si?" asked Gavin, the question that every sane person wants to ask when the lone survivor in any self-respecting horror movie decides to face whatever is stalking them rather than making a run for the hills. "I mean, why not leave it until tomorrow, once you've slept on it overnight?"

"Because I want to see what he's just seen," said Simon, not quite believing the strength of his own resolve. "I've been hoping that all this wasn't real, that it would just go away, but if Bill says that he's seen nine or more spirits down there, then I'd like to see just one of them. I want to know what it is that we're dealing with and, if I can, I want to talk to it. To them. I want to talk to them. To understand them. To help them."

"Great speech, well then I am coming," said Gavin, in a sudden surge of pride for his partner, knowing that he might soon live to regret such a snap decision. "Bill, can you please stand guard? In fact, it would be better if you sat, right here."

The two of them were soon wedged inside the cramped space, their one solitary halo of light projecting circles on the opposite wall just five feet away. The light from the lounge provided scant comfort through the bars of the closed cell door and every now and again they answered Bill's call, assuring him that they were okay and asking him the same in return. Until this moment, they had not taken a really close look at the stone-built cell, each building block separated by a thin layer of mortar, its clammy surface covered in marks and scratches that at first seemed to have no form at all.

"How long are we going to sit here Gav?"

"I dunno, its very quiet, isn't it? What do you make of all those marks?" he asked moving the light around the wall just a few inches in front of them. "Look at that one, is that a word? And look there." he said pointing, the light stopping over an unmistakeable double 'V' which overlapped to form a cross shape in the middle, but the letter was a 'W'.

"There's more than one of them," said Simon, "the same thing that we saw upstairs, you remember?" He motioned for Gavin to shine the light lower down the wall, where the same monogram was scratched into the surface, but inverted to resemble the letter M.

"Is that your heart I can hear," asked Simon.

"I wouldn't have thought so Si, though its going ten to the dozen."

"Maybe it's mine then?" said Simon, but he really didn't think so either. As it grew louder, it began to take on a certain familiarity, a regular drumbeat, like fingers on a pane of glass. Or feet pacing on stone. "Do you not hear it now? Tell me you can hear that."

"Yes," said Gavin as his hand clutched Simon's outstretched arm without warning and made him jump out of his skin.

"For fuck's sake Gav." he hollered too loud for the enclosed space, "don't do that you idiot."

"You two, okay?" It was Bill, his voice a welcome reminder that there was still a living, breathing world beyond their walls.

"Yes, we're fine," he answered, "it's just Gavin being a dick as usual."

"Help me."

There was no doubting the words and where they had come from. They had come from between them. Not from either of them, but from right between them, within the twelve-inch gap that separated them from each other. It was faint but undeniably female, the voice of a young woman, if not a child.

A voice from another age. A voice from another time.

"Oh shit." said Gavin, who was ready to bolt, but Simon was made of sterner stuff, and he gripped his friend's hand in a clear invitation to stay right where he was. They were going nowhere.

"This is what we're here for Gav," he said sternly. "This is our chance to sort this out once and for all. They're not going to hurt us, and we need to help them. Hello? Can you hear us? Knock on the wall if you can hear us."

The knock that came in return didn't seem to emanate from one place or from one hand. It came from everywhere. From all four walls and from the floor beneath their feet, even from the stone ceiling above, as if the room were full of souls and they had all reached out to rap upon whatever they could in the very same moment. Like a round of applause or more likely the roll of an executioner's drum.

"That's good," Simon went on, doing his best not to let fear find a foothold in his voice. "Don't be scared, we're not here to harm you, we want to help you. We're on your side."

"Did you die in this cell?" It was Gavin asking the question now, having plucked up the nerve to speak, but it was still as if he was surgically attached to his partner's arm, and he did not plan on letting go. "One for yes, two for no."

The response was confused, almost like a ripple of knocks, and it was Simon who thought he knew why. "Did only some of you die in here? Knock out the number of you that died in here if you can."

One. Two. Three. Clear as a bell.

"Three of you died in here. Were the rest of you hanged?"

Just like the first time, one knock from several hands resonated around the room.

"Were you hanged for witchcraft?"

The same response.

"Were you guilty? Are you witches?"

One. Two.

A definite, audible, and absolute, 'No'. It was like they had shouted it; it was like they had screamed it from the depths of their beings. It was like they were being heard for the first time in four centuries or for the first time ever.

"We found some names, listed in the back of a Bible that was left in this room," said Gavin, suddenly feeling more confident in himself and sure that what they were doing was the right thing, for everyone, living and dead. "Was that you, are those your names?"

One. Just the one knock, like an invisible show of hands.

"Alice Knight, are you here? One for yes ...," but they knew the drill. It was like taking a school register and as Simon began to recall the names that he could remember from the back of the Bible, the same singular response confirmed their presence. Elizabeth, Tabitha, Sarah, Poppy, Patience, Eleanor, Grace, Alice. He couldn't remember the rest and he apologised to those that he had forgotten, but he assured them that they were no longer forgotten.

They had been remembered.

And then they were gone. They hadn't seen them; they had seen nothing, but they had felt their presence, and in that moment, it was like the room had been emptied, as if they had simply left, or had been chased away.

"Let's get out of here." said Simon. Gavin didn't need telling twice.

"I don't know how much more I can take of all this," said Gavin as they reached the top and let the trapdoor fall back into place. "Look at me, I'm shaking." and he was, his hands vibrating violently like an infantryman at the onset of shellshock, or at the moment of going over the top. "I can't take much more," he said again, as if to ensure that his plea had not gone unheard.

"Nor me," admitted Simon, but he was right out of answers. "Nor me."

350

Saturday 10th July 2021

474 DAYS SINCE START OF UK LOCKDOWN

34 deaths reported in the UK – the total number of deaths due to COVID19 now stands at 133,678 with 4,586,497 people testing positive for the disease.

CHAPTER 42

Almost a month had passed since the incident in the cell and to their unbridled relief, by and large the house had slipped into silence. It was as if it had settled somehow, as if by making contact, by acknowledging its former prisoners and their dreadful fate that their need for attention had been satisfied. Not exactly at peace, but at least at rest, for now.

"Long may it continue," said Simon as they discussed it over breakfast in the newly refurbished conservatory, the rain beating down like stair-rods outside. It was still humid, but as is always the case with an English summer, the weather was its usual unpredictable self.

Not that everything had been all peace and harmony.

The day after that eventful evening, the prior residents' former housekeeper had beaten a path to their door and at first, they had thought it was the witchfinder himself that had returned to hammer on their freshly varnished hardwood.

"Good morning, Mrs …" but Gavin had not been afforded the time to complete his planned pleasantries.

"Don't you 'good morning' me." she'd blasted him, stepping across the doorstep to complete the job. "I am thoroughly disappointed with the pair of you. Where's Simon, I don't want to have to say my piece twice."

"Hello, Mrs Illsley, how are …," stuttered Simon as he came to greet her, a steaming mug of fresh coffee at the ready, but he too was cut off in his prime.

"I suppose you thought that locking that poor man down there in the dark was one of your witty larks did you, young man?"

He hadn't been called a 'young man' for quite some time and it had taken all his self-control to stop himself from laughing out loud, but to his detriment Mrs Illsley had sensed his amusement and that only served to spur her on.

It was a reprimand the like of which neither of them had received in a very long time.

"He could have had a heart attack, down there in the dark." she'd scolded, "and I don't care that that other boy had suffered the same treatment, two wrongs don't make a right. You should have both known better. The poor man, he was still shaking when he told me about it only this morning."

"We're very sorry Mrs Illsley." It was Gavin who had relented first, having decided that a slice of humble pie was the best option open to them. "We didn't really think that anything would happen down there."

"Clearly." she bit back, not yet ready to call a truce.

"And if we can do anything to make up for it, Dot," said Simon, taking a risk on a friendlier form of address. "We did apologise profusely afterwards and if it makes up for it all, we gave ourselves the fright of our lives as well."

"No, it doesn't really, but yes Bill did tell me all about it."

"We think we've figured it out," said Simon, hoping that she'd want to be the first to know about it and in doing so, pour some water on her flaming mood. "Not quite everything, but it seems to make sense, and things have been very quiet since so just maybe …"

It was Gavin this time who jumped in to stop him mid-sentence. "Maybe it'll stay that way, is what we were thinking."

A loud bang from upstairs seemed to scoff at the suggestion, but they didn't even flinch, taking it as another positive confirmation to yet another question.

"I still think you owe Bill an apology."

"So do we" said Gavin, "and so we've been thinking, the weather is supposed to improve over the next few weeks, so why don't the two of you come round for a barbeque, we haven't had a chance to get the beast out yet and I know how much Bill likes a burger. I tell you what," said Gavin as an idea sparked in his head. "They've just put the ending of restrictions back a month haven't they, so why don't we do it on 19th July? They're calling it 'Freedom Day' aren't they, so what better timing?"

"But what if this rain never stops?" asked Simon, a little irritated that the two of them had not agreed on the idea in advance.

"Then we'll do something indoors instead."

She had stayed for well over an hour after that, consuming two cups of tea and helping them to see off a packet of fruit shortcake biscuits, her favourites. But she had warmed to the idea of the barbeque and had already begun planning what she would bring along by way of dessert; a sticky toffee pudding was in prime position, but a New York style baked cheesecake had gotten Gavin's vote, though they knew she'd bring both.

"By the way Si," said Gavin, as the thought of puddings somehow reminded him that he had failed to update his partner on his latest research findings. "We found a letter 'W' scored into the walls down in the cell, which matched others that we have seen around the house," he said, bringing Mrs Illsley fully up to date, "but we weren't sure what they were."

"Well, I can tell you exactly what they are," said Mrs Illsley, not waiting to hear if Gavin was on the right track or not. "Mr Humphreys always used to say that they were to protect against evil spirits. Lots of the old houses around here have them apparently, its meant to be the Virgin Mother, the double 'V' creating a cross and upside down it stands for Mary."

Gavin was left feeling a little deflated, but also pleased that his research had yielded similar results. "That's what we thought too," he said, "but is it specifically to ward off witches or witchcraft or just an antidote for bad luck? Is it simply a good luck charm or is it darker than that?"

"Well, Tony Mountford had some questions about witches too," she recalled as she dusted the biscuit crumbs from her floral-patterned dress and made to leave. "He spoke to the late Mr Humphreys about it, but unfortunately, he was unable to help him much and then, well we all know what happened next don't we?"

"To Tony or Mr Humphreys?"

"Well, you know only too well about Tony, and you know about Mr Humphreys too," and though they nodded, she felt that her old friend was worthy of loftier recognition. "He was the village historian, lived local all his life, so he knew everyone and everything. You may have heard that he's passed away now I'm afraid," she said mournfully. "He got the COVID in the end, but he died of pneumonia. Such a shame. I said he wouldn't survive it - if he came down with it - his immune system was already shot-to-pieces because of his prostate, you know. He was the one that left that pamphlet that I gave you Gavin, the one about the Jurymen. You remember. Was it any use?"

"Yes." said Gavin, "I do. Most useful it was too Dot, most intriguing."

"If we're going to have a Freedom Day party, why don't we go the whole hog?" said Simon after she'd left. "After all, we were going to have a housewarming weren't we, so let's have a few people down from London, especially if the weather's going to be good. I need an excuse to sort out the pool and so we can ask some people to stay; they can make a weekend of it, and we get to show off the house?"

It had seemed like a good idea, but as always, these things had a habit of getting out of hand, and before they knew it, they'd invited a houseful and the 'quiet barbeque' had turned into a full-blown costume party with midnight fireworks on an eighties theme.

As usual it was Gavin who'd taken charge of the arrangements and whilst he'd been kept busy putting in the food orders at the local bakers and butchers and collating a playlist on their favourite music app, he had also been up to his neck in research.

The re-opening of the local archive centre was still a week or so away and so he'd been forced to mine the online resources even deeper, exhausting every avenue and line of enquiry that he could think of. The UK Land Registry had offered a promising start, but it soon became apparent that all that could be gleaned from it related to recent ownership and any flood risk, all of which was already reported to them in the searches on purchasing the house. The National Archives also over-promised, but under-delivered, with much of its content undigitized and only available from local record offices; and so, he ended up back where he'd started, at square one.

Tithe maps from the middle of the nineteenth century had also started off well, but in the end had proved fruitless, and whilst his browsing took him to a database of 'listed' buildings on which their house was registered, it again told him nothing that he didn't already know. Estate maps, enclosure maps, land tax records from the late eighteenth century, parish rate books and local rate books issued in support of the new Poor Law in 1834, all offered a tantalising glimpse of the past but fell short of providing him with any additional insights and the dates in question were often hundreds of years too late.

Finally, just when he was close to giving up, one set of records emerged to shed light on an almost uninterrupted window between 1662 and 1674. After parting with a few pounds of Simon's hard-earned cash, he was granted access to what he hoped would prove his theory; a theory that he had been harbouring ever since he had learned of Oliver Hunt and his politically minded older brother.

The hearth tax was introduced to provide the newly restored King Charles II with a regular income to avoid some of the conflicts over cash that had taken the country down an evil path that ultimately led to regicide. Vast wealth was concentrated amongst England's landed gentry, and so this new form of taxation was intended to tap into this reserve of funds, and to make it as 'fair' as possible, it was decided to base it on property size; as the name suggests, it was to be measured according to the number of household hearths. The *University of Roehampton* had put the database together along with their Austrian counterparts at Graz, and it seemed to Gavin to be almost poetic justice that it was these records that might ultimately prove crucial in unlocking the mystery.

After all, the chamber in which the accused had been held prisoner, was buried just a few feet beneath one of the very fireplaces on which the tax would have been levied. One shilling was payable every year for every fireplace, hearth or stove and as Gavin delved deeper into the digitised scrolls, preserved now for eternity in photographic and electronic form, he eventually came across the proof of residence that he was looking for.

In the first years of the levy, O.Hunt was listed as owner, his name scrawled in black ink across the annual evaluation of four shillings for each of the returns from 1662 to 1668, but after that there were no returns for the next five years. Nothing at all, as if the house had not existed, or as if it had been wiped off the face of the earth. Then in the final year of record-keeping, marked as 'the year of our Lord 1674', the name of R.Hunt appeared no less than six times. Six separate dwellings were listed, all of them with a single hearth to their name at an annual rateable value of six shillings gross.

"So, it seems that Robert Hunt may have taken ownership of the land, from his brother sometime around 1670 and redeveloped it?" asked Simon later. "He'd acquired some additional parcels of land during the enclosures of the forest to the north a few decades earlier and so it would seem, he had decided to make good on a few of his investments."

"That's how it looks," said Gavin, "And having checked through the burial records for the local parish church it seems that Oliver died in 1669, in fact he may well be buried in the village church."

"How do you know that?" asked Simon, not expecting him to produce an extract from the church records listing all *'baptismes and burialls'* for the year in question. The handwriting was beautifully crafted, each letter swirling into the next, the print still perfectly legible, and the date of Oliver Hunt's funeral was centred on the page above the names of three other women whose bodies were all put into the ground on the very same day three hundred and thirty-two years before.

"I went up to the churchyard to see if I could find their graves," said Gavin, "and there's a whole load of ancient headstones, and one or two Hunts in what seemed like a family plot, though most are so badly eroded that it's hard to be certain either way."

"And what about the women?"

"Paupers graves unfortunately," said Gavin with a rueful smile, "or possibly buried in unconsecrated ground if they'd been convicted as being witches."

"So, is that a 'no' then?"

"Well, I know roughly where they might be buried, in what's aptly named "Pauper's Corner," but there are no markers," Gavin explained. "They would have simply been dumped into a mass grave with any others who had died that week, so they're likely to be together if they did die on the same day, but there are no headstones to pinpoint where they were laid to rest."

"But why would they have all died together?" asked Simon perplexed.

"I mean I suppose the women could have all been executed, if indeed they were witches, but why Oliver Hunt too? It's a bit of a coincidence isn't it, that he died at the very same time. Unless it was Plague or something, but even then, to all have died on the very same day seems to me to be a coincidence too far."

"I doubt that they'd have been interred in the churchyard if the Black Death had got them either." said Gavin, thinking on his feet. "They'd have been buried in a Plague pit and covered in lime or burned together with all the others. No, I think there must be some other explanation."

"I didn't expect that he'd be buried in the graveyard." said Gavin, with a triumphant grin that had Simon wondering what new revelation his partner had up his sleeve. But he would have to wait a while longer long to find out. "He was from an important family remember; local landed gentry didn't get dumped in the earth outside to get urinated on by the local canine community. I tried to take a look inside, but it was all locked up."

"A sign of the times, sadly." said Simon, "but why don't we try again now? It's Saturday evening, there might be a better chance on a weekend that it will be open again, especially now that the restrictions have been lifted. C'mon, I can carry on working on this lot later."

CHAPTER 43

It was only a short walk up the lane to the centre of the village, then left up the hill and along the rutted path that led up to the Norman church. It was dedicated to Saint Peter and Saint Paul, as if the founding fathers had been unable to decide between those two great apostles and it loomed large over the busy road that encircled its crammed burial ground. From a distance, the stone building seemed unremarkable, a single square tower rising two stories to a turreted top, fortified at each corner with an ornately carved spike in keeping with a thousand others all over England.

The interior was also of its time, with a dozen sets of plainly carved wooden pews lining the nave before the high altar, in front of which a gold-plated candelabra, its candles long since replaced with electric lighting, hung steadfast from the vaulted ceiling high above. A series of arches to the right marked the line of a later medieval extension and as Gavin and Simon ambled respectfully beneath, they each began to read aloud from the stone dedications to forgotten wars and lost sons. The eastern wall, whose surface seemed to glimmer like gold in the glow of the afternoon sun, was adorned with a vast array of individual plaques, many bearing the colours of famous families whose coats of arms would once have been all too familiar to the worshipping masses the like of which had not been seen for many a year.

"Have you seen the floor?" Gavin pointed as Simon edged his way towards the antechamber at the end of the open walkway. "All those names, and just look at the dates."

"I really don't like it when they do that." said Simon, reading the inscriptions beneath his feet as he walked along. "It always seems so sacrilegious to me. I suppose they must have been short on stone, but all the same, it doesn't seem right to have them laid out like floor tiles."

The floor was a mosaic of former headstones, some of which may have marked the final resting place of pious members of a long dead congregation, among them those who were deemed to be deserving of a place within the walls of the family church, or simply those who had made sufficient tithes during their lifetimes to have been granted an indoor plot. Several surnames appeared over and over again, but not all of them were legible; many had been worn smooth by the passage of ten thousand feet, with just the faintest edge of a letter or number remaining to catch on the rainbow of light that streamed in through the leaded windows above.

"I haven't seen a Hunt yet, have you?" asked Gavin.

"Nope, not yet," said Simon, "but let's keep looking, there are so many dedications it'd be easy to miss one."

At the back of the church, in what would have been the oldest part of the building, stood a line of intricately fashioned and life-sized carvings of men and women, laid down to rest with hands clasped tightly together in prayer. Though short in stature by modern standards, judging by their hand-hewn dress they were fourteenth or fifteenth century, complete with ruffs on which faded shades of ochre and black still cleaved closer than the dust of centuries past.

For a moment, both Simon and Gavin hoped that they might have found their man, but once again the name they most wanted to see eluded them, as the prefixed surname of a French nobleman and his wife stared back at them in defiance. The unmistakeable outline of a knight, complete with helmet, shield and sword stared up at them, the name "de Percy" chiselled smartly into the grey stone surround, behind which a family shrine, complete with a line of sleek stone pillars, defied even the most determined of raiders to plunder its walls.

"C'mon Oliver Hunt," said Simon out loud to no one in particular. "If you lived and died around here, your name has to be somewhere."

And then right on cue, Gavin found him. "Look." he crowed, pointing up towards the vaulted ceiling. "Up there. Hunt."

"I don't see it" said Simon, frustrated. "Where are you looking?"

"There." said Gavin, pointing frantically. "Just to the left of the Boer War memorial."

It wasn't much to look at. A stone scroll, set in white marble, its edge marked out with a black and white marquetry border and the name within emboldened in the same sable script.

> *Oliver James Hunt Esq. 1631-1669 - Brother and Son.*
> *Late of this parish. A more God-fearing man never walked this earth.*
> *"Thou shalt not suffer a witch to live."*
> *Exodus 22:18*

The two of them stared at it for a while, before withdrawing their phones in tandem to snap at it from every angle just in case there was something that their eyes weren't seeing that the wonders of 21st century technology wouldn't miss.

"Anything strike you as odd about that Si?" asked Gavin, a puzzled expression on his face.

"Yeh," said Simon, "Brother and Son?"

"Exactly. No wife? No children?"

"Do we assume then that he died unmarried, aged 38?" asked Simon. "Seems unlikely in that age for a man of means not to be married much sooner, if not for love, then for status and wealth."

"Of course, it doesn't mean that he *wasn't* married," reasoned Gavin. "I mean it could just be that his wife didn't want to be acknowledged or that they didn't have any children. Not impossible, I suppose."

"No, but if he was married, then wouldn't he have been interred with her?"

"Not to say that he isn't" replied Gavin, "it's only a plaque, it doesn't say his body isn't buried somewhere else, maybe even in another church. The family seat maybe, or in the graveyard?"

"But what if there was no *body* to bury?" said Simon with a knowing look.

It was an interesting thought and not one that either of them had even considered up until that point, but as the two men stared up at the plaque perplexed, the weighty wooden door of the church swung inwards with a heavy thud.

A troupe of scouts poured inside, and in an irreverent rush they swarmed along the aisles, collapsing to the floor in turn, charcoal in hand, and tracing paper at the ready, each competing to find the oldest gravestone from which to complete their rubbing. It was a time-honoured tradition, and not one that Simon nor Gavin wanted to interrupt, so they skirted their way around the excited teenage mob and left them and their leaders to it, though Simon could not resist making a three-fingered salute to the beleaguered adults as they pushed their way out into the evening air.

"I didn't know you were ever a scout Simon?" smirked Gavin.

"South Wales's finest." said Simon with a wry smile.

Sunday 18th July 2021

482 DAYS SINCE START OF UK LOCKDOWN

60 deaths reported in the UK – the total number of deaths due to COVID19 now stands at 134,016 with 4,925,123 people testing positive for the disease.

CHAPTER 44

Summer 2021 had finally arrived in England, and it had already moved beyond warm to sweltering. Some were simply calling it just another heatwave but for others, it was further evidence that the planet was suffering from the long-term impact of the 'Greenhouse Effect'. Whatever the explanation, it was perfect weather for a pool party.

Simon had paid to have the pool thoroughly overhauled in the days leading up to their 'event of the year', as it had been billed – though the competition was meagre. A few tiles had needed replacing and the pump had also required a new motor, whilst a complete relaying of the surrounding paving stones had also set them back a few hundred pounds. In the end it had cost him a lot more than he'd bargained for, but they had both agreed that it had been worth every penny, for they now had a fully functional pool to enjoy for the rest of the summer.

The first couple arrived on the Friday evening. Lifelong friends from their university days, Jack and Penny had always been their go-to couple for weekends away and nights out in the West End and although the arrival of their twins had caused a rethink, it had been but a temporary hiatus. Now fully grown and away travelling the world, the girls for whom they were each a proud Godparent, were no longer a tie and so the four of them had continued where they'd left off, only for the pandemic to put paid to that. Now they hoped that normal service could be resumed.

On their arrival it had been hugs all round, none of this elbow tapping and virtual hugging that had become the new normal since March 2020 and within minutes it was business as usual, as the alcohol began to flow. They had dumped their stuff in the larger of the two spare bedrooms and decamped to the garden, to enjoy the last of the evening sunshine over a bottle or two of cold prosecco and assorted nibbles.

The house was of course immaculate. Every corner cleaned to within an inch of its life and the surfaces sparkling. An obligatory tour followed once they'd polished off the first bottle, but Simon couldn't help noticing how Penny looked ill-at-ease as they moved around the house, as if convinced that something was amiss. Once back in the garden, he couldn't help but ask her what it was that had been bothering her.

"Oh, it's nothing," she lied brushing a strand of grey-streaked hair from her face, but she was not about to fool either Simon or Gavin with such a poorly thought-out response.

"We know the place is haunted," said Simon plainly, "so if you saw something, it would be really good to know what it was that you saw."

"Or felt?" added Gavin, for good measure.

"She's always been a bit sensitive to that sort of thing," said Jack, butting in and at the same time, hoping to encourage his wife of nearly thirty years to open-up a bit. "Do you remember that time at Uni when she informed that exchange student that her room was haunted by a former resident."

"That's exactly why I'm interested to know what you saw," added Simon, "I remember that, and there have been other times as well. Remember that hotel in the Lake District?"

"Okay," she conceded, "well I don't know that I *saw* anything. But I definitely sensed something and I'm sorry to say that it didn't feel good. It was one of those corner-of-the-eye things, every time we turned a corner or left a room there was a shadow or a movement, as if it was lurking in the shadows and didn't want to be seen."

It was the starting gun for Simon to share all that they had witnessed since moving back in, whilst Gavin shared the headlines from his research, which as a history major, was sure to pique Jack's interest. They showed them the old Bible and the place where they had found it, though Penny refused to go down there on account of what she'd described as a dark shape on the steps, which no one else could see. Jack on the other hand couldn't get enough of it, spending ten minutes alone on the cold stone slab with the cell door closed, but he returned disappointed and with nothing of any note to report and bemoaning his conclusion that he must be 'spiritually dead'.

The next day more guests arrived in the form of Sarah and Chloe, a couple that they'd known since first moving to London and from their days when clubbing had been a regular weekend event. They had rarely missed, and most weeks they had joined forces in one or other of their favourite haunts in and around Soho. The couple had bagged the final spare room on the first floor and had wasted no time at all in donning their swim wear and heading out to enjoy the sunshine, where Jack and Penny were already soaking up the rays. Adventure was their middle name, and they had travelled the world together in the nineties, trekking up mountains and walking the ice fields above the Arctic Circle. To their friends they were fearless, and although Simon and Gavin had once joined them on a walking holiday in the Swiss Alps, when it had come to white-water rafting, skydiving and high wiring it through the Rockies, the boys had both left the girls to it.

As three mixed households was still the limit under the government restrictions until midnight on Sunday, the six of them had spent Saturday night and all-day Sunday in splendid isolation, enjoying each other's company for the first time in a year and a half and having a blast into the bargain. They'd managed to consume more alcohol than either of the hosts had thought possible and so, despite the generous contributions that their friends had made, Gavin had headed out to the local supermarket on the Sunday morning to replenish the wine and mixers ahead of Monday's onslaught.

"I'm taking it steady tonight.," Gavin had announced at Sunday breakfast, a promise that was met with almost universal approval, but by the time the evening came around they'd all got a second wind and the drinks were flowing once more.

"Well, it's too hot to sit around drinking water," said Simon, with a ready-made excuse, as he poured six gins and tonic into a newly acquired set of extra-large balloon glasses. "Ice-and-a-slice everyone?" Lime of course.

As he placed the glasses on the worksurface and turned his back to reach into the fridge for the tins of flavoured tonic water, two of the glasses slid together as if in a toast to their friendships. The sound was undeniable and the source unquestionable, and as Simon turned around to stare, the ice was still rattling around inside two of the six, whilst the others looked on unmoved. Of the guests, only Penny had noticed, and she regarded Simon with a knowing expression, as if she had seen more than she had heard.

"So how long has all this been going on?" asked Penny after raising their glasses together in a more traditional manner. "I mean, was it happening before you started renovating?"

"Yes, and before that as well" explained Gavin, "the previous owners had it worse, although they think it all kicked off because some holiday makers messed with a Ouija board here. Until then, it was always haunted, but not in a bad way." He opted not to tell them about the unexplained death; he didn't want to scare them away, but he could see that Penny wanted to know more and so, he took her to one side and told her all that they knew.

"And did they close the board down?" asked Penny, "after they'd used it, did they say goodbye and what about protecting themselves before they started, did they do all that?"

"We don't know," said Simon, chipping in from within earshot. "The family that they think were responsible died in a car accident on their way home. No one knows what they did, before or after, we only know what happened when the former owners held their own séance, against their better judgement, it must be said."

"Do you still have it?" asked Penny, much to the consternation of her friends, who were quick to rule themselves out of any parlour games, so it came as a relief to all of them when Gavin explained that it was long gone. "Well, that's a good thing if you ask me," she continued. "I've never gone in for it myself, but I've heard of people who have, and it never ends well, but if they failed to close it down – either the first time or the second time - then it could have opened a door and until it's properly closed, you might continue to have problems. And so might they."

It seemed to be getting even warmer indoors, as the natural light began to fade and as Simon flicked on the remote control to activate the LEDs above their heads, each one flickered in turn, sending shadows darting for cover.

As usual, it was Simon who did his best to lighten the mood. "And for my next trick." he said, feigning a theatrical bow to his audience, though no one laughed. Jack did take a seriously large swig of his cocktail and Sarah and Chloe edged their chairs a little closer for safety or comfort, it was hard to tell.

"Give me K2 any day over this." said Chloe, nudging Sarah who was nodding furiously in agreement. After all, mountaineering was one thing, but their very own paranormal reality show was something else entirely.

"Have you any idea what might be at the root of it all?" asked Sarah, plucking up the nerve to join the conversation. "I mean, if ghosts are spirits of dead people, do you have any idea who they might have been? When they were alive, I mean?"

Gavin looked at Simon as if seeking permission to answer, before launching into a long-winded explanation which he knew could easily last for the rest of the night. The resigned look that Simon offered in return seemed to suggest that he had no choice; at some point in the next couple of days the truth would out. "We know that there was once a different house on this land, and that it belonged to an Oliver Hunt Esq." said Gavin, "the hearth tax records show that he was the ratepayer back in the 1660s, but by the 1670s a Robert Hunt – who we think was his brother - was paying the tax on several separate dwellings."

"So, what happened to the original house – did it burn down or was it knocked down?" asked Jack, focusing in on the only two real possibilities.

"It might have fallen down for all we know." said Simon thinking of an unlikely third option, "but we really don't know. If I had to put money on it, I'd say a fire, these things were tinderboxes after all weren't they? Timber frames and open fires, it would have been an accident waiting to happen."

"All we know for sure is that Oliver Hunt died in 1669 and that he has a memorial in the local church where we know that three other women are most likely buried too. They died on the same day, though we can't say for sure that there's any link between the deaths, but a house fire is a strong possibility of course," said Gavin. "What we do know is that Robert Hunt was a known sympathiser who presided over the trials and sentencing of suspected witches on the Western Circuit, which is basically the whole of what we know as the West Country today."

"And he's best known for uncovering a *'hellish knot of witches'* not too far from here, up near Frome, so he's our prime candidate," said Simon. "Him and his brother, though hard evidence is hard to come by."

"And there's your link back to the Ouija board." said Penny, "so you think the people in your cell down there were accused witches, or at least people suspected of being witches?"

"It seems that way," agreed Simon, "but there's more, go on Gav, tell them about the Bible." All four guests turned as one to look at Gavin and as they did so, all of them screamed.

CHAPTER 45

The first object that smashed against the wall on the far side of the kitchen had come from the worktop; later on, they would all agree on that. The second had seemingly appeared out of nowhere, clattering against the range and sounding like crossed swords on a battlefield.

"I swear it came from nowhere." said Jack, on his feet now and instinctively backing away.

"We all saw it didn't we?" said Sarah, visibly shaken by what she had personally seen with her own eyes. The three others nodded, but neither Gavin nor Simon, whose backs were turned had seen anything, but they had heard plenty.

"What was it?" asked Simon, "there was nothing reflected in the glass, at least I didn't see anything, did you Gavin?"

"Okay then," said Gavin, shaking his head, "there's no doubting what you saw. The only question now is, who or what caused it?"

"Actually, I'd say that the only question is" said Chloe, pausing for effect as they waited for the punchline, "is there a *Holiday Inn* anywhere around here?"

"Seriously?" asked Jack, "how do you guys even live here? I'm not sure that I even want to stay another night."

"What choice do we have?" reasoned Gavin. "We've sunk all our money into this place, and we love it, don't we Si?"

"I'm starting to love it a little bit less than I did," said Simon only half-joking, but as Gavin kicked his shins he was persuaded to think again. "I'm taking the view that it can't hurt us, it can only scare us and so, if we're not frightened of it, then we're halfway to beating it."

"Let's go into the lounge," said Gavin, motioning them all to follow. "Before anything untoward happens to disprove that view Si." and he led their four guests nervously past the capped off well, and into the oldest part of the house, where the fate of long forgotten lives had once been sealed.

"I'll sort out this mess," said Simon, reaching for the dustpan to clear up what was left of the plate. "I've put the fans on in there so it's nice and cool and we can have a couple more drinks, at least that way we'll all sleep tonight."

"Damn fine idea Gav," said Jack, "but can you tell me, is it a bit more or a bit less haunted than this part of the house?"

"Much worse." said Gavin, "didn't you hear about the underground cell? And if this mess is down to you Oliver, then give it a rest, we've had enough of your antics for one night."

"You talk to it?" asked Chloe, in a rush not to be the last to leave the conservatory.

"Sometimes that's the best way," said Penny. "Acknowledge them but make sure that they know who's boss. Tell them off, say good morning, that sort of thing."

"How about telling him to 'fuck off'?"

"Yes Jack, that too."

"You were about to tell us about the Bible that you'd found …" said Sarah, once they were all comfortably seated back in the lounge, each with a double shot of whisky or brandy to settle their nerves. "Down there."

"I can do better than that." he said, reaching down beside his chair to wrest it from its hiding place. "I can show it to you." and with two hands he passed the leather-bound volume to Penny who was seated to his left. The others crowded around her, desperate for a closer look at a genuine piece of history. Gavin left them to leaf through its weathered pages, waiting for them to arrive at the dedication and the inevitable line of questioning. It was a long time in coming, but just when Gavin was beginning to think that they had skipped over the relevant pages, it was Chloe who finally settled on the inscription.

"So, this actually belonged to Oliver Hunt then?" she stated, "how amazing. And it was from his brother, but what does the bit in Latin mean? Here Sarah, you did it at school didn't you, how's your memory?"

Sarah took the weight of history onto her own lap and on seeing it, she was immediately drawn to the final word as she began to decipher the text. "Well, the last word is magic, I think, no it's not, it's *witches*."

"No way." said Jack, "what about the rest?"

"The first bit reads '*to my brother*', or 'because my brother' maybe. But I'm not sure of the other word."

It was Simon that filled them in. "It says, '*to my brother, killer of witches*'."

"Oh crap." said Chloe, summing up the moment nicely in two simple words, but it was Sarah who could not resist having the final one and she spoke each one perfectly.

"Quia frater meus," she whispered, "interfectorem maleficarum."

It sounded like a spell or incantation, and it had a similar effect. Later they would liken it to summoning an earthquake, as the doors began to rattle in their frames, the metal fittings vibrating like a wind chime in a storm. Then the newly hung pictures began to lift like a dozen cat-flaps around the room, as if a spectral litter was trying to force its way out of the solid stone walls of the cottage. Then the light show began, though the full effect could only be appreciated from the street outside, as every light fitting took a turn to trip itself on and off as the three couples sheltered in its shadows, as if from lightning. And of course, the reinstated witches bottles that were nestled into their nooks on either side of the fireplace shuddered and spoke like a dozen tuning forks being struck in a synchronised show of force.

"Enough." shouted Simon, more infuriated than fearful. "Enough you freak." he yelled, "leave us be. This is not your house anymore, this is mine, mine, and Gavin's. Get out of our house."

It stopped then as if shocked by the reprimand, but not before the rug folded up on itself like a snakeskin being shed, the trapdoor beneath straining on its hinges and flipping over to strike the floor with an almighty clatter.

"I'm serious now." said Chloe, "where's the nearest hotel?"

CHAPTER 46

"Have you ever heard of *'automatic writing'*" asked Penny, as they bid Chloe and Sarah a better night than they were expecting to have themselves. The local motel was only a ten-minute drive away and neither Simon nor Gavin could blame either of them for making a quick getaway. Jack and Penny, however, were clearly made of sterner stuff and for those that stayed behind, the night was just getting started.

After Gavin had plied them with another round of drinks, Penny took the opportunity to enlighten them.

"It's also known as *'spirit writing'* and it's said to date back, well for a long time" she explained to her dubious audience, "though the Victorians adopted it as another of their more risqué parlour games, along with the Ouija as part of their obsession with all things related to the afterlife."

"How does it work then?" asked Gavin, still unsure if it was something that he wanted to participate in or not.

"Well first of all I need a pen and a lot of paper," said Penny, sending Simon scurrying away to his study, to return a moment later with a ream of plain A4 paper and a selection of ballpoint pens. "And I need a flat surface, preferably a small coffee table if you've got one, or a tea tray if not."

Before long they were crouched on the floor above the trapdoor, believing it to be the heart of the house and therefore an ideal spot to conduct this particular psychic experiment. The largest of a nest of tables had been dragged into position and on its polished surface, Penny had carefully positioned her pad and pen, like a secretary poised to take the minutes to a long-awaited negotiation, where neither party was prepared to back down on its demands. They were in it for the long haul.

"Ready?" she asked breaking the silence, as a timely bead of sweat formed on her temple and began a steady slide towards her neckline. It wasn't getting any cooler, despite the lateness of the hour, and as the four of them readied themselves for whatever was to follow, Penny tightened her grip and, against her better judgement, tentatively closed her eyes.

"Breathe deeply everyone," she said, taking a long intake of humid air, "and out."

Simon had one eye open, regarding the scene before him with a mix of humour and horror. What are we getting ourselves into here, he thought to himself; a thought that he was determined to share with Gavin but now was not the moment for cold feet and so he determined to save it for later. So far, he'd been steadfast in his determination to see things through, certain that whatever they were up against could be thwarted somehow, that its curse – if that's what it was – could be lifted and the shadow that had been cast over their house for generations might at last be banished. But as the two couples sat crouched around the trapdoor, their eyes closed and their senses on high alert, he was no longer sure that all was going to end well.

As if sensing his reticence, Penny repeated the familiar mindfulness exercise several times, urging them all to clear their heads of all thoughts except one. To focus on the pen. To pour all their energies into it and into the object of the exercise; to encourage whoever might be listening, or watching, to scratch their message onto the paper beneath.

"Are you there Oliver?" she asked, for the first time addressing the person that she had only then dubbed as 'The Watcher'. Why, she had no idea, but the word had just come into her head, and so she accepted it without question. It just seemed right, but there was no response. "If you are listening to me Oliver, please can you send us a message? We are not here to judge you, nor to harm you in any way, we only want to understand why you haven't moved on. We can help you to move on if that's what you want?"

The pen jolted to the right and fell from Penny's grip. It seemed that she had hit a nerve with her last question, unless it had been the moisture on her hands that had caused her grip to loosen. Without hesitating, she retrieved the cheap biro and continued to call out.

"We know that you were a 'watcher' Oliver." she said accusingly. "Did your brother pay you for your services? Did he tell you the names of the poor unfortunates that he wanted you to accuse? Or was it all your own lie Oliver? Did you decide which of your neighbours you would 'bring to justice' all by yourself, or were you just acting on orders?"

Penny hadn't wasted any time in going for the jugular, and the three men had all opened their eyes to stare at her, convinced that she must have taken leave of her senses. Her eyes remained closed, and the pen remained unmoved, but something had changed in the room and Simon thought that he knew what it was, though his theory would have to wait.

When the pen eventually started to move it did so without warning, though to Penny's credit she didn't even flinch as the base of the pen began to be tugged, like a fisherman's float might do when a catch is imminent.

It was like she was in a trance, more so than any of the boys who were all staring transfixed at the scrawl that had started to slip and slide across the page. Her fingers didn't appear to be moving at all, but the plastic pen was jabbing back and forth, leaving a trail of black ink in its wake. Like a lie detector machine on a TV crime drama.

"Paper." she ordered, and Gavin reached over to pull the top sheet away, discarding it in the same movement to reveal a new blank canvas on which the spirits could make their mark. At first the pen was stopped in its tracks, as if the change in surface had thrown it off somehow, and when the motion began again, it was of an altogether different style.

It put Simon in mind of a graceful figure skater, a dancer on ice whose balletic poise leaves a faint trail in her wake. A trail of interlocking and ever decreasing circles, that careered across the page and into the corner, until the pen itself fell off the side of the pad. As Penny righted it back in the centre the circular motion began again, but this time it was as if it had learned its lesson and instead of sliding from the edge, the pattern stayed within its boundaries until it resembled a rising trail of smoke that billows up into a darkening sky.

It was a while before anything remotely resembling a word was formed and when it did, it was only a single letter. The letter 'O'; a singular mark left upon a freshly revealed piece of paper and until they refreshed the pad again, nothing else happened. It was as if whoever was coming through had wanted a fresh start, or a new record, and it was only when the nib next connected with the paper, that what seemed like words began to form in increasingly rapid succession.

s-r-e-h-t-o-r-b

l-a-y-a-r-t-e-b

s-s-e-n-k-r-a-d

e-r-i-f

The letters overlapped on the page, making it almost impossible to decipher if they were actual words or not, but it didn't take long for Simon to work it out and when he did, he shouted so loudly that Penny dropped the pen, and the link was broken.

"They're all written backwards."

"Really?" said Jack, "oh yes, you're right, look '*darkness*'." He had read the third word aloud, but it was Gavin who read the rest.

"Brothers. Betrayal. Fire."

"I'd say that's pretty clear." said Simon, regarding the others with something not unlike satisfaction, though his sweat lined brow told a different story. "But we still don't know if it's our man or not do we?"

"Let's try once more," said Penny, "and then I have to sleep, I'm exhausted." Once more they gathered around the table like school kids around a game of jacks, the pen at the ready and poised to print on a perfectly blank page. Again, nothing happened for a moment or two, but then something seemed to grip her hand, and her fingers moved with the word that was forming beneath; and this time the letters were not in reverse.

i-n-n-o-c-e-n-t

"That was extraordinary." said Gavin, as they tidied up the tables and glasses in readiness for bed. "I didn't know you had a gift for this sort of thing Penny, you've never said, though Simon always suspected."

"She's always been a bit that way inclined" said Jack, sensing that his wife was now too exhausted to speak for herself. "Though it's always very draining for her, emotionally. Every time it happens, she sleeps for hours afterwards as if her batteries have to be recharged or something."

"It's not something that I can control," she interrupted, "and not something that I go about advertising on social media or anything. But every now and again, when the moment is right, I seem to be able to make a connection."

"That's it." blurted Simon, "that's what was different in the room, earlier on, in the middle of that, exercise. It was trying to sweat us out."

"What are you on about Si?" asked Gavin perplexed.

"The electric fans, they're both disconnected," he said, pointing to the wall sockets where the 3-pin plugs lay on their backs like dead flies. "I thought that maybe they had just timed out, but they didn't, they've actually had the power cables pulled out of the wall."

"Now that is extraordinary." said Jack as he picked up the one that was closest to him, "and it's cold. Shouldn't it be warm to the touch, even if it's been off for ten minutes or more, it shouldn't be cold, should it?"

"Not that cold," said Gavin, taking the plug in his own hands for comparison. "It's freezing."

It was then that Penny burst into tears.

Monday 19th July 2021

483 DAYS SINCE START OF UK LOCKDOWN

76 deaths reported in the UK – the total number of deaths due to COVID19 now stands at 134,092 with 4,968,524 people testing positive for the disease.

CHAPTER 47

Freedom Day had started exactly how the previous night had ended. Hot.

As Gavin poked his head out of the curtains and through the open expanse of a restored sash window, there was not a cloud in the sky and though it was only seven o'clock in the morning, he could feel that it was going to be another scorcher.

He'd had a fitful night, but there was much to organise and so he wasted no time in getting dressed and heading downstairs to fix breakfast for their guests. He was hopeful that the aroma of sizzling bacon and fried eggs would tempt his husband from the sheet in which he'd become entangled, but it proved to be wishful thinking. Jack and Penny ate their fill though and joked they would be furnishing them with a five-star rating on their favourite travel app once the weekend was over.

For Simon, a cold bacon sandwich would have to do.

"I'm sorry for the state I was in last night Gav," said Penny. "Sometimes it gets to me that's all, and suddenly I just felt so …" the words didn't come immediately, and she took a mouthful of tea before continuing with the explanation. "So, lost and frightened. I suppose I was feeling what those poor girls must have felt all those years ago, with this monster on their tails. They must have been terrified; look at me, I'm tearing up again."

"Nothing to be sorry for Pen," said Gavin, taking hold of her hand. He wasn't sure if it was helping but he'd never been good with crying girls and usually ended up in tears himself, so he decided to cut it short by offering them both further refreshments. "Orange juice? Another cuppa?"

Having taken Penny and Jack up on their offer to clear up the breakfast things, Gavin left them to it and returned two hours later with another carload of alcohol and assorted nibbles, and enough ice to sink the Titanic. Although the ice machine in the kitchen was hard at work cranking it out by the bucketload, the temperature outside was already close to thirty degrees Celsius and the chest freezer was full to the brim. In a few hours' time the trugs would be full of bottled beer and the party would be in full swing, but as midday came and went the preparations were far from complete.

As he turned his attention to the outdoor lighting, he spotted Jack loitering amongst the raised beds and went over to join him with the brazen intent of enlisting more of his help.

"Sure," said Jack only too pleased to lend a hand, "but as you're here, you do know that these are original foundations for something, don't you?" He was pointing to the double course of weathered red brick that ran in two interlocking rectangles at the side of the property, which, according to Mrs Illsley had been filled with earth and used as vegetable plots for time immemorial. She had told them all about the prize-winning leeks and turnips which had sprouted from these very beds under the care of previous owners, but not that they lay in the very footprint of what must have been the old manor house.

"You can clearly see," said Jack measuring out the large and inconsistent span of several bricks with his hands, "that these are all handmade, pre-dating the industrial production of bricks and the introduction of the imperial measurement system. These are all locally made in individual wooden moulds, then kiln baked, but I'd say that this is all part of the original house that you were talking about last night. And they were expensive too, so were mainly for the foundations; wood was still abundant and so the timber frame provided the main structure, and the bricks were used to establish the outline and to provide stability."

"Well, I never." said Gavin, "have you told Simon yet?"

"No, I haven't seen him since this morning," said Jack, "but that's not the most interesting thing about this and he crouched down at the side of the nearest stretch of wall, encouraging Gavin to join him. "You see here?" he said, digging away at the dirt on the outside of the walls with his bare hands to reveal the layer of bricks beneath. "Look how black the bricks are here, and here," he was pointing in several places and revealing more and more of the old structure. "There can be no doubt, that there was once a fierce fire on this very spot, that almost certainly engulfed this building. I bet if you dig anywhere here, you'll find the same layer of black soil a few inches below the surface all around the outside of these beds."

Gavin retrieved the garden fork from the plot and began turning over the unframed earth to the left and right of where they stood and sure enough, the evidence was everywhere. "So, the place did burn down then?" he said, almost to himself, but Jack was there to confirm the theory beyond any reasonable doubt.

"Almost certainly," he said smugly "and I bet you that if you put a metal detector to work around here, you'd find some old pots, bottles and metal objects that would also show signs of being superheated. I'd say that you've found your smoking gun Gav."

"You mean you have." said Gavin clapping his lifelong friend on the back. "You see, I always told you that a history degree was not a waste of time."

"Liar," laughed Jack, "you always said the exact opposite as I recall. Anyway, let's get these lights up, where do you want them?"

It took them the best part of an hour to lay a trail of Christmas lights from the conservatory to the swimming pool, in what would form a twinkling path to guide their guests to and from the house. They would have to wait a few hours to see them in all their glory, but a quick test proved that they were all still in full working order and, with another job ticked off the list, they returned to the kitchen where Simon and Penny were waiting for them with their own tale to tell. After sharing Jack's find-of-the-century amongst the flower beds, it was Simon's turn to hog the limelight, though he too had their guests to thank for the discovery.

"I was showing Penny the book that you bought on eBay Gav," he said, handing it to Jack who immediately began to browse. "She noticed something interesting about the testimony of Elizabeth Styles. Well, you know that we thought she must have been illiterate, because she 'made her mark' when she signed her confession?"

"Yes?" said Gavin, unsure of where the conversation was headed but intrigued all the same.

"It suggests that she signed her name as the letter 'O'," and he leant over to open the book at the earmarked page, pointing out the pertinent line in the text. "Last night, whatever was moving that pen was making circles, but then on the fresh piece of paper it made one almost perfect circle. Some might say a perfect letter 'O'."

"Do you really think so?"

"Sounds like a strong possibility I'd say," agreed Jack, convinced that his wife was onto something. "I've heard worse theories in horror films anyway."

"It's got to be a possibility, hasn't it?" said Penny, frantically retrieving the relevant piece of A4 paper from the pile of what looked like scrap. "I mean, if she was illiterate in life, why would she suddenly be literate in death?"

Gavin regarded the automatic writing with a shudder, feeling more nervous now as he recalled the events of the night before than he had done in the moment itself. "I guess so." he admitted, unable to think of a reasonable argument against it, "after all her name does appear in the list at the back of the Bible and so if we believe that those women were all restrained here at some point after being held against their will by Oliver Hunt for goodness knows how long, then why wouldn't she be one of the people who are haunting the place?"

"Stands to reason if you ask me," added Jack. "They say that most hauntings are the result of tragic deaths."

"Or unfinished business," added Simon.

"Or both."

It was Penny who had tried to have the last word and she would have succeeded, had another thought not occurred to Gavin that would maybe trump them all.

"Innocent." he said, shouting rather more loudly than he had intended, causing a book to fall unseen from the bookshelf in the room above their heads. They heard it land, but refused to react, leaving it to lie where it was until morning. "Where's the Bible Simon?"

"Where you left it mate."

Gavin was back in flash, heavily laden with the book of books in his hands. He laid it on the table in front of them and with as much care as his excitement would allow, he made his way to the back and the list of names that had been added as a permanent reminder of their sacrifice.

"There." he said, pointing to the last but one name on the roll call. "Innocent Williams. We weren't being told that they weren't guilty, we were being told that there is one amongst them that was not illiterate. We need to make contact with Innocent Williams."

CHAPTER 48

"That's a bit of a strange name, isn't it?" asked Penny.

"Not really," explained her husband. "Lots of the new church denominations, especially the Quakers, started using names like Patience, Prudence, and Innocent, particularly in the years after the Reformation. It's unusual though, I'll grant you that."

The caterers had just arrived, providing a welcome distraction for Simon and Gavin as they began carting tray after tray of freshly made sandwiches and salads through the house and into the conservatory in readiness for the onslaught. The doors had been wedged wide open to encourage what little breeze there was to keep the room cooler than the rest of the house, though both fans were re-employed at either end of the table to provide a constant stream of chilled air.

"I swear it's getting hotter out there." said Gavin as he placed the last of the prepared food on the table. "I hope this stuff stays fresh until everyone is here."

"Let's just get started early," said Simon. "If we take the covers off at six-thirty, everyone should be here by then. I'm glad we ditched the costume party idea, it's way too hot to wear anything but shorts and a t-shirt."

Sarah and Chloe were first to arrive, immediately making a beeline for the garden where they would remain for the rest of the night, and where they hoped to be out of reach of the house and its former occupants. Others followed soon afterwards, a rag-tag collection of friends old and new, many of whom were heading out of London for the first time since the lockdown had begun over a year before. The excitement was tangible and as the hosts hugged and bumped elbows and fists as each familiar face pulled up outside, the buzz began to build, and the party vibe got started.

They'd told everyone to bring their swimming costumes for their re-labelled 'pool party' and some had wasted no time at all, taking the opportunity to cool off after a long drive. Others preferred to stand and chat, or simply to dip their feet, sitting on the side of the pool where they could catch up with old acquaintances and on old times.

The drinks were soon flowing, and the multitude did not stand on ceremony when Gavin announced, rather theatrically, that 'dinner is served', descending like a proverbial plague of locusts to devour almost everything in sight within the hour.

"I told you we hadn't ordered enough," said Simon ruefully, as he surveyed the scene. "I'll put the rest of the crisps and snacks out, though I doubt they'll last."

"And at least they'll have room for dessert," answered Gavin, returning with several trays of sweets of every description – including Mrs Illsley's homemade cakes - much to the delight of those nearby who wasted no time at all in tucking into a spread that would not have looked out of place in a Paris patisserie. As the last of the sticky buns and iced tarts were spirited away, Gavin cranked up the music to fill the lane with a succession of bass-heavy nineties club anthems that soon had everyone letting their hair down as the light outside began to fade.

Mrs Illsley and Bill became more and more inseparable as the evening wore on, each feeling a little uncomfortable rubbing shoulders with an eclectic array of under-dressed partygoers. Both felt rather out-of-place in a flowing chiffon floral print and short-sleeved-shirt and chinos respectively, and as neither had made plans to take a plunge, they had no intention of changing into their swimwear. Bill had been presented several times as 'the man that made it all happen' by Gavin and as 'Bill the Builder' by Simon, the latter of which never failed to kick start a drunken karaoke competition that Bill did his best to ignore.

Mrs Illsley had received far less hype, but had nameplates been distributed on arrival, then she would almost certainly have been labelled as their 'former housekeeper' which, though not exactly true, conferred on her a status that was not unwelcome.

The first sign that something was wrong came when one of Simon's old schoolfriends on returning from the upstairs toilet had asked 'who the guy was that didn't get the memo?'

"Who's that?" said Simon, immediately sensing that something was amiss.

"The guy in the Salem costume," he went on without flinching. "When you said 'eighties', I didn't think you meant sixteen eighties. Great outfit though, very convincing, got the boots, the hat and everything, but he must be boiling in this weather. I told him, 'rather him than me'."

"And what did he say?" replied Simon, immediately wishing he hadn't asked.

"He didn't," said the guest. "He just smiled at me, as if he appreciated the joke."

Simon searched the house from top to bottom and then, after suggesting to Gavin that there might be a stranger in the house, the two of them circled the garden, looking for the appropriately dubbed 'man in black'.

Neither was surprised to find that no one fitting that description was anywhere to be found.

"Do you think he was mistaken?" asked Gavin, clutching at straws.

"No," said Simon with an air of absolute authority, "he saw what he saw. He was so certain that it was a real flesh-and-blood person, that he wasn't even scared, and so I thought it best not to suggest to him that he might have seen a ghost."

"Do you think it was our man then?" he asked, putting a name to the face. "Do you think it was Oliver Hunt?"

"Yes, I do," said Simon, "but why now, why tonight? When he could have appeared at any time in the last year, why does he choose the hottest night of the year to make his full technicolour feature-length debut?" There was a seed of an idea in his sentence, but it needed time to germinate and as the evening's festivities were about to culminate in a long overdue fireworks display, duty called.

A succession of rockets, Roman candles, Catherine wheels and whizz-bangs lit up the sky in an explosion of colour and despite there being no children in attendance, each one was greeted with an outpouring of astonished joy. As is so often the case the spectacle was short-lived, but the assembled gathering continued to make their own entertainment, drawing circles in the air with their sparklers and hurling their fluorescent head and wrist bands into the sky only to watch them fall to earth like an arrangement of multi-coloured fireflies.

Even Bill was joining in, wearing his own like an Alice-band, which made his greying hair seem white against the darkness of the sky. "It's been a really nice do," he said to Gavin, "thank you for inviting me, I'd forgotten what it was like to have an evening out and I haven't had this many beers in quite a while I can tell you."

"I'm glad you could come," said Gavin honestly. "It wouldn't have been the same without you and Mrs Illsley. Talking of which, where she's gone, she hasn't left already has she?"

Bill had been engrossed in the fireworks show and so had not noticed her slip away. "She was right here just a minute or two ago," he said, looking around at the silhouettes to see if he could spot any of the right size and shape. "Maybe she's nipped to the loo?" he wondered aloud, though he did not recall her excusing herself, and he felt sure that she would have. "She wouldn't have gone without saying goodbye to you both, I'm sure."

As the minutes passed, Bill was clearly starting to get agitated at her continued absence, and so Gavin enlisted Penny's help to check out the bathrooms, just in case the old lady was in difficulty. "I hope she hasn't bumped into our Puritan friend." he said quietly, turning to Simon who had been keeping up with events at his side.

When Penny returned shaking her head a few moments later, all of them dispersed like a formation of display planes, heading towards every corner of the garden as if prompted by a starter's gun and when a woman's scream pierced the muted music, they all bolted in the direction of the sound.

The swimming pool.

Gavin turned through the line of trees that stood in the shadow of the house just as Simon launched himself like an Olympic swimmer into the pool. Then his eyes drifted over to the swirling mass of floral material that was floating on the surface like grey algae in the semi-darkness, and he raised his hand to his mouth in an instinctive intake of air.

"Oh no." was an insufficient exclamation for the medical drama that was unfolding before their eyes, but in the moment, it was instinctive and a prelude to worse.

Simon had already turned her over and was dragging her limp and lifeless body to the side as Jack leapt in to help, whilst Bill stayed on the side, tugging her onto dry land with all his might. "Please no, God please no." he cried, as Sarah and Chloe arrived on the scene and in an instant knelt to clear her airways, bringing their lifesaver training to bear.

Gavin was on the phone to emergency services, pleading with the operator for speed, but as he explained the situation as clearly as he could - giving the location and as many details as he could muster – he heard a horrid but unmistakeable retching sound, as the kiss of life brought the old lady back from the brink.

Immediately, the two women turned Mrs Illsley into the recovery position, and Bill fetched beach towels to cover her up, as the shock of what had just happened hit home like a thunderbolt for everyone who had witnessed it. Someone had had the sense to switch off the music. The party was officially over, and when the ambulance crew finally arrived to attend to Mrs Illsley, she was already sat up and nursing a hot cup of tea in both hands.

It was only then that reality began to bite.

From a safe distance away, Gavin could see that Mrs Illsley was talking now and although he could not hear what she was saying, nor lip-read through the breathing apparatus she was now clinging to, he could feel her agitation as each paramedic did their best to calm her. Though he was desperate to know how she had ended up in there, he didn't want to crowd her and so instead waited patiently for one of the first responders to update him. In the end he was pleased that it was Simon.

"How?" but he didn't have to finish the sentence.

"She says she was pushed," said Simon, combing his fingers through his still wet hair. "Said that someone placed both hands in the small of her back and gave her an almightily shove, and then pulled her down in the water so that she couldn't breathe. The paramedics have called the police and they'll need statements from everyone, so I need to ask everybody to stick around, and we'll need to give them a full list of guests."

"Shit." said Gavin, thinking that some people had already left. "But thank God she's alive. I really thought she was a goner there for a minute Si, didn't you?" Simon nodded as the two of them embraced, and then a huddle formed as they were joined by the three girls who had been next on the scene. Chloe was crying, and both Penny and Sarah seemed close to tears too. All of them looked fraught and not a little terrified.

Bill had stayed by Mrs Illsley's side and had also kicked up a stink to be allowed to accompany her to hospital, not wanting to leave her alone for another minute. As they lifted the stretcher into the back of the waiting ambulance, they all raised a hand and wished them both good luck. Though he'd won the battle to be at her side in the ambulance, they all doubted that given current restrictions, he'd be allowed onto the hospital ward itself.

"I'll call you Gavin," he promised, as the doors closed, making an old fashioned telephone sign with his fingers which looked uncannily like horns, and as the blues-and-twos began to silently swirl, the vehicle lurched up the unmade service road that ran behind the cottage.

"Let's get a cup of tea." said Gavin, motioning all of them indoors, and into the arms of the waiting watcher.

CHAPTER 49

The police came and took their statements, initially from those who had been witnesses to the incident itself and then just the names and addresses of everyone else who had stayed behind, telling them that local officers would be in touch over the coming days if they had any further questions. Gavin complied with their request for a full list of attendees, having already written it down a week before; he had simply crossed out the names of those that had not turned up and handed it over.

By two o'clock in the morning the same six that had started the weekend together were left sitting in the very same space, each cradling a stiff drink and considering their next move. The house was strangely silent and unmoved, as if in shame of what had taken place that night or in fear of the judgement that was still to come.

"I wish we had that Ouija board Si," announced Gavin. "After tonight I want some answers."

"I know what you mean Gav. I'm fed up with all these unanswered questions. This fella has got a lot to answer for and I don't want to let it go any longer." said Simon, his hair a tangled mess and his shirt and shorts stained with something that looked like blood but was probably just dirt. "I thought it couldn't hurt us, but it would seem that I was wrong on that score and so I'm thinking that it's time we stopped messing around."

"We could always make one." said Penny, "it's easy enough to do, just fetch me a large piece of stiff cardboard and a marker pen, and a glass tumbler."

"I'm not sure that's a great idea," said Sarah, looking to Chloe for support. "I've heard some bad things about them, people being followed home by demons and all sorts of weird shit."

"That's because they haven't asked for protection first," said Penny, repeating herself, "or because they haven't closed the board down properly at the end and they've unwittingly left the door open."

"I'd rather we didn't knock on the door in the first place." said Chloe, "in fact if you're going to do that, I think we'd rather leave you to it, right Sarah?"

Sarah was not about to disagree and so, as Penny began to mark out the makeshift board, Chloe put an order in for an Uber which, to their undisguised delight, arrived within ten minutes. "I'm sorry guys, it's just not our scene," said Sarah as the two of them hugged their hosts in turn. "Thank you for a lovely evening," she started to say, before correcting herself. "Well, to a point, anyway. I hope that she's okay, send her our best if you do hear from them and let us know if there's anything more that we can do."

"We will and well done to you, too." said Simon, "it's not every day you get to save a life. Thank goodness you were here, that's all I can say."

"You sure this is a good idea, Pen?" asked Jack, as six became four, but it was Gavin who jumped in to defend her.

"I agree with Simon," he said, "we have to try something. I'm fed up with it all, tonight was the last straw. It has to end now, and so if we have to open the door to slam it shut again, then so be it."

And that's how the four of them ended up sitting cross-legged before a makeshift Ouija board in the early hours of a Tuesday morning, with Penny praying for protection against whatever evils might be lying in wait. It was not how they had expected the night to end, but it wasn't over yet, and as they each reached out a finger and placed it on the base of the upturned glass, the temperature in the house suddenly seemed to have peaked.

"Innocent Williams are you there? Elizabeth Styles, do you want to talk to us? Use the board to make contact." It was Penny who had taken the lead, somehow this seemed to be her field of expertise though in all truth, she had never before taken part in a séance of any description, so the perils of a homemade spirit board were far from familiar territory. "Oliver Hunt, do you have anything that you want to say to us?"

Had the glass shivered? Or had one of them accidentally caused it to move? The improvised surface was not the best, the smallest table in the house again deployed as the base and so whilst the glass might not slide quite so freely as it would have done across the polished surface of a purpose-built board, they were hopeful that it would do the job. Again, the slightest shimmer seemed to grip the glass, but it didn't move from its central spot.

"Was that you tonight?" asked Simon directly. "Did you harm our friend?"

The movement was so rapid that two of the four fingers fell off their perch, as the tumbler sped to the place that was marked 'Yes' and there it stopped, as if it's path was pre-ordained. Penny picked it up and placed it back in the centre urging them all to continue before Simon asked out again.

"Why her?" he asked. "Why not one of us?" but he realised that wasn't an easy one to spell out an answer to, so he asked a more direct question. "Did you think she was a witch? Were you testing her?" He hadn't shared his idea with the others beforehand, but they were all on his wavelength.

It seemed like a bloody good question, and it had the same effect as the glass returned to the same spot without hesitation. As before, Penny returned it to the centre and once it was settled back on its spot, the follow-up question was even more revealing.

"She floated, didn't she?" said Simon, continuing to test his theory. "What does that mean? Does that make her guilty?"

This time, the glass seemed to elevate above the table. All four of them felt the full force of its upward thrust and it seemed to hover back to the 'Yes', where it rotated like a spinning top, forcing their fingers to fall away. That was unnerving enough, but when an unseen hand hurled the glass against the wall where it shattered into a thousand pieces, the quartet were scattered like mice from a cat. When they had finally recovered their nerve sufficiently to reform the unbroken circle, it was to close the board down and to usher in a period of calm.

"We can't leave it there." said Simon, "let's take a break, but I want more answers and I think that we should seek them down there." He was pointing, but he didn't need to. They all knew very well what he meant.

"Why don't we try the automatic writing again?" said Gavin, fearful but determined to uncover the truth this time. "But this time let's hope that it's Innocent Williams that's on the other side of the door."

CHAPTER 50

"Innocent?" asked Penny, the biro bending in her intense grip, her voice demanding a response. "Innocent Williams, did you die in this place?"

The three men were listening from the top of the steps, though Jack was sat on the underside of the trapdoor itself, just in case forces beyond their control should try to slam it shut. Simon and Gavin had each taken-up position on alternate steps, their sights fixed on Penny, who was sat in the crosshairs of two separate beams of light, like an actor on a West End stage. The heat was unbearable, even the walls themselves seemed to be radiating heat and two of the men had already unbuttoned their short-sleeved shirts to the waist.

"Innocent?" she called out again, "I know you're there. Please answer me. I want to help you, we all do. We know what he did to you and others, and we are here to bring him to justice."

That did the trick. A low moan seemed to emanate from the foot of the steps as the last word worked its magic. A deep guttural choking sound that hardly sounded human at all, but which was no animal either, because the name that clung onto its trail was as clear to Penny's ears as the bell that had once tolled to mark every hanging in England.

"Hunt."

It was hard for the others to keep track of what was happening in the enclosed space beneath their feet, but it seemed encouraging, as Penny continued to call out and the filled-up pages started to fall. With no one by her side to help, she was tearing at the pages with her left hand as she struggled to keep her writing hand balanced on the pad, the pen dancing from left to right and dragging her hand along in its wake, as if it had a mind of its own.

"What was his first name Innocent?" they heard Penny ask, her breath short and her voice shaking as she began to beg. "I need his Christian name. I need to know his name if you want to be rid of him. Write it down, tell me his name."

She sounded desperate now, but she also sounded different, her voice deeper somehow and her intonation more accented. "Tell me *your* name bitch."

"Get her out of there." yelled Jack, leaping into the stairwell to join Gavin who was already at the foot of the short flight. "I told you this was a bad idea." As he leant inside the cell and grabbed his wife by both arms, her head sprung back, and he recoiled at the sight as a stranger's lifeless face stared back at him.

An aged face; a man's face. A dead face.

The vision was only temporary and as Gavin reached forward and reasserted control, the two of them pulled her bodily from the hole and pushed her up the stairs, her body sagging like a sack of spuds which Simon did his best to haul up and out into the sitting room. Gavin went back for the papers, snatching up a dozen or more that were scrawled black under swirling lines of ink, but which were begging to be deciphered.

"Penny." yelled Jack, "Pen, can you hear me?" He gently slapped her face, shaking her by the shoulders as he called her name over and over, coaxing her back to life. Finally, she began to murmur and opened her eyes, but at first, she failed to recognise her surroundings or the faces of the men who were regarding her with a mix of concern and real fear. "Thank God," said her husband, kissing her full square on the lips as he drew her into him, holding onto her for dear life and nuzzling his face into her sweat soddened neckline.

"What happened?" she said in a daze, "Jack? What happened to me?"

"Sorry guys," said Jack, looking up at their lifelong friends. "But we're leaving. I've had enough of this."

"No." said Penny, with more strength that she had left to spare. "We must see this through Jack, we have to send him packing, or he's not going to leave us alone. We must send him into the light, and the girls are going to help us to lure him there."

༄

Sorting out the mess of papers into a logical order was beyond anyone's capabilities and so, as they each took turns at pouring over the unmistakeable stream of words and half written sentences from an earlier age, it revealed only a partial picture of the women's fate. But it was better than nothing, and it proved beyond all reasonable doubt, that Oliver Hunt had been behind the abduction, imprisonment and ultimate conviction of countless women and girls whose only crime was that they were different.

Listen to this said Simon, reading aloud from the crumpled scrap of paper in his hand.

"He saith I did bewitch them, I did not. He saith I did have discourse with Lucifer, I did not. He saith that the Devil did have carnal knowledge of my body, he did not."

"He did press me, so said I [illegible] no instrument of his, so he did press me more, though I did [illegible] the very truth and could speak no more of it."

"Hunt Oliver [illegible, could be Informant] did such violent acts upon my flesh."

"Prisoner [illegible] confesseth [illegible] not for stripes at his wicked hand."

"No purpose to put her out of her life [illegible] intent to have kill'd her, so accus'd, indicted and arraigned upon our oaths for using and practicing of witchcraft upon the body of [illegible] his wife."

"He holds us still, though innocent I am now and innocent I was, of all defame."

What followed was a stunned silence as the incredulity of what had just transpired between them began to settle. Gavin had fetched them each a glass of cold water, which they all drank down in one as if from an oasis or mountain spring after an arduous trek. Refills were required, but they would have to wait.

"There's no doubt about it then" announced Gavin wearily, "Oliver Hunt was an informant in the witch trials, but I bet that he did his own 'interrogations' too, here in this house."

"I think there's no doubting who was in league with the evil one." replied Simon, feeling increasingly wretched at the thought of what had once been done in the name of God and King here, in their home. "If we'd have been around back then Gavin, I bet they'd have come for us. Just for being different, and you too Penny, without a doubt, you'd have been singled out as a prime suspect, just because of your gift."

"I think anyone who was in his way would have been accused" sighed Penny.

"He sounds like a psychopath" said Jack, as a glass smashed in the kitchen, but he didn't even flinch. "Yeh, we're talking about you Oliver Hunt, you sadistic bastard. Don't think you've gotten away with it either, we're watching you now and if that's the best you can do, then ..."

"GET OUT."

The sound was demonic, and it spat hate from beyond the grave. It sounded like it came from within the room, between each seat where they all lay slumped, hot, exhausted, and ready for the dawn. This time, it spurred them into action, somehow unperturbed by the latest outburst and as Jack and Simon stood to attention, Penny and Gavin remained seated but on high alert, their shoulders steeled for a fight.

"I think we've got him rattled," said Jack, "don't you?"

"Yes" said Simon, recovering some of his former resolve. "As I said, this is our house, mine and Gav's and no one tells me to 'get out' of my own place. Hey Oliver, why don't you go fuck-yourself, you murderous son-of-a-bitch."

Another glass went flying in the kitchen, followed by what sounded like crockery, as the cupboard doors began to clatter open and shut in an orchestrated show of strength. Jack and Simon were at the edge of the lounge now, closer to the action and ready for anything. Simon pulled out his phone and started to film the impressive display of paranormal activity, which if he ever uploaded to the internet would no doubt be debunked by experts from around the world as being 'obviously' fake.

"You're gonna need some new glasses Si." said Jack as another tumbler smashed against the hard floor, but it was the last and as the storm began to abate, Simon stepped forward to start the clean-up exercise. There was glass and broken ceramics everywhere and for now, he simply brushed it into the corner, sweeping the mess off the surfaces and onto the floor for good measure. "I think you're scared Oliver, aren't you?" said Jack, as he taunted their ephemeral friend, "but I've got news for you buddy. Attack is not your best form of defence, you need to run, you need to hide, because we're coming for you."

"What did she mean by 'he holds us still'?" asked Simon. "How does he hold them, why can't then move on?"

"I guess they're trapped somehow?" said Gavin, "being held here against their will."

Penny began to leaf through the discarded pages again, intent on finding something, but she wasn't yet ready to share what it was that she was looking for. By the time she had, there was a pile of paper next to her in a misshapen mound. "What do you think this says Jack?" she asked, passing the unearthed piece to her husband.

"Looks like *'battle'* to me." he said, a single word that was poured out across the page in an overlapping line like in a hall of mirrors, the vision continuing into infinity. "What do you guys think?"

"That's not *battle*." said Gavin, "I know what that says." The others stared at him, desperate for him to reveal the truth that might finally provide an answer to four centuries of torment. "It says *bottle*, and wait a minute, it's repeated ten, eleven, twelve, thirteen times."

"So, what do you think that means, Gav?" asked Jack, as another glass shattered in the kitchen as if to gain their attention. To distract them from their purpose. But this time, it didn't work.

"I get it." said Simon, "those witches bottles aren't there to protect us from them at all. They're meant to keep the women in their place. They're there to keep the women earthbound, imprisoned here or more likely, down there."

Without a second's hesitation all four of them leapt to their feet and stepped towards the fireplace, reaching out in unison to grab at the bottles with only one intention. To smash them against the walls and floor in a mad dash for freedom, but he was too quick. The first one hit Penny square between the eyes, sending her crashing to the ground, stunned and not a little sore as the bottle fell limply to the floor, its fall broken by the collision. The next struck

Jack in the eye, leaving him blackened and bruised by morning but again failing to break apart, as its landing was cushioned by the thick rug beneath. Two more were hurled by unseen hands in the direction of the homeowners; somehow Simon saw his coming and caught it in mid-air, flinging it in one movement against the stone wall to his left where it erupted in a burst of light.

Gavin's reaction was less graceful though it had the same effect, as he tripped over the hearth and collided with the fireplace grazing his hands and forehead, but it was enough to see the bottle with his name on it sail over his head and shatter into a thousand shards on the far wall of the snug. "Own goal you dickhead." he shouted, as he rubbed vigorously at his brow.

Later they would not be able to recall who had done what, but the three men grabbed a bottle in each hand and hurled them against the flagstones at their feet, like football players celebrating a touchdown and before the minute was out, all the remaining vessels of antique glass had been destroyed. As a recovering Penny picked up the final unbroken bottle from the floor at her feet and in one victorious strike smashed it against the centre of the fireplace, the sound that defied them was like nothing any of them had ever heard before or would again.

Rage could not fully describe it. The wrath of ages past, a thunderous fury of unbridled anger that seemed to press in on them from every side, filling the snug space until the very stone that surrounded them seemed to flex as it bowed under the pressure, like water pressing against a dam.

"Jack." It was Penny, she was on her feet and facing away from him and towards the fireplace, where a darkness was starting to form. It was as if a slice of the night had been forgotten by the rising dawn, a tear in the fabric of the firmament through which a form was starting to squeeze itself out. It was like a black satin sheet hung up on a washing line as the wind whips it up into a frenzy of movement, a turning tide of billowing blackness.

All four of them were now stood before it, their feet planted at the lip of the closed trapdoor, like some troupe of superheroes on the brink of victory. "What is it, Pen?" asked Jack, expecting that she might have been in possession of some insight that they all lacked. "Is it him? Is it Hunt?"

She didn't answer at first, but she closed her eyes and ordered each of them to do the same. She had no idea if it was him or if it wasn't or whether such a parlour trick would even work, but it was worth a try. "Visualise a ball of light." she commanded. "A small circle of light at the top of the steps, like a ball of lightning. Hold onto it in your mind's eye, and let it burn there, like an imploding star. Intense white light. Burning. Turning."

They were unaware of the vision that had formed before them, fearful and desperate, like a man standing before the magistrate's bench and praying for clemency. He was clad in black and white, a simple black hat upon his head and square white cloth lapels around his shoulders, from which a thigh length buttoned coat led down to darker pants atop long leather boots. His face was contorting, as if enraged, his mouth open and teeth gnashing as he seemed unable to move from the spot on which he had been summoned to stand. Wailing like a banshee in chains.

"Now imagine bringing our lights together," said Penny, her eyes tightly shut, "gently now, closer, and closer until they are caught in each other's halo. Then let them merge. Bring them all together as one fiery light, one massive supernova of whiteness. Now when I tell you to open your eyes, don't lose that picture, keep the vision before us of one single sun, hovering above the trapdoor in front of the fireplace. Are you ready?"

"Yes," the boys all said as one.

"As ready as we'll ever be." said Gavin, sweating profusely.

"Open your eyes."

They all saw him then. A perfectly formed and solid vision of a man, a man from another age, a Puritan who was anything but pure. A magistrate's informant, a vile witch-finder's watcher. An evil purveyor of injustice whose only aim in life had been to abduct and abuse innocent women for the glory of others and to further his own perverted desires. They saw him for what he was, and he was not frightening, he was frightened, because he knew what was coming. What he'd been hiding from for four hundred years.

Judgement day.

"Now push our light into him, into his chest, into his heart."

They all knew what she was planning before she said it and so as soon as the order was given, they had begun to send him back, to send him on, towards whatever fate awaited him. To stand before another bench where a celestial judge had been waiting patiently to pass sentence for four long centuries.

"I'm burning up." screamed Gavin out of nowhere, and it was almost enough to break their concentration, but Penny held them together.

"It's just a trick Gav." she snapped, "don't pay it any attention, keep concentrating".

"But he's smoking, like a fucking chimney." yelled Simon raising the alarm as steam began rising from Gavin's skin like smoke in the semi-darkness of the room. "Mate, are you okay?"

"I am for now, but I'm not sure for how much longer." he whimpered. "It's like I'm being burned alive. Let's get this thing done with before it's me that ends up going up in smoke."

They each watched enthralled as the light enveloped the man of their nightmares, slowly swallowing him up. His form began to shrink and fade, as a host of other lights, thirteen in all - each shining in a glorious rainbow of colour – crowded around him, hastening him towards his final act. Until they too began to fade and merge into the whiteness and were gone. In the end, it was all over in seconds. There was no final retaliation, no sudden surge of bile and spite, no threat of vengeance or retribution. He had no power. He had no lifeforce. His only power had been the fear that he had invoked in others, and the free reign to do harm that he'd been granted by a twisted and corrupt society. He was gone and the women too, free to pass over, free from the misery of their imprisonment. Free.

Penny fell to her knees, drained of colour, and wracked with tears. Gavin too was sobbing, but thankfully no longer smoking, as Simon poured what was left of the water over his head and shoulders and dashed to the kitchen to fetch some more so that he could repeat the trick. Jack stood and watched in awe and wonder, staring into the fireplace as if waiting for the hearth to erupt in flame, but all was quiet.

The light from outside had begun to seep into the corners of the room, and as Penny and Gavin were both helped to their feet by their respective partners, they came together in a cluster of joy and remorse. Joy that those convicted of the crime of witchcraft, for which they were not and never had been guilty, were finally released from the curse of pain and torment; remorse for a time when so many innocents had gone to the gallows for crimes which they could not have committed, judged by unholy men who were themselves inspired by wicked motives – amongst them lust, greed, and selfish desire.

As they broke away from each other's embrace with no other thought but to find their way to bed, it was Penny that spoke up to herald in another day of trauma.

"Can you smell burning?"

Epilogue

"A firework?"

"A firework." said Gavin, "that's what the man said."

"A stray firework is going to cost me fifty grand?" Simon was incandescent at the prospect that the insurance company were not going to pay out. They were of the learned opinion that, by having a firework display so close to their cottage and its thatched roof, that the customers had invalidated their insurance. Not a single pound was coming their way.

"Well, I'm getting our solicitor onto that for starters." raged Simon, his face crimson.

"At least we weren't asleep in bed when it took hold Si," said Gavin, "we would have been toast. Had we not been up until four doing what we did, that smouldering firework would have been the death of us all."

"I suppose so.," Simon admitted with a sigh. "But fifty grand."

"It could have been the whole house and not just half of the roof that was destroyed," said Gavin, "look on the bright side, it's only a redecoration job now that the thatcher has finished, it could have been much worse. And it's not like we can't afford it, is it?"

"Yeh, and we have Penny's acute sense of smell to thank as well" nodded Simon, "I didn't smell a thing until we stepped outside, and we were all so tired, with nothing else to disturb us we'd have gone out like a light. For the last time."

"Permanently."

"Do you think that *'he'* had anything to do with it, Gav?"

"What, with a stray firework that had gone five hundred yards up into the air and then landed back in our eaves, like a direct hit?" It sounded stupid when it was said out loud, but the whole thing would have been non-sensical to a rational logical minded person. "I dunno, and who knows, he's gone now and that's all that matters. The house is ours."

"I'm just glad we put a stop to it." said Simon.

"I still can't believe that we did it," said Gavin, "but whatever 'higher authority' it was that stopped Robert Hunt in his tracks, maybe they also had the foresight to stop his brother first. At least in their lifetime."

It had been quiet since the events of Freedom Day and the party to end all parties. No noises, no breakages, no visions. A few creaks but that was only to be expected. It was after all, an old house.

"I popped into see Mrs Illsley yesterday," said Gavin, a large tabby cat nestled on his lap. "She seemed well, though she's vowing never to set foot in our house again."

"Can't blame her for that I suppose," said Simon, "near death experiences tend to do that to a person."

"She's still of the view that she was pushed," reported Gavin, raising his voice above the gentle hum of their recently rescued cat's contented purr. "By person or persons unknown, though she's now saying that it was the dreaded 'man in black' that was behind it all, though the police are putting that down to an hallucination."

"Thank goodness for that." sighed Simon, "though we know better, don't we?"

"Indeed, we do," agreed Gavin, "but that's not the worst of it. She reckons when she was underwater trying to fight him off, there were other women grappling with him, she thought it was Sarah and Chloe, which has convinced the police that she was getting it mixed up with when they resuscitated her on the side of the pool, but she says that the man told her that they were both witches, like her. And that's where the police packed up their notebooks."

"I've just had an email from Mrs Mountford by the way," said Simon nodding as he changed the subject. "She seems good and was pleased to hear our news. She said that since she returned the key there have been no more disturbances, and she's getting married again it would seem. A new bloke that she met on a grief counselling course would you believe?"

"That's good to hear," Gavin answered, before sharing some news of his own. "By the way, the booksellers think they might get ten grand for the Bible, so that'll help towards the cost of the roof. Funny thing is though, they'd advertised it online as being in 'mint condition', so I called them up as I was concerned that if they sold it, we might have a problem when the new owners realised, well, that it isn't."

Simon looked up from his iPad, as his interest stirred.

"They said something really peculiar, I was sure they must be mistaken, so I asked them to check again."

"And ...?" asked Simon, sensing what was coming next.

"Nothing." said Gavin. "The dedication from Robert Hunt to his brother is still there, but there is no list of names. Simply gone, like they were never there in the first place."

"Well surely, they've just ripped out the pages at the back?" said Simon, still refusing to accept that writing from almost four hundred years ago and ink that had been infused into the paper on which it was written, could simply disappear.

"That's what I said, and they said not," shrugged Gavin, "they said that there's no sign of any pages missing, and the stitched nature of the binding would not allow someone to simply remove the page without leaving evidence of it behind."

"Well, I never." said a flummoxed Simon. "On the subject of the names, weren't you going to go down to Taunton, to the record office, to see if you could come up with a list of Robert Hunt's convicted witches, just to close the circle?"

"I was" said Gavin, "but do you know what? I've changed my mind. They're all at peace now, I think I'd rather leave it that way; after all, I don't want to go and stir anything else up do I? Not now that we've finally got our house to ourselves."

"Do you think anything has changed Simon?" asked Gavin, in philosophical mood. "From then to now. Those women were persecuted just because they were vulnerable, because they were different. You could even say that Mrs Illsley was of the same mould; an old widow, with money, but with no family to stand up for her. Nowadays, it might not be about women being accused of witchcraft, but prejudice and hatred is just as rife, isn't it? It's not that long ago that Jews were being rounded up and murdered, or ethnic minorities like in the Balkans, and it's still going on in Africa and other places. People like us too. It's not changed that much, has it?"

"How many would have been accused today?" wondered Simon out loud, "had we held the same views about witches and wizards. How many would have been tried in kangaroo courts around the country for bewitching their neighbours or for bringing down God's wrath on their towns and villages?"

"Thousands." guessed Gavin. "Hundreds of thousands even."

And on that point, they were both agreed. The world is still an evil place.

Acknowledgements

The Witches of Selwood – Andrew Pickering, printed by The Hobnob Press 2021

Witches: The History of a Persecution – Nigel Cawthorne, printed by Arcturus Publishing Ltd. 2019

Witch Hunt: The Persecution of Witches in England – David and Andrew Pickering, printed by Amberley Publishing, 2013

The Annotated Daemonologie: A Critical Edition – King James (expanded in modern interpretation with an introduction and notes by Brett R Warren), 2016

Witch Hunting and Witch Trials – C.L'Estrange Ewen, ORIGINALLY printed by Stephen Austin and Sons Ltd and then by Lincoln Mac Veagh, The Dial Press, New York in 1974

Maleficium: Witchcraft and Witch Hunting in the West – Gordon Napier, printed by Amberley Publishing, 2017

<u>Original sources:</u>

A Guide to Grand Jury Men – Richard Bernard: 1st edition 1627, 2nd edition 1629, printed by Felix Kingston for Ed Blackmore, and are to be sold at his shop at the Great South Door of St Paul's Cathedral

Saducismus Triumphatus, or, Full and plain evidence concerning witches and apparitions in two parts: the first treating of their possibility, the second of their real existence – Joseph Glanvill 1636-1680, 1st published in 1681

All statistics on Coronavirus taken from the official government information at <u>https://coronavirus.data.gov.uk/details/cases?areaType=nation&areaName=England</u>

Hearth Tax survey – centre for Hearth Tax Research – University of Roehampton at <u>https://rohu02addon115irprep.azurewebsites.net/research-centres/centre-for-hearth-tax-research/</u>

<u>Back cover image</u> is loosely based on a Daisy Wheel inscription found at All Saints Church, Litcham, Norfolk, England as part of the Norfolk Medieval Graffiti Survey – see <u>www.medieval-graffiti.co.uk</u>

Author's Note

The Burning is of course a work of fiction set against a background of historical fact.

Persecution of accused witches was rife in England in the seventeenth century and the references to the cases and trials in Somerset, Wiltshire and Dorset are real, though the records are scant as much of the paperwork for the Western Circuit was indeed lost during a night raid in Exeter in the Second World War, where the documents had been taken for 'safe keeping'. The role played by Robert Hunt, one time Sheriff of Somerset and MP for Ilchester, is unclear but he was labelled as a zealot by his contemporaries and said to have uncovered a "hellish knot of witches" in the mid 1660s, but to what extent he can be called Somerset's witch-finder is lost to history.

His brother Oliver is entirely fictitious and bears no relationship to anyone living or dead, though Robert did come from the area and had brothers and sisters, Oliver was not one of them.

The works of Andrew Pickering and Jonathan Barry - who have both been recognised for their significant academic research into the witchcraft cases of the Western Circuit – were most useful in setting the scene when writing this account and to the likes of Richard Bernard, Joseph Glanvill and others for their long-forgotten insights from a world that is largely lost to us, but where belief in the Devil and his interactions with the living were a widely held truth.

After all, King James I of England and VI of Scotland and self-proclaimed King of Great Britain, and his compendium of witchcraft lore – *Daemonologie* – was hugely influential across the Kingdom and as such, lit the fire and then fanned the flames for a century of witch trials and persecutions which led to at least 1,000 innocent people losing their lives courtesy of the hangman's noose, or like Elizabeth Styles, in the filthy gaols of England's county towns.

At the end of the 1st quarter of 2023, a full 3 years since the first lockdown began, there had been almost 21 million cases of Coronavirus recorded in the UK and almost 280,000 deaths where COVID19 was mentioned on the death certificate. Like the Great Plague in the 17th century, it had struck without warning, but unlike those days, witchcraft was never cited as a potential cause and no witches were accused, tried, and murdered as a result.

This book is self-published and though it has been thoroughly reviewed and edited there may yet be some dreaded typos. If you find any, please do email me at robertgderry@gmail.com so that I can edit the manuscript.

Finally, a request. If you enjoyed this book, please consider leaving an honest review on Amazon.

And if you did enjoy it, please check out my previous novel – The Waterman – published by Austin Macauley Ltd. in 2021 and also available on Amazon in both paperback and eBook formats via this link.

Printed in Great Britain
by Amazon